Praise for Mark Kimmel's writing...

Mark Kimmel's emphasis on the spiritual implications of extraterrestrial contact adds an important dimension to the discussion of this, the most important event in human history.
— Dr. Steven Greer, The Disclosure Project

Fiction is perhaps the most palatable way to break the ice on the whole subject of our place in the cosmos.
— Brian O'Leary, Former Astronaut

Mark Kimmel has not only crafted an exciting story, but courageously takes us into possibilities that each of us should ponder.
— Dennis Weaver, actor, author, environmentalist

Trillion is a captivating story that will inspire readers to create a sustainable future for themselves, and for this planet.
— Robert S. Ivker, D.O., President
— American Board of Holistic Medicine

What an inspiring amazing hybrid human he is! His books should be made into phenomenal visionary films! He has such inner grace and majesty and an inner knowing and compassion about the alien agendas.

— Naomi Semeniuk, New York

Trillion reminds me a lot of the Celestine Prophecy, but with a cosmic point of view.

— MK, Book Distributor, Green Bay

From successful conservative businessman to fiction writer, Mark has not only succeeded in transitioning himself, but has written a wonderful story about the larger purpose to our lives.

— Debra Benton, Author - *How To Think Like a CEO*

I couldn't put it down, a real page-turner. It was like reading about the past four years of my own life.

— Commercial Airline Pilot, Denver

This is a story that carries you along on an exciting adventure that will keep you involved.

— Gerald L. Evans, Boulder, Colorado

Trillion includes vitally important truth, woven into the framework of a fascinating fiction story.

— Jill Hull Strunk, Minnetonka, Minnesota

Decimal

Knowing the truth changes everything.

Mark Kimmel

PARADIGM BOOKS

BOULDER, COLORADO

Decimal

Mark Kimmel

Book II of the Paradigm Trilogy

www.cosmicparadigm.com

Kimmel, Mark
Decimal / Mark Kimmel - 1st Edition
p.cm

ISBN NUMBER 0-9720151-1-6

1. Paranormal — Fiction 2. Metaphysical — Fiction

I. Title

First Printing
August 2004

PARADIGM BOOKS
BOULDER, COLORADO

*For Heidi who supports me in my quest for the truth,
for my two sons who are my joy,
and for the many non-human conscious life forms who assist us all.*

Earth is but one among many spheres occupied by conscious life forms with highly developed civilizations. However, Earth is unique both for what has been accorded to it, and for the ways in which its human inhabitants have responded to these gifts and burdens.

AUTHOR'S NOTE

The President of the United States, the Federal Bureau of Investigation, Central Intelligence Agency, National Security Agency, Defense Intelligence Agency, Air Force, Army, Navy, USGS, Customs and Border protection Agency, various media organizations, and the Boulder County Sheriff's Department are of course real. While based on fact, the people and organizations in this book are fiction. The technology described either exists or is being developed. The author has depicted non-human life forms as accurately as his present understanding permits. Liberties have been taken in describing actual places, organizational structures, and procedures to facilitate the telling of the story.

PREFACE

Decimal is the continuing story of Ryan Drake and his off-planet friends, Sarah Smith and Peter Jones. For a detailed account of their previous adventures, and for an understanding of the cosmic paradigm, read *Trillion*, the prequel to *Decimal*

Many readers of *Trillion* believe the tale in that book is mostly true. Most readers find that the cosmic messages contained within its pages present them with hope for the future of this planet.

Synopsis of Trillion: In a remote corner of the Navajo Reservation in northwest Arizona, Ryan becomes acquainted with Sarah and Peter. As rogue Federal agents invade their home, he helps them escape into the desert wilderness. It is there he learns that his very human-like friends are from another planet, Phantia. They tell him that the universe is ubiquitously inhabited, orchestrated, and friendly, and that they are here to help a troubled planet. When they finally escape their pursuers, he takes them to his home near Boulder, Colorado.

Ernest Steiger, a member of the group that controls the major media in the United States, the same group that has been covering-up extraterrestrial contact for the past fifty years, discovers Sarah. The clash between those who know about cosmic reality and those who would conceal it begins. Steiger's men kidnap Sarah.

It is time for a new generation of leadership, to cope with new problems and new opportunities. For there is a new world to be won.

— JOHN FITZGERALD KENNEDY

ONE

The two hundred pound boulder did not belong on the expensive blue and white Navajo rug. Chunks of black mortar still clung to it. Someone had pried it lose from the moss rock fireplace. In its former resting place was a dark crater.

Then his eyes were drawn to the three chocolate leather sofas in the center of the great room. Long slits had opened their armrests, backs, and seat cushions. Someone had methodically pulled out the white polyester stuffing; tufts of it were everywhere. The sofas now hung on their frames like deflated brown dirigibles.

While Ryan Drake paused on the ceramic tile of the foyer of his mountain home, the buzzing of the security system attracted his attention. He knew he had only thirty seconds to punch in the disarm code, thirty seconds before it would sound an alarm at the monitoring company who would, in turn, alert the Boulder County Sheriff. In a stupor from the twelve-hour drive from Scottsdale, Arizona, he started to take another step, but halted. Sarah's words gave him pause.

As they had waited for the wrought iron gate across his driveway to open, she had said, "Something is wrong with your house."

Ryan had seen nothing other than tiny red flashes, probably an indication that his eyes were weary from the drive. He blinked a couple of times and the reflections disappeared. Disregarding her warning, he had pulled his Jeep around the circular driveway to the front of the house. Unloading here meant fewer steps than lugging their belongings from the garage.

"Ryan, be careful." Sarah had grabbed his arm as he had reached to open the driver's door. The only other time he had seen that look in her eyes was when the Immigration and Naturalization Service had chased them across Fortress Mesa, when she had been afraid of being captured and exposed. He had seen nothing like it during the past six weeks.

He had ignored her concern, walked the short distance from the Jeep to the front door, and opened the house.

Now, he stood transfixed.

His home had been ransacked.

The security system beckoned him — he had twenty-five seconds before the alarm sounded.

The destruction around him produced a sinking feeling. He and his ex-wife, Vicki, had spent so much time and effort constructing and furnishing this house, the myriad details, long hours, and, yes, bitter disagreements. "This is our dream home," she had said when at last it was finished, six years ago.

How had intruders bypassed the house's security system? Why hadn't the Sheriff's Department already responded to the break-in? Why would intruders bother to reset the security system?

Ryan took in the assaults to the house and its furnishings. Two ficus trees, that had formerly framed his floor-to-ceiling picture window, lay on their sides. Their root balls had been exposed, crushed open to reveal anything secreted there. Next to the glass wall, the baseboard molding had been torn away, the interior of the wall probed with something that had dislodged clumps of pink insulation.

He caught a whiff of the unmistakable odor of propane.

On the right, Native American pots, each a pricey collector's item, had been smashed on the floor. Framed southwestern originals that had adorned the walls of this spacious room had been torn from their frames and discarded into a heap along with the pottery. Shards of glass and terra cotta littered the expensive hand-woven carpet. The pottery and pictures alone would have fetched an ordinary thief thousands of dollars.

Finally, Ryan got it.

In fifteen seconds, the alarm was set to go off.

He bolted out the door.

His white Jeep Grand Cherokee was parked ten feet away. At the end of the sidewalk leading to the entryway, Sarah Smith and Peter Jones stood watching him.

"Get out of here," he shouted. He grabbed an arm of each and yanked them away from the house, away and across the snow-covered knoll within the circular driveway, away from whatever was about to happen when the alarm went off.

Boom! Whoosh! They had managed but a dozen steps, had crested the two-foot high mound, and were headed down its far side.

With a fiery blast the house exploded. The force of the concussion caught all three, pushing them like some unseen hand. As Ryan stumbled he threw himself over Sarah.

Chunks of metal, wood, and glass rained around them.

Ryan felt something smash into his leg. He winced.

Crash!

A reverberating grind as part of the structure collapsed.

Silence...

Slowly Ryan raised his head and looked back at the house. One section of the green metal roof was peeled back as if a giant can-opener had been put to work. Smoke began to seep from holes formerly occupied by windows and doors. Then like kindling in a campfire, the interior ignited and flames burst forth from every opening.

He rolled off Sarah and asked, "Are you okay?"

"Uh huh." She took a deep breath and struggled to a sitting position. The front of her white blouse was damp from her fall onto the snow-covered ground. "Except for being squashed."

Even in her disheveled condition he thought her beautiful. Her light blonde hair fell to her shoulders. Her delicate nose and lively mouth blended into a defined jaw line. Large gray eyes surrounded by light lashes blended perfectly with her flawless bronze skin. Her eyes had an intensity to them that hinted at the years of wisdom beyond her youthful appearance. To Ryan she was the most beautiful creature in the universe — and he had always paid attention to natural blondes.

He looked at his leg. A jagged spear of wood, about nine inches long, protruded from his calf. The back of his jeans was covered with shards of glass. When he pulled out the spear, he winced at the sharp pain.

Ryan saw no cuts or blood on Sarah. He reached out and gave her a hug. The pleasant odor of vanilla filled his nostrils. He had told her he liked the fragrance of this new lotion.

"Ouch," Sarah said. She pulled her hand from Ryan's wool shirt. Slivers of glass clung to her palm.

He turned toward Peter who lay on the snow next to them. "How about you?"

Peter lifted his head and muttered, "Fine. Just fine." He said it in an excellent imitation of Humphrey Bogart. During their stay at Danielle's, Peter had watched Casablanca and all the other old movies her husband Dick had collected. Peter had decided that Bogart's gruff exterior suited him well. Like the accomplished performer he was, Peter had delighted those gathered for Christmas by switching between characters.

The effect had been marvelous. Peter had brought himself to a level where ordinary people of this planet could relate to him, not as some vastly superior being, but as a brother from another planet. Ryan had watched as his son Darren, the determined bachelor from Orange County, California, and Dick, Danielle's husband, opened up to Peter's message. Sarah had accomplished much the same by developing an intimate bond with Danielle and her children. The instinctual fear of extraplanetary beings had given way to a loving relationship.

"Maybe next time you'll listen to Sarah." Peter's tone was still that of a disgusted Bogart. He pointed to the burning house. "The violence of this planet — it solves nothing."

"Yes," was the only reply Ryan could muster. He reached over and laid a hand on Peter's muscular shoulder.

He noticed a red trickle edging across the side of Peter's shaved head. A chunk of glass had imbedded itself in the exposed skin. His leather jacket, another attempt to imitate Bogart, and blue jeans had saved the rest of him.

Peter too was handsome. His perfectly shaped hairless head contrasted with bushy dark eyebrows. Like Sarah his skin was bronze. But his mouth was severe, thin lips, a determined set to his jaw. His gray eyes had a depth to them that spoke of his other world experiences. As usual, he clutched his maroon book in his left hand.

Ryan reached to pull the glass from Peter's skull, but stopped when he realized he would need something to close the razor thin gouge. He said to Peter, "Don't touch your head. I'll be right back."

"Now what?"

"Stay put. I'll take care of it when I get back."

The newly fallen snow about them was littered with everything from a window frame to a small chunk of green metal roof. The three were fortunate to have avoided contact with any large pieces of flying debris.

He was amazed to see an unbroken dinner plate lying in the snow. Almost as if it were a leftover from a recent picnic.

Ryan hobbled to his Jeep. One of the oak front doors to his house had slammed into its side. The heavy, nine-foot high, lacquered door had cleaved off most of the Jeep's right front fender. The headlight, turn signal, and a portion of the bumper were scattered nearby. The Jeep's side nearest the house had been scarred by smaller pieces of debris; one window was broken, all were cracked. His Jeep had helped shield them from the force of the explosion. The other half of the front door, the one that he had opened, hung from the doorframe by a single hinge.

He saw that a chunk of some sort had landed in one of the two Ponderosas that framed the entrance. It was just smoldering, had not burst into flame.

From the vehicle's rear, Ryan retrieved his first aid kit. He grabbed his cell phone from the front seat. Maneuvering around glass, wood, and unrecognizable fragments of his former dwelling, he returned to the pair on the ground.

He dialed 911. With a hurried voice, he reported the fire and requested paramedics. He also asked for a sheriff's car. He gave the operator precise directions to his location. In a few moments he heard the siren atop the volunteer fire department station at the bottom of the hill.

After they moved a few yards further from the house, Sarah extracted the glass from Peter's scalp.

"Ouch," the bald Phantian said. "What are you doing to me?"

"Stay still while I work on you," Sarah said. She placed a Band-aid across the gouge in his scalp and pulled the sides of the wound together.

"Thank you," Peter said to both Sarah and Ryan. He now spoke with the words of a celestial traveler. "Ryan, I know this fire and destruction makes you angry. But you must leave behind the paradigm of good and evil, where one human is battling another. There is another way, the way of the cosmic citizen. Beyond this world, in the advanced realms, there is no good and evil; there are only brothers and sisters."

Ryan pulled up his pant leg. Sarah bandaged the bloody hole she found there. She checked the back of his shirt to make sure no more fragments of glass were clinging to it.

Remembering her warning before he went into the house, Ryan asked Sarah, "How did you know?"

"Remember those red lights you glimpsed when you opened the front gate?"

"Yeah, I thought I was seeing spots." At the time that was exactly what he thought he was seeing, spots, spots from being very tired. Well, he certainly wasn't tired any longer — the explosion had taken care of that. He squinted through burning eyes. Ash and smoke drifted about them. "So?"

"A warning," Peter said. "From now on, you must pay close attention to such things. You must learn to be sensitive to the assistance that is available from non-human life forms."

Ryan blamed himself for what had just happened. He had relied on possession of two books and the fact that their owner was hospitalized, in a coma. He had thought that the threat of revealing the books' contents to the public would protect them. Obviously, it had not.

"Are we in immediate danger?" Ryan directed the question to both Sarah and Peter, but he knew she would be the one to respond. Over the past weeks, he had watched, as she rapidly attuned her superior abilities to her new home planet.

She closed her eyes before answering. "Whoever did this is no longer in the area."

Ryan stood and looked at the flames. Anger welled within him. This was no accident. Someone had deliberately set out to kill him, to kill all of them. He would find whoever it was, and they would pay.

He felt his face redden, his hands double into fists. He squinted his eyes and stared at the burning structure.

Reading his intentions, Sarah said, "We must not stoop to their level."

"Sometimes being nice doesn't get the job done," he retorted.

"Please, no violence." Sarah stepped to Ryan and laid a hand on his arm. "I know it's hard, but the end result of tragedy is always some greater good. Remember the ways of the cosmic citizen."

Ryan turned and walked away from her. He had tried their non-violent way, shielded them from capture by the INS, harbored them at this house, and rescued Sarah after Ernest Steiger had kidnapped her. And he had made sure no one got hurt in the process. He felt sure that Ernest Steiger's trip to the hospital was due more to the man's age, ailments, and overweight than to anything he had done to him that day.

But now someone had decided to play a different game, a violent game. In his experience tough guys reacted only to strong countermeasures. Every movie, every fight, every war was based on the ancient code of an eye-for-an-eye. It remained to be seen if the ways of people from another planet could be applied here.

What he resented more than the destruction of his house was that it pulled him back into his old paradigm. For the past six weeks, Sarah, Peter, and he had found ways to see the good in his world, to see the promise in its future, to see others as fellow journeyers. It had been wonderful, as if the spirit of Christmas had extended the entire time. If he allowed his anger to take over, the high road he had foreseen would disappear like manicured landscaping before the onslaught of a tornado.

By the time the first chartreuse fire truck roared into the circular drive, both Ponderosas were ablaze. Flames lashed through the openings that had been his front entrance and windows. The firefighters from this first pumper, which was equipped with water only, strung its hose to the fire hydrant just outside the gate to Ryan's property.

In another few minutes, a paramedic unit followed. Ryan motioned for it.

While three men in yellow jackets scurried to attach hoses and pump water through one blown-out window, a fourth firefighter frantically requested assistance on his truck's radio. Waving his arms, he described the fiery scene.

After the paramedics cleaned and re-bandaged his leg, Ryan hobbled to the Jeep to retrieve their heavy jackets. Feeling the garage door opener in his pocket, he pressed the button. The door to the space where he normally parked the Jeep opened.

Boom! The force of an explosion burst from the first empty space. Additional blasts ripped open the other two doors of the garage. These openings exposed the burning wreckage of his red Porsche in one stall and Sarah and Peter's car in the other.

Within a few minutes, two additional fire trucks, lights blaring, sirens wailing, came barreling into the driveway. A Boulder County Sheriff's car followed them.

Any fire in the wooded hills west of Boulder was a threat to nearby homes. A few years previously, an out-of-control fire had blackened over a hundred acres and destroyed fifteen homes.

The new arrivals carried equipment to make Class A Foam. After they towed his Jeep out of the way, the two trucks began pumping a smothering white blanket into his house. A fourth tanker arrived and began spraying the two Ponderosas.

"Hello, Mr. Drake. Looks bad." Deputy Sheriff Andy Milliken greeted Ryan as he emerged from his car. From within, the radio crackled with indistinct conversation.

Milliken was six feet tall, with a friendly smile under a full mustache. Broad shoulders filled his tan uniform. As they stood face-to-face, Ryan smelled coffee.

He had met Milliken when President-elect Carlton Boyle had spoken at Sanitas Technologies in October. Milliken had also been involved when Mitch Young reported that Sarah had tried to abduct him.

"I arrived to find my house had been trashed," Ryan said. "Furniture slit open, pottery smashed. I stepped in far enough to hear the buzzer on the security system and smell propane. Got out just in time."

At Ryan's comment about the buzzing of the security system and the smell of propane, Andy raised both eyebrows. He extended the microphone of the car's two-way radio, requested a crime scene unit, and reported the situation to Boulder County Sheriff, Tom Ertl.

After determining that Sarah and Peter were okay for the moment, Ryan approached his blazing three-story dwelling. White foam leaked from windows and door openings. The thick timbers of the walls seemed to be containing the fire. The clear lacquered finish on the exterior of the fourteen-inch diameter logs was largely untouched except where smoke had blackened it on the top story.

The green metal roof had buckled over the great room and flames leaped upward through the seams. The massive chimney that had dominated this room was intact. It protruded through the smoke and flames like the thick mast of a schooner trailing green sails.

The net effect of the sturdy log construction was to contain the fire, and thoroughly roast the interior of the house. Ryan wondered if the people who had caused the explosions had planned it that way. With damage from smoke, fire, water, and foam, there would be little evidence of their mischief. He wondered who other than Ernest Steiger wanted to kill them.

Because his lot sloped acutely downward to the east, the firefighters were prevented from attacking the fire from that direction. The best they could do was to pour chemicals through the front and sides. The blaze was so intense that no one dared enter the structure or climb onto the roof.

On the north side of his house, two Junipers were ablaze. A firefighter was foaming them from a handheld canister. If he could contain it here, the snowy ground would prevent the fire from spreading to other trees or bushes. As a mandated fire prevention method, Ryan had cut brush and trees forty feet away from the house. Forest fires were a constant threat to the homes in the hills west of Boulder, Colorado due to years of below-normal snowfall.

Ryan climbed down the hill behind his house, staying well away from the structure. As he stepped over scraps of glass, metal, and wood, he noted the sliding glass doors next to the indoor pool had been blown out. They were the entry to the walkout basement. The recreation room, furnace, water heater, and pool were on this lowest level. He visualized his entertainment center with its large screen television ablaze.

Memories of his daughter and her high school friends playing in the pool flashed through his mind. In the summer months the family had barbecued on the deck. Vicki and he had hosted gatherings of his business associates, catered dinners, and staged events. There had been happy times before his divorce, happy times before the fire.

There was no way to tell whether the intruders had jimmied a lock or gone in through a window. They obviously knew how to manipulate his home security system.

And what about the perimeter security around his eleven acres? And the motion detectors? He was sure they were engaged when he had departed ten days ago. Brauk Braukington, Sanitas's interim manager and technical guru, had shown him how to make sure they were working properly.

He remembered disengaging the perimeter security when they re-entered through the main gate. During the ten days they were away, someone had defeated his very expensive installation.

Sarah, Peter, and he had spent the Christmas and New Years Holidays with his daughter, Danielle, and her family at their home in Scottsdale, Arizona. They were happy days — the happiest since Ryan and their mother, Vicki, had separated. Equally important, no one had threatened them the entire time.

They had departed Scottsdale early the morning of January 2nd. By taking Interstate 40 through New Mexico, and then Interstate 25 north to Denver, they had avoided the Four Corners area, the location of Harmony Center, and the site of their encounter with the INS.

He stared at his flaming house. Their friendship had almost resulted in all three of them being killed. What a way to end an otherwise happy vacation. What a way to start a new year.

As he stood looking at the smoking ruin of his house, he foresaw that he would likely die in the process of helping Sarah and Peter bring truth to his planet. Regardless, he was determined to plunge forward.

He stepped into a shallow hole and tumbled to the ground. Looking around he saw that the slope was full of holes, covered by the three-inch blanket of snow. Marks of heavy equipment were faintly visible at their edges. The intruders had not been content with ransacking his house; they had gone after buried treasure. Ryan picked himself up and circled back to the front of the house.

"The Sheriff would like you to wait around," Milliken said when Ryan returned to the commotion in his driveway. "He'll get here as fast as he can."

"I'm not going anywhere."

Sarah and Peter looked like royalty that had been flushed from their palace. Both were wrapped in wool blankets supplied by the paramedics. Sarah stood tall and proud. Peter, shorter by six inches, retained his air of authority. Reflections from the flames of the burning house danced across their faces. They stood, arms around each other's backs, observing the burning house and the firefighters at work. He walked over and greeted them with a gentle hand on each.

'This is a great loss to you,' Peter communicated. None of his Bogart imitation came through when he communicated mind-to-mind, just the unvarnished truth.

'It could be worse,' Ryan communicated back. *'At least we are still alive.'* Over the past six weeks his ability to grasp the mind-to-mind communications his extraplanetary friends used had improved markedly. At first it was only a few words and only in a meditative state, then he found he could carry on a conversation while fully conscious.

'I would like to have spent more time here,' Sarah added without speaking.

The streams of foam were dampening the fire, but smoke still poured from each opening in the stacked logs. His heart sank. After the explosion and damage from foam and water, all of his valuables, his records, his collections of pottery and paintings, and his business files would be worthless.

But it was not so much the thousands of dollars worth of valuables. Scattered about the house were pictures of his kids at various ages, birthday photos, photos of important events. In a cabinet in the dining room were scrapbooks and trophies from Darren and Danielle's school years. These were not particularly valuable except to a father who treasured these mementos of an earlier time.

But the most important items were none of these. He had locked them in the small safe in his home office. Someone had methodically torn apart his house. He had to assume they were searching for the books.

"I hate these damn metal roofs." Ryan overheard one of the firefighters say.

"Yeah, good for preventing a fire," the other said, "but once it gets going on the inside, it's like putting a lid on a frying pan."

In another hour, the house was reduced to blackened horizontal logs covered with white foam. Most of the roof had collapsed. Two additional fire trucks had responded, adding their personnel and fire suppressant chemicals to the fight. Firefighters were just now entering the house, searching out the remaining hot spots. The crime scene unit was busy stringing yellow tape.

The one-story wing with Ryan's master bedroom and home office was largely untouched. This end of the house and the surrounding trees had been heavily foamed. It reminded Ryan of the sagging chocolate cake, with globs of white frosting, that Danielle, age six, had proudly made for his birthday.

By the time Boulder County Sheriff Tom Ertl arrived, the temperature was dropping fast. Ertl climbed out of his car to talk with a firefighter who sat in the cab of one of the pumpers. The Sheriff moved like a man in charge, a man used to having subordinates. He was dressed in a dark suit with white shirt and patterned tie. He appeared to have come from some official function.

Ryan recalled his first conversation with the Tom Ertl about extraplanetary beings. "The government couldn't cover-up anything as big as extraterrestrials," Tom had said.

"And if it's true?"

"If it's true, it would change everything." And everything had changed for Tom Ertl when he encountered Sarah Smith and Peter Jones. His first reaction had been wonder, his second fear, and his third acceptance that he was somehow important to them and to their mission. Ryan had watched Tom's evolution and had recognized that it had happened to him also, albeit in a much different way.

After a brief conversation with the firefighters, the Sheriff drove to where Ryan, Sarah, and Peter stood waiting by Ryan's Jeep. Tom Ertl stood as tall as Peter, three inches shorter than Ryan; both men shared baldness. Tom Ertl came by his naturally. Only a dark ring remained above his ears and at the back of his head. In the style of

Phantia, Peter shaved what remaining hair he possessed.

After Tom made sure they were okay and got their version of the incident, they retrieved their personal items and threw them into the trunk of his official vehicle. "You were really lucky," he said.

They all agreed.

"Let's find you a hotel room."

"And some food," Peter added.

"The Colorado Bureau of Investigation will have people here tomorrow," Tom said as they drove through the front gate of Ryan's property. "I've already talked to them. Under the new rules, I'll also need to report this to the FBI — possible terrorist activity."

No one paid attention to the dirty white van parked a hundred yards down the gravel road that led to Ryan's house.

Before men can come to Utopia, they must learn the way there. Utopia, I see, is only a home for those who have learnt the way... it is not the place for men who grow wealthy by intercepting, but by serving.

— H. G. WELLS

TWO

That night they stayed in a small one-bedroom suite at the Hilton Hotel in downtown Boulder. Peter and Sarah shared the bedroom with its twin beds. Despite closed draperies, noise from the street filtered through the window. The room, the last one at the hotel, was badly situated. The manager had promised they could move into a larger suite tomorrow.

He had meditated the way Sarah had shown him, but Ryan still tossed and turned his six-foot frame on the uncomfortable sofa bed in the suite's front room. What most concerned him was not the metal bar in the middle of his back; he was wondering whether the intruders would be satisfied with trashing and burning his house. He had borrowed a pistol from Tom Ertl; it rested on the coffee table. Tomorrow he would retrieve his revolver from his house.

Ryan sat up. He bounded out of bed, grabbed the phone, and dialed the familiar number.

"Hello." The voice was filled with irritation. People did not welcome calls at 2:45 AM.

"Aza, this is Ryan."

"Who?"

"Ryan."

"Why the hell are ye callin' me in the middle of the night?"

"Where did you put those papers we took from Steiger's safe?" Ryan asked. "No, hold on. Don't tell me. This phone could be tapped. All I need to know is do you still have them?"

"Ryan." The sleepy voice had less irritation in it. "So are ye back from Arizona?"

"Sorry to bother you, but it's important."

A long pause, then, "I made a couple a copies, just like ye suggested. Put one in my favorite hidin' place."

"Okay," Ryan said. "Go back to sleep."

"What's goin' on?"

"I'll explain everything when I see you. Just watch out for anything unusual."

Aza had accompanied Ryan when he had rescued Sarah and taken Ernest Steiger's diary. If the old man harbored a grudge against Ryan, he probably had an even larger one against Aza — for it was Aza who had married Steiger's only daughter, Lucia, and had then divorced her.

"Look, I'm awake now," Aza said. "What do you mean?"

"They burned down my house."

"Jesus and Mary. Say that again."

"When we were away, somebody trashed my house," Ryan said. "Set bombs rigged to my security system and garage door opener. We were almost in the house when they went off. It was probably Steiger's people."

"Are you okay? Sarah? Peter?"

"Yeah, we were lucky. But I'm guessing I lost everything. I moved all my business stuff out of Sanitas before we went to Arizona."

"Where are you now?"

"At the Hilton in Boulder."

"You want to come stay here?" Aza asked. "I got plenty of room."

"You and I've got our date for coffee in a couple of days; let's talk it over then. I'll see what Sarah and Peter say. Just watch yourself."

After they rang off, Ryan tried calming his mind again, tried meditating. The sound of a car horn outside his window interrupted his concentration. After twenty minutes, he returned to tossing and turning. He hoped his insurance would cover the house and its contents. He thought he remembered placing the policy in his safety deposit box.

Now that he was without a regular income, Sarah and he had been discussing how to achieve a sustainable lifestyle, something that did not involve the huge mortgage and expensive utilities of a fancy house. Something to set an example of "xiaokang," Chinese for living moderately well, an example that money was not the goal. Well, without his mountain home, life sure would be a lot more moderate.

They had been lucky this time. Sarah's warning had given him just enough time. But how was he going to look out for her, and for Peter? His belief, that the house with its expensive security system afforded them some measure of safety, had been shattered. "I cannot hide," Sarah had insisted repeatedly. "We do not have much time. Peter and I must step up our efforts."

Peter had repeated his concerns about the self-destruction of Earth, an extinction of life that could happen with years. He had told Ryan that another planet, an inhabited planet from another star system, had self-destructed. Peter insisted that its destruction had come from actions such as those that were ongoing here on Earth. For the first time in Earth's history, humans had the capacity to adversely impact the air, water, and ground of the entire planet. With nuclear devices in the hands of so many, violence could easily escalate into a holocaust.

He had learned many things from the two extraplanetary beings in the six weeks since he had rescued Sarah from Steiger — during the time when no one had been hounding them. As the Phantians had laid out more of the larger truth, he thought of himself as trying to drink from a fire hose. Ryan eventually fell into a troubled sleep.

The transparent walls of his jail cell confined him. As had happened in every episode of this bizarre dream, he could watch the people next to him, above, and below. Guards in black uniforms sat watching the inmates, looking through their cells to other cells and on to other guards watching other inmates.

But the dream had changed. Before he had accepted it, now he fought to escape. No longer did he compliantly go about his prescribed activities. No longer did he get up at home, go to his office, drive his car, and fly on airplanes. One moment he felt free from the jail; the next moment he was securely confined.

The cells were without sound barriers, and he could hear others make observations about him. Their comments were much more critical than when he had conformed to the norm. But he reacted less to their censure; no longer did he modify his behavior to please them. Now, he commented on their mundane activities and attempted to influence their actions with his new insights. He and friends in adjacent cells helped each other to break free of the ever-present gaze of the guards and the other prisoners. From time to time, the jail walls faded and he felt no longer confined. However, he knew he was not free, knew the diaphanous cocoon within which he existed was ever ready to smother him, knew that when he was acting under its influence he was not truly himself. Somewhere deep within him, his real "me" tried to make itself known.

Ryan startled awake. He had heard something.

A faint scraping sound.

In the slit of light under the door to the hall, he glimpsed a shadow of movement.

The scraping sound again. Someone was trying to open the door.

Dressed only in his boxer shorts, he picked up the gun and crept forward. Through the peephole he could see the top of a head of black hair.

"What do you want?" Ryan asked.

A moment's hesitation, then a booming voice responded. "What are you doing in my room?" A florid face filled the peephole.

"I think you'd better check your room number."

"Is my wife in there?" The man began to pound on the door.

Smiling, Ryan stepped to the phone and called the front desk. He informed them that a drunk was at his door.

A few minutes later, the pounding and yelling subsided. Ryan went back to bed, wondering if the man was really a drunk or a clever intruder.

Morning sun, filtering through the two burned Ponderosa pines, cast strange shadows on the circular driveway and the vehicles parked there. Ryan Drake surveyed his gutted house, absorbing the damage.

Investigators from the Boulder Fire Department, who had been at work since daybreak, were showing him wires and remnants of a device they had found on the lower floor where heavier propane fumes had concentrated. "There is little doubt your security system was set to trigger it. Pretty standard stuff. It'll be hard to trace."

One of them had found an explosive triggering device in his garage. "The garage door opener was still wired to this piece." The investigator handed him a metal object with a burned wire attached.

"Ry, looks to me like somebody wants to kill you," Sheriff Tom Ertl said.

"Does look that way. Sure went to a lot of trouble."

"What about your friend Steiger?"

"Not too likely," Ryan said. "I called his son Nick. He said his father is still in the hospital — in a coma. Ernest Steiger is the only one I can think of; I can't figure any other reason for someone wanting to search the house."

"Something doesn't add up."

Carlos Romero, Ryan's insurance agent, finished his tour of the damage and joined them. He had brokered not only Ryan's house insurance, but also a large life insurance policy. He was not happy. "It'll take me a few days to work up numbers on the structure. Any idea on contents?"

Ryan thought for a minute. "I have an appraisal from my recent divorce. My wife's attorney insisted on it — so she could show the judge everything Vicki was leaving behind in the house."

"That'll do. So, are you going to rebuild?"

"Don't know." Ryan turned from the insurance man and stared at the shell of his formerly beautiful home.

"My firm's nervous about your life insurance," Romero commented as he walked to his car. "You live too dangerously."

Ryan was sure the man was not joking. If the insurance company had been privy to his association with two extraplanetary beings, they probably would already have cancelled.

"I want to go in," Ryan started for his house.

"Hold on. Why?" Ertl grabbed his arm.

"To check on something."

"Where?"

"In my office."

"You're sure?"

"Yeah."

"All right, I'll go with you."

Ryan and Ertl went around to the master bedroom wing. The smell of smoke was everywhere. They climbed onto a balcony and were about to go into the white-foamed, black jumble through an open French door.

Boom! The force of the explosion knocked both men to the deck.

When they struggled into a sitting position, both were covered with a mixture of black debris and yellow-white foam.

"You two okay?" The head of one of the fire inspectors popped up over the edge of the deck.

Ryan nodded.

"We're fine," the Sheriff replied. Turning to Ryan he added, "Romero was right, hanging out with you is dangerous."

"John's in there," another fire inspector yelled.

"Better wait until I see what happened." Ertl went to see if he could help.

A few minutes later he hurried past Ryan, raced to his car, and called for a medical unit.

Within a few minutes, a paramedic vehicle, lights flashing, arrived. Two men raced to where the explosion had occurred. A short time later, they came through the door with a stretcher and a body.

Ryan lent a hand getting the stretcher off the balcony. When he his hand touched the black bag, he knew the bomb had been intended for him. Bowing his head, he wished the man God speed on his celestial Journey.

Tom Ertl came to Ryan and put a hand on his shoulder. "It was wired to your bed."

"Bastards."

Ryan stepped inside and headed for his home office. Because it was distant from the center of yesterday's fire, and the recent explosion had been confined to the master bedroom, it was relatively intact.

He moved cautiously amidst the ruin. Each drawer of his desk and file cabinets hung open and empty. There were no ashes indicating their former contents had burned, not one charred paper. The keyboard, mouse, and display were still on the desk, but his computer tower was missing. And he could find none of his back-up disks.

Ryan pointed at the small fire-resistant safe in the corner. Still firmly bolted to the floor, its door hung open. It was completely empty, no papers, no leather bound volumes of Ernest Steiger's diary. "They got them."

"What?"

"Steiger's diaries," Ryan said, "and everything else."

"Leaves you kind of naked doesn't it?" After he had rescued Sarah from Ernest Steiger, Ryan had told Tom how he and Aza O'Sullivan had taken the two leather-bound originals of the old man's diary as insurance. Ryan had told Ertl that he believed threatening to publish the diary would shield Sarah, Peter, and him.

"Yeah, I'm feeling pretty exposed right now."

"So what was in those diaries that Steiger, or his crowd doesn't want out?"

"Names, dates, and the truth behind certain events."

"Names? Names of who?"

"The diary names men who control our country, the world, names of men behind the scenes, the shadow government, the puppet-masters."

"And you think knowing those names makes you a target?"

"Yeah."

They walked through the master bedroom. The closet had been emptied. The clothes, along with the contents of his dresser, were piled at the foot of the bed, or what was left of the bed. Most were singed; all were soaked. The drawer of the bedside stand stood open; his .357 magnum was gone.

They stepped toward the center of the house along a hallway that had been Ryan's photo gallery. He picked up a dozen pictures of his kids; all were blackened and wet.

Ryan's photo collection of hiking companions, at the top of

Colorado's fourteeners, had been smashed in their frames. Men and women, most of them from other businesses — hearty people who enjoyed a challenge. He extracted a few torn remnants.

"Whoa." Ertl grabbed his shirt and pointed at the gaping hole. Ryan pulled his foot back onto the singed carpeting of the hallway.

The dining room, along with part of his ultra-modern kitchen, had collapsed into the pool below. Pieces of the metal roof hung from the walls like flaps of a giant tent. Ryan could tell from the pile of canned and packaged goods in what remained of the kitchen, that the contents of each cupboard and drawer had been emptied. Some of the wallboard showed slashes, opened to reveal the pink insulation behind.

A fire inspector explained that this pattern had been repeated in each of the five bathrooms, and in the laundry room and downstairs bar. In each bedroom, the beds had been stripped and the mattresses and box springs slit open. Clothes were removed from drawers and closets; gaping holes opened in walls. Tiles had been pulled up around the indoor pool and in the shower and bath areas.

After they had retraced their steps to the outside, Ryan said, "I wonder if they'll try anything more, now that they've recovered Steiger's diary."

"Wondering won't keep you alive," Ertl said.

"They could have shot me."

"Now that they have the diary, they can do anything they damn well please. Ry, if someone decides to take a shot at you — well, no one can protect you from a sniper. Are you sure you want to keep pushing this cosmic paradigm?"

"Tom, I understand a lot, a lot more than I've even told you. Now that I know this stuff, I don't think I have a choice."

"You might wind up dying."

"I know."

In spare moments, over the past six weeks, Ryan had read every word on the pages of Ernest Steiger's diary. He had taken a copy with him to Arizona, leaving the original volumes safely at home. The contents of the copied diary, each page carefully authenticated by the clerk in Ryan's attorney's office, were an eye-opener for the formerly conservative businessman. Until now, he had only the faintest idea of the power games being played behind the scenes, games with the lives of his fellow citizens, with his own life. A vast conspiracy of those who considered themselves elite.

In addition, Dr. Adamson had furnished him with all of Steiger's older diaries, neatly stapled into volumes, and dating from 1947. They too had been authenticated, by a legal firm in Paris who used oversized paper to include their certification at the bottom of each page. Combined with the more recent copies, they made a stack five inches high. Starting with the earliest years, Ryan had devoured the diary page-by-page.

In it he had discovered how Ernest Steiger's father had educated and trained his son as an elitist –- destined to become a member of the World League, an organization of those who secretly ruled the world. While the elder Steiger lay dying of cancer, he had made arrangements for his only son, Ernest, to replace him on the board of the media affiliates, one of the League's subsidiary organizations. Ernest had shown his abilities, and within twenty years he was running the most powerful influencer of public attitudes and behavior ever conceived. Ernest Steiger had become an expert at mass mind control. He was also a member of the Board of Governors of the World League, the very top of the elite secret organization.

Ryan discovered how the media affiliates had manipulated the major media, as well as Hollywood, with unrelated breaking news to hide important events, with spin control to modify the truth about events, with bogus investigations with predetermined results, with front organizations, with true information provided first to disreputable sources, and with packaged misinformation provided to reputable sources. In the process they had built an artificial world to shape the way people reacted.

He saw how the World League had packed media organizations with men and women from the intelligence agencies. He discovered how the media associates, at the direction of the League, had over the years entrapped and manipulated politicians. Just before Christmas, he had read the last page in the copies of Steiger's older diaries. They ended at February 15, 1998.

The volumes he had taken from Steiger's mansion picked up on February 16th. They showed the old man becoming impatient with others in the World League. He was getting older, wheelchair bound with heart disease and diabetes; they still had not accomplished their ultimate objective.

He had maneuvered his protégé, John deBeque, into a position of influence only to discover that deBeque now had divided loyalties, and was asking too many questions. There were comments on his meeting with Ryan and the mysterious box from Harmony Center, and how he had tried to intimidate Ryan into disclosing the whereabouts of Sarah Smith. The diary detailed his obsession with capturing "the alien" and his disappointment when she would not tell him the secret of her communications technology. The last notation was Steiger's directive to begin using a new class of drugs to probe Sarah's mind.

One of the more telling revelations was the role Ryan's father, Albert Drake, had played in Steiger's machinations. Steiger had sought out his old army buddy after they had been discharged. From his first job with a law firm in St. Louis, Albert Drake had become Ernest Steiger's personal attorney. From that initial assignment, Albert's role had grown into confidant to the powerful media mogul. Ryan now understood one of many secrets his father had kept from his family.

Between what he knew about the cosmic paradigm, and what he knew about the World League and people like his own father, Ryan Drake was a very dangerous man. But like the key player in a crucial game of football, he knew he had no choice but to see it through to its end.

A dark sedan pulled into the driveway and stopped next to them.

As two men alighted, Ertl said to Ryan, "FBI."

"Great, just what I need."

"All they know is that your house was bombed." Ertl said in words so low that only Ryan could hear them.

The two Special Agents introduced themselves, Jake Ashton and Howard Billings. Both were from the Denver office.

"Any idea who?" Ashton pointed to the blackened structure.

"No." Ryan shook his head. He was not ready to talk to the FBI about Ernest Steiger. It was better to see what they could turn up. He was sure the men who had ransacked his house had left some evidence. The bad guys always made mistakes — at least in the movies.

When Ashton asked who else was living in the house, Ryan explained that he and two friends had returned after being gone for ten days.

"We'll need to talk to them." Ashton jotted down their names.

"They're pretty shaken by all this. Can you give it a day or two?"

After a few more questions, the two FBI agents went off to talk to the fire inspectors. Ryan watched them go and wondered whether they really were who they said they were, whether their real interest was in a possible terrorist attack, or whether they were secretly working for Ernest Steiger and the World League.

Thought transmission is the purest form of communication, as the conversation may not be manipulated into something it is not.

— PTAAH

THREE

J'Li D'Rona ate dinner that evening with Z'Rv, who was known on this planet as Peter Jones. The members of her team had chosen names to fit comfortably with the inhabitants of the region where they were assigned. Saying that he had something to attend to, Ryan Drake had not accompanied them to the hotel's restaurant.

After the explosion of the bomb under Ryan's bed, Sheriff Ertl had assigned deputies to watch over them. One of the Sheriff's men waited in the lobby of the restaurant.

It was late when they returned to their suite. There was a message for her from Tom Ertl. When Sarah returned the call, to his home number, he said, "Jake Ashton contacted me. He's one of the FBI guys that Ryan met this morning. He wants to meet with you."

"Not Peter?"

"He requested you. Didn't mention Peter. I find that a little strange because Ryan gave him both of your names. It won't hurt to meet with him. Maybe we'll find out something."

Trusting Ertl's judgment, Sarah agreed to come to his office the next morning.

"Somebody's meddling," Ryan said after she hung up. He had returned to the suite as she was talking. "I've got a bad feeling about this." He offered to cancel his meeting in Denver with Aza O'Sullivan and accompany her, but she declined.

The hour was late, so they talked briefly. Then with a kiss to Ryan's cheek, she turned and walked to her room.

Both Peter and she were in the habit of meditating before sleep.

She knew, without consulting her celestial friends, that they had been warned about the explosions because Ryan had a vital role to play in transforming this planet. She thanked her guardians for sparing her also, so that she might continue her mission.

Tapping into universe mind Sarah went to check on the two daughters she had left behind on Phantia. She saw that all was well with both families and that B'Tric's new baby was thriving. She so longed to hold her grandchildren in her arms. These frequent "visits" served to keep her updated, but they were a poor substitute for being present physically.

Returning from her visit, she thought of the human in the next room. There was Peter, of course, sleeping in the adjacent bed, but Ryan Drake was the closest thing she had to family on this planet, and she treasured their relationship.

'*Good night, Ryan,*' she communicated to the sleeping Earthhuman. '*I do love you.*' Before she realized it, she was asleep.

"That guy gives me the creeps. He is just butt ugly."

"I agree, but he always has something to offer," Günter Von Hedemann said.

"I don't care, he's creepy. You can never tell what he's thinking — those blank eyes." He mimicked the blank stare of the one they had just visited. His living quarters were on the lowest level of the underground facility. "And that other one that's usually with him — sometimes it seems human, other times it's like a ghost."

"Look, the alien eats and craps just like you and me. Get over it. He may have given us a real tidbit on this guidance control thing. Give it a try — the way he wants it."

"Don't I always."

"And don't they usually work?" Von Hedemann asked his assistant. He had known the other man for many years and had recruited him as the head of research from a lucrative corporate position. They interacted daily.

"After a lot of screwing around. He chewed my ass because we still haven't got the last thing right."

"Well, do you?" It was only when conversing with his trusted assistants that Von Hedemann felt comfortable dropping his thick German accent.

"Like I told him, we're working on it. But no, that's not good enough. I'm telling you, we need more time. This technology hasn't even been imagined by anyone on this planet. Now he wants me to implement it like..." Von Hedemann's assistant snapped his fingers.

"We have to play along. In time he'll give us the rest of picture."

"And I think he's stringing us along."

Wes and Jenny Bailey had just turned off US 191, a few miles north of Monticello, Utah. The back road headed east and then jogged in the general direction of Slick Rock, Colorado. Their modest ranch straddled the Colorado Utah border.

"Awake, honey?" Jenny asked as she stared at the lonely road ahead. Both Wes and she were on the lookout for deer, or other wildlife that might be crossing this deserted strip of gravel.

Wes yawned and drained his can of Coke. "We're almost there." They had driven this road many times in their five years of marriage. The nearest super market was back at Monticello.

He hated these late night returns from his in-laws place in Flagstaff. He had enjoyed the five-day visit and the bowl games on New Year's Day. As usual, his wife's parents had doted on Jenny, their younger daughter, and insisted they stay another day. But damn it, no matter how many days they stayed, they always left late, and they always wound up driving home at night.

"I could drive," she said.

Wes re-centered the vehicle in the middle of the deserted road and drove on. He shifted in his seat, moving his left leg into a more comfortable position.

Without warning, the dash lit up like a Christmas tree, every indicator turned on. Then every light, including the Chevy's headlights, blinked out. The engine stalled. They coasted to a stop in the middle of a snowy patch.

Suddenly he was wide-awake.

"Great spot for car trouble," she said, trying not to sound critical.

"But I checked everything before we left," Wes said defensively. He kept the car in good shape. "We didn't have any trouble going down." The four-year-old vehicle had just rolled over sixty thousand miles. Growing up on a ranch, miles from the nearest service station, Wes had learned to maintain all kinds of equipment.

The powerful lights of a huge truck came barreling down on them. They did not get much truck traffic out here, an occasional delivery, or a truck to pick up a load of cattle. Since he had turned off the main highway, there had been no traffic.

He pumped the brake pedal, but saw no red indication to the rear. "We better pray he sees us."

Without a sound, the big rig halted behind the Bailey's vehicle. It did not dim its exceptionally bright lights.

"He stopped."

"Thank God."

Before either Wes or Jenny could say more, the lights on the truck took on a strange greenish cast. Intense, they illuminated the interior of the car like daylight.

"What's happening?" Jenny sounded the alarm.

At first, Wes saw only fuzzy shadows in his side mirror. As they came closer, he could tell they were about six feet tall and thin. His mind flashed to the science fiction movie they had seen in Flagstaff. In it, aliens had terrorized some ranch folks just like Jenny and him. The images separated, going to each side of the vehicle.

Jenny screamed when a face with over-sized, almond eyes peered in her side window. When the alien pointed his weapon at her she fainted. She would later recall that she had been taken on board a space ship where gray-skinned aliens had sex with her. It had been a disgusting and painful event.

While he kept one eye on the big-eyed alien that had come to his window, Wes groped under the seat for his pistol. As he brought it up, a blinding headache forced him to reach for his temples. The gun went rattling to the floor.

Two silver-skinned aliens opened the door and dragged him from the car. All the time a tremendous headache pounded his head. He would remember how they had taken him aboard their space ship, restrained him on a table in a white operating room, and inserted a long probe up his nose. It was a painful, frightening experience, accompanied by threats on his life, an experience he wasn't sure he would survive.

When Wes awoke, he was laying at the side of the road, not far from the back of his car. He struggled to his feet, still holding his temples.

The car door was ajar and he climbed into the driver's seat. Jenny was slumped in the passenger seat, unconscious. He felt helpless to do anything more than reach across and gently touch her. Examining himself in the rearview mirror, he saw that blood was crusted on his upper lip. He had not dreamed this awful experience.

When he turned the key, the Chevy started. Wes slowly drove home. Checking his watch, he noticed that two hours had elapsed.

In about a mile, Jenny stirred and began to rub her temples. "Did they take you too?" she asked.

"Yes."

"Are you okay?"

"Got one hell of a headache."

"Me too."

When they reached home, they both took aspirin and collapsed into bed.

The next morning, as the first signs of daybreak awakened them, neither Jenny nor Wes could bring themselves to speak of the incident. Wes had a splitting headache. Jenny had cramps from the sexual assault.

A bit later, that same morning, J'Li D'Rona walked the few blocks from the hotel to the Boulder Justice Center on Canyon Blvd. She wore large dark glasses to protect her eyes from the sun's powerful rays. Along the way she passed a young mother dragging a screaming two-year-old boy. The young woman yelled at her son, reached down, and slapped the youngster.

J'Li approached them. "Your son has a sickness in his throat." Sarah reached down and put her hand on the child's head. The child immediately stopped crying.

The young woman stared at the tall blonde woman. She opened her mouth to say something, but decided otherwise.

"You too can learn to cure sickness. My name is Sarah Smith. Call me." She handed the woman a card which told where she could leave a message.

Stunned, the young woman could only utter a simple,

"Thank you."

When Sarah arrived at the Boulder Justice Center around 9:00 AM, Sheriff Tom Ertl was again dressed in a suit and tie. Eight inches shorter than herself, he appeared to be much more muscular than Peter. The Sheriff carried himself like one of the prizefighters she had seen when she had studied videos at Harmony. Unlike Peter, Tom's head was not completely bald, he had a skirt of dark hair over his ears. He wore small rimless glasses.

He took her into his office and explained that there was a second FBI agent, Rita Martinez — a woman from their Phoenix office. "I checked her out with my contact in Arizona. You need to know, she was there the morning of the raid on Harmony."

Ertl went on to tell Sarah several other things he had learned from his friend in Arizona. The internal investigation by the U.S. Customs and Border Protection Agency, a recent combination of the former Immigration and Naturalizations Service and the Customs Service, had concluded that since there were no witnesses, they had no choice but to believe Raul Viejo's written report that stated the shooting of George Tomichi was in the line of duty. The Agency was prepared to return Harmony and to make suitable reparation for the damage caused by their "investigation into Mexican illegals."

When Tom Ertl and Sarah Smith entered the room, the two agents politely introduced themselves. Now, on the opposite side of the polished wooden table, they sat ramrod straight, a yellow pad in front of each of them. A recording device, which she recognized as a dictating machine like the kind Ryan used, sat on the table between them.

Rita had disheveled dark hair and dark eyes, and wore a dark gray suit with a green scarf about her neck. Although Sarah was not a good judge of Earth-human age, she appeared to be about thirty years old.

Jake Ashton had on a light gray suit, white shirt, and blue tie. His lighter skin and neatly trimmed brown hair contrasted with the more swarthy rumpled appearance of his associate. Sarah thought he looked about forty. His intense green eyes looked at her through tiny rimless glasses. She sensed that he was a man of integrity.

They were in the conference room next to Ertl's office. Sarah noted that the chairs were padded, unlike the interrogation scenes she had seen on television. And the lights were not terribly intrusive, more like the lights at the hotel. With the exception of Raul Viejo and Luis Litchfield who had rudely interrogated her at Harmony Center, this was her sole face-to-face conflict with the authorities of this planet. She was glad that Tom Ertl sat next to her.

Sarah recalled when she had pictioned for the Sheriff. He had resisted at first, but gradually calmed enough that she was able to proceed. She had shown him her voyage from Phantia and a little of life on her home planet. When she released him from her piction, he had sat stunned, unable to speak. His whole worldview had been turned upside down. Since that time he had taken special care of Peter, Ryan, and her.

"Sarah, where were you on the morning of October sixteenth of last year?" Jake Ashton asked.

Sarah thought for a moment and replied, "I was in the desert."

"Where?"

"Several miles southeast of Harmony Center — that's in Arizona."

Rita raised one eyebrow and asked, "With Cody Tsotsie?"

"Yes." Weeks ago, a celestial ally had informed her that, as part of their routine follow-up, the FBI had obtained a record of the INS's rough interview of Cody Tsotsie, her Navajo guide. Cody had told the INS that he had guided Sarah and the others in the desert.

Jake Ashton interrupted to explain that, because everybody thought they were dealing with Mexican illegals, the Immigration and Naturalization Service had primary responsibility for securing Harmony Center the morning of the raid. However, the killing of George Tomichi, a Navajo, had changed things. The FBI had jurisdiction when problems with Native Americans were involved. Their investigation was being hampered by their inability to find Raul Viejo, the INS agent who had led the raid.

Before Ashton could say more, Martinez shot a question at her. "Why were you out in the desert?"

Sarah saw that it was intended to catch her off balance and did not react. Rather, she calmly responded, "I had been threatened by Raul Viejo. We obtained advanced warning of the raid and chose

41

not to offer resistance."

Sarah was about to volunteer more, but before she could, Martinez asked, "Why did George Tomichi remain at Harmony?"

While Martinez asked her questions, Ashton made notes. Martinez made no notes.

"We pleaded with him to leave," Sarah said, "but he didn't want to abandon the garden inside the bio-dome."

"What do you know about the circumstances of his death?"

The questions were coming so rapidly she had no opportunity to formulate a complete reply. On Phantia, questioners always allowed someone to respond fully, to elaborate, and to tell the whole story, even if it took days. She began to understand that a series of rapid questions and answers were the way interrogators worked on this world. There was no time for "pointless" expounding. She had seen this form of interrogation in videos where it was assumed that the people being questioned were trying to hide something.

Her parents had trained her that integrity was the only way, regardless of the pain or consequences — the Phantian way. Sarah intended to respond to their questions within the full scope of her knowledge — she had no training in evasion, and before coming to Earth, no model for that type of behavior. Integrity for her meant supplying additional information that helped to clarify the situation, even if it meant disadvantaging yourself. On the other hand, she was happy that they were not questioning her about her off-planet origins.

Everywhere she turned on this world, people were less than totally truthful. Advertisers did not reveal the whole truth about the products advertised. Witnesses answered only the questions asked of them, volunteered nothing else. Ryan had told her that in business, it was common to "finesse" others — not tell the whole truth. Many of the problems of this planet would be solved if people just dealt with complete integrity.

She returned to Martinez's question and said, "I visualized Raul Viejo shoot him."

Ashton and Martinez exchanged glances.

"Can you say a little more about that?" Ashton asked.

"I have the ability to remotely view. That morning I saw George enter the greenhouse by the rear entrance and try to stop Viejo from overturning his newly planted seedlings."

Before she could go on, Martinez asked, "What was your relationship to Andria Hernandez?"

"I don't know who that is."

"She was found unconscious near Harmony. Her coat was found in your facility."

"Oh, the Mexican woman. I didn't know her name. I did hear about her trouble in the desert, a terrible thing," Sarah said. "I did not meet her, and she was never at Harmony."

"You're sure about that?"

"Yes."

"How do you think her coat got there?"

"I don't know for sure. But I suspect it was planted there to make us look guilty, and to help justify the raid. I did not remote view it happening."

Martinez shook her head, "Just answer the question, please."

"What's the purpose of this line of questioning?" Ertl interrupted.

"As we explained, we are completing our inquiry into the death of George Tomichi," Martinez said. "There are things about the whole Harmony Center affair that don't make sense."

"Aren't you a little late? This all happened months ago."

"There's no statute of limitation on murder."

"Murder?" the Sheriff said.

"We haven't ruled out murder in the death of either George Tomichi or Andria Hernandez."

"Despite what Customs and Border Protection has concluded?"

Martinez gave Ashton a glance before she replied. "Despite their conclusions." She obviously did not like the fact that Tom Ertl, a local sheriff, was as well informed as she.

"Were there FBI agents at the scene?" Ertl bored in.

"Yes," Rita Martinez responded, "I was one of them."

"What's your version of what happened?" Ertl asked.

"Neither my partner nor I witnessed the incident." Martinez's response was icy. "We were busy elsewhere."

"Was there an Amelia Lighter at Harmony?" Ashton asked Sarah. He obviously wanted to take back control of the interrogation from Ertl.

Sarah paused for a moment and then said, "Yes. She lived with —"

Martinez jumped in with another question. "Where is she now?"

"Amelia graduated the night before the INS raided our facility."

"Graduated?"

"I believe you use the term 'passed on.'" Sarah said.

"And her body?" Martinez asked.

"Her body combusted. When she determined it was time, she went to the incinerator at Harmony — to avoid causing a fire somewhere else within the facility."

Ashton wrinkled his forehead and squinted at her. "In the event of a death, the authorities need to be notified, a death certificate needs to be filed. It's illegal to cremate a body without authorization."

"Amelia was very sick," Sarah tried to explain. "Since she could no longer contribute, she decided to leave. When she made that determination, her body combusted. That is the best I can explain the process."

"What do you mean combusted?"

"Are you familiar with the process of spontaneous combustion?"

Ashton rolled his eyes and asked, "What was she sick from?"

"Her system was allergic to certain chemicals and —"

"There were no human remains in the ashes at Harmony." Martinez studied her face for a reaction to the question.

"If spontaneous combustion is allowed to run its course, there are none."

"Okay. Okay." Ashton put up his hands indicating they were getting nowhere with this line of questioning.

Ryan and she had discussed Amelia. He had told her that without a body or other evidence, the authorities had no case for any wrongdoing. He also told her not to expect the authorities to believe her story about spontaneous combustion.

"What about Victor Adamson?" Rita Martinez asked.

"I do not know where he is at the moment. He travels extensively."

Martinez scowled at her response, then asked, "And Peter Jones?"

"He is at the hotel," Sarah said. "I'm sure he would be happy to answer your questions."

The two agents glanced at each other, and then indicated they would like to interview Peter.

"But first," Sarah asked, "when will Harmony be released?"

"Customs and Border Protection is prepared to release Harmony, after we inform them of the results of our investigation."

"When do you intend to wrap this up?" Ertl asked.

"I'll be frank, Sheriff Ertl," Martinez said, "there are a lot of loose ends." She glanced at Ashton. "I think we need to talk to Peter Jones."

"There is one more thing," Ashton said. "Tell us what happened at Ryan Drake's house."

Sarah related what she had seen.

"Do you have any idea who booby trapped it?"

"Booby trapped?" Sarah had not heard the expression before.

Tom Ertl came to her rescue, "Placed the bomb."

"Oh. No, I do not know." They had not asked about her suspicions, and she did not wish to speculate, so she did not offer more. Ryan had asked her to remote view the placing of the bombs. When she had done that, she found that two men were responsible. One of them was the same man who had kidnapped her.

More than anything else, Sarah wanted to tell them about the cosmic paradigm and all the other wondrous news she had brought to Earth, about the paradise that Earth could become. But both Ryan and Tom Ertl had advised her to let the agents lead the discussion for now. "There will be another time," Ryan had said. But she was impatient; the seconds of her existence on this planet were ticking away. Even if she lived out a normal life expectancy, which was not at all likely, she had much to accomplish, and little time in which to do it. Conditions on this planet were worsening daily; people simply did not realize how close to extinction they were.

The two FBI agents walked with them to the hotel. There they interviewed Peter, without her present. When they departed, they told Peter and her not to leave the State.

Comparing their impressions, Peter and she decided that their interviews had been most strange, particularly by Phantian standards. They could not tell whether the two FBI agents were dedicated to finding the truth about the raid on Harmony, or whether Rita Martinez was under pressure to arrive at a predetermined outcome.

We can easily forgive a child who is afraid of the dark; the real tragedy of life is when men are afraid of the light.

— PLATO

FOUR

At the same time Sarah was being interviewed by the FBI, Ryan was waiting for Aza O'Sullivan at the coffee shop in the Brown Palace Hotel in downtown Denver.

Studying the faces of those around him reminded Ryan of his second trip to Phantia. Sarah had once again pictioned for him. It was after he had rescued her from Steiger's mansion, after she had recovered her strength.

This second time the pictioning was different. This time he had the opportunity to watch Sarah interact with other Phantians, to see how human they were, to see that they had personal lives, concerns, and loves.

As before the piction had started at Harmony. This time the trip from Earth to her home planet was at high speed, a snippet as Earth receded into the background, a quick view of the stars as they shifted into unfamiliar patterns, a slice of the Milky Way Galaxy as they skirted its periphery, and a bit of the approach and landing on Phantia.

This time she took him to a restaurant on her home planet where she was seated across the table from a man and woman. This time, his more highly developed mind-to-mind communication skills had enabled him to understand their conversation.

The woman appeared younger than Sarah. Dark hair against a bronze complexion, beautiful grey eyes with a hint of violet, high cheekbones, and a mouth that was perfect for her face.

Her companion was similarly young and handsome. Ryan could not tell if they were married. Except for light eyebrows and eyelashes, his perfectly shaped head was devoid of hair. His eyes were also gray, a pale gray. Like others on Phantia the eyes of the man and woman were slightly larger than those of Earth-dwellers.

'We leave soon. Are you excited?' the woman communicated to Sarah. She took a bite of what appeared to be green salad with pieces of things Ryan could not identify. He did see what he thought were tiny dark dots of caraway seeds.

'I am having a hard time leaving A'Dr and B'Tric and the children,' Sarah communicated.

'How are my two nieces taking it?' The man too was chewing while conversing mind-to-mind.

'A'Dr is upset, does not want me to go. B'Tric is sad, but concurs. Their mates side with each. The children are simply too young to understand.

'I have told them of the opportunity to transition this other planet, as we have already experienced the great transformation here. But A'Dr has heard stories about the planet's history of violence and is afraid for me. I can only hope her anxiety, and that of others, does not transcend the distance. We do not want to give energy to those on that planet who encourage fear. My community of D'Ct-Elds has suspended teaching to focus positive energy on our mission.'

'Our entire world has been sending regularly scheduled positive energy to that other planet every day since your mission was announced,' the woman communicated. *'I think it will be much easier than anyone suspects. After all, they have lived in wretched circumstances for thousands of years. I'm sure our sister world is ready for a change.'*

'Our sister world,' the man communicated. *'I kind of like the ring of that. For my part, I foresee that this other planet will not be much different than living here. As you know, before this opportunity came up, my next position was to help the less developed people of a small village in the southern hemisphere. They are lagging behind our planet-wide transformation.'*

Sarah reached across the table and touched his arm. *'Haven't you been paying attention to the previews of our new home? The entire planet has yet to experience any but the first stages of its transformation to enlightenment.'*

'Yes, older sister, I have been paying attention, but how hard can it be, really?'

'Did you hear about the disturbance in Tibnap?' the dark haired woman asked. 'Two families got into a fight over some silly antique. One man stabbed the other with a knife; then two people from his family retaliated. The local authorities had to intervene. It's one of the few times three people have died at one time since the compact one hundred twelve years ago. Physical violence has become so rare on our sphere.'

'It's no wonder,' Sarah's brother communicated. 'Tibnap is the last undeveloped place. That's where I was supposed to go, before this opportunity came up — clear on the other side of the globe. Do you know that some people down there live at fifty percent of the world standard of living?'

'And they burn hydrocarbons to produce electricity,' the dark haired woman communicated, 'and have more than two children per family.'

Sarah had pictioned further, taking him to a collection of large buildings. He had thought at the time that they reminded him of some of the buildings in Washington, DC. Offices surrounded the three main buildings with their large meeting halls. Other nearby buildings were filled with courtrooms.

Men and women, tall and short, thin and fat, but all with similar skin coloring — a light tan, or bronze, not unlike Sarah's — scurried about. They were dressed in a wide variety of clothing from flowing robes to skin-tight garments. All were handsome, all appeared to be quite happy, and all looked very human.

Now, as Ryan sat at the coffee shop, he wondered what had happened to Sarah's brother and the dark haired woman. They must have come to Harmony, then what? He made a mental note to ask Sarah about them.

When they had talked about the buildings, Sarah had explained that what he had seen was Phantia's seat of world government. The three large buildings were the home of Phantia's world legislature. One house was elected in accordance with economic function, another was elected by social organizations, and the third was made up of distinguished people nominated for their dedication to service. The court system was broken into those dealing with socioeconomic issues and courts of law. One wrinkle in Phantia's democratic system that Ryan liked was the idea of conferring additional votes on individuals who had distinguished themselves in terms of service or wisdom.

Planetary administration was a mixture of human and celestial. Everyone acknowledged the greater wisdom and experience of the celestials and intraplanetaries who had been at work for thousands, if not millions, of years. Fellow humans carried out the details of day-to-day administration.

Could Earth evolve to a place like Phantia? It seemed like such a stretch. As it was, the political and economic structure was fragile, more delicately balanced than the average person realized. International banking depended largely on the strength of the American dollar, which in turn, since it was no longer backed by gold, depended on the confidence of the American people. With this scheme, the Treasury and Central Bank of the United States effectively controlled the money of the world. The stock market, a similar creation, was subject to political and economic gyrations, as well as psychological whim. The Internet, which was becoming more important every day, was constantly subjected to hackers and viruses. Yes, the structure of his world was fragile, but somehow it worked. How radical of a change could it accommodate? New inventions had taken years to be absorbed. Would the existing structures have to be torn down, before they could be rebuilt? Would acknowledging the presence of extraplanetary beings knock everything off balance?

The Phantians had achieved an absence of nations and competing political entities in their planetary government. Was that the key? How had they managed to get everyone to give up their weapons? He knew from Sarah and Peter that they relied on forms of energy barely known on Earth. Would exposure to the cosmic paradigm be enough to initiate the process? How would it play out?

Glancing at his Rolex, Ryan saw the time. Aza was forty-five minutes late — that was not like him. Ryan flipped open his cell phone and called Aza's house.

A strange voice answered. "Hello."

Putting aside his temporary confusion, Ryan asked, "Is Aza there?"

"Who's calling?"

"This is Ryan Drake. Is he there please?"

"Mr. Drake, this is Detective Sergeant Michael Martin. We are at Mr. O'Sullivan's home investigating his death. What is your connection with the deceased?"

Ryan dropped his cell phone. It clattered to the tile floor loudly enough that several people looked around.

When he had retrieved it, Martin asked, "Mr. Drake, are you all right?"

"Yeah, I'm okay. But my best friend was just murdered."

There was a pause, and then Martin asked, "Where are you right now, Mr. Drake?"

"I'm at the coffee shop in the Brown Palace."

"Please wait there, I'll have one of my men come pick you up. Please identify yourself to the hostess."

"Why? What's going on?"

"Just stay put. An officer will be along shortly."

A uniformed Denver Police Officer arrived in a few minutes. Ryan was on his second cup of espresso and had wolfed down a bowl of oatmeal and a piece of toast.

"Mr. Drake, Mr. Ryan Drake?"

Ryan looked up to see a large black man in the blue uniform of a Denver Policeman. "Yes."

"I'm Officer James Manville. Will you come with me please?"

They went to the black and white parked at the curb. Ryan expected to be driven to Aza's house, but Manville drove him to the Denver Police sub-station on South University Boulevard and ushered him into an interrogation room.

As he sat looking at the sterile walls, Ryan wondered if the people who had killed Aza were they the same ones who had planted bombs at his house.

Detective Sergeant Michael Martin arrived in ten minutes. Martin was a big man in a tweed sport coat and dark blue slacks. His red tie was loosened about the collar of his pale blue shirt. He plopped himself down across from Ryan, turned on a tape recorder, and began to ask questions.

"Where have you been since seven PM last night?"

Ryan smiled and then began. "At seven I was just finishing dinner with friends at a Boulder restaurant. I walked to my room at the Hilton in Boulder. At about nine I said good night to my roommates and went to bed. I awoke at six this morning, did some work in my room, showered, dressed, and at about eight thirty headed for my appointment with Aza."

"Let's narrow it down a bit closer, where were you at about two AM?" Martin asked.

"Asleep."

"Can anyone vouch for the fact that you did not leave your room during the night?"

Ryan smiled and replied, "There was a Boulder County Deputy stationed outside my room. I can get his name if —"

"You're serious?"

"Yes."

"Damn." Martin slammed his hand on the recorder. He sat staring at Ryan.

After Martin did not speak for several moments, Ryan said, "What made you think I was involved in Aza's death?"

"On the phone, you told me he had been murdered — I hadn't told you how he died."

"Murder," Ryan said, "was a reasonable assumption, given the police were there."

"Maybe, maybe not."

"All right, Detective Martin, now that we have that out of the way, why don't you tell me what happened to my friend?"

A long pause during which Martin tried to figure out how far he was going to allow Ryan to probe. "Why was a deputy outside your room?" he asked.

"Because, two days ago somebody booby trapped my house and tried to kill me. You can verify everything with the Boulder Sheriff's office. So, what happened to Aza?"

Martin hesitated, heaved a sigh, and then said, "This is off the record, okay. If you repeat any of it, I'll deny I ever told you anything."

Ryan nodded.

"A neighbor of Mr. O'Sullivan's reported gun shots at about two this morning. A patrol car went to investigate. They found the front door open. When they went inside, they found him dead."

"Shot?"

Martin nodded. Ryan figured the detective had offered all he was going to about the crime. "Why were you meeting him?"

"He had —" Ryan stopped short. "We had breakfast every week or so. We were good friends."

Ryan wasn't ready to tell the police that the reason for their meeting was so Aza could supply him with copies of the material they had retrieved from Ernest Steiger's safe. He had thought about it at the coffee shop after he had heard the news, and again in the interrogation room while waiting for Martin.

No, if those papers were so valuable that Aza had died for them, he was going to put them to a better use than explaining about them as part of a murder investigation. If the murderer had not taken them, the police might find them in Aza's house, but it would take them a while to discern what they were all about.

Ryan needed them now.

After Detective Martin returned him to the Brown Palace, he retrieved his rental car and drove to Aza's facility in Commerce City. Fearing that the policeman might not have totally believed him, Ryan checked the rearview mirror every few minutes. No one appeared to be following.

"My favorite hidin' place," his friend had said the night before last on the phone. Ryan thought he knew where Aza might have hidden a copy of the papers.

When he arrived at the front entrance to Aza's company, Western Enclosures, there were two Denver Police vehicles parked in front. He did not stop, but drove through the open gate at the side of the office building and into the fenced area to the rear of the main manufacturing building. He parked his rental behind a shed used to store the large pieces of metal for fabricating cabinets for electronic equipment. As he had hoped, Aza's fishing boat was parked back here.

He climbed into the twelve-foot skiff and went straight to the built-in fishing tackle box. Once, when they had been out on Dillon Reservoir, Aza had opened the box and pulled out a wad of cash. "My stash," he had said. "In case the banks go south. Plenty of beer money." Ryan had estimated there was at least ten thousand dollars in small bills.

He knelt before the box; a sturdy lock secured it. Keeping an eye out for the police, Ryan went to the rental car and found the lug wrench. With it he twisted off the hasp.

Opening the box, he pulled out layers of fishing gear until he reached the false bottom. The bills were still there wrapped in neat plastic lock bags. Beneath them, lay a plastic folder. Ryan opened it and thumbed through the stack of papers. It was exactly what he had remembered: copies of the media affiliates' agreements with Congressmen and Senators. Yes, in memory of Aza O'Sullivan, his best friend, he would put them to very good use.

Lost in thought about Aza's murder, and the folder of papers on the seat beside him, Ryan Drake drove back to Boulder on US 36. As the speed limit increased just past Sheridan Blvd., he put his rental car into cruise control to maintain 65 MPH. OFFICE DEPOT, BEST BUY, WAL-MART. The signs to the north of the highway zipped past.

After he had retrieved the papers, he had deposited a large check into an account at one of Denver's major banks. It was his final payment for his years at the helm of Sanitas Technologies. He had arranged the meeting at the Brown Palace to show the check to Aza.

Over the past six weeks he had concluded his affairs at Sanitas, moved out his personal belongings, and signed the final papers for the acquisition of Sanitas by TTT Instrumentation, Inc. of Boston, Massachusetts. A chapter of his life had ended. He was disappointed that he had not been able to share the event with his best human friend.

Keenly aware that the perpetrators who had rigged his house and had tried to kill Peter, Sarah, and him were skilled operators, he had left instructions that, when the check cleared, they were to disperse the funds into five separate accounts at different institutions. Ernest Steiger's agents had previously gotten to his bank account and credit cards; he did not want to give someone a chance to get to this significant sum.

Ryan ruminated on recent events. The problems began when he returned from his visit to Arizona, found that his house had been ransacked, and twice had barely escaped with his life. Then the FBI had requested an interview with Sarah — he had yet to learn how that had gone. And this morning he found out about Aza's death.

If Steiger's men were behind this, couldn't they understand that he would make good on his threat to publicly expose the media affiliates? Were they stupid enough to think he hadn't made a copy of the diary? And now, now he had a copy of additional incriminating evidence against Steiger and his media gang. But how could a man in a coma be pulling the strings? Had he issued orders before he lapsed into it?

Ryan concluded that the papers next to him were the secondary targets of the intense search of his house. He understood the potential impact of the incriminating evidence against well-known politicians.

The toot of a loud horn startled him. Ryan glanced in his rear-view mirror. An eighteen-wheeler was on his rear bumper; its massive grill filled his rear window. He checked his speedometer: 65 MPH. He looked for an opening and moved to the right lane behind a dirty white van. The lettering on its rear doors read, HUBBLE PLUMBING.

The big rig followed him into the right lane. He noted that it was a tractor without a trailer. What was this guy doing? He couldn't be more than a few feet from the rental car's rear bumper.

The larger vehicle closed to within a foot. It was so close Ryan could no longer see headlights, just the chrome of a massive grill and the top of the truck's huge bumper. Ryan accelerated, but the big rig stayed with him. He had read about road rage, but what had he done to deserve this?

Ryan felt the car lurch. The truck had bumped into him.

With the white van immediately ahead, he looked for an opening in the left lane. A black Dodge Ram with an extended cab and an extra long bed was next to him. It blocked any hope of maneuvering in that direction. Although there was no sun, he noted that both the driver and passenger of the pick-up wore sunglasses.

His car lurched again. The truck was now pushing his vehicle. He watched his speedometer rise to 75 MPH. As if they were in sync, the black pick-up and the dirty white van accelerated along with his car. His front bumper remained only feet from the bumper of the white van.

The hair on the back of his neck stood out; fear gripped him.

Fear so strong he was thrown into panic. He felt dizzy, disoriented.

Some instinct reminded him that death had little hold on him since Sarah and Peter had explained what awaited him on the celestial Journey. He focused on that; the fear subsided.

His car's speed was now at 80 MPH and the truck was still pushing. He thought of braking, but realized it would do no good, and he could easily lose control.

These guys are trying to kill me. The thought settled with a thud in his awareness.

Fear again caught him, greater than bolting from his house in the face of an explosion, greater than looking down from a narrow foothold on the side of a mountain, greater than he had felt racing through the jungle in Vietnam.

Then he recalled his encounter with the celestial messenger from Michael, recalled that he was to help his world. The fear again subsided.

Ryan saw that the embankment on the right sloped sharply downward a good twenty feet. The truck was edging his vehicle toward that drop-off. His right wheels were already on the shoulder. He cranked the steering wheel and brought his vehicle back into the lane.

If he went over the edge, at 80 MPH, he was sure he would wind up dead.

He looked left. The black pick-up was edging into his lane.

He had nowhere to maneuver.

104th CHURCH RANCH ROAD. The green sign flashed past.

His speedometer read 85 MPH.

BUTTERFLY PAVILION NEXT RIGHT. Another green sign.

The speedometer was just touching 90 MPH.

EXIT 45 MPH. A yellow exit sign.

Ahead the concrete supports for the Church Ranch Road overpass were not that far off the highway. If they maneuvered him into those, he was dead.

Ryan pushed the car's accelerator to the floor. The rental responded sluggishly, but it momentarily edged away from the grasp of the truck and smashed into the van's bumper. At the last second, he touched the brake and swerved away from the van, careening onto the exit ramp. He missed the asphalt, but remained on the shoulder. He braked hard.

Loose gravel captured his front wheel. He lost control.

The car flipped, rolled, and skidded on its top.

It encountered the embankment of the exit ramp and rolled again.

Ryan Drake's memory of the incident ended when the vehicle's air bag deployed and his face was smashed into it.

"Are you okay?" The voice of the female Colorado Highway Patrol officer sounded far away. He looked to see an upside down face peering at him through the cracked side window of the car.

"Uh, I think I'm all right," Ryan said haltingly. Around the deflated air bag, he could see the shoes and pant legs of a small crowd. They too were wrong side up.

The officer tried to open the door of the rental, but it was jammed.

"Don't try to move, sir. Paramedics are on the way."

They finally freed him using power tools. As they pulled him from the wreck, he reached out, snagged the folder of papers, and pulled them to his chest.

Despite Ryan's protests, the paramedics hustled him to St. Anthony Hospital in Arvada. There an emergency room physician examined him. The man wanted to keep him overnight for further observation. Ryan protested and called Gordon Moore, his personal physician, who had an office in a clinic in nearby Westminster.

It was three hours until Doctor Moore arrived at the hospital to examine him. "That seatbelt bruise may hurt, but it probably saved your life."

Ryan had known the doctor for several years. Although not personal friends, they related on more than a purely professional level.

"I'll sign whatever I need to," Ryan said. "Just get me out of here."

"I'll see what I can do."

The hospital insisted that Ryan use a wheel chair to the front entrance. Moore walked him to the replacement the rental car company had delivered to the hospital.

If you have integrity, nothing else matters. If you don't have integrity, nothing else matters.

— SENATOR ALAN SIMPSON

FIVE

"Ryan's 'accident' would appear to have been well planned," Dr. Adamson said, "It sounds as if they used psychotronics to create fear and disorientation."

Dr. Adamson sat across the table from Sarah. He was dressed in a wool shirt, his full head of white hair complementing his tanned face. As he spoke with that rumbling voice of his, there was sadness in his intense blue eyes that she had not seen before. She wondered how many other times in the course of history the intraplanetary being had attended such a fateful meeting.

"Psycho what?" Ryan asked.

"Psychotronics is a form of mind control. From your description, I would say your bouts of fear were caused by equipment in one of the vehicles involved in harassing you. This is important; it indicates that people from the intelligence community or certain 'black' operations are involved."

"Who? Why?"

"I do not know, but I will find out. You all must be very aware of your situation from this moment on. Do you have any residual effects from the incident?"

"I'm sore where the seat belt got me."

"Any further sensations of fear?" Dr. Adamson asked.

"I think that's it, just the soreness across my chest and around my middle. My head doesn't hurt that much."

"Pay special attention to your body for the next few days," Dr. Adamson said. "Psychotronics can leave lasting marks; it is tuned to exacerbate any of your body's weaknesses." Turning to Peter and her, he said, "Ryan seems to have done well. The use of these weapons has become very refined; they are often much more subtle and harder to detect. You must teach him to remain centered so that they have little or no impact."

She nodded her understanding. The dangerous game on this planet had taken on a new dimension. With highly developed mind-to-mind communications, psychotronics were unknown on Phantia. She had learned of them only after coming to Earth. She wondered why they had not been applied to some peaceful purpose like enhanced learning, rather than being used to cause fear.

Ryan, Peter, Dr. Adamson, and she were meeting in a conference room at Sanitas, where Ryan had been CEO until the company was acquired. Brauk Braukington, the co-founder of Sanitas and Ryan's former business partner, had assured them that this room, deep within Sanitas's facility, was secure from prying listeners. Before he left them alone, the technical genius behind Sanitas's success speculated that the people who were trying to kill them were probably using everything from tracking devices, to remote listening devices, to satellite imaging. Ryan had told her that part of Brauk's expertise was keeping abreast of such things.

The room was furnished with thick carpeting; the chairs were heavily padded and very comfortable. The table around which they sat was a reddish wood. Ryan told her that it was from the cherry tree. On the walls were pictures of equipment that bore small nameplates with dates and the names of customers. In accordance with Peter's and her wishes, the lighting was subdued. Ryan had told her this was the room where the Board of Directors of Sanitas had met. They would meet no more; now TTT Instrumentation owned Sanitas. Ryan's only tie to his former company was a consulting arrangement.

Since October, as measured in Earth time, she had learned much about the Earth-human who sat next to her. She had watched as he switched from being a successful entrepreneur, the head of Sanitas Technologies, to a champion of her mission. She had learned that he was uniquely capable of forecasting the impact of her message on Earth-humans, and that he possessed leadership skills that he was ready to apply toward transforming his planet. She also had come to realize that he was easily distracted from their mission by threats to her welfare.

Tonight, as always when he was highly focused, Ryan had a determined set to his jaw. His usually well-groomed appearance had a slightly ruffled look to it. The gray hairs about his temple were out of place, probably where a nurse or doctor had brushed them while examining his head. His blue eyes were clear, as always, but there was a hint of concern she had not seen since he had rescued her from the clutches of Ernest Steiger.

He wore a camel hair sport coat, over a striped shirt. As had become his custom, he wore these with blue jeans. She had seen the racks of more formal clothing in the closet at his mountain home. With the fire, much of it had been discarded or donated to charity. But since she had known him, since their time in the wilderness, she had not seen him wear a suit, or a tie.

Her position on this planet was precarious. Both the people she had pictioned and Ernest Steiger knew an extraterrestrial was living here. There was no way to predict how unscrupulous men might use that knowledge. Ryan Drake was the only human she knew she could count on; he had proven that more than once. Others, like Tom Ertl, had yet to be tested.

During the month of December, she had pictioned for over fifty men and women. Many of them had become instant "knowers" — those who knew the larger truth, rather than merely believing it existed.

A pulsating caused her to shiver. Something dark had entered the room. She sensed that someone was remote viewing this meeting. She tracked it back to its source, a young woman in a state of deep concentration. She reclined on a couch in the basement of a building.

By focusing her own energy on the youngster, Sarah broke the young woman's concentration. Then remote viewing her in return, Sarah warned her against trying it again. Stunned by the repulse of her efforts, and the sudden appearance of such a powerful personality, she collapsed in a state of exhaustion and began to cry.

Sarah relayed this drama to the others present in Sanitas's conference room. It reinforced the group's conclusion that someone more powerful than Ernest Steiger was monitoring them.

Ryan began the formal part of the gathering, taking charge as someone comfortable with being the leader. "The fire at my house was deliberate. Not that we needed anyone to tell us, but that's what the fire investigation team has concluded." He encircled the index finger of his left hand with those of his right. "The explosion was rigged to go off after we entered — planned to kill us. The garage was a second set of explosives, in case we came in that way. My bed was a third.

"Aza's death was not an accident. According to the police, he was shot three times." His right hand grasped the middle finger on his other hand. "I'm not sure whether the intruders knew about the documents from Steiger's safe, or not. Remember, I had let Aza keep those, in case someone retrieved the diary. In doing so, I believe I caused his death."

She laid a hand on his arm. "How is that?"

"I used the phone in our hotel room to call him."

Ryan looked at her, at Peter, then at Dr. Adamson. "I feel the noose is being tightened." He kept going down his list. "This was no accident this afternoon. I'm sure they were trying to kill me." The knuckles of his right hand were white as he gripped his ring finger.

When Sarah tightened her grip on his arm, she felt taunt muscles beneath his clothing. She immediately sent warm, uplifting energy to Ryan. His muscles relaxed one notch.

Just as her celestial allies had forecast, Ryan had become her protector. In the initial phase, before he discovered she was from another world, it had been his attraction to her blonde hair. Afterwards, after he had understood her mission, he protected her and Peter because he genuinely wanted them to succeed. But it was more than that, and she knew it. She knew that Ryan Drake, Earth-human, was in love with J'Li D'Rona, extraplanetary being. And despite all her training, her dedication to her mission, Sarah Smith had to admit that she had come to feel the same about him.

"Why," Sarah asked. "We have done nothing except tell people about the cosmic paradigm."

"I think they are more interested in me than you. I think it's what I know from reading the diary."

"Maybe," she said, "But the explosion at your house could have killed all three of us."

"But this afternoon was for me alone."

"True," Sarah said. "But maybe they did not know you would be alone. They might have used a tracking device to pinpoint you. It's like Brauk said earlier, they may be using all kinds of technologies."

"Look, I apologize to everyone." Ryan looked from face to face. "I really thought we had bought more time. Those six peaceful weeks went awfully fast."

"I too believed Ernest Steiger's diary would shield you," Dr. Adamson said. "Remember, I was the one who told you about it."

Sarah was not surprised that the white haired intraplanetary was present for this meeting. Somehow, despite his many duties, Dr. Adamson seemed to know when to make his appearance. A bear of a man, who appeared to be in his mid-sixties, he had appeared in the corner of the room and seated himself in a chair that had been pulled back from the edge of the table.

Like other intraplanetaries, Dr. Adamson was able to enter any space, and observe what was taking place. He could materialize or not as he chose. The only limitation she had observed was his inability to directly affect the physical — he was incapable of picking up so much as a sheet of paper. For tasks like that, he relied on physical beings.

It had been just prior to Thanksgiving when Ryan had rescued her from her cell in Steiger's mansion. No one had confronted or pursued them after that — until the explosion at Ryan's house.

Both Ryan and Dr. Adamson had been so convinced that possessing Steiger's diary would shield them. But the original of the diary had been retrieved by whoever had searched Ryan's house. What the intruders did not know was that Ryan also possessed copies of the earlier volumes of the diary, copies of the volumes that Steiger had faithfully sent to his daughter, Lucia, in Paris, copies that Dr. Adamson had obtained from the secretary of a Parisian attorney.

Sarah and Peter relayed their interrogations by the FBI. "They were nice enough, but had no rationale for their tardy interest," she said. "I think someone directed Rita Martinez to seek us out. I think agents for Ernest Steiger instigated this. Martinez knew to look for me in Boulder."

"Last I heard, Steiger was in a coma," Ryan said.

"Who else could get the FBI to do his work?" Sarah asked. She recognized that she had slipped into the fear trap and immediately regretted it. It had been so wonderful after her rescue; she had been able to focus on the higher ways of seeing, had been able to convey to all a true cosmic perspective.

As if reading her mind, Peter said, "It matters greatly how we proceed from this moment. I see that the drama of our struggle against our unknown adversaries has invigorated us. As we became addicted to this excitement, we failed to notice that we were avoiding the way to peace. What we are really doing is to participate in drama that deadens our ability to see clearly, to move forward.

"The members of the World League are not an enemy to be resisted and fought. As we sit here focused on those that oppose us, we fail to notice that they are but men who are following that which they perceive to be true.

"We must forgive those in power, for they do not foresee the results of their actions; their only concern is retaining power. It is time to let go of anger toward the institutions that prevent the awakening of this planet. We are supporting the existing paradigm in that we too are judging others. It is our message, and only our message, that we must deliver to the people of this planet. We must convince them to awaken."

Both Ryan and she nodded their understanding of what Peter had said. They had discussed this approach during their six-week hiatus. Sarah was amazed at how quickly she had been led away from the higher perspective when Ryan's house exploded.

Peter and she had been working on an explanation for Earth-humans' tilt toward fear, toward judging, toward violence. They were at a loss to explain why their message kept getting lost in people's xenophobia. She suspected it had something to do with the unique psychology of the humans of this planet. She made a note to talk more to Ryan about his dream of the transparent jail.

"I regret that I have been occupied in California." Dr. Adamson interrupted her musing. "I have not had time to check in with Ernest Steiger."

"Let me try to view him," Sarah said.

She leaned back into her chair and closed her eyes. After settling into a meditative state, she willed her mind to see Ernest Steiger's hospital room. In an instant she was there. The old man appeared to be asleep. She checked to see that he was breathing.

A man was seated beside the bed. She gasped. It was the man who had kidnapped her from her apartment, the man she had viewed as he wired the bomb for Ryan's house. He too appeared to be dozing. She willed herself out of the remote and into the present moment.

"Ernest Steiger is still in the hospital. But there is something else. Let me piction it for you." She extended shaking hands, one to Ryan, the other to Peter. Dr. Adamson joined to form a closed circle.

Then she replayed the visit she had just made to the hospital room.

When they were all back present, Ryan said, "I recognized the guy with Steiger. The last time I saw him, he had on a blue sweat suit. He was following me around Boulder."

"We must now take the next step," Peter said. "We must proceed before they stop us."

"I reluctantly agree," Dr. Adamson said. "You can wait no longer."

After a lengthy discussion, the four developed a plan, a way to insure their safety. But even this was no sure thing.

"Then we will proceed," Peter said.

Sarah studied her mentor. He had helped her so much during those years after the death of her mate, M'Adan. He had taught her to speak out about cosmic truth, had helped her advance her teaching career at the Academy. She had gone to him when this trip to Earth was first proposed. He had immediately seen the potential and had volunteered to accompany her.

Peter was the one who had outlined the steps required to complete a planet-wide transformation. He had studied how it had occurred on Phantia and believed the lessons could be applied to Earth. What neither Peter nor she had foreseen, was the grip that fear and violence had on their new home planet, and how groups of elitists were using this fear and violence to keep themselves in power.

Earth had the potential of becoming a place of tranquility like other advanced planets. The transition would not be easy; two hundred thousand years of self-indulgent behavior, violence, and fear would be difficult to overcome. The only hope they had was to initiate a worldwide connection between people who saw the truth, who saw that there was an alternate way, and who were willing to begin to live as if it were already accomplished. Would the knowledge that theirs was not the lone inhabited planet, knowledge of a peaceful cosmos, knowledge that another planet had transformed be sufficient to get the people of this sphere moving in the right direction?

The commotion surrounding their planned actions would be felt around the world — that surely would buy them more time. But would it advance their mission? Equally important, could they stay alive long enough to put the plan into effect?

The next morning, Ryan tracked down Sam Wellborn. He was in Washington with the President-elect. Carlton Boyle had named Ryan's childhood friend as his Special Assistant. Sam was busy helping to prepare the new administration to take over in a few days, but he took Ryan's phone call.

"Arrangements were made between a number of Senators and Congressmen and a group called the media affiliates," Ryan said. He was calling from an office at Sanitas and had taken precautions to make sure Sam spoke on a private line as well. "I can deliver copies of those agreements to you, if you'll do something for me."

"I'm kind of busy."

"Sam, listen to me carefully. I have copies of arrangements with Senators and Congressmen who were elected in November."

"Arrangements?" Sam finally woke to the conversation. "What kind of arrangements?"

"Financial contributions in exchange for votes."

"And you say they're in writing?" Sam asked.

"Yeah."

"Signed by the candidates?"

"Yup. And by the people who supplied the money."

"Wow, those could be most useful."

"That's what I figured." Ryan wished he were there with Sam to see the expression on his old friend's face.

"How'd you get them?"

"That would take more time than we have. Now, I need something from you."

Not far from President Boyle's transition office in Washington, DC, a conversation of a very different sort was taking place. "I want to know more about the workings of those computers." John deBeque said to Patty Nelson, his operations manager. "It seems to me that we have lots of excess capacity."

He stood looking through the glass door at racks of machines. Styled dark hair, dark eyes, a determined set to his jaw; his white shirt and club tie reflected in the glass. He had left the jacket of his dark suit in his office on the floor above.

Ever since he had taken the job as the coordinator of the International League, deBeque had wondered at the amount of computing power that took up half the suite beneath him. This was the first time he had found an opportunity to raise the issue.

He knew little about the technical workings of computers; his Degree from Harvard had been in political science. But he knew enough to recognize modern hardware, and these were certainly not outdated models of anything. The five racks of equipment seemed excessive for his organization, the International League, a lobbying organization that depended on contributions from corporations scattered about the world. As for the editors that worked for the clandestine media affiliates, their needs were met with their personal computers, telephone calls, and email.

The messaging center had been in place the day he arrived. Outside technicians appeared periodically. One of the women who worked for the media affiliates told him that the equipment had been modified on two occasions since he had come to work; both times he had been out of town. None of his people touched either the hardware or the software; Patty said she did not even have a key to the glass-enclosed room. Although he had no control over its budget, the computer facility should report to him — after all it was occupying his space.

Something did not feel right. He had glimpsed the telephone

bill for last month that had come to Patty. The International League was being charged for thirteen telephone lines and four DSL connections. With a hundred members of the International League, all of whom contacted each other infrequently, why did they need this much communications gear? He had checked around and found that this was more capacity than some Internet nodes. It did not matter to him that there were sufficient contributions to cover the expense. Something did not feel right.

John deBeque's job description read, Secretary of the International League. He was the organization's lobbyist and coordinator. Beyond that, and unknown to outside observers or members of the International League, he was part of an organization that disseminated insider information to the media. A third responsibility involved arm-twisting Senators and Congressmen to whose campaign war chests the wealthy members of the media affiliates had contributed funds.

"One of the service guys told me that those racks on the left are routers and sorters." Patty Nelson pointed to cabinets full of blinking lights. A multitude of cables came from the floor into them. "Next to them are processors and data storage. As I understand it, the whole system is just a message center. It receives messages, and forwards them on. It all works automatically."

His six employees, who placed information tidbits in the hands of reporters, editors, and producers, occupied the rest of the suite on this floor. They were housed in offices that faced the short hallway running from the entrance. That entrance was designed as a "man trap" — only one person at a time could enter. There they were scrutinized by a guard with a full view of the area within the bulletproof glass entryway.

John DeBeque sensed that he was not getting a straight answer from Patty Nelson. He was undecided as to what to do. "And this is all just for the International League?" He suspected that excess capability was being sold outside, and he wanted to know if the International League was being properly compensated. It might affect his budget.

"Yes, amazing isn't it."

"I'd like to see the details." His brow furrowed. "Something that will tell me about the stream of traffic, who's getting all these messages, where they're coming from."

"I'm sorry, John, You're not cleared for that."

"What do you mean cleared? This is my organization; you re-port to me."

"You do not have a need to know. Ernest Steiger instructed me that you are not to have access to these details," Nelson said.

"Ernest Steiger? He's in the hospital, in a coma. I'm the Secre-tary of the International League. Now I want a detailed report on my desk tomorrow."

"It won't happen. I can't do it."

DeBeque stormed back to this office. He called the senior mem-bers of the International League. To a man, they told him they did not know anything about the computer system.

The four-story, tan brick building sat at the corner of 18th and Illinois Streets, in Golden, Colorado, adjacent to the Colorado School of Mines. Large cottonwood and pine trees indicated that the struc-ture had been there for more than thirty years. At the rear of the building were three large satellite dishes. A sign in the window adjacent to the entryway read: SCIENCE FOR A CHANGING WORLD. A smaller sign, on the other side of the double glass doors said: SMOKE FREE BUILDING. Concrete planters, arranged across the broad sidewalk leading to the entrance, blocked it from pos-sible terrorist assault.

This building housed the National Earthquake Information Center. The Center was part of the United States Geological Sur-vey that was, in turn, part of the United States Department of the Interior.

Twenty-four hours a day, the USGS received reports on seis-mic activity from around the world, via satellite and through the Internet. It was recorded automatically. In an average year twenty thousand seismic events were recorded. Some of the tremors were large enough to be felt as an earthquake, sometimes a devastating one; most of them were below the problem threshold. The largest event recorded by the center was the 9.5 earthquake in Chili in 1960. Japan, on the far side of the Pacific Plate, had experienced an 8.0 tremor in 2003.

John MacDonald was making a periodic check on the seismometers, seismographs, recorders, and clocks that filled one room of the building. He noted a magnitude 3.5 quake in the Portland area. Similar tremors were reported in Chili, New Zealand, and Japan. Stepping further around the room, he paused in front of a computer display. He hurried across the room and looked at readings from several seismographs.

"We're getting strong readings off the Juan de Fuca," MacDonald said. He was on the phone to his boss on the floor above. "You might want to take a look."

The Juan de Fuca tectonic plate was sandwiched between the Pacific Plate and the North American Plate. Tiny by comparison, it encompassed the coastal areas of Oregon and Washington, taking in parts of Northern California and British Columbia. About three times as long north to south as it was wide, it extended into the ocean for many miles. A few miles out to sea, forty to fifty kilometers below sea level, it dipped beneath the continental plate. The eastward thrust caused activity far inland. Its most notable creation was the Cascade Range. The last time it had exhibited activity like this, Mt. St. Helens had blown her top.

After a few hours of deep sleep, Sarah awakened. She required less sleep than Earth-humans. Peter had not awakened so she laid still and thought about the decision Peter, Ryan, Dr. Adamson, and she had made. Rather than rehash it, she turned to an event that had occurred not long before Peter, Ryan, and she had returned to Boulder, Colorado.

In the days before Christmas, shortly after they had arrived in Scottsdale, Peter and she had taken Ryan's Jeep to wander around Phoenix. It was different from Boulder or Denver, and totally different from Ur'Geary, the largest city on Phantia. Ryan had not accompanied them, preferring to spend time with his children, Danielle and Darren, grown kids who he saw much too infrequently.

The night after Christmas, December 26th, she had suggested that Ryan, Peter and she venture into the desert to the north of Scottsdale. The three of them had taken their heavy "Colorado" clothing in anticipation of lower temperatures that night.

As they drove north through Carefree and headed out toward Horseshoe Dam, the population dwindled until they were beyond city lights and dwellings.

'*Turn here,*' she communicated to Ryan who was driving. She was using the mind-to-mind communications that Ryan and she had been practicing.

They rode for a mile along a deserted dirt road where Peter and she had ventured on one of their expeditions.

'*This will be fine.*'

Ryan pulled off to one side of the road. They bundled up and then walked a few yards into the desert.

'*We will pause here.*' She stood quite still and quieted herself. She was instantly in a deep meditative state, but still totally conscious of her immediate surrounding. Sarah had learned this technique when she had trained as a D'Ct-Elds, the high order of teachers on Phantia.

With her conscious awareness, she saw Peter smile and motion to Ryan that he should enjoy the multitude of stars and the crisp desert night.

Before long, a small orb, about four inches in diameter, appeared and hovered near Ryan. It was transparent gray and appeared to have mechanical workings within it. After it went around and checked out Peter and her, it disappeared.

Peter and Ryan continued to survey the clear night sky with its blanket of stars reaching from horizon to horizon. Ryan pointed out Orion, Canis Major, and the Pleiades.

In about ten minutes, she received what she had requested. '*Follow me,*' she communicated.

They walked for two hundred yards up a rocky arroyo. Although Ryan stumbled once, Peter and she walked confidently. Their eyes functioned much better in the dim light than did Ryan's — one of the advantages of growing up on a planet where its sun was less intense.

'*We are here.*' Sarah paused and indicated that Ryan and Peter should come to either side of her. Unaware of what was about to happen, Ryan went back to surveying the glorious night sky.

Suddenly, tiny, sparkling blue-white lights blossomed to fill her view. In another instant, a circular craft materialized not more than fifty feet in front of her.

It was about a hundred feet in diameter and hovered four feet off the ground. Brilliant blue lights circled its periphery. It made no sound.

Standing close to Ryan, Sarah observed his entire body shake with excitement. It was one thing to have pictioned for him, or to have transported him to the Between worlds holding Dr. Adamson's hand; to see an extraplanetary craft up close was another matter. She had learned that first contact of this sort always triggered a visceral feeling that let Earth-humans know this was not something normal.

While she watched, the details of the craft became more apparent. Rounded bumps, top and bottom, protruded from the main donut. Its glistening skin was without markings.

'Do not approach,' she warned Ryan. *'It is very active and would burn you.'*

The skin of the craft became translucent and they could see beings moving inside. A hatch opened and a ramp descended to the ground.

A tall, thin life form appeared and walked down the sloping surface toward them. Not human, but walking upright, she looked somewhat like a praying mantis.

Startled, Ryan gasped and took a step backward.

Sarah grabbed his arm. "Peter and I are like you in appearance." She spoke the words in English to comfort him. "However, there are other races who appear quite different. She is a friend."

She heard Ryan take a deep breath and felt him squeeze her hand.

As the being got closer, J'Li could make out a friendly face with large eyes and a small mouth. She had communicated with Argyle mind-to-mind, but had not met the unusual looking being in person. Now as she faced her, she would describe the extraplanetary being as "beautiful and loving."

'I will not harm you,' Argyle communicated.

The message was directed to Ryan. Sarah sensed his body relax a notch.

'I am honored to meet you, immigrants from afar.' The large eyes of the preying mantis caught hers.

'And we are honored to meet you, historian of this planet,' Sarah communicated.

'*I have observed your efforts; the battle for the minds of the Earth-humans is most difficult.*'

'*We are making progress,*' Peter communicated. '*But powerful people oppose us.*'

'*It has been thus since the beginning. Those who have power are reluctant to give it up.*'

'*Tell us about the beginning. I think our friend, Ryan Drake, will be most interested.*'

Argyle began, '*This planet was selected as a life modification sphere, the tenth in the rotation of creation, a decimal planet.*'

Sarah had trained Ryan to receive mind-to-mind communications from Peter and her. Generally they were short, cryptic messages. What he was now receiving from the tall extraterrestrial were not just words; they were concepts. She hoped Ryan could understand what was being communicated.

'*Billions of years ago, before life in any form existed on this sphere, the life carriers set out to create a race of free-will, intelligent beings, mortals modified in subtle ways never before attempted. They were to be warm-blooded mammals of type twenty-three. It was, of course, done with the full knowledge and agreement of Michael, the Sovereign of the Local Universe. Their goal was a hearty race, a race capable of great empathy, a race destined to innovate.*

'*As they had done for other spheres, they brought to this lifeless planet the essence of life, basic building blocks encoded with the ultimate forms, and deposited them in the primeval seas. As these life forms evolved, certain strains, considered unsuitable for this world, were terminated.*

'*The life carriers worked very hard on their project for millions of years. Until the ancestors of modern Earth-humans appeared one million years ago, evolved from those first seeds of life, the life carriers did not know the outcome of their experiment.*

'*Today's Earth-humans possess the characteristics encoded by the life carriers.*' She motioned to Ryan. '*On my home planet, we too were evolved from the seeds brought by the life carriers. On each successfully developed planet, life carriers remain to monitor evolutionary progress. On your planet, as on my home planet, extraplanetary influences have further modified conscious life forms.*'

'*Unfortunately, the result of the life formation process on this planet is a race of Earth-humans whose instinctive reaction to anything unusual is fear. Xenophobia, of course, is derived from your animal origins — but, for reasons that the life carriers did not anticipate, fear has been retained as a basis for action long after its normal cessation, long after its usefulness as a natural defense. Aggression is due to the persistence of testosterone, primarily in the males of the Earth-human race, long past prime reproductive and athletic years, long after its usefulness. When Earth-humans fail to master this aggressiveness, violence results.*

'A second factor derives from the first; the persistence of testosterone in the males of the Earth-human race contributes to over population. On planets such as Phantia,' she motioned a long arm at Peter, *'the human sexual urge diminishes rapidly after age thirty. This has two desirable results. First, there is a reduced urge for breeding. This coupled with more conscious choices from seeing the larger picture results in a smaller, but higher quality population. Second, without an unbridled sexual urge, men turn to more noble pursuits.*

'You do realize that the population of this planet is not sustainable, don't you? Resources are being consumed at an alarming rate. The ecology is rapidly deteriorating. Measures must be taken, and soon. In this there is no choice, both for this world and for the universe.

'The Creator provided you a beautiful sphere. Rejoice that you have been allowed to partake in its bounty. And work to establish a community of humans who live together in harmony with the grand plan of the Creator.'

With that last concept transmitted, the extraterrestrial closed her eyes and bowed her head.

'Thank you,' Sarah communicated. *'Your insight is most valuable.'*

'For Earth-humans such as you,' the tall extraplanetary being opened her eyes once again and looked at Ryan, *'fathoming cosmic truth is like a marine animal at the deepest part of the ocean trying to discern the flight of an eagle high above the surface of the water. At best you might see shadows through the intervening marine layers and atmosphere. If the eagle were to descend to your level, you would hardly recognize the saturated feathers and distorted body as a magnificent bird capable of soaring in the clouds. Yet his lofty existence is every bit as real as yours at the bottom of the sea. I wish you well on your Journey, Ryan Drake.'* The tall life form closed her bulging eyes again, signaling the interview was ended.

Ryan was too stunned to communicate anything. After Peter

and she had said their good-byes, the tall extraterrestrial turned and glided back to her ship. An instant after the portal closed, the twinkling lights of dematerialization replaced the solid structure of the craft. Then the three of them were alone in the desert.

On the way back to Danielle's house, Peter and she talked while Ryan drove silently. Sarah knew that this meeting had touched Ryan, that he now felt a connection to other races of his off-planet brothers and sisters, a connection that Peter and she could not have produced.

Suddenly Ryan blurted out, "Why this planet? The more I understand about this place compared to a more typical world, I keep asking God, 'Why this planet?' Why couldn't I be born in some normal place?"

Sarah smiled and said, "Because you have a desire to serve. Because that spark of the Creator within you knows that you will make a great contribution — a contribution that was determined before you were born. And because adversity hones maturity. Peter and I consider it a great honor to have been invited to come to this troubled planet."

"Like Earth, Phantia too was the subject of the decimal protocol," Peter said. "That is why we resemble you. But there is a difference: On Earth the decimal protocol was modified and left its unique mark on this planet. It is from this mark that the idea of original sin originates. The mark is a genetic flaw, not the action of some distant ancestor."

Ryan made no reply.

Sarah and Peter went back to their discussion. "Anger stems from deep seated animal fears," she said to Peter, 'or because the other person is not doing something the way you would like. Given Earth-humans' predisposition to anger, it is easier to understand the violence that persists on this planet. We must recognize the fear component, then go beyond it to recognize that each person, angry or not, has a spark of God within him or her, and we must honor their free choice. The best we can do is speak out, and hope that those who are open to the cosmic paradigm will hear. Unlike those in power, we cannot use xenophobia to frighten or control."

Ryan again interrupted. "How is the ETs explanation for our basic nature different from original sin?"

She thought for a moment and then replied, "A minor flaw in the design of Earth-humans is quite different than claiming all Earth-humans are flawed as the result of what some distant ancestors chose to do. The design flaw is not the fault of Earth-humans, living or deceased."

"OK. And what about this population thing?" Ryan asked.

"The population of this world is not sustainable at its present level," Peter said. "Even if there were no problems associated with the burning of hydrocarbons, other resources are being consumed too quickly."

"What about mining the moon, the asteroids?"

"You assume that you have a right to do that?"

"You mean there could already be someone else there?" Ryan asked.

Neither Peter nor she replied. Sarah knew that their silence indicated that Ryan had stumbled on another important fragment of the larger picture. In subsequent days, she had explained to Ryan that just as Earth-humans could not continue to exploit their own planet, neither could they assume they had a right to take over and exploit another.

Ryan's final query was just before they arrived back at Danielle's house. "Is that creature a celestial?"

"As we have told you before," Peter said. "You must not confuse mortals, wherever they may come from and however they appear or behave, with celestials who were created as immortals. Although she will live for thousands of years, Argyle is a mortal; she will experience the death of her physical form."

Recalling this event made Sarah smile. Before meeting the extraplanetary being, Ryan had voiced his confusion about his role as a leader of a worldwide transformation. After he got over the reactions to that meeting in the desert, she had seen Ryan's self-confidence and understanding assert themselves. Both the information about his planet's origin and the presence of nearby extraplanetary civilizations had once again changed his paradigm, awakening him to greater possibilities.

Naturally, the common people don't want war, but after all, it is the leaders of a country who determine the policy, and it is always a simple matter to drag people along whether it is a democracy, or a fascist dictatorship, or a parliament, or a communist dictatorship. Voice or no voice, the people can always be brought to the bidding of the leaders. This is easy. All you have to do is tell them they are being attacked, and denounce the pacifists for lack of patriotism and exposing the country to danger. It works the same in every country.

— HERMANN GOERING

SIX

"What's the problem?" Warren Ophir asked. He had agreed to make this trip because he did not trust the answer to the question anywhere near his office in Washington, D.C.

"An unsettling new development," Von Hedemann replied.

With his right hand, Ophir hung onto the side of the blue golf cart to steady himself against the sudden lurches caused by Von Hedemann's erratic driving. In his other hand he grasped the engraved gold top of his cane. They had just passed through a checkpoint where his identification, and that of Von Hedemann, was again verified against pictures, fingerprints, and retinal scans. Had they not been identified and searched, the security guards would have been "relieved from duty."

The picture on the I.D. that hung from his neck showed him with the closely trimmed beard he currently wore. As usual he wore a black suit with a black tie. His dark brown hair had been styled. Dark eyes betrayed little of his thoughts or emotions. In a hidden compartment in his briefcase, he had a passport and government identification papers with a different name and a picture of him without the beard.

Many of the security people here were his former employees. Secretly, some still were; they kept him advised of developments. The fact that Ophir's people had developed and installed the elaborate security for the facility did not exempt him from a thorough check, nor did the fact that he had visited the installation numerous times.

Warren S. Ophir's unacknowledged special access program was buried three layers below the purview of the Senate Oversight Committee on Covert Operations. His immediate superiors knew of its existence, but could not demonstrate the need to know its details. He had merely to satisfy them that he was performing his duties as a good intelligence operative.

His covert operation was connected to other secret, compartmentalized programs hidden within other covert operations around the globe. Informally known by its members as "the intelligence affiliates," they were the world's most complete repository of knowledge about the existence and activities of UFOs and aliens. Because of its tight focus, the intelligence affiliates were much more cohesive and effective than any single country's official intelligence agency.

"They forced back number one eleven," Von Hedemann said in heavily accented German. With one hand on the wheel, the other gesturing wildly, he swerved to miss a piece of equipment.

"Not the first time."

"This time they escorted it right back to us. I want you to see the flight video. And hear about it from the crew."

Ophir heaved a sigh. An occasional setback was to be expected in a program of this magnitude. At least it was nothing worse than he had imagined. But what kind of a game was Von Hedemann playing by insisting that he make a special trip to the middle of nowhere? There had to be more to it.

The two men expended no further words in expressing their frustration. Long ago they had agreed that their progress was much like that of the first fish learning to maneuver on dry land, evolving to become a reptile. For that daring fish, there had been setbacks and casualties, but ultimate success. They thought their program was of similar significance to human progress. The other fish in the ancient oceans took little note of what the daring fish had done. But recognize this program others would — and very soon. Then people would honor him as a visionary and a pioneer, and would acknowledge the World League as the rulers of the world. Then his world would dominate the other races in the universe, and carve up the galaxy to suit itself.

Günter Von Hedemann was a study in the unconventional. Except for his short blonde hair, he looked and dressed like a young Albert Einstein, rumpled suit, white shirt, and stained blue tie. He had spent his entire life in the United States, yet he cultivated the German accent he had learned from his deceased father, Gerhardt, whose memory he worshipped. Today, Ophir thought Von Hedemann smelled like an old man; he wondered if the German was wearing a suit handed down from his father. The tie looked like it had been around for more than a decade.

The elder Von Hedemann had been a brilliant scientist, an associate of Werner Von Braun. Both Von Braun and the elder Von Hedemann had come to America after World War II with the remnants of the German rocket program. As members of Project Paperclip, they had developed America's first successful rocket.

But Günter Von Hedemann had acquired more from his father than a dedication to technological innovation and scientific genius. He passionately believed Hitler's doctrine on the Aryan race and looked with disgust on the immigration policies of the United States. "Shame on you for allowing the dark races to corrupt your people," he often repeated. For this reason, he had agreed to involve himself in projects not officially sanctioned by the government, projects undertaken within the darkest corners of the covert world, projects designed to advance the plans of an elite ruling class.

Von Hedemann drove his midnight blue golf cart along a broad corridor in the underground facility. It had no emblem or marking, but from the way people scurried out of its path, it clearly had a priority. He wove it through groups of men in white overalls, past carts of different colors, and around heavy equipment.

The corridor was standard military/industrial construction — unfinished concrete floor and walls. The twelve-foot ceiling, supporting three hundred feet of rock, was laced with overhead pipes and wires. A copper wire mesh, designed to block electromagnetic signals, was embedded in the concrete. The facility was as secure as modern technology could make it.

Ophir's Lear jet had landed on a runway six miles away. His pilot had then taxied it into a hanger concealed under the lip of a nearby mesa. There, Ophir had boarded the underground train that had shuttled him to this facility. A dilapidated structure disguised the air-conditioning system for this extensive complex; from a distance it appeared to be the remains of an old mine. Neither the airstrip nor the surrounding area was detailed on any Jeppeson chart.

In fact, this whole region of Utah was designated as a "no-fly zone." Civilian aircraft were routed around the forty-square-mile military preserve. There were no surface roads in or out; tunnels connected various operations. In cooperation with Ophir's counterpart in the military affiliates, equipment to construct the complex had been flown in from bases in the western United States. LNR's security forces guarded the eight-foot high fence surrounding the perimeter of the preserve.

This underground facility was one of almost a hundred in the western States. Beginning with World War II, various military contractors had constructed most of them. In 1992, LNR, a consortium of three aerospace giants, had this one constructed to its specifications. Funding for this facility had come from the budgets of several black projects. But funding for its research was strictly from the companies' treasuries, whose coffers were, of course, replenished through government contracts. This research was conducted in Nevada, at Papoose Mountain, a very black facility. Because the private corporations making up LNR were funding the research and development of the ARVs, LNR maintained ownership of the technology. If, in the future, certain governments of the world were allowed to procure the unconventional craft produced here, they would pay a very high price.

The world's military forces, including those of the United States, continued to receive conventional weapons manufactured by armament and airframe companies. LNR intended to present the world with fully functional crafts, crafts that would dominate the atmosphere and could dominate space beyond the solar system. By proceeding in this manner, the World League intended to become the reigning force in world politics. The genius behind all this was that it was being done within private corporations, corporations that existed on government contracts.

The reasons for an underground facility were legion. Among them were keeping non-authorized people from prying into its activities.

Another reason was internal security. Many of the men who worked here were top scientists from Russia, acquired for a fraction of their worth. Some were ex-military who had been dishonorably discharged. However, the majority of the senior people were hand picked from corporations and the military. Some of the latter had not come willingly.

All personnel were routinely subjected to mental hygiene exercises. Their sleeping quarters were fitted with psychotronic devices that subliminally insured their compliance with the routine of the base. Ophir's staff had overseen the development and installation of that equipment. Since construction of the facility, there had not been one incident.

One more reason was to avoid Congressional oversight. If a facility did not exist, it could not be monitored. However, the most important reason was to hide the manufacturing of alien reproduction vehicles from the real aliens.

Seven-foot high doors parted and the two men turned into a side hallway with viewing windows. The hallway skirted the brilliant white, main building of the facility, a five hundred foot long by two hundred foot wide space. Through the tunnel's windows, Ophir could see the huge steel beams that supported a ceiling forty feet overhead. Ophir thought of it as a building even though it was a cavern under several hundred feet of desert sandstone and six feet of copper mesh laced concrete.

Three disk-shaped craft were in various stages of construction. The numbers 122, 123, and 124 were posted next to their assembly area. The manufacturing operation reminded Ophir of an aircraft assembly line, except that everyone wore sterile clothing similar to that required in a semiconductor manufacturing facility. During his last visit, he had showered and donned one of those white suits. Then he had toured the floor of the busy operation, had been shown the electro-gravitic mechanism that propelled the craft, the unique power generator, and the guidance system. Today there would be no need for that; he already knew enough to appreciate the splendid crafts' capabilities.

Each craft was approximately twenty-five meters in diameter with a raised center for the four-man crew. Their underlying structure resembled circular aircraft. When they were finished with this phase of the production, they would be moved into a chamber where their sleek skin would be "grown" over the framework. This final stage completed the ultra-pure fabrication of the craft, depositing metal as pure as the ingots grown for semiconductor substrates.

Conventional instrumentation and controls were used to facilitate training the crews who would man them. Hopefully, the next generation would feature the more advanced man-machine interface that the LNR partners were trying to copy from ET craft.

The backs of the crew's seats formed a rectangle, giving them visibility to all points of the compass. They communicated with the vehicle using helmets like helicopter gunners and gloves like those employed in video games.

Von Hedemann and Ophir drove from the production area past hangers built into the side of the mesa. The doors to these empty spaces were open and Ophir glanced out into the uninhabited desert valley beyond. Each hanger was situated under overhanging cap rock. Satellite images would not reveal their presence.

One of the prototype ARVs was in the seventh hanger. Although far from space capable, for the past twenty years, it had been used to stage "abductions." While real aliens contacted people, they rarely left memories of such contact. This ARV, along with its crew, was intended to leave a never-to-be-forgotten memory of an alien abduction.

"Hold on for a minute." Ophir's hand signaled Von Hedemann to halt. "Is my crew staying busy?"

"Night before last, they did the routine on that informant's family." Von Hedemann rubbed his hands together in a gesture of satisfaction. "Understand the boys had a grand time with the woman. Scared the shit out of the guy."

A whistle-blower from within one of the Air Force's top-secret programs had come forth. She had offered evidence about an extensive covert operation not included in any Congressional black budget. If an investigation were allowed to get under way, it might prove embarrassing to certain military commanders that Ophir depended on. Yesterday, a man, whose identity was unknown to the whistle-blower, had called and detailed the abduction of her younger sister. After a call to her sister, the whistle-blower had claimed it was all a mistake.

"Just another fun-filled day." Ophir motioned to Von Hedemann to move along.

They passed through another set of doors and into a brightly lighted hanger. At its center, a disk shaped vehicle floated three feet off the floor. Serial number 111 was the eleventh craft of the new design.

There were no visible wires or support structure. This aspect of these strange ships, more than any other, contributed to their mystery. It was straight out of a science fiction movie; except it was not science fiction, it was science fact.

Ophir stepped from the cart and walked to the craft. Its gleaming surface showed few lines and displayed none of the rivets or seams common to conventional aircraft. From flying saucers that had crashed in the forties and fifties, they had learned about the extreme purities of the metals used in their construction. It had taken years to replicate it. Reverse-engineering extraterrestrial craft had required bringing many technologies to a new level of perfection, as well as a new understanding of physics.

He did not touch the vehicle. Its skin might be "hot." The outer surfaces of ARVs were charged, by their electro-gravitic systems, allowing them to fly into a vacuum of their own creation and enabling stupendous speeds in the atmosphere. As he circumnavigated it, he dreamed of the day he would fly in one to show the rest of the universe that the humans from Earth were superior to any of them.

"The men are waiting," Von Hedemann said.

The words startled Ophir, but he did not acknowledge them. It was good to make others wait.

"How's the man downstairs?" Ophir asked.

"Still cooperating. We're working on his latest tidbit."

"So he's happy?"

"I believe so — snug as a bug in that hole he likes to call home."

After another longing glance at the sleek craft, Ophir walked to the adjacent conference room. Stepping from the presence of an

ARV to the common realm of men always caught him. It was as though there were two worlds: rarified existence and ordinary reality. He liked to think he functioned well in either.

In his late forties, Warren Ophir was in reasonably good shape considering his disability. His right ankle had been shattered by a land mine in Afghanistan. He had been a CIA field agent at the time of the Soviet occupation.

They had recruited him as he laid in the hospital in Germany, three men who said they were with a sister agency. He knew his days in the field were over; he listened as they talked of their plan. He told them he would think about it. After he returned to the U.S. for physical therapy, the leader of the trio contacted him again. This time Ophir listened with renewed interest. His other option was a desk job at Langley.

With further persuasion, and a promise of juicy financial rewards, he accepted a position at the Defense Intelligence Agency. At first they asked him to do simple tasks, accomplished with assets outside his department. Within five years he was running a black budget operation, carefully buried within the Defense Intelligence Agency, carefully funded with money from black budgets. After ten years, still an employee of DIA, he had clawed his way into the position as head of the intelligence affiliates. Along the way he had made good use of his skill in wet work to eliminate competitors.

Remembering the name, Bill Johnson, on the picture I.D. that hung from Ophir's neck, an I.D. that portrayed him as a U.S. government official, Von Hedemann introduced Ophir to the four men who had flown the craft. Only a few people knew Warren Ophir's real name. There was no need to divulge it to these men.

What these men did could not be called flying, nor would Ophir call the ARV a craft. For Ophir flying was connected to airplanes, helicopters, or awkward rocket-propelled launch vehicles. His cousin at NASA worked on improving those outdated monsters. No, the ARV in the adjacent room could barely be called a craft. The ARV in the other room was a miracle, a miracle he and his associates intended to put to good use.

As he shook the hand of each crewmember, he congratulated the man and said, "You are very brave. Your country thanks you."

The men who flew the ARVs had not been informed that they were no longer members of the United States Air Force, that they now worked for LNR. For them, Mr. Johnson was simply another military intelligence officer.

When all were seated, Günter Von Hedemann said, "Brad, tell Mr. Johnson what happened earlier today."

Brad Trenary, a crew-cut man of about twenty-five, stood. "Yes, sir. Well today, sir, we got to the neighborhood of the moon before they stopped us."

"And just how did they stop you?" Ophir asked.

"Like the other times, we lost forward progress and slowed to a standstill. Just hung there. Three of their craft buzzed us. Then one of them settled directly in our path. We found we couldn't move in any direction other than back to Earth."

"Did they communicate?" Ophir asked.

"Yes, sir," Trenary replied, "but it was that funny mind-to-mind stuff they do."

"What'd they say?"

"We received an image. Each of us saw the same thing. It was like a pyramid."

Ophir looked at the other men. Each nodded his concurrence.

"A pyramid with stairs." One of the other crewmen, Jason Cotter, the youngest of the four, passed a sketch across the table. It resembled a four-sided pyramid with a square platform on its top. The edges were a series of small steps leading upward. Ophir had seen similar structures on Mexico's Yucatan Peninsula. He crushed the paper and stuffed it into the pocket of his suit coat.

"Godless bastards."

"Let Brad finish," Von Hedemann cautioned.

Ignoring Von Hedemann, Ophir asked, "What do you make of this pyramid?" He pointed to the sketch, and then looked at the men. "Anyone care to guess?"

"I think it represents the four of us," Cotter, said. "I think they're trying to tell us to take it a step at a time. I think they're saying that we have a long ways to go. We're at the bottom level of a learning pyramid."

"Oh, bullshit," Ophir said. "Don't give me some psycho babble. Go talk to the psychiatrists if you want to put out stuff like that.

"The pyramid is a symbol of power." He walked over to Jason Cotter and, leaning on his cane, stood over the young man. "Don't you see, they are acknowledging our power — that we are powerful enough to have mastered their technology — that they handle you carefully because they are afraid of our power — that we are soon to be powerful enough to be their equal."

Cotter slumped in his chair and dropped his gaze.

Ophir walked back to the other side of the table and calmly said to Brad Trenary, "Please continue."

"Well sir, when we headed back toward Earth, instead of coming here, we decided we'd try something else. We acted like we were coming back, but when we got back into the atmosphere, we went around and headed out the other direction."

"The other direction?"

"Yes sir, away from the moon. We headed out from Earth in the opposite direction. Got out the same distance — the moon's orbit — before we were intercepted again. Looked to be the same three craft — you can't really tell differences because there's no marking. This time our controls froze and we stopped abruptly, like hitting an invisible wall.

"Our life support continued to function, but nothing else. And they didn't communicate. For two hours, they just kept us there, cooling our heels. I don't know, maybe they were waiting for instructions.

"Anyway sir, after two hours, they took us in tow — no power of our own. They escorted us all the way here, even knew which hanger to plop us into. We have a video of the whole thing."

"Let me see it," Ophir said. He was not about to recant his remarks about power. Screw the damn aliens. LNR would master this technology, and their specially trained men would take a fleet of ships out there and show them.

Von Hedemann pushed a button on the console in the center of the table. The lights dimmed and a large screen television came on.

The video, taken from the crew's perspective, reinforced the story they had relayed. As an ex-helicopter pilot, Ophir appreciated the feeling of speed the video conveyed. The views of space were crystal clear. The pictures of the alien craft were sharp and their maneuverability — wow. LNR's vehicles had a ways to go; nonetheless, the ARV was truly a miracle.

"They didn't harm you?"

"No, sir. It was like they were real concerned about us. They didn't get too close or anything. But I have to tell you — they were in charge. No doubt about it."

The discussion went on for another hour. The crew examined every aspect of the trip and compared it to the other flights they had taken over the last month. To Ophir's disgust, the crew concluded that as long as they stayed in the atmosphere, or close to Earth, they were allowed to test their craft. But, each time they ventured out from near space, they were hounded and sent back. Everyone was upset that this time they had been escorted to their home hanger — it reflected badly on the program.

"How did they know to bring you here?"

"We don't know, sir. They just did."

For what seemed like a long time no one spoke. At last Ophir said, "I want to thank each of you. You are real patriots. In time, when we can tell the people of this country, this world, they will appreciate what you're are doing against the invaders. I don't think I need to remind you that we need to keep a lid on this — even from other people at this facility. No one is to know that the aliens are aware of this facility."

Ophir stared at each of the four crewmen until he was sure he had their unqualified agreement. These men had been chosen not only for their skill and daring, but because they had no close family attachments, and they had the right psychological make-up to enjoy participating in secrets. It was unlikely they would ever return to their USAF squadrons. Retiring them to civilian life was equally out of the question.

Ophir and Von Hedemann returned to the blue golf cart and drove back through the underground maze. Three hundred men worked in this operation. Many saw the light of day only when they were taken to LNR's private resort on the coast of Mexico. There they were treated to any type of recreation they desired, anything except drugs. With his history as a dealer, Ophir had made sure the underground facility was drug free.

When they were about to part company, Von Hedemann said,

"We must arm an ARV. We cannot allow them to thwart our destiny."

"Arm an ARV?"

"I have a plan." He outlined the simple idea for Ophir. "Once they see we are serious about controlling our region of space, then they will leave us alone."

The intelligence man studied Von Hedemann. "You're crazy, absolutely crazy." What he did not say was, "but you might be right."

"This planet and the space around it are our birthright." It was Von Hedemann's turn to pontificate. "God gave it to us. We cannot allow aliens to taint what is ours. We must control it."

"What happens if they fire back?"

"We fire on them all the time when they come near our facilities. They don't fire back. I believe they are unwilling to start something."

"But they have shown they can disable our missiles." The records under Ophir's control showed that UFOs had disabled intercontinental missiles — in their silos — and that a UFO had intercepted a nuclear warhead on its way to the moon.

"If we put it in an unmanned ARV, they'll think it's part of the ship's energy source — until it explodes." Von Hedemann waved his arms to show the explosion. The ends of his smile curled upward.

"What about radiation fallout?" Ophir stroked his beard.

"We are at war. We may have to sacrifice a few lives to secure our rightful territory — this is, after all, our planet."

"How would we report a nuclear explosion in space?"

"Simple," Von Hedemann said, "have your friends in the media affiliates make up a story. Tell the public a foreign power, China, exploded it. Make a big deal of it, lots of publicity. Gives the government further ammunition for the dollars it needs to upgrade the strategic defense shield, maybe get some more satellites monitoring deep space."

"I'll discuss it with the others," Ophir said as he climbed back onto the underground train.

Midway through the dark the train stopped at a brightly lighted platform. A guard in a black uniform checked his picture identification against a computer display, then returned with the intelligence man's handgun. It was the tenth time Ophir's I.D. had been checked during his visit; he was pleased that his security force was following procedures. The bones of the ones who had not followed them to the last detail were bleaching under the hot desert sun.

After he exited the guard station, He pulled the crumpled sketch from his pocket. "A four sided pyramid," he said to himself. "I think we just got our first interplanetary proposal. So, they want a four-way power sharing. Well, I'll just have to think about that." He smoothed the paper and, after folding it, placed it into his breast pocket.

On his flight back to Washington, Ophir called the other members of the Board of Governors of the World League. Only he and the other governors knew these identities and phone numbers. Each had a highly secure email as well as emergency contacts. They were somewhat unconcerned about someone spying on them, as they had control over most intelligence assets. But it never hurt to be careful.

He told them about the long ARV flight. It was not the longest, but in recent years they had been increasingly restricted to near Earth. The twelve reiterated their agreement to gather two weeks hence. Ophir did not tell them that the ARV had been returned to its hanger, about Von Hedemann's latest not-so-crazy idea, or about the four-way proposal.

By the time he arrived back in Washington, Warren Ophir had made appointments to talk with the other members of the intelligence affiliates. These were men who directed black operations within various government agencies, U.S. and foreign, men with compartmented top-secret knowledge about UFOs and aliens, men with an understanding of the "silent war" being waged against aliens who had dared to invade this planet. They had never met as a group, and did not plan to. It would require trips to several foreign countries to complete the circuit of one-on-one meetings he planned.

"Sounds like we're stuck," Monte Pfingster said. The Central Intelligence Agency man walked beside him along the concrete next to Washington's famous Reflecting Pool. He was a member of Ophir's intelligence affiliates.

"We know we can go further, but they won't let us." As with others, Ophir carefully structured the information he supplied to Pfingster.

"Look where we've come. In the forties and fifties, we were totally in awe of them. Now, we are implementing some of their technology."

In the early years of the program, before the creation of LNR and the most recent innovations based on reverse engineering, pilots from the black ops had flown a captured alien craft as far as Jupiter. The aliens had figured out what was going on and the craft never returned to Earth. The crew was found wandering along a deserted beach on the coast of California.

"Von Hedemann wants to arm one of the disks," Ophir said. "See what happens if we explode a nuclear device and take out a few of their craft."

"As usual, he's crazy." Pfingster spun his forefinger around his temple. "The repercussions from such a move might expose all of us. Political suicide. Media repercussions. Besides, where are you planning to get such a device?"

"That's why we're talking. I'm aware that your people have recently acquired four quarter-kilo devices." Ophir forced his best smile. "If I'm not mistaken, they're the ones our Russian friends misplaced."

"I say we take it slow and easy. Keep flying into space regularly. Keep trying to get out further. See how far we can push them. Hey, they're not fighting back and I don't think they're going to start anything."

"As I recall, our military downed one of their ships, out there in space."

"That was a conventional weapon," Pfingster said. "We had a killer satellite in orbit and we got lucky. It hasn't made them back off. I think they have a damn good idea where our technology stands."

"So, will you look into a nuke, or do I have to go somewhere else?"

"I'll think about it."

A people that values its privileges above its principles soon loses both.
— Dwight Eisenhower

SEVEN

"Any change?" John deBeque asked as he entered the hospital room.

"The same," Nick Steiger replied. "Doctor says his vital signs are strong. Doesn't know if he'll ever come out of the coma."

DeBeque noted that Nick slurred his words. As usual he was on something, probably popped a few pills before coming to the hospital. The dark bags, almost as black as his eyes, spoke to the fact that he had been missing sleep. His clothes had a rumpled look about them.

"Has he said anything new?"

"No. His ramblings stopped weeks ago. Don't know if that's good or bad. Only recognizable words I ever heard were 'diary' and 'aliens.' His grunting stopped before the holidays."

"Diary and aliens?"

"Yeah. He must have said those words fifty times in the first week. All jumbled together with other words I couldn't make out." Nick's face showed little emotion as he gazed down at the still form. From telephone conversations, deBeque knew that Nick had been visiting his father twice a week since the old man had entered the hospital.

DeBeque looked at the man in the bed, Ernest Steiger, seventy-nine at his last birthday. He had been unconscious since the paramedics brought him to Northwestern Memorial Hospital. The emergency room physician had diagnosed heart attack. His doctor had added diabetes and severe overweight.

Ernest did not appear to have lost much weight; his complexion looked normal. In fact he looked better than he had the last time deBeque had seen him. A saline drip ran under the sleeve of the hospital gown; an oxygen line assisted his breathing. The two men watched as a nurse checked her patient's pulse and blood pressure. She shrugged to indicate that nothing had changed.

Ernest's private suite, located at the end of a quiet hallway, had many luxuries not commonly found in most hospital rooms. Gregor Hauptman, Ernest's security chief, occupied the attached room. One of Hauptman's security team sat at a small desk just outside the suite; from there he monitored everyone entering and leaving.

"How long has it been now?" DeBeque asked the question to make conversation with Nick. He knew the exact date. November 17th was chiseled in his memory. He had been one of the first that Hauptman had notified.

He removed the pile of magazines from the plush armchair and pulled it next to the bed. Hauptman must have been reading as he kept his boss company.

DeBeque had visited frequently in the early days. Since the year-end holidays, his visits had averaged once per week. Each time he had left feeling a sense of loss. The old man had been an important feature in his life for a long time. Ernest Steiger had watched over the development of his protégé. Now it was his protégé's turn to watch over him.

Strictly speaking, John deBeque was not a member of the Steiger family. When his parents died in an automobile crash, his junior year of college, Ernest had informally adopted him. The old man had helped pay the cost at Harvard, made sure he had the right job in military intelligence, and later found him jobs within Steiger Enterprises. His current position as Secretary of the International League was at Ernest's instigation. And it was Ernest who had supervised his work with the media affiliates.

DeBeque's mission to "bump into Nick" had caused him to change his regular visit day from Saturday to Monday.

"He's been like this for over seven weeks," Nick said.

After exchanging a few more pleasantries, deBeque asked,

"What's this about a diary? Do you know if he kept one?"

"Don't think so. Didn't say anything about it to me. We weren't exactly close, you know. He probably wouldn't have told me anyway."

DeBeque studied him. It was important to find out how much Nick knew about his father's affairs. If Ernest died, Nick, his sister Lucia, and his brother Richard would most likely split the multibillion dollar media empire known as Steiger Enterprises. DeBeque did not know whether or not he would be included in some portion of the split. Pending Ernest's demise, Albert Drake, the old man's attorney had refused to allow anyone to review the details of his will.

For the moment, DeBeque was not concerned with the disposition of corporate assets and trust funds. He was on a mission to find the location of two items.

"I'm looking for a file that I loaned him," he said. "Haven't been able to locate it."

John deBeque was interested in recovering a certain set of papers. They were copies of arrangements with members of Congress, members who had been compromised by offers of campaign funds. After the agreements were signed, deBeque had kept the originals safely at his office. Just before the robbery and Ernest's heart attack, the old man had asked to look at them. DeBeque had shipped off the more recent ones to his adopted father. He had told no one he had done this.

"Don't ask me." Nick Steiger had a hangdog look about him. In recent years, few things had gone well.

"And nothing about a diary?"

"Nothing."

"What does the word 'alien' mean to you, anyway?"

The biological son thought out his response. "Look John." Nick raised his head and stared at deBeque from within the dark hollow of his eyes. "Let's not kid ourselves, we both know my father was importing Mexicans for various operations within Steiger Enterprises, and selling the less desirables to other companies. If you want to know more, talk to Richard. He's in charge of that dirty business. I think my father was referring to all the aliens he's imported over the years — maybe he's got a guilty conscience over the way he treated them. A fair number of them died, you know. Maybe he wants to be sure the Steiger reputation isn't smudged." Nick chuckled at his last remark.

DeBeque joined in the humor. Ernest Steiger was certainly the last man to worry about his reputation. During the eighteen years he had known the man, he had discovered Ernest's involvement in all kinds of off-color activities. Ernest always contended that money could buy him anything. And the old man did have money, lots of money, and lots of connections to the right people, and lots of power. During the last twenty-four months in Washington, deBeque had uncovered more than a sampling of this.

By comparison to his father, Nick was pitiable. He ran the Steiger Family Trust, by no means an insignificant job to the average person. But as one of Ernest Steiger's sons, he could be doing so much more. Steiger Enterprises, wholly owned by Ernest Steiger, controlled television and radio stations in major cities, had newspaper, book, and magazine publishing operations around the world, and dabbled in a variety of other enterprises. Yes, there was so much more, a multi-billion dollar empire. But Nick's drug habit barred him from an active role — the old man had seen to that. Now this druggie was scheduled to inherit a fortune. How long would it last?

"I wonder," deBeque said more to himself than to the other man. "I wonder if that's what he's trying to tell us." Raising his voice, he addressed Nick. "Let's assume for a moment that he wrote a diary. Where do you suppose he would have kept it?"

"Locked up somewhere, maybe the desk in his study."

"Hauptman let me search in there for that file I loaned him."

As soon as he learned that Ernest had been taken to the hospital, John deBeque had flown to Chicago and, under the pretext of recovering borrowed data, had searched Ernest Steiger's office in the Hancock Building. But neither the diary nor the missing file was there.

Then he had gone to Ernest's mansion in Winnetka. There his investigation had been more restricted. Gregor Hauptman had stood over him, demanded that he limit the search to the drawers in the old man's desk and a single file cabinet.

In both instances, he had glimpsed a wealth of current information about Steiger Enterprises. Just scanning the financial statements had helped him understand the unbelievable profitability of the conglomerate. But the search had surfaced neither file, nor diary.

"Maybe the safe in my father's study?"

"Hauptman doesn't have the combination, or so he says."

"Then, I have no idea," Nick said. "Why are you so interested?"

"Just curious," deBeque lied. "Like you, just curious about what he really thought, what he believed in, who he knew, what he did that neither of us knows anything about."

"My father, the mysterious Ernest Steiger." Nick shook his head and looked at the floor. "Do you buy the burglary bit?"

"No. How could anyone get into that house?"

"I think some of my father's friends from the intelligence community paid him a visit that night."

"The house is a fortress," deBeque said.

"Always has been."

"Even when you were growing up?"

"Yeah, even then he was paranoid as hell."

"Hauptman's not saying much." DeBeque glanced at the closed door to the adjoining room.

"That what he gets paid for. As long as there's any hope of father's recovery, Hauptman will wait for orders. You won't get a thing out of him until the old man orders it, or until he dies. They were real close."

"Hauptman wouldn't let me look around the house, said it was off limits. I really got into it with him."

"Just like it's always been: no salesmen, no firemen, no police. I remember when I had just started to drive. I wrapped my car around a tree and the police brought me home. My old man made them leave me at the front gate, refused to talk to them."

"Do you think whoever was part of the robbery hurt him, caused him to wind up here?"

"Could be, but his health hasn't been good since my mother died."

DeBeque had been observing Nick. Unless he was a very clever liar, he really didn't know anything about what had happened to his father, or about a diary. Nick was more interested in his father's money and paying for his drug habit. DeBeque was not about to bring up the subject of the highly confidential file to someone who had distanced himself from Ernest Steiger, and Steiger's life's work, someone who might sell a secret for drug money. John deBeque was quite sure he knew far more about Ernest Steiger than any of his biological children.

Ernest moved his arm. John deBeque and Nick looked at the comatose man. The old man's eyelids quivered ever so slightly. Suddenly his eyes popped open — eyes that were as clear and alert as deBeque had ever seen them. His right hand reached up and pulled the oxygen line from his nostrils.

Nick Steiger and John deBeque were speechless.

A moment later Gregor Hauptman was at the foot of the bed. "You rang, sir?"

"Yes, I've heard enough. Show them out."

DeBeque stood up and glowered. "You're not sick?"

Nick stammered, "All the hours I've spent here, and you weren't unconscious after all?"

As deBeque stood speechless, Ernest threw off the sheet and light blanket. With little effort, he swung his thick legs over the side of the bed. He was dressed in dark slacks with a fresh press. When he pulled off his gown, the line from the saline drip came with it. Beneath was a white sport shirt.

"Gentlemen," Hauptman said. "This way."

"No," deBeque said. Standing with his hands on his hips, he faced his adopted father. "You owe me an explanation."

"What have either of you done for the past seven weeks?" Steiger looked hardest at Nick. "Hanging around. Waiting for me to die."

"I've been busy in Washington," deBeque said. "I'll show you the reports and —"

"I've read all of your reports and memos. They're a bunch of mush and you know it. All you do is rehash whatever those bastards give you."

"That's the job you asked me to do, remember?"

"You've become a lackey for the Washington crowd. They're trying to shove me out. Think I'm too old. Well, I'll show them. And why are you so interested in whether or not I have a diary? Huh."

"My investments are going well," Nick said. Hauptman had him by the arm, edging him toward the door.

"Liquidate them," Steiger sneered.

"But they're not ready, they need —"

"Cash them out. I don't want to play that game any more."

"What am I supposed to do then?"

"I don't care." The old man sneered. "I really don't care. Now, get out, both of you. I've got things to do."

Ernest slid off the edge of the bed and slipped into loafers that he pulled from the cabinet beside the bed. A uniformed guard, one of Hauptman's men, rolled his wheelchair into the room.

Without further words, Hauptman ushered them out the door of the suite.

John deBeque was crushed to think that Ernest had deceived him. Until a few moments ago, he had believed that his adopted father was the one person in this crazy world he could predict. For eighteen years, he had played the role of adopted son. He had worked the jobs the old man assigned him, reported on people the old man questioned, given the old man the loyalty and acquiescence he had demanded. He may not have agreed with Ernest's tactics, but he complied. Now his mentor had turned on him.

He looked at Nick. Steiger's younger son was equally crushed, but for a very different reason. It was clear that Nick had hoped his father would die. He liked getting out from under his thumb, planned on inheriting part of an empire. John deBeque hoped that Nick hadn't already spent his inheritance.

Steiger's private nurse gave them a Cheshire-cat smile as they passed her in the hallway. DeBeque stopped to question her, but she brushed him off and hurried toward the door of Steiger's suite.

"So how's our little inquiry going?" Warren Ophir asked. He had heard something in deBeque's phone call that signaled an immediate meeting was advisable. He hoped deBeque had learned the whereabouts of Steiger's diary.

They were seated in John deBeque's Washington, DC office. Before they sat down, he had made sure that deBeque engaged the white noise and electronic interference equipment. It was 7:00 PM; the reception area and outside office were empty.

Ophir could have suggested another meeting place. But that might have alerted deBeque to his keen interest in their little project. Better to play it casual and see what he could learn. There were always more intrusive and painful ways to get information — in case he decided deBeque was holding out on him.

The desk between them was dark mahogany with gold trim. DeBeque sat in a maroon leather chair that towered two inches above the young man's head. The desk was clear of papers. On the credenza behind him, a screen saver with modern art played across a computer display. Prints of well-known Picassos adorned the walls. To a casual observer, the International League was just another trade group, a collection of multi-national corporations with common interests. To a casual observer, John deBeque was just another of Washington's many lobbyists, albeit an apparently well financed one.

What the casual observer could not discern was that this office was the focal point of the media associates, and that John deBeque was its point person. DeBeque's youthful appearance and enthusiasm masked the aging members of the media affiliates, masked their powerful positions. The "insider information," that deBeque supplied to selected members of the media and Congressional staffers, was understood to come from credible sources that the young man could not disclose. DeBeque was a prized source of such information; the people who used the information left it at that.

What John deBeque did not know was that the International League, in addition to acting as a cover for the media affiliates, was covering for a much more important operation, the World League. In fact, as far as Ophir knew, John deBeque did not even know the World League existed.

Ophir's confidant on deBeque's staff, Patty Nelson, reported that things had been proceeding as planned. DeBeque was reasonably content acting as the focal point for the manipulations undertaken by the media affiliates, and, despite his inquiries, had not discovered the true scope of the messaging center that resided on the floor below. To anyone examining the system, the information appeared to be emails between commercial entities and their far-flung interests — the publicly acknowledged members of the trade organization known as the International League. If one knew where to look within these communications, they might find messages between the members of the media affiliates, messages between men of influence in television, newspapers, and Hollywood, messages that did not concern deBeque. Buried deeper yet were encrypted communications between the members of the Board of Governors of the World League.

Ophir pulled out a Cuban cigar, lit it, and relaxed into the plush leather chair. He pulled his left ankle onto his right knee, making sure his black suit coat hid his gun. High-ranking government officials were not supposed to carry such things.

Ophir could tell that his relaxed attitude perturbed deBeque. That was exactly what he intended.

"You talked to Richard?"

"Yes, I talked to him." At Ophir's request, deBeque had flown to Des Moines, Iowa to interview Richard, Ernest Steiger's elder son. Richard ran all of Steiger Enterprises' magazine and book printing operations, as well as a few smaller subsidiaries. "Doesn't know anything about any diary his father might have been writing. In fact, he doesn't know much about his father's life at all, except his micro-management of Steiger Enterprises. When we talked, he seemed kind of happy the old man was in a coma."

"And Nick?"

"Nick and I had a most interesting conversation this morning."

"This morning?"

"Yeah, I called you on my way back from Chicago," deBeque said.

Ophir knew enough about deBeque to suspect that the younger man was torn between his loyalty to the International League and media affiliates that employed him, and gratitude for all that Ernest Steiger had done for him. This assignment had been the perfect way to test that loyalty.

"In the middle of our visit, Ernest got out of bed." DeBeque's broad grin stretched from cheek to cheek.

It took a moment for the news to settle in on Ophir. "You're kidding." He jolted forward and crushed his cigar into the ashtray.

Ophir could see that John deBeque was enjoying this.

"Nope. Opened his eyes, threw off his blanket, and got up. Then he tossed us out of the room." DeBeque leaned back in his chair and put his feet on his desk.

"So the old bastard is alive, and he didn't tell anybody." Ophir got up and began to pace.

The news had caught him, and he didn't like it. His men had bugged Steiger's room, but Hauptman had found them before any useful information was recorded. Then Hauptman had installed a twenty-four hour guard and access was restricted. Ophir had bribed the hospital staff, but no one seemed to know what was going on. Now he suspected that Hauptman had gotten to them first, with larger bribes. He kicked himself for not using one of his remote viewers on Steiger.

He should have suspected the old man was pulling the strings. The telephone taps had been silent except for Hauptman communicating with his men. That was probably how they did it — used the security force as messengers.

"Damn. I should never have believed those hospital reports. Damn it all to hell. And Hauptman didn't say a thing."

"Hauptman? You've been talking to Hauptman?"

"One of my men spotted him in Boulder after Ryan Drake's house exploded." As was the case with many events, Ophir had told deBeque about the explosion at Ryan Drake's house in case they needed to fabricate a cover story. He had not told him the rest of the situation. "Why? Did Steiger say why?"

"He thinks people are trying to maneuver him out of the media affiliates," deBeque said.

Ophir observed the slightest twinge at the corner of deBeque's right eye. Yes, the young man needed to be closely watched. He smiled inwardly at the truth of deBeque's words; the other members of the Board of Governors had, indeed, determined that the media mogul in the wheelchair was to be replaced.

"So, how did Nick react?"

"He was more surprised than me. He's been visiting Ernest twice a week."

"Before we go any further, did Nick know anything about a diary?"

"Nothing," deBeque said. "We talked about it before Ernest

threw off his covers. Didn't know his father was writing one. Has no idea where he might have kept it. What makes you so sure Ernest had a diary?"

"We have our ways."

"Why are you so interested?" deBeque asked.

"We want to make sure there are no leaks, nothing that could impact the media affiliates. Steiger's been around a long time. He knows the players, the issues, the methods. It was stupid of him to write it all down."

"Nick should have suspected his father wasn't in a coma," deBeque said. "He told me he'd been getting inquiries from Hauptman and that attorney, Albert Drake. They never issued orders, just asked lots of questions."

"So Albert Drake was in on it too?"

"It would appear so," deBeque said. "Actually, when you stop to think about it, it was rather clever. Ernest probably found out a lot."

"I wonder." And Ophir did wonder. Something smelled. How had Steiger found out he was going to be shoved aside?

Now that Steiger was alive, it gave him another way to track down the diary. Its contents could be the most threatening thing that had happened to the World League since its founding at the conclusion of World War II. Was Steiger going to use the diary as a negotiating tool to try to keep himself in power?

"So, now what?" deBeque asked.

"Ernest Steiger has obviously chosen to go his own way. He's no longer a team player."

"Says who? I thought he was one of the founders of the media affiliates, untouchable."

Members of the World League's affiliate groups were always changing. People died, retired, lost their positions of influence, or became less useful. Ernest Steiger was the patriarch of the media affiliates. He had held that position for the last sixteen years. But Ophir believed Steiger was getting old, and he was equally sure that Steiger, one of the Board of Governors of the World League, would never back his personal ambitions.

Ophir realized that deBeque might have figured out a few too many things. Only members of the media affiliates were supposed to interact with the young man. With the exception of himself, no one from the other affiliate organizations was to have any contact. But he participated in meetings of the media affiliates, knew who they were. And deBeque's people were the ones who spun the insider information that was forwarded to them. Ophir concluded that deBeque already knew too much. In the final analysis, would he be loyal to Steiger? Or had Steiger's rejection opened him to a new loyalty?

"Did anything else come up?"

"Nick said that Ernest had mumbled something about aliens. Nick thinks he was referring to all the illegals Steiger Enterprises employs."

Ophir chuckled and said, "What do you think?" In the two years deBeque had been on the job, Ophir had made sure that nothing about UFOs or aliens had found its way to the media affiliates. The ET situation was handled in other ways, ways that did not involve John deBeque.

"All I know is that before he went into the hospital, he was trying to track down some supposed alien woman. Had Hauptman out looking for her. I didn't pay much attention — too much other stuff going on."

"And you didn't tell me about it?" Ophir gave deBeque a look that was meant to intimidate.

"There was nothing to tell," deBeque responded, "I don't think he ever found her. I'm sure he would have told me about that."

Ophir thought. DeBeque was useful where he was. However, the communications center for the World League would have to find a new home, and soon. When that was done, and only then, would he feel more comfortable about John deBeque.

Breaking the quiet, deBeque asked, "What about Lucia? Maybe she knows something about the diary."

"One of my men is getting to know her. That inquiry will be a bit different than the way you've approached Richard and Nick. She has, shall we say, certain weaknesses." His man had already started to romance Lucia.

Ophir was exploring several avenues that did not involve John deBeque. The tape recording of the break-in at Steiger's mansion had triggered his interest. His man had followed Hauptman's people when they searched the home of Ryan Drake. It was his man who had overheard Hauptman's people discuss the diary and the suspected aliens who lived at the house. Ophir had decided to step in. Drake had obviously read Steiger's diary; Drake was too dangerous to allow him to live.

"I want you to go to Steiger. Find out where he keeps his diary." Ophir looked for the twinge, a reaction to his suggestion. There was a single flicker, then nothing more.

"I can try. Remember, he threw me out of his hospital room."

"So you told me. But keep after him." Ophir sat back and folded his arms over his chest. "He'll eventually talk to you. Just don't tell him about our conversation."

Ophir rose and walked around the desk. He towered over deBeque. Bringing his face very close to the young man's he said, "I am going to be watching you very closely these next few days. Be sure you pay attention to what's really important. If you screw up, you know the consequences."

Then he straightened and gave deBeque one of his best smiles. "An interesting presentation is going to be held, tomorrow evening, in Denver, Colorado. I want you there."

Ophir went on to tell deBeque that a man named Peter Jones would be making the presentation. He stressed that deBeque needed to be present, to report back on what Jones said. Reports on Jones' prior presentations had been disturbing.

Over the next few days, Ophir intended to test deBeque's loyalties in every way possible. He also needed him out of his office, because he intended to relocate the World League's computer center.

Be ye therefore perfect, even as your Father who is in heaven is perfect.
— MATTHEW 5:48

EIGHT

Aza O'Sullivan had arranged for this Friday evening presentation weeks ago, after he had listened to the first of Peter's talks. Ryan Drake's recently murdered friend had family and business acquaintances around Denver with whom he had wished to share the Phantians' message. In addition to fulfilling its original intent, tonight's presentation was to serve a second purpose.

Twice while they were driving to the site, Sarah had told Ryan to take an unexpected turn at an intersection. Since the catastrophe at his home, he had been paying attention to the warnings from her invisible allies. A Boulder Sheriff's car trailed behind them.

She also informed him that she had viewed a healthy Ernest Steiger. He was back at his home in Winnetka. Things clicked into place for Ryan: His question about who might want to kill him. The motives behind the bombing of his mountain house. The big question was why they hadn't tried again — but maybe they had, maybe Sarah's foreknowledge had thwarted them.

With the two Phantians in tow, Ryan Drake arrived at the theatre prior to the arrival of their guests. Boulder Sheriff Deputies had opened and secured it.

What they were about to do, would balance things. Tonight, Ernest Steiger would find that Ryan Drake was no pushover. Tonight, Ernest Steiger would find out what he had unleashed when he kidnapped Sarah Smith, and then, failing that, had tried to kill them all. While Ryan was convinced that a recovered Ernest Steiger had instigated the bombing of his house, the assault on him, and Aza's death, it did not explain Dr. Adamson's insistence that people from the intelligence community were involved in his "accident."

From Steiger's diary, Ryan had learned how the World League was master manipulator. The process had its roots in the propaganda machine developed during World War II. The media had cooperated with that war effort by shading its stories and withholding certain information. This had escalated during the Cold War as the world's intelligence services had engaged in various techniques of mind control. The World League had organized the media affiliates to extend these techniques to all aspects of modern life. They had constructed the "box" in which most Americans, and increasingly others around the world, were allowed to function.

A half-hour later, the audience was filling the seats of the theatre while Ryan paced the stage. He had worn the only dark suit that had survived the fire. Even after a cleaning, the navy blue pinstripe still smelled of smoke. It was the first time he had worn a suit since returning from his trek across the desert with Sarah and Peter. The collar of the yellow shirt rubbed his neck and the red tie felt uncomfortably tight. He had struggled with his dress for tonight, but finally decided he needed to portray himself as a solid businessman — his former role. He was going to give the audience enough to think about, without them wondering if he had somehow "lost it."

He nodded to a man he recognized and motioned for him to take a seat down front. The fellow headed up a software company in Colorado Springs. Ryan had introduced Sarah and Peter to him. Another man, using crutches to support a broken leg, came half way down the side aisle and plopped into a seat. Ryan had heard his injury was the result of a skiing accident at Aspen. A woman, wearing a dark business suit, came and sat in the second row. Ryan knew her from the Boulder Chamber of Commerce. Somehow she had managed to be at Peter's first talk in Boulder. Sarah had pictioned for her. So far he had seen no one who was not vaguely familiar. Maybe the opposition would not show up.

Sarah, Peter, and Ryan had invited everyone they knew to attend what could be "a real turning point in the transformation of the planet." Aza had advertised this event to his friends as an event for anyone interested in "a larger view of the world." Ryan hoped Aza's invited guests would attend out of his memory. He really missed his Irish fishing buddy.

"I hadn't expected such a turnout. You're sure you want to do this?" Sheriff Tom Ertl wore a tweed sport coat and dark slacks. Outside his jurisdiction, the coat covered his shoulder holster. Ryan had briefed him on the plan for the evening.

"Yes." Ryan replied without hesitation, but he was worried. The risks were enormous. After this evening they would be totally exposed. If it did not work, he did not know what else they could do to protect themselves.

He had not received the package he had requested from Sam Wellborn. Sam and he had talked about it several times. Sam's efforts to retrieve the documents had repeatedly been thwarted. But at Ryan's insistence, Sam had made one last attempt, through a different channel. Ryan had heard nothing since then. Tonight's event would be a lot more credible with the information Sam was to obtain.

"The whole world will know," Ertl said.

Ryan sensed the Sheriff was staying close, offering a modest form of protection. "I've thought about that." And he had, day and night for the past two days. "We've been through it all. I see no other choice."

"Well, okay. Good luck." Tom Ertl sauntered to a seat between two of his deputies.

They had struggled with other ways to counter the person, or persons, who had tried to kill Sarah, Peter, and him, and had succeeded in killing Aza. It now appeared Ernest Steiger was at least partially behind it. He had decided that whoever the guys were who had tried to kill him on the highway, were probably worried about the things he had read in Steiger's diary. Would the media affiliates squash news of the astonishing event that was about to happen? Or would the sheer magnitude of the event force them to acknowledge it?

Peter, Sarah, and Ryan waited for people to settle in. How many in the audience had transcended their old beliefs, had become "knowers" of the truth? The time had come to let the rest of the world know about its greatest secret. Someday there would be a whole planet of knowers. He glanced at his gold and stainless steel Rolex, the sole piece of jewelry he now owned: 6:55 PM.

They had discussed whether they should explain the whole situation to some law enforcement agency, like the FBI. Tom Ertl had advised against that course of action; someone like Special Agent Jake Ashton would only embroil them in months of red tape.

Ryan stepped to where Peter and Sarah stood. He encircled them in a warm hug. The three of them had been through so much, their flight across the desert, Peter's slow recovery, Sarah's kidnapping. He briefly thought about spiriting them away to some isolated island. That thought passed quickly. Tonight was the reason the two had come a trillion miles; it was just happening way sooner than they had planned.

'*Everything will work out,*' Sarah communicated.

'*One way or the other,*' Ryan communicated back to her.

'*This is but another small step on your Journey. Enjoy the experience. A million years from now, you will look back upon it and wonder why you were so anxious. Remember, you do the work of the ruler of a universe.*'

In her cream-colored robe, with the delicate gold chain about the middle, she looked like an angel. Her only other jewelry was the three concentric circle pendant that hung from her neck. Her blonde hair flowed like a crown atop her lithe body.

He smiled at her and wished he could kiss the lips that smiled back at him, delicate lips in a classically beautiful face, high cheekbones, bronze skin, and those incredible large eyes with blonde eyelashes.

'*I'm just honored to be included,*' he communicated. He would keep this attitude toward it all, for it gave him strength, steeled his resolve, and helped him say the right words. He felt like an instrument in the hands of a great musician, playing the notes clearly with just the right pitch, with enthusiasm. Yes, he would help move this world forward. He would no longer avoid the limelight.

The stage on which Ryan, Sarah, and Peter waited was a few feet higher than the first row. The padded seats rose from there and wrapped two-thirds of the way around the center pit. Sanitas's founder, and now TTT Instrumentation's chief technologist, Brauk Braukington was on the left, three rows up. Two of Ryan's former employees were next to him. The three had flown in from Boston to be here tonight.

It took him a moment to recognize the face. Seated on the right aisle was Jake Ashton, the FBI agent he had met at his burned out house. Ryan heaved a sigh. Things could get real interesting tonight. Was it a coincidence that he was seated next to Gordon Moore, M.D.? A few weeks previously, Moore had confided in Ryan that he had heard an interesting speaker in Boulder. Not wanting to jeopardize Sarah's security, Ryan had not admitted that he knew Peter. Well, so much for security. That phase was all ending tonight. Ryan could only hope the two would not exchange stories about him.

Ryan recognized many people he had met through his association with Sarah and Peter. More than a few business acquaintances were sprinkled in the crowd, friends of both Aza and himself, some he had never imagined would attend something like this. He judged the theatre might hold four hundred. The seats were almost filled. He had lost track of those he recognized and those he did not.

The crew he had hired readied the large broadcast-compatible video camera in the center aisle. The two television reporters he had cajoled to attend were in the second row; they appeared to be sharing a private joke.

A pretty dark-haired woman approached the platform. She wore a dark blue skirt and jacket with a bright red scarf. Tiffany Wheeler, Sam Wellborn's assistant, introduced herself. She explained that they had met briefly when Carlton Boyle was campaigning at Sanitas. "I'm intrigued with the cosmic paradigm. I've written a position paper on it for President-elect Boyle," she said with a perky cheerfulness.

"So I understand." When Sam had figured out the origin of the material on which Tiffany was basing her recommendations, he had forwarded a copy of it to Ryan. "You're staying for tonight's presentation?"

"Wouldn't miss it. I'm anxious to see what happens with this." She smiled and handed him a thick brown package.

He opened it to find multiple copies of the file from the archives, just as he had requested of Sam. He glanced at the typed pages and pictures from fifty years earlier. Without Dr. Adamson's assistance they might have been buried until some scholar found them, a hundred years hence, or until the World League destroyed them. Leaving one copy in the envelope, he laid the others on top of the pile of papers beneath the podium.

Ryan retrieved a sealed envelope. He handed Tiffany the agreements that Aza and he had taken from Steiger's safe. When she paged through them, her eyes went wide. "President-elect Boyle will love these," she said.

"Tell him to use them wisely."

"I'm sure he'll remember who provided them. Thank you."

As Tiffany took her seat, Ryan looked out on the audience. This was the end of the old. The new would begin in a few minutes. At Peter's first presentation Ryan had let Aza introduce the Phantian. For each of Peter's subsequent presentations — there had been three between Thanksgiving and Christmas — other people had introduced Peter.

Thus far, Ryan Drake, high-profile business executive, had remained on the sideline, out of the glare of publicity. Many in the audience either knew him personally, or knew him by reputation. To them, he was a businessman, the former President of the highly successful Sanitas Technologies. Few knew of his connection to extraterrestrials.

To this point, he had rationalized it as one more way to shield Sarah's whereabouts, but tonight marked the end of all that, the end of his old life. Tonight, he began fulfilling his commitment to the celestial messenger — he would help lead the transformation of his world.

'Everything will work for the best,' Peter communicated. *'We have friends in high places.'*

Ryan looked across at the bald Phantian. Like Sarah and himself, Peter was seated in a high backed chair. He smiled at his cosmic brother reassuringly and communicated, *'It is the only way open to us.'*

Ryan began the presentation with a moment of silence in honor of Aza O'Sullivan. He mentioned that his friend's funeral would be held tomorrow.

Then he thanked those who had returned to hear more from Peter and welcomed the newcomers. He announced that tonight was a special occasion and suggested that everyone should stick around to the very end. Should anyone need help staying awake, coffee and tea were available in the lobby. He welcomed representatives of the media and acknowledged that tonight's presentation was being taped. The he turned the stage over to Peter and went to sit next to Sarah.

If anything, Peter's enthusiasm and power had increased over the course of his four previous presentations. Like Sarah he wore a cream-colored robe. The garment was a heavy weave, fashioned in the style of a monk.

His commanding presence mesmerized the audience from his first words. The bald Phantian continued to amaze Ryan. Compared to the stumbling figure of their desert trek, Peter had transformed into a powerful captivating orator, the equivalent of a Robert Schuler or a JFK.

He explained the five elements of the cosmic paradigm: First, there was much more to reality than the physical that we are able to sense. It was true at the individual level; it was equally true at the cosmic level. Conscious life forms, individual personalities aware of their existence, existed on a spectrum from the purely physical to the celestial.

Second, the cosmos was teeming with life: Other races, other civilizations of mortals, and many types of celestials ubiquitiously inhabited planets throughout the universe. Contact with non-human conscious life forms was more common than generally acknowledged on this planet. Most contact was very subtle and left only impressions. By design, there was seldom a memory of extraplanetary contact, but a residual impression remained in the subconscious. Anyone who remembered extraplanetary contact, whether with a spirit or a mortal, knew it as an unforgettable experience.

Third, the cosmos was organized and overwhelmingly friendly. There were trillions of celestials wiser and more powerful than the humans who inhabited Earth. Most mortal extraplanetaries, who visited Earth, were highly evolved spiritually.

"All extraplanetary beings," Peter said, "all non-human conscious life forms, recognize the reality of The Divine One. God has many names: the Creator, the Source, Divinity, and the Universe

Father. The Divine One created the universe. The Divine One not only set the universe of time and space in motion, but also upholds and governs this vast creation down to the spinning of each and every atom. But The Divine One does not stop there; within every conscious life form there is a spark of divinity. No, you are not divine, but you have the potential to become perfect as a unique personality, a highly evolved spirit. In all of this it is best to think of The Divine One as a loving Father, a loving Mother, a Divine Parent. For indeed, The Divine Parent of all is present in each of us, providing a direct, instantaneous connection.

"Stop for a moment and think about this one truth: Realize what that means, realize what is possible. You in conjunction with that fragment have the ability, the power to accomplish anything you choose. Stop and think about the possibilities."

Peter paused to allow his words to take root. He then continued enumerating his five points. Fourth, Earth was being called upon to grow up and join with other enlightened planets. The people of this planet were not in charge of the universe, or even of this planet. Despite being one among many races, Earth-humans exerted a powerful impact beyond this planet.

Fifth, the human inhabitants of Earth were the only ones who can help make the proper transformation of this planet. It had happened on other planets; it could happen here. They could leave it up to their current leaders, to their current institutions, or they choose to rally about a higher truth. The choice was theirs.

He emphasized that Earth was at a critical juncture: It would evolve spiritually, or it would self-destruct in a massive extinction of life. Given ongoing trends, the time was short for making that determination, short for people waking up to the reality of the situation — and making a collective decision about the future.

People shifted uncomfortably in their seats, some leaned forward, some to one side. Ryan saw no one drift from paying close attention.

Peter explained that celestials were personalities that functioned at a higher, more powerful frequency rather than their historical image as inhabitants of some mysterious realm. He pointed out that the mortals of every planet were connected to those on other planets through the functioning of universe mind — a gigantic "computer network" that pervaded time and space — and that the well being of every planet was important to the balance of the universe. He said that the humans of this planet benefited from celestial guidance, as did the mortals of all inhabited planets — and that they could get more of this guidance, if only they would open their hearts and minds to it.

He disclosed that the universe of time and space had been constructed for the sole purpose of fostering the progressive ascent of mortals upward and inward to home of The Divine One. He revealed "Between worlds," specifically designed celestial spheres, where mortals would find themselves after their time on this planet. The many stages of the celestial Journey were intended to perfect those who had begun life as mere mortals. Mortals were not destined to be gods, rather they were to perfect their uniqueness.

The bald Phantian then painted a picture of what an evolved planet would be like. "There is another way, the way of the peaceful cosmic citizen. Picture yourself moving into that role. Pay attention to the perfection around you, from the orbiting of the planets to the spinning of the atom. Nothing is your exclusive property, or is worth the effort to covet or protect, for it has been given to you. If you would live in harmony, perceive the need of your brother or sister and give it to him or her, knowing they will do the same for you. Internalize the knowing that when another flourishes, so do you.

"Imagine a community of your brothers and sisters who live in harmony because they revel in that understanding. Imagine a world in such harmony. When your hearts and souls passionately hold such an ideal, all within the universe will support your vision. This is the only way in which you can rescue your world from its downward spiral."

These remarks caused some to nod; others shook their heads at the impossibility of such a utopian view.

Peter then challenged each person in the audience to wake up and acknowledge what was going on around them. "How much better are you treating each other than your ancestors did a thousand years ago? Yes, there has been some progress. But such progress is racing against planetary self-destruction." He challenged them to see the cosmic paradigm as a motivator that could transform this planet into the veritable paradise it was intended to be.

Peter summarized his talk into three major points: Citizens from the organized, peaceful universe were visiting this planet. All non-human conscious life forms knew that God was very real and in charge of the cosmos. It was time for the children of Earth to grow up and join with the enlightened planets.

As Ryan sat listening to Peter, he thought back to his meeting in the desert. He had learned there about the decimal protocol, learned how it had left its mark within each Earth-human. How much harder was it going to be — this transformation of Earth to an enlightened planet — with each of its citizens marked by the decimal protocol? Yet each human had a spark of divinity, the ability to accomplish anything they chose. Was that not more than an adequate compensation for the mark?

As soon as Peter stopped speaking, hands went into the air. Several people stood, yelling to be recognized. Not only newcomers had questions; those that had been at his earlier performances questioned Peter's statements. A microphone was passed around so that their questions might be recorded. Ryan waited patiently as Peter fielded each one. Ryan noticed the two reporters speaking into their cell phones.

The questions were winding down when Peter pointed to a man sitting behind Brauk. He stood, grabbed for one of the microphones, and spoke in a rough voice with a strong Southern accent. "I've been listening to this discussion and it appears to me that we're talking about some sort of aliens coming here and taking over. I think freedom's the real issue here. I fought in Korea and in Vietnam. I'm proud to be an American. I believe, as do all Americans, that everybody should be free to do his own thing, pursue his own life. This cosmic cooperation stuff doesn't do a thing for me, and I don't plan to let it affect me one bit."

Peter said, "I know that your soul connected with the larger truth this evening." Peter pointed to his heart. "If you will listen to your inner voice, it will —"

"Mister, I don't think you heard me; what you're talking about stomps all over my personal freedom. That to one side, I don't think your high minded stuff makes one bit of sense, or difference to me personally. I suspect I speak for others in this gathering." The man returned to his seat.

Murmurs went through the audience.

Peter walked to the edge of the stage, to a point closest to the man. "Is the wisdom of the mortals of this planet the highest of which you can conceive? Are the institutions of men the highest to which you can aspire? Is the behavior of your fellow man based on love for one another? If not, then I suggest you listen to the accumulated wisdom of the cosmos. There is a higher way to live than focusing on your personal freedoms.

"Your freedoms are proscribed by those in power. Your freedoms are limited by the box in which you live. Truth has been withheld and manipulated by your leaders. How can you choose freedom when you do not know the truth? Cosmic truth is something beyond those daily activities that make you 'feel' secure, comfortable, and free. On enlightened planets, freedom is treasured as the opportunity for all to seek out their highest path, and to rejoice when others attain their goal. On enlightened planets, beings serve others before they seek their own welfare.

"Does it make any difference to you that new technologies, technologies based on revised science, technologies that could alleviate your energy crisis, are being withheld? Does it make any difference to you that the truth about extraterrestrial contact has been hidden away and ridiculed, and that this truth could change the way in which you view your world, your life? Does it make any difference that other planets are veritable paradises, utopian worlds? And that people from these other civilizations stand ready to offer their lives to help the people of this planet? These truths do affect you. They affect you very personally."

A man in a suit stood and turned to the man with the gruff Southern voice. Ryan recognized him as a fellow entrepreneur, the president of a very successful chain of health food stores. "Friend, I don't know you, but I think you need to listen to what Peter is saying. I think he makes a lot of sense. After I heard him talk in Boulder, I decided to make a few changes in my life. I decided to stop "doing my own thing" and start looking at the consequences of my actions. I saw that I was doing things largely because I wanted to do them, not because they were necessarily good, true, or helpful. I was more worried about competition and what others would think, than doing the right thing, than serving others. I started focusing on what's really in the best interests of my employees, my customers, my community, and my world. I suggest you try it. You see, once you truly awaken, you don't have a choice but to help transition this world to the utopia that Peter is describing."

The gruff man did not respond.

Searching through the few remaining hands, Peter pointed to a man at the rear of the church; Ryan had not noticed him before. He stood and said loudly, "The things you are proposing are in conflict with all tradition, not to mention the legitimate government of the United States of America." His precise ivy-league intonation resonated off the bare walls. "You don't have any special knowledge. This is a ruse to undermine our beliefs, to criticize our great country, to get our money."

Ryan rose and came to the microphone. "Good evening, Mr. deBeque. I was hoping you, or some other representative of the media affiliates, would be here tonight. You see we have something rather special planned and I would have hated for you to get it second hand. I invite all of you to listen for the next few minutes, then decide if what we are disclosing undermines your beliefs — or enhances them."

DeBeque sat down. A murmur went through the crowd.

Ryan handed the microphone back to Peter and nodded to him. The bald Phantian walked to where the camera crew would get their most direct picture of him.

At that moment, a television crew burst into the church and headed for the front. One of the reporters, a woman, greeted them.

Ryan signaled Peter to pause until their camera was ready and its red light blinked on. The camera that Ryan had commissioned had not stopped its taping. Ryan noted that the second camera, like the first, did not have a live feed.

"Before Ryan proceeds, I want to answer this man's question." Peter pointed to the gruff-voiced man. "I know about the larger truth because I was born on another planet." He spoke in a measured tone, not unlike the way he had delivered his earlier speech. "On my home planet, Phantia, everyone knows the truth about the cosmic paradigm, and about true freedom. That knowledge has created a beautiful planet with sustainable peace and prosperity for all."

Peter paused to allow his words to hang in the air.

Ryan heard gasps from the audience. The erudite speaker who had captivated them only moments ago was now revealing that he was an extraplanetary being. How could that be? He looked so human. Ryan could relate to their shock, and disbelief. That was the way it had struck him that day, three months ago, in the desert wilderness.

"About time this all came out," Ertl said to his deputies with enough volume for those around him to hear.

"Sarah Smith and I traveled trillions of miles to deliver the cosmic paradigm to you." Sarah rose and joined him at the edge of the stage.

Peter continued, "We are here to prove that a friendly universe exists, a universe orchestrated and nurtured by celestial beings. Look at me. You can see that I am not of this planet." With that he parted the top of his robe to expose his slim body. "Humans on your planet have navels." He pointed to his sleek, hairless, uninterrupted abdomen. The camera zoomed in. "On Phantia, we are born without umbilical cords."

Sarah slipped open her robe, dropping it to her elbows. With her left hand, she pointed to the smooth belly between her jogging shorts and top. Ryan was immediately jealous as the willowy body of his favorite extraplanetary being was displayed for all to ogle.

The audience froze. Dead silence, then whispers.

Some leaned forward to get a better look; others reared back, afraid.

Ryan realized how few of those present had received a pictioning session from Sarah. For those who had not, Peter's announcement was a real jolt.

For some it confirmed beliefs in the reality of extraterrestrials. For most, the realization that beings from another planet stood before them was astonishing. Ryan recalled his own experience with Sarah and Peter — it had been a real shock, an emotional thunderbolt.

"I know they're extraterrestrials." Ryan recognized Brauk's voice and smiled. His former business partner, and now corporate executive, was on his feet, waving with his usual wild gestures. "I've seen their home planet."

People turned to see who had spoken. The few who knew what he was talking about smiled and nodded.

Sarah closed her robe and said, "Our hands are unlike yours, as are our eyes." She and Peter edged forward, hands outstretched.

People in the front row shied from them. Out of respect, the two Phantians did not advance further.

"I'm afraid." A woman in the fourth row said to her husband.

"They look so human," he responded.

Ryan stepped forward and said, "I also know these two are from Phantia. They are indeed extraterrestrials. I can vouch for them. They have been living with me for the past three months."

People screamed out questions. Sarah, Peter, and Ryan tried to respond. A woman, still wearing surgical scrubs, walked forward to examine Peter's stomach. She also checked his hands and eyes.

"These are most unusual," she commented. She went to Sarah and did the same.

Six people scurried out a side door. One of them was the gruff-voiced man. He caught Ryan's eye as he slid through the door. The man turned and made a gun with his forefinger and thumb.

Peter wrapped his robe about himself, but continued to answer queries. Every question was about his origins. He offered details about himself and Phantia. Yielding the floor to Peter, Sarah returned to her chair.

"You can't fool me," deBeque shouted. He was on his feet again. "It's a make-up job."

"Sample our DNA," Peter replied. He stretched out his arm.

The woman in scrubs turned to deBeque and said, "They are not made up."

The businessman with crutches struggled to his feet and turned in deBeque's direction. "Mister, you are way off base. I met this gentleman and his partner several weeks ago." He pointed to Peter and Sarah. "They have given me a vision of their home planet — a peaceful, sustainable, beautiful place. And showed me how this world could be like theirs. I signed up as soon as I understood how much better it would be for my family, how much better it would be to live on a planet without violence. Sure, it's going to cause some real disruptions, some dislocations, and some people are going to fight it like hell. But it's inevitable. Eventually it'll happen.

Why not now? Why not on our watch?"

Ryan took the microphone from Peter and said, "Now that we have your attention." He smiled. Nervous laughter came back. "I remember my first exposure to Peter and Sarah — we were out in the desert, all alone. I want to tell you, it left an indelible impression." A few joined his light heartedness.

"Thank you all for staying with us," Ryan said. "I know the hour is late, but we're not finished yet. Some of you have known me for years, others knew Aza, and others have come to know Peter or Sarah. I can assure you that everything they told you is true. In fact, people from Phantia are trained to relate with complete integrity.

"However, we have a problem and we need your help. Certain people want to stop Peter and Sarah from telling you about the cosmic paradigm. These people don't want the existence of friendly extraterrestrials to be known — it serves their purpose for you to think of all ETs as evil aliens who are intent on abductions or conquering Earth. For many years, they have hidden the truth about extraterrestrials who visit here, who have visited here for thousands of years, extraterrestrials who want to help us evolve this world. In short, these elitists don't want you to know the truth.

"Very recently there have been attempts on our lives. As many of you know, our good friend Aza was recently murdered. He had met and accepted Sarah and Peter for who they are.

"We need your help to make sure that this uplifting message is delivered, and that Peter and Sarah are no longer threatened." In his left hand Ryan held the package Sam had obtained for him.

"Please help Peter and Sarah." Someone shouted. It was Tiffany Wheeler, the young woman from Sam's office.

"I have here some information that I'm going to pass around." Ryan stepped off the stage and passed copies into the audience. There were too few to accommodate everyone. "Try to share. If you didn't get one, contact me and I'll make more copies available." He made sure each reporter got a copy. He walked to John deBeque and handed one to him.

Returning to the stage, Ryan said, "What you have in your hands are copies of documents retrieved from the government's archives. They have been labeled top-secret and hidden away for the last fifty years. Certain government officials have known about them, but 'neglected' to tell you."

He waited as people passed around the material.

"No, the photos have not been retouched. No, the documents have not been altered. What you hold in your hands is conclusive proof that an alien ship crashed near Roswell, New Mexico in 1947, and that the government has been covering up its knowledge of the off-planet life forms from that crash. I call upon President-elect Boyle to open the Roswell files to the public."

A round of applause greeted his remark.

"And I ask you, if they can cover up something as vital as this, what else are they hiding? And who are 'they?'"

Reactions were loud enough that Ryan had to call for quiet.

When the din had subsided, he said, "Now, I have other information I want to share with you."

He reached for the stack of papers. This time it looked like there might be enough copies to go around, so he asked the people in the front row to pass them out.

"These are copies of pages from the personal diary of Ernest Steiger. Mr. Steiger owns the controlling interest in Steiger Enterprises, a multi-billion dollar publishing and communications empire headquartered in Chicago. In this diary, we see a man who has devoted his life to manipulating and controlling each one of us. Mr. deBeque, over there, is the chief spokesman for a group known as the media affiliates. His bosses are influential men, like Steiger, who control the media, movie production, and advertising." Ryan pointed to the dark suited young man. Heads turned.

"No, you've probably never heard of the media affiliates. Neither had I, until they started to threaten my friends and me. Read the pages from his diary and learn how Ernest Steiger thinks of us ordinary people as 'cattle.' Learn how he and his media affiliate gang manipulate the truth for their own purposes. And ask yourselves if you are ready to rise above a paradigm wherein they tell you what to believe, wherein they define your life, wherein you are controlled, wherein you believe you are free, but you are not. Then ask yourselves if you are ready to grasp the cosmic paradigm, a new paradigm that will enable you to move this planet to where it can join with the other peaceful, beautiful planets of the universe."

Although he wanted to say more, Ryan carefully stopped his remarks at this point. He had read enough of Steiger's diary to know the problems went much deeper than the media affiliates. But he had selected only those pages that illustrated the media affiliates and their activities. He did not want to use all of his ammunition quite yet.

John deBeque rose and marched from the rear of the theatre, sheets rolled tightly in his right hand.

Ryan pointed at the camera, "Ernest Steiger, I know you will eventually view this event. If you or your friends harm Sarah Smith or Peter Jones, you will pay for it even more dearly than this brief expose tonight. We have additional pages of your diary, and we will make them public."

Ryan extended his arms and said, "I hope the American people will take this exposé to heart. All of you deserve better from those you have elected to govern, from the media you allow into your homes, and from those you have made wealthy."

He motioned for Sarah and Peter to join him. "In the name of my brother and sister from Phantia, I hope that tonight will be the beginning of the transformation of this planet."

Questions lasted until 1:00 AM. Most of the audience stuck around until the very end. Some of the newcomers became brave enough to approach Sarah or Peter.

After the camera crews packed up their equipment, Tom Ertl and his deputies escorted Sarah, Peter, and Ryan back to their hotel in Boulder. Ryan suggested that Ertl pass along a copy of the pages from Steiger's diary to policemen friends in Chicago. He wondered under what circumstances he would next run into John deBeque.

Television newsmen are breathless on how the game is being played, largely silent on what the game is all about.

— J. K. GALBRAITH

NINE

The following morning, Saturday, Ryan scanned the television channels; cartoons played on many of them. The few news programs, local or national, featured news, weather, and sports. There was nothing about extraterrestrials in Denver, nothing about information from a government archive, nothing about Ernest Steiger.

Frustrated, he turned on the radio and checked various news, talk, and music stations. The area's largest station was broadcasting a monologue about how the wrong person had stolen the Presidential election and what terrible consequences were in store for the country. The public broadcasting station had a program about creating more jobs. One FM station was broadcasting Orson Welles' "War of the Worlds." Ryan listened for a moment. It was good drama but far from the reality he now understood. Beyond that, there was just the usual.

Ryan opened up his new laptop — he had bought it to replace the computer he had lost in the fire. After thirty minutes he tracked down a site which had posted a written summary of the events that had taken place the prior evening. A reasonable account of Peter's presentation, it included scanned copies of the documents Ryan had passed out. There was a message on the site that stated that its manager had been in the audience the night before and could vouch for the accuracy of everything.

Ryan sent a thank you to the site's email address. He forwarded the site's address to Tiffany Wheeler's office, and to as many of the people who had been there last evening as he had addresses for. In this, he was hampered by the loss of his computer, disks, and files. He had taken only a written phone list with him to Scottsdale.

Ryan picked up the phone and called, Colette Dupree. She was the reporter from the local network affiliate who had called in the camera crew last evening.

He found her at her desk. "This is Ryan Drake. Why's nothing on the tube?"

Ryan heard Colette cover the mouthpiece with her hand and mumbled words. "Hi, uh, can I call you back?"

He gave her the hotel's number.

Five minutes passed before the phone rang.

"Sorry about that," Colette said. "This place is crazy. My producer was hovering over me. He has orders to make sure nothing about last night gets on the air and, I'm afraid, he doesn't completely trust me. I'm in the ladies room on my cell phone."

"Nothing on the air? What happened to the tape you made?"

"I am so upset. Nothing like this has ever happened before to me. My boss sent the tape to New York."

"New York?"

"Yeah, New York. U.S. Broadcasting owns this station. They're a subsidiary of Steiger Enterprises. Someone at the top put a squelch on everything. My guess is that it's temporary; they can't keep something this big under wraps forever. They're just crafting the right spin. Ryan, everything you said last night about the media affiliates is so true."

"You know about this kind of stuff?"

"Sure, it happens. We don't see it so much here in Denver, because we rely on the networks and news services. But when I was interning in New York, I saw it happen at the time of the World Trade Center. By the way, do you have the tape from the other camera?"

"It's with the firm I hired."

"It may be the only true record of what happened. Get your hands on it — fast."

Ryan hung up and called Mile High Productions. He had hired this small independent with the idea that they would create a record of last evening's proceedings for historical purposes, or in case he wanted to show it to some friends.

On the tenth ring, an Oriental voice said, "Hello."

"Is Hosyu there?"

"No. He not here. He go away."

"This is Ryan Drake. He made a tape for me last night. I need to get it."

"Other man, he come. He pay for tape. Good bye."

"What other —" The line was dead. He threw the handset onto its cradle. "Damn it."

"What is it?" Sarah was leaning against the doorway to the second bedroom. She was dressed in a yellow bathrobe and appeared to have just showered.

As she moved toward him, her robe parted to reveal a few inches of bronze calf. Ryan was instantly distracted. He was not sure whether or not she was aware that her quite normal actions created such a distraction for him.

To him she was a beautiful woman, not a visitor from some far off planet. He found her intoxicating. They had discussed the situation. For her part, Sarah was pleased with his attention and said she felt attracted to him. But in the interests of the mission, they had maintained their distance.

He forced his eyes from her leg and looked up. "Both video tapes are missing."

"What do you mean?"

"They're gone. The television channel sent theirs to New York. Some guy bribed my production house into surrendering the one they made."

The hours that followed were some of the most bizarre of Ryan's life, a yo-yo of events and emotions. He had a second television set brought to the room. As they were dressing, they scanned the channels for any tidbit of news.

The funeral for Aza O'Sullivan was held at St. Thomas Aquinas Catholic Church in southeast Denver. After the family members spoke, Ryan told a story about Aza's kindness to the homeless of Denver. What most people did not know was that he single-handedly financed a shelter north of the downtown area.

After the service, Ryan talked to several people who had listened to Peter the prior evening. Some of them had connections and promised to call the media people they knew.

On the way back to their hotel, Ryan stopped at Eads, a Boulder newsstand, and picked up one of every daily publication. On page five of both the Rocky Mountain News and the Denver Post were small articles. The headline read, "TWO CLAIM TO BE ALIENS." The story was a purely skeptical piece about the prior evening, questioning the truth of Peter's presentation and claims. There was no mention of Ryan, the Roswell material, or Ernest Steiger's diary.

Reflecting on the situation, Ryan was not entirely surprised; media conglomerates owned both papers. But because it was local news, they could not ignore it entirely for fear some other media might beat them to the story. Instead, they had chosen the ridicule and discredit route.

In independent papers, like the Colorado Daily and the Longmont Daily Times-Call, he found stories with various slants. He speculated that they were the result of second-hand information; none of them reproduced the material from the archives or the diary. And, neither of them treated the subject as the extraordinary, world-changing event he knew it to be. Again he was not surprised, and kicked himself for expecting more. The media had become so conditioned to crazy, unsubstantiated stories about UFOs and aliens that factual reports were treated with little respect.

Late morning, Sarah, Peter, and he ordered room service and talked about the situation. They told him the way things were handled on Phantia, showed him the way things might be different without the twisted influence of the media. The two Phantians constantly brought him back to evolving Earth to its full potential — if truth were allowed to assert itself, if people would function with integrity, if service replaced self-involvement.

"I continue to be amazed at the intellectual pollution offered by your media," Sarah said. "It is not just the way in which the truth is twisted, it is the way in which things of little or no substance are repeated, over and over again."

"Mental smut," Peter said. "How many commercials do I need to see for erectile dysfunction? How many depictions of gory shootings? Don't people understand that what they put into their heads is as critical as that which they put into their mouths? This drivel is more effective than the circuses used in ancient Rome. How can people find the truth about over-population, resource depletion, environmental problems, nuclear proliferation, and violence when they are fed lies? When they are fed only the sensational? Television numbs them to the truth."

Peter turned to Ryan, "I fear for your planet."

In the early edition of the news, one of the local television broadcasts mentioned that aliens had reportedly appeared at a Denver gathering. They treated it like another crazy UFO sighting. No other television station referenced it.

That evening, two of the major networks, with little prior announcement, ran specials about UFOs; the others stuck with their regular programming. The UFO programs were slanted to cattle mutilations and abductions, incidents that had been reported in the fifties and sixties. Both implied that aliens were hostile monsters.

Later in the evening, on one of the network interview shows, a USAF spokesperson assured everyone that there had never been verifiable sightings of UFOs, that over-worked government employees were not hiding anything, and besides the government did not have money to spend on such things. Ryan found it coincidental that, on another channel, a Pentagon spokesperson was talking about the latest technology that was being deployed in orbit "to detect and shoot down enemy craft."

Ryan found a local radio talk show personality who had discovered the web site. Ryan Drake, formerly of Sanitas Technologies, was mentioned as an accomplice of "Peter and Sarah, the aliens." No mention was made of the cosmic paradigm or any other parts of Peter's talk, nothing about government archives, or about Ernest Steiger. One caller demanded a witch-hunt to find people without navels.

Later in the talk show, people began to call in and discuss Ryan Drake. An old business associate blasted him for perceived wrongs in connection with a job dismissal. Several former employees came forward with stories of the iron fist with which Ryan had ruled Sanitas, stories of how he had misused people, stories about his rotten family life. One woman claimed he had fostered her six-year-old girl. A fourteen-year-old boy claimed he was Ryan's son and that his mother was an alien.

At 9:30 PM, Peter, Sarah, and he went to bed.

"I don't care how old a friend he is. If I'd known what he was going to do with that file, I would never have given it to him" Sam Wellborn's curly brown hair receded from his high forehead. At 11:45 PM and fifty years of age, he was showing the stress of his job as Special Assistant to the President-elect. He held the briefing paper that she had written on her laptop during her early morning flight from Denver. "If the media finds out that Ryan got that file from us, the opposition will crucify us. We'll never get a bill through Congress."

"Sam, you and I both know, we never would have found that file, if he hadn't told us to look in that box labeled employment statistics — probably the only reason it hadn't been destroyed."

"That has nothing to do with the repercussions."

"You liked the agreements with the Senators and Congressmen didn't you?" Despite the long day, Tiffany Wheeler was alert and enthusiastic. Her dark eyes scanned the various papers spread out on Sam's desk.

"That's different. They'll never be made public."

Tiffany's briefing document detailed the sensational disclosure by the two extraterrestrials, the material from the top-secret archives, and the pages from Ernest Steiger's diary. Any one of these was explosive in the face of the impending change of administrations. Combined they created the rationale for a major redirection of United States policy — at least that was what she had stated in her conclusions.

Sam and she were seated at his desk in Carlton Boyle's transition office in Washington, DC. Although she was positive he had read it, he had avoided the topic since she had handed the document to him about midday. His whole focus had been on the agreements and what they could do with them. Finally, she had demanded they talk before he went home, and had waited outside his door until he acknowledged her.

The room was plain, plain walls, plain carpet, and plain furniture — standard rented furnishings. Nothing like the space they would occupy in a few days. She had toured their new quarters in the White House office wing. Her office was small, but it was close to Sam's, and on the same floor as the Oval Office.

She felt clammy in the clothes she had worn for the past thirty-six hours. Not willing to waste time going home, she had come straight to the office from the airport.

Unwilling to show that she was steamed at being put off all day, she smiled deferentially and said, "Sam, don't you see, Ryan Drake's doing our work for us. He's doing what no administration has been willing to do — expose covert control of the media and information manipulation, not to mention the cover-up of aliens and UFOs."

She was sure he had not shown her write-up to the President-elect, and had not brought it to the attention of others. Although she was his assistant, there was much about his interaction with the President-elect that he did not tell her.

"It's all about repercussions, Tiffany. Hell, Boyle hasn't even been sworn in yet. The timing couldn't be worse. The public will hang us with the years of lying to them."

"But it's not President Boyle's problem," she said. "He can blame it on the current administration, on predecessors going back to Truman. If he does this right, blows it wide open, he comes out looking like a hero. 'The President who finally had the guts to open up the secrets about UFOs and aliens.'"

"We're dead in the water until he's sworn in," Sam said. "No one's giving us any more buried secrets until then, and even then maybe not — at least not at first. They'll all be covering their butts. Damn it, Tiffany, we haven't solidified the Cabinet yet. This could raise doubts, create defections. Let Sixty Minutes or CNN break the ice."

"The media's stalling," she said. While she waited, she had scanned the channels and checked with her friend, the assistant to President-elect Boyle's Press Secretary, Emma Roth. "Everyone's looking for direction. I think a statement, from Emma, would help set the proper tone, show we're really on top of things."

"No way. Without more facts, we don't know if it's true. I'm sorry, but we can't rely on Ryan and his two supposed ET friends."

"What about asking for a briefing?"

"From who? From military or intelligence people who don't report to Boyle yet? From an administration we just defeated in an election? They'd love that. I say we sit on it until we're in place."

"What if the media breaks it the wrong way?"

"It'll just look bad for the outgoing administration, not us. We have nothing to lose by waiting. On the other hand, as soon as we're in, maybe, and it's just a maybe, I can be persuaded to find out what's really been going on the past fifty years."

Tiffany was crushed, but she knew Sam well enough to know he wouldn't budge. Clinging to a ray of hope, she flashed her best smile and said, "I'll hold you to that."

"Media affiliates can't contain this much longer." Warren Ophir said. "Good thing today's a Sunday."

The three men of the hastily assembled task force sat at one end of the conference table, a table normally used by Generals and Admirals when discussing national emergencies. The table resided in a secure conference room on one of the lower levels of the Pentagon. Actions from the first Gulf War to the invasions of Afghanistan and Iraq had been considered and coordinated from this room.

Ophir pulled the sleeve of his black sweater down so that it touched his wrist. He was dressed in his weekend attire, a sweater over a long sleeved shirt and black slacks. He always wore long sleeves, except when he was alone. The elites of the World League might not understand his tattoo — a monstrous red and black devil that twisted from his right wrist, up his arm, and across his back. He had paid dearly in both money and pain to have the part of it removed that showed above his collar level, and at his wrist.

He had acquired his tattoo as a youngster and had worn it proudly. When his mother, the widow of a prominent Cleveland industrialist, and wealthy in her own right, had discovered it, she had shipped him off to live with relatives in a far less prestigious neighborhood, far from Shaker Heights and her socialite friends. He had hated the new school, but his tattoo identified the new kid as a bad dude.

Ophir had checked his gun when he had first entered the building. He felt undressed without a weapon; he had carried one, on his person or in his vehicle, since he was sixteen. In those long ago days, it had ensured that neither his customers nor his suppliers took advantage of him. Along with the tattoo, it had made him the badass, an image he had played to the hilt. Two of the spoiled brats from his mother's neighborhood, who he had supplied with drugs, had died. Some of the other kids knew who had supplied the drugs to them. He had used his gun as a threat to keep them quiet.

In many ways, he had come far since those days. In other ways, it wasn't such a great distance. Spying, keeping secrets, intimidating others were the same today as they had been in tenth grade. But now instead of pretending to be the bad dude to hide that his mother had disowned him, now he was pretending to be an upstanding member of the World League.

Thirty-one hours ago, at 2:51 AM, Saturday morning, John deBeque had telephoned and given him the highlights of the performance by Ryan Drake and the two aliens.

"I've already contacted our key media people," deBeque had said. The two had developed a list for just such circumstances. "They'll take care of the video. I'm just calling to keep you informed."

DeBeque had spent the next thirty minutes giving him the details. The young man told Ophir nothing that his own people, who had attended Peter Jones's talk, had not already conveyed to him.

"Good man." He had smiled and raised a clinched fist as he disconnected. Maybe there was hope for deBeque after all.

He had waited until morning, a few hours later, to inform the Governors of the League, until one of his men had secured the video that Drake had made, until he had ordered additional men to Colorado.

"Keep an eye on them. Don't interfere; just watch," he had directed them. Ophir smiled. By now, Ryan Drake and his two alien friends would be unable to hold a conversation, make a telephone call, send an email, or connect to the Internet without their every word being recorded and analyzed. He had also directed his corps of remote viewers to stay on them.

After that was done, he had alerted the other intelligence affiliates throughout the world. He had told them that he had reason to believe the two aliens were genuine. With his resources positioned, he had asked for this meeting. By prior agreement, no one had informed Ernest Steiger.

"There's no telling how people are going to react when they hear about this," Jonathan Olson had come directly from church. The impeccably manicured gentleman was dressed in a dark suit. On the little finger of his left hand, he wore a huge sapphire embedded in gold. Olson was the head of the financial affiliates.

"There could be panic," the investment banker continued. "The stock market. I say we get the President to declare martial law. There's got to be a way to make it go away." What he did not say was that he intended to short a number of stocks prior to the market opening on Monday.

"This could be the window we've been waiting for," retired Lieutenant General Delta Kingman said. "'When there's blood in the streets, we ride to the rescue.'" These last words were straight from the League's plan of action. Kingman was fond of quoting them. He had one for every situation.

Kingman, a stocky man in his late forties, was in uniform. Since he had arranged for the conference room, he occupied the seat at the head of the table. As one of the triad who ruled the World League, he would occupy a seat of honor in any gathering of its Board of Governors.

He was a large man with hard blue eyes and an ego that filled any room. During his years in the service he had been rewarded for taking risks. But his "shoot-from-the-hip" attitude had stymied his career. This morning he puffed on his second monstrous Cuban.

Since his retirement, he occupied himself, full time, with the League's overall strategy. The other two members of the League's governing triad, a retired diplomat and a corporate executive, were charged with government and business relations. They were out of the country and would be briefed by Kingman at the conclusion of this meeting. If needed, they were prepared to jet to Washington in planes owned by the League.

Among the three present, Kingman saw the new world order as the logical outgrowth of the World League's control of the United States, the lone super power. An elitist, he felt it was his duty to force the American way into every corner of the world. The World League rode very nicely on that horse called the American dream.

A second quote from the League's plan was, "What's good for the World League is good for America. What's good for America is good enough for everybody else."

As he had told Ophir many times, the new world order would result in everything being meted out under the World League's enlightened control: organizations, population, money, security, freedom, work, education, health care, religion, and entertainment. He and others had argued long and hard about a future role for "free enterprise."

On the other hand, Jonathan Olson was dedicated to preserving the status quo. His financial empire functioned best when world events were only slightly unstable. Change was bad. Things like wars were too extreme, wars caused people to choose sides, wars interrupted the free flow of funds, and wars destabilized stock markets. Although he had profited from past wars, he preferred a stable world, preferred the existing structures, and preferred dealing with the people now in power. After World War II, Olson and his group had wrestled control of world economics from certain European families; he had no intention of relinquishing it. A convulsive route to the new world order was more than the financial man was prepared to support.

The go-slow approach allowed him to manipulate everything from the stock market to the finances of third-world countries. He had even turned recent terrorist activity to his advantage. From the intelligence information he received, he had predicted the exact timing of terrorist attacks and sold stocks short the prior day.

"So, what about the President?" Olson pushed on Kingman.

"The President doesn't want to do anything," Kingman said with an air of resignation. He had a raspy voice, and it always grated on Ophir. "I talked to his Chief of Staff an hour ago. He's worried about his legacy. He wants to make it Boyle's problem."

"People are going to be pissed at the government for hiding things," Ophir said. "They're going to demand someone's head, a very powerful someone's."

"Great, give them Boyle's," the financial elitist said. "No telling what that bastard's going to do once he's sworn in. This is the perfect way to usher him into the Oval Office, and back out." He leaned back in his chair and laughed. "Maybe he'll quit and make room for the deuce."

"We have to hope that people bought our evil alien scenario," Ophir said. "The last thing I expected was to have two ETs politely announce their presence at a public gathering." He studied the faces of the other two men, faces that would have been hard to read if he had not known them so well.

Ophir's people had been watching Sarah Smith since he had figured out Ryan Drake's role in the tussle at Steiger's mansion. Before that, the surveillance of Steiger had been so lax that Ophir's people had failed to detect her presence at the mansion.

Since her return to Boulder, his people had detected little about her, or her friend Peter Jones — nothing more than a couple of activists — worth keeping an eye on, but not dangerous, certainly not an alien. His people had observed the invasion of Ryan Drake's house with interest, but assumed that Hauptman was acting on his own. When his people had reported preparations for Peter Jones's presentation, Ophir had smelled something amiss and had sent two of his people to it, along with John deBeque.

"By gawd, we can't allow fifty years to go down the drain just because our intelligence operation is asleep." Delta Kingman eyed him.

"If I hadn't sent my people to Denver, you would have read about it in the newspapers," Ophir retorted.

Kingman snapped his fingers. "We are so close. We cannot afford any screw-ups."

"And just exactly how did I screw up?"

"You should have known about these damn aliens — before they had a chance to go public. Now, we've got four hundred people in Denver that believe there are real live aliens living among them. And those four hundred are not going to be exactly quiet."

"This is not getting us anywhere," Olson intervened. "What are we going to do?"

They had two problems: Any expose would awaken public awareness to the reality of aliens. So far the public's knowledge of aliens had been handled by denials and ridicule. However, Peter Jones and Sarah Smith were tangible threats to that effort. Were they working alone? He was anxious to get back to his network. He had directed his people to find out if there were any others like

Jones and Smith.

Public awareness of aliens would also raise all kinds of questions about other things the government had been hiding. Ophir laughed to himself. When it all came out — if it all came out — people would be so amazed at how little "the government" really knew. It was people like him, people buried deep within covert projects who really knew the whole story.

The second problem was Ernest Steiger's diary — it identified Ophir as well as others by name. He cursed himself that he had become aware of the existence of the diary only when he'd listened to the tape of Steiger and the two men — Ryan Drake and Aza O'Sullivan — after they had broken into Steiger's mansion.

Drake's name had come through on the voice-activated bug, as had references to Sarah Smith. But detailed analysis had failed to decipher the action of that evening. He had not been sure who the other man was until Drake had called O'Sullivan from the hotel in Boulder. He still did not know what O'Sullivan possessed that Drake wanted to keep hidden. His man had botched the job and had fled before searching the house.

"I don't know how much of Steiger's diary Drake copied," Ophir said. "He may not have a copy of it all. Only passed out five pages — fortunately, they were all about Ernest Steiger."

"I think he's warning us," Olson said. He loosened his fashionable tie. "He has more."

"The most immediate thing is to retrieve all the copies," Ophir said. "The only thing we know for sure is that there were no other copies at Drake's home. If there were, they're ashes now."

Kingman held up his hand in a restraining motion and asked, "When did you learn of this diary?"

From past conversations, Ophir knew that Kingman did not trust him. But they had reached an uneasy accommodation; this time he replied truthfully. "When Drake and another guy snatched it from Steiger's safe."

"Two guys busted into that fortress?" Olson said. "What is this world coming to?"

"Eliminate Drake and the second man," Kingman said.

"I got the second guy. Tried to get Drake a couple of times. Now, we'd just make a martyr out of him."

"What about deBeque?" Olson asked. "He was Steiger's fair haired boy."

"Even deBeque didn't know about the diary until I put him on the scent."

"He was like a son to the old man."

"Yeah," Ophir said. "Steiger's real sons didn't know either. We've interrogated them."

"So, you bugged Steiger's study?" Kingman smiled.

"Yeah."

"How many more of those little devices do you have around?" Olson asked.

Ophir smiled but did not reply.

"Who burned down Drake's house?" Kingman asked.

"Hauptman," Ophir said. "When Steiger regained consciousness, he told Hauptman to get the diary back from Drake. Incinerating Drake's house was Hauptman's idea of a warning."

"Sounds like Drake was supposed to die in the fire," Olson said.

"The copies Drake passed out to the whole world were fairly recent," Kingman said. "Do we know when Steiger started writing this damn diary of his?"

Ophir opened his briefcase and produced two leather-bound volumes. He examined one and closed it. He opened the other to the initial page. "This one starts February sixteenth, nineteen ninety eight."

"Where did you get those?" Olson held out a hand to receive the leather volumes with the gold edging.

"I persuaded Hauptman to hand them over." What Ophir did not tell the other two was that Hauptman had informed Steiger he had not found the diaries at Drake's house. Ophir suspected that Steiger's security chief had planned to use them as job insurance, or as blackmail. When Hauptman learned that pages of the diary had been posted on the Internet, he had called Ophir. They had rendezvoused just over an hour ago.

"Where's Hauptman now?" Kingman asked as he paged through one of the volumes of the diary.

"He is my guest, not far from here," Ophir said. "I convinced him to give me those."

"Question him," Kingman said. "Everything he knows about Steiger, family, company. Anything about Drake and his alien friends. Then find him a job in Alaska."

"I've arranged for a nice underground job in Utah."

"That will do. And I want a copy of these."

"Me too," Olson said.

Another item Ophir failed to mention was that Hauptman had told him that Steiger was a different man after his encounter with Ryan Drake in the study at his mansion. Steiger had confided in Hauptman that he was afraid of Drake and the aliens. That was why he had directed Hauptman to kill them. It was not out of revenge.

"In your opinion, where are we with the media affiliates?" Olson asked.

"Right now everybody's playing the game, slowly leaking information. But, sooner or later, one will break ranks and spill the whole story."

"Can we stop them?" Kingman asked.

"Probably not. We have both videos that were made that evening," Ophir said. "I've had my associates spruce them up a bit. I'll get them into the right hands. That'll buy us a few weeks."

"What about these?" Kingman pointed to the two leather volumes.

"Five pages doesn't provide a lot of testimony to their authenticity," Olson said. "I say we come up with our own diary and publish it."

"The only problem is we don't have Steiger's older diaries — I doubt he started this diary thing as recently as nineteen ninety eight."

"Do we know if these supposed aliens are genuine?" Kingman asked.

"Steiger captured one, the one who calls herself Sarah Smith. According to the diary, Steiger had a doctor examine her. The doc's convinced she's an alien. I plan to send him to Utah along with Hauptman." What Ophir did not share with the others was that his people had acquired a sample of Sarah Smith and Peter Jones's DNA. For a small payment, a maid had supplied pieces of dirty laundry. His people had analyzed it and found that the DNA was alien. Ryan

Drake's DNA was human.

"The media's questioning that," Kingman said. He held up a copy of the Denver Post article.

"The spin that deBeque took it upon himself to put out." Ophir rotated his index finger in a counterclockwise direction.

"Not too bad," Olson commented.

"By gawd, I want it changed," Kingman said. "From now on they're aliens, enemies, evil beings who intend to conquer us. We've had too much of the Air Force insisting they were benign. Now's the time to slant it the other way — it'll unite the whole world."

"Yeah, like we just discovered aliens are really bad after all?" Olson leaned toward Kingman. "Come on, Delta, I'm afraid the media has already promoted too many scenarios."

"'Confusion to our enemies,'" Kingman quoted.

"Confusion's the best we can do for now," Ophir said. "Until we figure out where we really want to direct this." What Ophir did not say to Kingman was that he already knew where he wanted to direct the whole alien agenda.

Nothing in human affairs — whether it is the conquest of a nation, the changing of a single mind, or the pursuit of a love — can be accomplished without a struggle.

— TOM CLANCY

TEN

On Monday morning, the start of the third day after their disclosure, the 6:00 AM news on one of the alphabet networks had a brief item about new information that had surfaced about the crash of an alien craft in Roswell in 1947. A young, enthusiastic reporter claimed to have seen documents that had surfaced, documents from the Eisenhower years. It played again at 6:30 AM. Ryan was unable to find it again at 7:00 AM, to show it to Sarah and Peter.

When he departed the hotel at 9:00 AM, on his way to his former company, Sanitas, the absence of media was eerie. At the very least, by now, he had expected a few reporters and cameras. But, there was no one.

He waved to Andy Milliken and his woman partner, both in uniform. The two Sheriff's deputies sat in the lobby, drinking coffee and looking bored. As he crossed the street to his new rental car, he caught a glimpse of two other deputies in a Sheriff's vehicle. It followed him when he drove away.

The Police Department from the City of Boulder had complained to Tom Ertl that he was usurping their jurisdiction. But he had stood his ground; his men and women, and only his men and women, would continue to guard Peter, Sarah, and Ryan.

When he cleared Sanitas's front door he asked the guard behind the desk, "Anything unusual going on?"

"Nothing, Mr. Drake."

Two employees and a handful of visitors milled about the lobby. Each displayed a badge. Nothing seemed out of the ordinary. Ryan signed in and went for a cup of coffee from his old espresso machine in the executive kitchen.

There he ran into Brauk. "Saw the morning news. I think it's about to break."

Despite his promotion to TTT Technical Director, Brauk led Ryan to the same office he had occupied before Sanitas had been acquired. It was still piled with papers and pieces of equipment, but Brauk wore fresher clothes than Ryan remembered. It appeared that his new duties and an office in Boston at TTT's research center had wrought a few changes.

"I hope so," Ryan said. "I've never seen anything so carefully managed. It's got to be driving the editors and producers nuts." When they had talked by phone yesterday, Ryan had explained his frustration.

"Yeah," Brauk said.

"I need some help," Ryan said.

"Sure."

"Are you still in touch with Abe Russell?" Ryan was not sure who was managing the company's important contacts since he had stopped being Sanitas's CEO.

"Sure, he and I talk almost every week, have a beer whenever I get to Washington."

"I need you to call him for me." Ryan went on to tell Brauk what he needed from Major General Abe Russell, one of the Air Force's top procurement officers.

They reached Russell just as he was leaving for lunch. He spent a few minutes advising Ryan how to deal with the intelligence crowd and others involved in top-secret operations.

When they finished the call, Brauk said, "How about giving everyone here a preview? Let them in on it, before it breaks on the TV."

"That could be fun. Sure, let's do it."

Brauk gathered Sanitas's senior people. As the only official employee of TTT Instrumentation, the parent company, he was the senior person in residence. TTT had yet to appoint an individual to take Ryan's place. At the moment, each of Sanitas' departments reported to someone at TTT's Boston headquarters.

The first to enter the conference room was Karen Borden-Banes. His former administrative assistant was now working for Brauk. She rushed forward and gave him a hug. "Nice to see you."

After the others had said their hellos and settled into one of the conference room's chairs, Ryan said, "I'm going to give you a preview of today's news. I'll start with the UFO crash in Roswell. Take a look at these." He passed out copies of the information from the government archives and waited.

As they scanned the pages, Ryan glanced at the faces of his former employees. They were dedicated men and women. He had recruited each of them personally, known most of them since the early days of Sanitas. Now they waited for him, their former boss, to continue.

"Now comes the real interesting part," Ryan said. "For the last few weeks, I have been learning all about extraplanetary beings first hand. I've been associating with two of them, Sarah Smith and Peter Jones. They've been living at my house."

"I met them both," Brauk exclaimed, his youthful enthusiasm spilling out to interrupt Ryan's presentation. "They're extraterrestrials all right. Really cool."

Ryan still saw questioning looks on the faces of the others. He smiled and continued, "Yes, I said extraterrestrials."

"You're serious," Bill London, Sanitas's vice-president of sales said. Normally he spent most of his time on the road. It was happenstance that he was in the office this morning. Fritz Hildebrand, his counterpart who headed field service, was in France working on a problem of some sort with TTT's technical people.

"Really? You have, um, aliens in your house?" Glen Castillo, Sanitas's Chief Financial Officer, asked. He winked at Sanitas's controller, Ginny Markham.

Brad Bateman who headed manufacturing said, "I was there Friday night, when that good looking one showed us her stomach. Blew me away. I liked the way you put down that smartass from the, what do you call them, media something or other?"

"Media affiliates." Ryan supplied the name.

"Anyway, I like the way you put him in his place. And that

one that calls himself, Peter, man does he have a way with words."

Josh Neuman from quality control merely stared at Ryan, Brauk, and now Brad.

"I know one of them," Karen said quietly. "She's a very special person."

Ryan nodded to Karen. He had long ago forgiven her for her role in Sarah's kidnapping.

Maggie Perkins from public relations made a note in her day timer and stared at her fingernails. Ryan imagined what a headache he was creating for her. Fortunately, Sanitas no longer employed him.

Magdalena Quintana from personnel broke the tension with a chuckle, "And I thought illegal aliens from Mexico were bad."

Ryan acknowledged her remark with a broad smile. He remembered how the INS had found two illegals in its surprise visit to Sanitas's facility last October. At the time it had given him a scare, made him think the INS might have uncovered his extraplanetary friends. But that incident was nothing compared to what he was mixed up in now. Now he was publicizing that there were extraterrestrials living with him.

After a few more awkward moments, his former employees began to probe this unexpected news from their former boss. By the end of an hour he felt he had made a few cracks in their conservative business facades. He knew he would hear more from some of them in private.

"The next few days are going to be difficult." Ryan said. "Eventually the media will break the story. Unlike UFOs, resident extraterrestrials are too big to keep quiet, or to ridicule out of existence. When it hits, all hell will break loose. They'll be probing everything. Journalists are not stupid; they know they are being fed stories much of the time. They know there are whole areas of the government and private industry to which they are not privy, stories their editors won't let them publish. Why do you think they dig so relentlessly into people's personal lives? They're hungry for scraps of real truth."

Several heads nodded. Maggie Perkins closed her eyes and massaged her temples.

"Each of you will be questioned about everything imaginable, about me, and about my relationship to Sanitas. The way I intend to respond to such questions is no comment — for anything that involves Sanitas. I am sure TTT management will encourage you to do the same. But feel free to express your personal opinions, just be sure you label them as such."

The meeting lasted until lunch. Brauk and the other managers set up procedures for security, mollifying customers, and handling suppliers. They resolved questions about telephones, the lobby, and the shipping-receiving area.

After lunch Brauk asked all employees to gather in the cafeteria and Ryan went through his story again. Most said they had believed in this kind of stuff for years and were not surprised. Only three, techies who virtually lived on the Internet, were aware of the web site Ryan had found. They said they had seen the information, but had not said anything to anyone else because they did not want to seem weird.

Brauk's assistant, Kim Jong, had been at the Friday night presentation. He told his version of what had happened. He commented that Sarah was, "a real looker."

Ryan knew they still saw him as their leader, and a local celebrity. To him, his public appearance with Peter and Sarah had been an irrevocable statement of his allegiance to the cosmic paradigm. He told them he was honored to be associated with the effort, and that he still found it hard to believe that a lone web site carried the truth about extraterrestrials in Denver and of Ryan Drake's involvement with them.

On his way out of the meeting, two former employees, a man and a woman, approached him. Both said they had seen UFOs. The man claimed he had been abducted. Ryan talked to them for a while and discovered that the man was suffering from the shock of being repeatedly contacted by an extraplanetary being. Nothing unpleasant had happened, but it scared him every time. Ryan told him about his contact experiences in the Arizona desert.

Karen intercepted him in the lobby and asked, "How is Sarah?"

"She is well. I know she'd like to see you."

"But I caused her kidnapping, almost got her killed."

Ryan put his arm around Karen and said, "She would love to

hear from you. Just know that if it had served a purpose, Sarah would have willingly given up her life when Steiger had her. But that was not to be, and things worked out. Go ahead, call her at the hotel."

"You must stop this anti-American campaign," Albert Drake said when Ryan returned his call that evening. They had not spoken in six months. "You are ripping the very fabric of our society."

"Do you know many of the media affiliates?" Ryan asked. "How about members of the World League?"

Albert Drake's name had been sprinkled throughout the Steiger diary. Their relationship went back to 1947 when they had both been at Roswell, New Mexico, and had been involved in recovering material and equipment from a downed extraterrestrial craft.

"The ones I know are fine men and women," Albert said, "patriots, philanthropists, leaders. I am proud to have represented some of them for years. Through them, I have come to understand that the threat from hostile aliens is very real. You are being terribly mislead."

Ryan remembered visiting his father's study, whirling clouds of pipe smoke, dark wood. His father always wore his vest; even with his coat off, it remained buttoned to the top. Ryan also recalled meetings with mysterious men in dark suits behind the closed doors of that study.

One evening he had listened at those heavy doors. The men had argued about something surrounding the death of President John F. Kennedy. His mother had found him and pulled him away before he could hear more. As he reflected on the incident, he now understood the depth of his father's involvement with the media affiliates.

"I'm disappointed in you — the lies you've told me all my life," Ryan said.

"I did it for you, for the American people."

"You did it for yourself."

"We live in a very dangerous world," Albert Drake insisted. "The alien threat just adds to our problems. I am on the side of those fighting to preserve America, preserve civilization."

"Don't try to use patriotism to defend the mess you and your

141

friends are making of a really great country."

"Because you have unearthed the media affiliates will not lessen their power."

"In time it will," Ryan said.

"Please stop."

"No."

"Then I cannot save you." With these final words, Albert Drake hung up.

Tuesday morning, Ryan rose early and sought out the newspapers. SHOOTING AT HIGH SCHOOL. SNOW PACK TRIVIAL: WATER RATIONING TO CONTINUE. TERRORIST ALERT REDUCED. Nothing about extraterrestrials in Denver, or anywhere else.

On page seven of the Wall Street Journal, he saw the article about the death of the eminent Ernest Steiger, industrialist, philanthropist, and head of Steiger Enterprises. It painted him as one of the preeminent forces in the media world.

The article said he had died when a semi trailer, loaded with beef, collided head-on with his limousine on a Chicago side street. The driver of the truck had left the scene; police had determined that the truck was stolen.

The obituary recounted his brilliant college days and his outstanding work with several charitable institutions. A summary of Steiger Enterprises disclosed a conglomerate with interests throughout the world. Steiger's estate was estimated at $10 billion. He was survived by two sons, Richard and Nicholas, and a daughter, Lucia.

Telling Peter they would return in a couple of hours, Sarah and Ryan went for a mid-morning run. They passed a Sheriff's deputy on the steps to the ground floor. Exiting by a side door, Ryan glanced at the front of the hotel. More Sheriff's deputies were keeping protesters and media from the front entrance. Several people had placards: ALIENS GO HOME. ALIENS SUCK. Their running outfits, hats, and dark glasses enabled them to slip out without being spotted.

The path along Boulder Creek was alive with runners and bikers. Although it was winter, it had been unusually warm for the past few days. There was no evidence that it had ever snowed. In silence they ran east for two miles, turned north for a half mile, and headed west on Jay Street. This had become a daily ritual since they had moved into the hotel. Weary of potential assaults, Ryan chose a different route each day. It felt good to work off the accumulated adrenalin. After about an hour of running, they found a sunny spot and sat down.

"Nice to be away from the television," Ryan said. "I'm going nuts wondering how they're going to spin it next."

"It is disappointing that they are unwilling to present the facts and let the viewers make up their own minds."

"I think it's been that way for lots of years. It doesn't seem to matter what the issue is, conservative or liberal, national or international. All you can be sure of is that every piece of news has a spin to it — I'm not even sure about the weather. And, of course, there are some topics that never even make the news. We'll see if that young reporter can get back on the air or if anything about Ernest Steiger's diary appears in a major newspaper. After what has happened so far, I seriously doubt it."

It was at times like this he could see Sarah's two guardians, faint shimmerings that stood behind her. She had told him that they advised her of danger, helped her make connections, and kept her centered.

He shifted on the hard ground and said, "That was good news about Litchfield."

Tom Ertl had stopped by their hotel room to tell them that Louis Litchfield, of the Bureau of Indian Affairs and one of the two who had organized the raid on Harmony, had made a deal with the FBI to become a witness in their case against Raul Viejo. He had admitted that the raid on Harmony was a diversion for smuggling activities — for which he had never been paid anything. Viejo, the mastermind of the raid, was still missing. Litchfield believed he had fled to Mexico.

Tom said his policeman friend in Chicago thanked Ryan for the pages from Ernest Steiger's diary. They would add it to the file of alleged illegal activities that Steiger Enterprises had engaged in. It was too bad the old man had died before he could be brought to justice.

Tom also reported that he had received a call from the Governor of Colorado. He had asked Ertl to stop wasting manpower shielding Ryan and the Phantians. Ertl had refused.

"We must accept that Viejo is missing," Sarah said. "But I do not wish to believe that he is beyond help. When he advances to the Between world, he will be asked whether or not he wishes to continue his Journey. I wonder how he will reply? In the meantime, I will send him positive energy."

"You are a very good person," Ryan said.

"I am doing what is right."

"The media could sure use some of your rightness," Ryan said.

In their first segment of the Tuesday morning news, the first of the alphabet networks had played parts of Peter, Sarah, and Ryan's presentation, without mentioning that it had taken place three and a half days ago. Within an hour, all the others played clips from the presentation. Each version was a sound bite or two, all taken out of context, each slightly different. Ryan analyzed the spin that each newscast gave to Peter and his presentation of Friday evening. One portrayed Peter as a religious zealot; another questioned whether or not he was really an alien; the remaining offered speculations that Peter and Sarah might be advanced scouts for a pending invasion. All the networks treated it like one news item among many, and went on with their regular morning shows.

Ryan's cell phone rang. He stood to answer it. It was Brauk calling to say that Truman Thompson had just cancelled Ryan's consulting contract with TTT Instrumentation.

Ryan smiled and said, "Sure, no problem."

"He still wants to have that little visit with you. Can't understand why you would trade a successful career for associating with people impersonating aliens. Ryan, please don't get me wrong, I really like Sarah and Peter. I think they are way cool. But I need to pay attention to my new job, okay?"

"Sure, pal, I understand." And he did.

TTT's newly appointed technology guru was headed back to Boston, would probably be very busy, and might not be able to talk to Ryan for a while. He cautioned Ryan to be careful. Ryan thanked him for yesterday's visit with his former employees.

After he hung up, he realized how sorry he was to see his friend and former business partner slip back into the box prescribed by the dominant paradigm. Ryan thought back to how dedicated he had been as the CEO of a thriving, high technology business. He had really enjoyed it, and had relished the success he had wrought. In a similar situation, he too would have found it hard to associate with a weird bunch of people, including some off-planet ones.

Once Ryan had learned of the cosmic paradigm, he had turned his back on the box prescribed by the dominant paradigm. He had no regrets about that decision, but there were still moments he wished he were still at the helm of a company rather than wandering through the un-chartered waters of transforming a planet.

Ryan had no sooner finished with Brauk than the phone ran again. It was Ben Tsotsie. His Navajo friend had called to say he had read a piece about Sarah and Peter in that day's edition of the Navajo News. He told Ryan that the U.S. Customs and Border Protection Agency had moved out of Harmony Center and that Dr. Adamson was recruiting local contractors to restore it.

Referring to the publicity surrounding the Phantians, Ben asked if Ryan was upset that he had been the one to involve him with them. Ryan replied that he had long ago forgiven his Navajo friend for his match making.

Ben said he was back working his dig full time. They agreed that Ben would keep in touch and report on conditions at Harmony.

The third call was from an unidentified caller. Since he gave his cell phone number only to close friends, Ryan wondered how the man had found it. "Mr. Drake, I wanted to let you know that we have Ernest Steiger's complete diary. The pages you handed out don't seem to match the original. Just thought I'd let you know."

"I'm happy to learn that they didn't burn up in the fire," Ryan said.

"I assure you, they are in remarkably good condition."

"Nice try," Ryan said. "However, I have copies of all of the pages of Steiger's diary — copies of the originals before your people modified them. A law firm here in Colorado certified my copies; I'm quite sure they will withstand scrutiny by any court. Ernest Steiger's writing is quite distinctive, don't you think? I really marvel at some of the details."

The caller hung up without further words.

"I wish to talk about the dream you keep having, the one about the jail," Sarah said, after they had discussed the third phone call.

Ryan described the transparent jail. Then he told her how the dream was evolving, how he was no longer fully a prisoner.

"Your dream sounds much like the prison described by Michael Foucault."

"Who's that?"

"A French philosopher," Sarah said. "I read one of his books at Harmony when I was learning about this planet. Foucault's theories revolve around power structures. I am interested because Peter and I are unable to figure out why the people of this society cling to their old ideas and behaviors after we have exposed them to the cosmic paradigm. The people of Phantia made a quick transition after learning the larger truth."

"I think people are afraid to change," Ryan said. "I think they value their safety and comfort. They don't like someone telling them what to do."

"It is more than that. I believe they are trapped in some kind of cocoons, diaphanous cocoons from which they seem unable to escape."

"The media affiliates' work?"

"Yes, but there is more than that," she said. "Your transparent jail holds part of the answer. Everyone is a tied into, and everyone is contributing to the problem."

They looped back to the hotel on side streets. Most of the people Ryan observed appeared to be going about their daily business of conforming to the conventional paradigm.

'I am concerned at the way they are portraying you in the media,' Sarah communicated.

'I have nothing to be ashamed of,' he communicated back. *'Like I've told people, I'm honored to be included.'*

The media were broadcasting everything they had managed to dig up on Ryan Drake, "friend of the aliens." They had his high school picture, interviewed old friends, examined his credit standing, bank account, income tax returns, and details of his divorce. Some of Sanitas's internal documents found their way into the press, but none of Sanitas's management had commented on Ryan Drake.

Ryan had always thought of himself as a normal person. Now, he was being characterized as a cosmic zealot, an alien lover. One commentator accused him of being a traitor to humankind. For years he had been in charge of his life. Now, things were beyond his control.

He thought back to his recurring dream of the transparent jail. Even with his knowledge of the cosmic paradigm and the celestial Journey, at times he still felt like a prisoner, felt that others were trying to control his behavior, trying to dictate how he thought. The grip of the dominant paradigm was very strong for anyone who had grown up within the media affiliates' carefully designed box. Even with his understanding of the mark that had influenced man's development on this planet, it was still hard to get beyond the self-involved, day-to-day grind of life — he still had to eat and sleep. Somehow, he had to find a way to express his newfound insight so that people could use it as a basis for their personal transformation. Somehow, he had to find a way to help his brothers and sisters to see how much better life was outside the box.

He made a mental note to talk to Peter about how people on Phantia had come to their form of planet-wide government, a government that gave economic and service representatives equal weighting, a more directly participative worldwide government where nations had no voice.

'*I'm much more concerned about the way the media is treating you,*' Ryan communicated.

'*All Peter and I can do is tell the truth.*'

Ryan knew that if he were asked to judge the truth from the media, it would have made no sense at all. The only consistent thread throughout was the absence of further references to the media affiliates.

The Phantians' message of a friendly, organized universe was not actively suppressed, but it received little notice. Instead, the media focused on abductions — people who claimed they had been abducted by "greys," had implants inserted in their bodies, and had been sexually molested.

They stopped at a flower shop not far from the hotel. Ryan bought a dozen yellow roses. The sales clerk packaged them in a long box. When he presented the flowers to Sarah, she said, "Romms, my favorite," and gave him a big hug and a kiss on the cheek.

When they returned to the hotel, a media truck had positioned itself at the side entrance. A reporter was ready with a microphone. A small group of college students, some of them smoking pot, others drinking beer, had gathered around him.

Someone recognized them. "There's one of them." A young woman pointed to Sarah and said, "Show me your alien powers."

Pointing to the flower box, another said, "Is that an alien laser gun? Where are the others? When is the invasion coming?"

Sarah said, "Yes, I am from Phantia. I am here to help you transform this planet."

"Transform? I don't want to transform," the girl said. "I like it the way it is." She held up her can of beer; the others giggled at her words.

One of them, a college student with tangled hair, began to chant, "ET go home. ET go home." Before long the others followed his lead.

Ryan and Sarah pushed past the deputy who was manning the door. In the deserted hallway, a second deputy stopped them. When they removed their dark glasses, he smiled and allowed them to pass.

Among the many messages taped to the door of the hotel room, was one from Sam Wellborn. Ryan returned the call on his cell phone. After a quick greeting, Sam transferred him to President-elect Carlton Boyle.

"Mr. Drake, thank you for those papers you passed along. They are very important. Did you read them?"

"No, Mr. President-elect," Ryan responded, "with everything else going on, I just glanced at a few of the more recent ones."

"Did you keep a copy?"

Ryan noted the cryptic words of the President-elect. Was the man soon to be President of the United States worried as to who might be listening? He replied in kind. "Yes, sir, I did."

As he spoke these words Ryan had an inkling as to why the President of the United States had called him. He wondered if Detective Martin had found the copies that Aza O'Sullivan had kept at his house.

They talked briefly about Ryan's two extraplanetary friends and the position paper Tiffany Wheeler had written. Ryan briefed him on his views of the Phantians and their mission. Boyle listened intently, but made no comment. He thanked Ryan again for providing the papers to him. As they were winding up, Ryan asked him for a favor on behalf of his two friends from Phantia.

Boyle replied, "I'll see what I can do."

"Why are you doing this to yourself?" Ajax Johnson asked the woman seated across the table. From the balcony of their condominium they watched giant cargo ships ply the waters of the Pacific Ocean as they headed into San Diego Harbor. The sails of small boats seemed to dance on the sun-lit water.

"Being myself." His companion, a more-than-attractive woman, did not look well this morning. Circles surrounded her large eyes; her dark hair was a tangled mass. She cradled a steaming cup of coffee. "This planet is so great. I just want to experience it all."

"Your new boyfriend is scum."

"He's going to make me a star," Ethete Johnson replied. She stood and bowed to her companion. "Introduce me to the right people."

"He has no idea who you are. Thinks you're Hunter McKenzie, some small town girl from America. What's he going to do when he finds out?"

"Like Ethete, Hunter's just another name. We both know your name isn't real either."

"You're not being true to our mission."

"You should talk," she said. "You're all wrapped in that silly game. Just what do you think the National Football League's going to do when they figure out who you really are?"

It is very easy in the world to live by the opinion of the world.
— RALPH WALDO EMERSON

ELEVEN

Sarah and Peter agreed to a TV interview on the condition that the details of the cosmic paradigm would be aired. When they entered the ballroom for the taping, there were a dozen media representatives there.

While Peter and Sarah tried to talk about their cosmic perspective, the interviewers questioned them about their home planet and their trip to Earth. At one point, Ryan almost stepped in, but Sarah stopped him. *'We will try it this way,'* she communicated. *'Maybe good will come from it.'*

When clips were aired, two hours later, they focused on the story of Sarah and Peter's travel to Earth. A brief summary of the cosmic paradigm was provided, almost as an after-thought. Each network presented the interview differently. Ryan noted that the spin was coalescing about a central theme: These are two curious creatures. We're not sure whether they're from another planet or not. We don't know if we can trust them, or what they say.

One enterprising researcher had investigated the Phantians' backgrounds. He found that both Peter and Sarah had Arizona driver's licenses and that the Phantians were in this country on visitors' visas based on passports from Antigua. He was unable to trace the paper trail further.

The next day, Jake Ashton, Rita Martinez, plus two other Special Agents from Washington, DC, came to visit Sarah and Peter at the hotel. They interviewed Peter and Sarah separately, excluding Ryan from the interviews.

On his way out, Ashton stopped to talk with Ryan. "The first time we met, I sensed there was something different about you." The FBI man studied the ex-CEO with the practiced eye of a trained investigator. "Then I interviewed Peter and Sarah, and my sense of something odd really began buzzing. I was at your presentation the other evening — well done, by the way. Rita and my two associates from Washington aren't so sure, but, for what it's worth, I believe you and your friends."

"I'll keep that in mind," Ryan said.

Then the other three FBI agents came along and Ashton was swept along with the group. Ryan looked after them, wondering why Ashton had confided in him.

When Sarah and Peter returned to the suite, they told Ryan their version of the conversation. Ashton had been friendly; Martinez and the two from Washington had not. Most of the questions centered on the Phantians intentions: Why had they come here? How long were they going to stay? What did they intend to do?

The openness with which the two extraterrestrials had answered the FBI's questions apparently amazed the two Washington agents. They had been investigating "alien phenomenon" for some time, but claimed they had been thwarted by others within the FBI and by various government agencies' lack of cooperation. At the conclusion of the meeting, Martinez informed Sarah that the FBI had okayed the release of Harmony.

Soon after the FBI agents departed, Tiffany Wheeler and Sam Wellborn showed up unannounced. Sam took Ryan aside and began to ask him about the media affiliates, the World League, and how he had obtained copies of the arrangements with Senators and Congressmen.

Ryan said, "From what I have been able to gather from Steiger's diary, this whole World league thing is closely knit gang: they are all sworn to secrecy about each others' identity. The media affiliates, the most public of the affiliate groups under the umbrella of the World League, has an office in Washington, run by that guy, John deBeque. It hides under the guise of The International League, a lobbying group. DeBeque's people take information from the other

affiliates, spin it, and disseminate the lies to the media in every corner of the world. The heads of the affiliate groups gather periodically to exchange information and update their plan for creating a
new world order."

"A new world order?" Sam raised an eyebrow.

"Yes."

"According to who?"

"According to the Governors of the World League. They plan
to create a single world government."

Sam crossed his arms over his chest and glanced away. He
was obviously lost in thought.

"I got a call from an unidentified man, my second," Ryan said
when Sam had not spoken for a full minute. "He claims that his
group will not impede further reporting about Sarah and Peter, if I
promise not to publish any more of Ernest Steiger's diary."

"Sounds interesting — on the surface."

"Something tells me he has that much power. I told him I'd
keep my copy of the diary handy, until we saw how things shook
out. I also suggested that the World League put their agenda to a
vote."

"I'm sure he was all in favor of that," Sam said with a note of
sarcasm.

"Right." Ryan gave him a few of the names he had been able
to glean from Steiger's diary, prominent people, both Democrats
and Republicans.

Sam stumbled into the nearest chair. He stared at the floor for
a long time, then haltingly said, "I don't think one government for
the whole world is in anyone's best interests. Why the —"

Ryan interrupted him. "Sam, a single world government is
inevitable; it happens on every planet. In time, it will happen on
this one. It is the only real way to achieve peace. It can come from
the grass roots, or people like the elitists of the World League will
force it to happen their way. In the later case the gap between rich
and poor will increase, and we will continue to have dysfunctional
societies. If they prevail, things could get a lot worse for the bulk of
humanity. Our only hope is to get the ten percent of the people who
understand what's going on, and who really care, to convince the
other ninety percent to follow a new path, a path that doesn't in-

volve powerful men telling the rest of us what to do. The Phantians hope publicity of their presence will shock ordinary people into coming alive and acting along these lines."

"You're talking about a whole new international structure, new forms of government, new economies. I doubt that I'll live to see that."

"Don't be too sure. America needs to start paying attention to the real needs of the rest of the world, not just how things affects our security and economy, not whether they are consumers or low-cost manufacturers. It's called peace and sustainability for everyone on the planet. After we get to that status, the rest of the cosmos will let us join them."

"You've exposed the media affiliates. Won't that slow down the League?"

"It might," Ryan said. "But stop them, no. As long as people let them get away with it, they will. President Boyle needs to become proactive, needs to help make it happen the right way."

"That's political suicide. He's beholding to his own set of money interests. Don't get me wrong, he's not in Steiger's pocket, but he is a politician."

Ryan nodded. "Sam, somebody has to stand up to them."

"You told me the World League had kept other Presidents in the dark, threatened them," Sam said. "What makes you think it'll be any different this time?"

"That's what you and I are going to figure out."

When Sam and Tiffany exited their meeting with Peter and Sarah, they both looked dazed. Ryan instantly knew what had happened.

Sam Wellborn, key member of President-elect Carlton Boyle's staff, walked over to his boyhood friend and gave Ryan the tightest hug that he had ever experienced. "They really are ETs," Sam whispered in his ear.

When he pulled away, Ryan saw that Sam had tears in his eyes. "Now I understand," he said. "You were right, we're going to get this show on the right path, even if we have to uproot every agency in Washington."

The next day Ryan observed the line of men and women

queued-up to see Peter and Sarah. They had shown him credentials that they represented the Army, CIA, NASA, Air Force, and Navy, and other less known agencies. Then he had routed them through the metal detector and requested that they check their guns. The routine that Major General Abe Russell had suggested worked like a charm; military people responded to discipline.

Reporters and cameramen hung around, remaining as close as Tom Ertl's deputies and government security personnel would allow. The nervous representatives of the various agencies refused to talk with them or to be photographed.

Three men from the Air Force Office of Special Investigations tried to force their way into the room where Sarah and Peter were being interviewed. They challenged Tom Ertl and two of his deputies when the Sheriff demanded that the military men submit to having their briefcases searched. Ertl remained adamant; the Air Force backed down. Ryan suspected Tom enjoyed enforcing the procedures that General Russell had suggested to them.

Among the people on the various teams, Ryan noted a man in a black suit with a cane who came as a member of the CIA contingent. His badge read, "Bill Johnson." He had been most reluctant to give up his pistol. As his group had waited for the Army contingent to come out, Johnson spent the time eyeing Ryan. Ryan had a feeling there was something sinister about him. Later he checked with Sarah and Peter, they recalled the man and had similar impressions of him.

The various interviews lasted until midnight. Peter told Ryan that the military people had all been interested in his knowledge of zero point energy and electro-gravitic effects. "As I explained to them, I could talk to them about the historical development of these technologies on Phantia, but not about the scientific details. But, they did not seem interested in learning about Phantian history."

"Or about the cosmic paradigm," Sarah added.

The early morning call from Sam Wellborn awakened Ryan from a deep sleep. A call from the Special Assistant to the President-elect apparently trumped his request to the front desk of the hotel not to be disturbed. The clock read 5:00 AM.

"The President wants to meet them."

"What are you talking about?" Ryan was barely awake.

"Carlton Boyle wants to meet Sarah and Peter. I told him about Phantia — he wants to meet them."

"Where? When?"

"He's got a meeting with the Vice President-elect at his farm in Southern Illinois. He doesn't want it public. You have to get there without being spotted. Can you do it?"

"When?"

"This afternoon."

"This afternoon?"

"Yeah." Sam gave Ryan specifics about the meeting place.

Ryan turned over and wrestled with the logistics of getting Sarah and Peter to Southern Illinois.

Ryan's friend Evan Bromley flew Sarah, Peter, and him to the airfield at Mt. Vernon, Illinois in a rented Lear Jet. Evan had a hole in his otherwise busy schedule of piloting executive aircraft in and out of Jeffco airport.

A member of the President-elect's secret service team greeted the plane and drove Sarah, Peter, and Ryan to Richard Tyler's family farm. They were escorted into the dining room of the farmhouse and Tyler's eighty-year-old mother offered them coffee.

Sam appeared fifteen minutes later. "He's made a short time available. Follow me."

"Nice to see you again," President-elect Boyle said as he greeted Sarah. "I remember our little chat in Denver.

"And you must be Peter. I understand you could show me a few tips on giving speeches."

"And Mr. Drake. It seems I owe you again." He greeted Ryan with a warm handshake.

Turning to Sarah, he said, "Tell me about Phantia."

According to Ryan's watch, the conversation lasted a total of seventeen minutes. During that time, the validity of the Phantians' origins was never raised.

As they exited their interview, a heavy-set man with a friendly smile was drinking coffee at the kitchen table. Carlton Boyle introduced them to Vice President-elect, Richard Tyler as some friends of his from Colorado.

During their interviews with the military and intelligence people, Sarah and Peter had agreed to non-invasive medical examinations. The day after their return from meeting Carlton Boyle, they drove to the University of Colorado Medical School in Aurora. Experts from various branches of medicine had been rushed in from sites around the country. Gordon Moore, Ryan Drake's doctor friend, acted as a watchdog to be sure the examinations did not involve drugs or anything more invasive than drawing blood, x-rays, ultrasound, and MRI. At one point he called a halt when the medical team was preparing to inject a local anesthetic for a biopsy.

A summary of the examination was in the following day's edition of most papers. The team of medical experts from Wright Patterson Air Force Base were quoted as, "Some of the physical evidence — their reproductive organs — supports their claim of off-planet origin. Their DNA is marginally different from human DNA. We will require more study to determine anything conclusively."

Teams from the Mayo Clinic and Harvard Medical School concurred. They went on to speculate that the Phantians distant ancestors might have been some type of heretofore-unknown primate, and that they might be a new species of humans from this planet. The self-proclaimed experts from Wright Patterson stated that breeding humans from the two planets, if indeed these very human-like beings were from a different planet, might be an interesting experiment. They even held out the possibility of creating a superior race.

Ryan voiced his reaction to the news. "Beautiful. Get a team of experts, and they don't say anything."

"I believe they are shocked by the similarity of our DNA," Peter said.

"I'm not so sure," Sarah said. "When they were examining me, they made several comments that lead me to believe I am not the first extraplanetary being they had examined."

President Carlton Boyle was inaugurated on January 20th. The ceremony and the inaugural balls were telecast live. None of the network hosts mentioned the paradigm-shattering events that had taken place in Denver a week earlier. Ryan watched the coolness with which the President treated Richard Tyler. It confirmed his suspicions that there was more to the meeting at the Vice President's farm than a chance for Boyle to meet two extraplanetary beings.

The next afternoon, Sam called Ryan to say that Boyle's military, science, and intelligence advisers had met with the new President to give him their standard initiation speeches. The two-hour meeting was designed to intimidate the incoming office holder with insider facts about the true state of the world, and to bolster the status of the advisors.

Sam had attended the meeting; he was appalled at the posturing that was intended to form the basis for running the country. Later, with Tiffany Wheeler's help, they managed to present the President with a more balanced picture that included the reality of extraterrestrials, the black operations over which neither the President nor Congress exercised control, and the World League who wished to call the shots — as the League had already done with certain Senators and Congressmen. They also persuaded Boyle that it would do no harm to honor Ryan's request, and it might help him determine who were his real friends in Washington.

People Ryan had seen at Peter's presentation had called and left messages. These he returned on pay telephones, suspicious that some intelligence agency might be recording calls from the hotel and even his cell phone. All talked about the ways in which the Phantians' celestial perspective had touched them. They admitted that they had been afraid to speak out publicly to this point, but that all the crazy publicity made them want to help.

"Just tell your personal story to the press," Ryan said. "The more people who verify the impact of what Peter is saying, the better. Maybe now you can understand just how badly you have been mislead all along by the media."

Several people who claimed they knew details of the history of the UFO cover-up called. Ryan listened and referred them to an organization dealing with that type of information.

He also returned calls to several influential friends and fellow entrepreneurs who had not attended Peter's presentation. They questioned him about his involvement with extraterrestrials and why he had left the world of high tech management. He explained what he had discovered and asked each to remain open-minded. Two said they suspected that they had experienced contact with extraplanetary beings, supported what he was doing, and offered to use their positions of influence to help. They also mentioned they would only feel comfortable helping if it could be done secretly.

Three days after President Carlton Boyle's inauguration, Ryan staged a press conference in front of his burned-out mountain home. Not willing to risk being upstaged, each of the major networks and print media sent reporters and cameras. The late January day was cool, but cloudless.

A contingent of Sheriff's officers checked identifications and kept the gathering confined to the grassy knoll in the center of the circular driveway. Debris had been cleared, but like the lone survivor of a bloody battle, the massive moss rock fireplace stood guard over the blackened shell of his log home.

Waiting until the camera crews signaled they were ready, Ryan stepped to the assortment of microphones. Sarah and Peter stood on either side of him. Next to them were their hazy, non-human guardians; certain highly conscious individuals had reported "seeing" these phantasmal images. For Ryan Drake, the guardians were faint reminders of Sarah and Peter's exalted mission to shift this planet to a new paradigm.

Ryan thanked the members of the media for coming; then he introduced Sarah Smith and Peter Jones.

"Tonight, go out and look at the vastness of the universe. Understand that most of the stars that you can see with your naked eyes have planets orbiting them. Know that intelligent humanoids inhabit many of those planets. Imagine someone on one of those distant planets, someone not too unlike yourself, enjoying the view of their night sky.

"Moving to our own backyard, during the last century this noble experiment which we call the United States of America, helped to defeat Nazism, totalitarianism, and communism. I am grateful to have lived to witness such auspicious events as the fall of the Berlin Wall and the end of the Cold War. America has now become the lone super power; the other peoples of this planet look to us as an example. It can truly be said that we hold the future of the world in our hands."

Ryan paused for dramatic effect. He had delivered many speeches, but this one was, by far, his most important.

"I want to speak to you today about building on what's good about America, building on it in light of a cosmic point-of-view, building with the knowledge that millions of extraplanetary beings from angels to mortals are present on this planet, present and offering to help us."

Ryan went on to tell them about the grave danger to their country from a misguided few who were twisting all that was good about America to their own ends, a danger that threatened to engulf the entire world. He pointed out how wealth, corruption, and special interests had gradually chipped away the basics embodied by the founding fathers in the Constitution. This had resulted in the emasculation of most Americans, and that, in his opinion, the people of America no longer governed themselves. He said he was here to ask people to join him in building on what was right and decent about America, leading the entire world to a better place.

"Do not lash out against those in power; neither should you fear them. See that they are men and women just like you and me. See that they are pursuing a vision which they believe is right. See that they pursue their vision from a self-centered point-of-view, a view from inside cocoon constructed to conform to the conventional paradigm of force, wealth, and privilege. See that they are afraid to open themselves to the larger truth. Do not condemn them for we are the ones who give them their power. All of us are 'guilty' for having allowed this situation to develop, for the denial about it that is in place. And when you have taken this into your heart, then forgive them. Forgive them, but do not dismiss the reality of the situation."

Ryan paused again — to allow these last words to sink in. He saw a knowing smile on people in the crowd. The red lights on the video cameras glowed back at him without emotion.

He continued, "As an entrepreneur, I pursued my dream of creating a better world. I overcame my failures and created my successes. Now I have come to understand that I must apply the lessons I learned as an entrepreneur toward a larger purpose in life, to creating a peaceful and sustainable existence for everyone on this planet. As an entrepreneur, one of the great lessons that I learned was that I could successfully attack the status quo, attack it and create something new. We must all apply that lesson to creating a new world.

"For a moment I would ask that you envision a world without violence, a world where all people participate in the abundance that we in America have come to expect. I see that this kind of a world can only be accomplished with a single government for all. Bypassing existing governments that are composed of competing political entities, I see a worldwide government comprised first of elected representatives from the sphere of economics and second of elected representatives from the social sphere. These two bodies of representatives would be balanced in their legislative power by a third comprised of appointments from those among us deemed to be the wisest, those who have served their brothers and sisters best. I see a worldwide system of equal and fair justice for all, and an administrative arm that functions in concert with celestials who possess abundantly more experience than we Earth-humans. This is a model from the cosmos; I suggest we adopt it."

Sarah, Peter, and Ryan had each invited a number of close friends to the press conference. Some among that group clapped at his proposal.

Ryan took the hand of Sarah and of Peter. He smiled at wonder of two extraplanetary beings standing next to him.

"Non-humans have been working with us for many, many years. They appear in many forms, from pure spirits to human-like mortals. Repeatedly, they have provided us with conclusive evidence of their benign intentions: They do not fire back when we shoot at them. They heal people of everything from minor cuts to major illnesses. They have shielded us from natural disasters. With their superior technology, if they had wanted to dominate us, eat us, they could have done it at any time — besides, we would have tasted better a hundred years ago."

A smattering of laughter rippled through those assembled.

Ryan continued on. "Are there some from the cosmos who do not share the benign attitude of the vast majority? Who are not aligned with the grand plan of the universe? Yes. There are certain rogues who try to turn situations to their advantage, to recruit humans to their cause. But they must be invited into your consciousness. You can say 'no' to their intrusions.

"Are they numbered among the celestials? No. God is love, and those who do his work are loving. It does us little good to focus on those, from this world or from the cosmos, who would lead us along a dark path. For to do so lends them power.

"We, the people of America, need to grow up and look beyond fear. We must see that our high level of consumption is not some sort of a unique right. We must move beyond violence as a means of solving disagreements. We must grasp this pivotal moment, and to make sure we are creating a sustainable prosperity — not only for ourselves, but also for our children, for the entire world.

"We have it within our power to awaken the world to a larger vision: First, recognize that despite reassurances from those in power, we are on a path to destruction. This planet it at a point where it cannot sustain the humans living upon it. We are losing animal species at an alarming rate. We are destroying vital forests. The polar ice caps are melting at an alarming rate. Increase your awareness of these issues and seek approaches to solving them.

"Second, find what feeds your sense of hopelessness, your sense that you are powerless. Do not allow hopelessness to rule you. Rather, focus on what is good, what is possible.

"Third, do not allow governments, multinational corporations, or the media to ignore issues important to your brothers and sisters in far off places. We here in the U.S. do not live on an island.

"Fourth, let us try a different way; let us use empathy, forgiveness, and love to heal our planet, our home. Visualize that which we wish for this planet, for all inhabitants of this planet. By affirming this vision, make it a reality.

"Fifth, your safety in this undertaking is assured, for as children of The Divine One your immortality is certain. Look beyond your immediate needs to ways in which you can serve all.

"Finally, understanding this situation, do not go back to sleep, do not go back to ignoring its impact on yourselves and your loved ones.

"These two courageous people, Sarah and Peter, have traveled far to bring us a message of hope and understanding. Some of you have heard their words. Many of you have had your own experiences with extraplanetary contact, celestial messages, or a knowingness. You already understand that we have a higher destiny than tending to our personal security and comfort.

"It will require courage to act on these higher truths. Look inside and ask yourself if you want this world to continue its downward spiral. If you would break this spiral, join us in making the positive transition of this planet a reality.

"The universe is opening itself to us. We are being called to become citizens of the cosmos along with peoples from other worlds. If we are to meet the challenges of the forthcoming years, we must grow spiritually. We must set aside our fears, our attachment to material things, and take control of our destiny. This planet can be a bountiful, beautiful, and peaceful place for all.

"I am hereby announcing the establishment of a permanent home for my friends from Phantia. I intend to rebuild this burned–out hulk of a house behind me into a place from which they can carry on their work. It will be called the Cosmic Paradigm Center. Its goal will be to train 'knowers of the truth,' train them how to create a world where people treat each other with integrity, kindness, and love, a world where the larger picture is used to guide the behavior of all."

Ryan turned over the bank of microphones to Sarah. Her long cream-colored robe accentuated her flowing blonde hair. For Ryan, she was the embodiment of cosmic truth and love. She was also a very beautiful human being.

"I bring you greetings from your brothers and sisters on Phantia," she said. "I know that many of you, numbering in the millions, have had contact with extraplanetary beings. Most of you do not remember this contact because its startling impact often renders people ineffective — thus it was purposely hidden.

"Peter and I, humans very much like yourselves, are residing on this planet to reassure you of the benign intent of contact, to reassure you of the love of the celestial administrators of the universe. And we are paving the way for upcoming events of undisputable worldwide contact with extraplanetary beings. As Ryan said, the universe is indeed opening to you."

"Events of undisputable worldwide contact," Ryan had not

heard these words before and was taken back. It made sense, but how? When?

Sarah continued, "We came here, in person, to tell you that you are part of an orchestrated, nurturing, and friendly universe. The inhabitants of the other planets desire that the people of this planet mature and join with them in peace."

She stepped away and Peter moved in front of the microphones. He stood proudly. Standing next to him was Dr. Victor Adamson. He too was dressed in a cream-colored robe.

Peter said, "The celestial rulers want each of you to know that, after your time here, you will be welcomed on the Between worlds. The graduates of this planet are highly esteemed for the difficulties they must overcome in pursuit of the truth and in the practice of love.

"Rest assured, the people of this planet can rise to become brilliant, enthusiastic, and wise citizens of the cosmos. I ask you to join with all your cosmic brothers and sisters to make that vision a reality. Once you accept that you have an immortal destiny, you will not fear to risk your mortal lives for truth and love."

Peter motioned to his white-haired companion and said, "This is Dr. Victor Adamson. This planet is his home; he and others like him are its caretakers. They have lived here for thousands of years, largely without anyone's knowledge. They have nurtured your ancestors; they continue to nurture you."

The white-haired apparition stepped to the microphone and said, "Sarah and Peter are my guests on this planet. I ask that you treat them with the honor you would accord a guest in your home."

The camera crews motioned wildly and asked for a pause. Something was amiss. Their sound systems were picking up Dr. Adamson's voice, but the technicians who were monitoring the video signal could not see his image on their screens. The cameramen were at a loss. They were able to see him quite well when they viewed him directly.

While the cameramen fiddled with their cameras, three silver disks appeared overhead. They hovered silently in a triangular formation, two on the bottom, one on top. As Ryan watched, their color changed to an iridescent blue. Everyone in the audience began to point and comment. Reporters reached for their point-and-shoot cameras.

Then the extraterrestrial craft took off straight up. None of the video cameramen were quick enough to capture them for the television audience.

After the commotion subsided, Ryan asked if Dr. Adamson could resume. Stepping away from their cameras in frustration, the cameramen signaled that he might as well go ahead.

The white-haired apparition continued in a deep voice, "The sole rationale for the universe of time and space, the larger purpose for your lives on this planet, is to advance you from here to Paradise, the home of The Divine One. Your path will not be readily apparent nor will it be easy. There are many distractions and urgencies that would seek to pull you away from your larger purpose. However, finding and following your unique path, perfecting yourselves, is what The Divine One requires of each one of you. The universe of time and space was created as a playground in which you each are called upon to make your unique contribution.

"This planet was created as a place of great beauty, a bountiful and peaceful home for you. Despite fear and violence, despite pollution and poverty, it still maintains that potential. Your technology can be made to work in harmony with the natural grandeur of this world. Your hearts can embrace the least of your brothers and sisters. I encourage you to take control of our world, to grow our world to that which it can become.

"In this effort you are assisted by many extraplanetary beings who follow the grand plan of The Divine One. Honor them for their assistance, for their friendship, and for their sacrifices.

"Do not forget that within you is a fragment of The Divine One. Your relationship to The Father of the Universe can be as intimate as that with your earthly parents. Make use of this link as you seek to transform this planet." Dr. Adamson faded from the view of those present.

Ryan stepped back to the microphones and said they would take a few questions. With hands raised, several among the media blurted out questions. Peter, Sarah, and he patiently answered each.

"What you're proposing is anti-American — it gives business too much power." The question was directed to Ryan.

"On the surface, it might seem that way," Ryan replied. "However, I think my proposal recognizes the role of economics in our current world, the ways in which it has brought us a higher standard of living, the ways in which it has shrunk our globe. I am proposing a balance to economic power with social power, and with wisdom."

"We can't have a one world government. What about America?"

"America has no preeminent right. All of your brothers and sisters are created your equal. Learn to anticipate their needs, and give to them before they request. When they blossom, you too will blossom."

Tiffany Wheeler from President Boyle's staff stepped forward and handed a document to Sarah. "This was one of his first official acts as President. I flew the red-eye to get it here."

After she studied the words, Sarah passed it to Ryan. He scanned the official announcement that he had requested of the newly inaugurated President. It conferred diplomatic recognition on Sarah Smith and Peter Jones, *Ambassadors from Phantia*. Tiffany attracted the attention of the networks, introduced herself, and read the proclamation.

Ryan breathed easier. Now in addition to lots of public exposure, his friends would have legal protection.

"President Boyle rushed this through," Tiffany said. "There are a number of people who are upset about it."

Sarah went to Tiffany, hugged her, and whispered, "Thank you for your courage. Thank the President."

A bald man and a blonde woman approached Ryan. They said they were from Oregon. They offered to lend their support to the new Center and spoke of a rising consciousness among Earth's people. They assured him he was not alone in wanting to spread the word about the cosmic paradigm. Then they went and hugged Sarah and Peter.

Gordon Moore extended a hand to Ryan. "Most impressive." The doctor was among the group of non-media friends that Ryan had invited. "Are you going to run for office?"

"No, I have a much larger job in mind."

"Well, good luck. I think I'm going to take on the task of hounding the government to open up the truth about ET contact."

"In that case, good luck to you too." Ryan hugged his doctor friend.

Looking over Moore's shoulder, Ryan noted several people he did not recognize. They did not appear to be members of the media, who were in the process of loading up their equipment. He could only surmise that they were from one of the intelligence or black operations.

The next morning, Ryan drove to Eads, a mile away from the hotel, on 28th Street. He retrieved the local newspapers from around Boulder and Denver as well as the New York Times and Wall Street Journal. An article was on page one, section one, of the Rocky Mountain News; above it was a photograph of Sarah, Peter, and him with three large silver disks overhead.

The announcement of an "Alien Institute" in Colorado was big news. The main theme centered on its impact on the Colorado economy and the number of jobs it might create. The accompanying story carried a tinge of incredulity, an unspoken wonder at such an eccentric decision by a respected businessman like Ryan Drake. It also speculated about the motives of the aliens from Phantia, and why the President had recognized them as ambassadors.

The New York Times article was small, buried on page five. It spoke mostly about President Boyle awarding diplomatic status to two people who were purportedly from another planet.

Upon returning to the hotel, Ryan turned on the television. After watching four morning news programs, he turned it off, disappointed. None of the programs had mentioned the Cosmic Paradigm Center or recognized the newest ambassadors to the United States.

The smart way to keep people passive and obedient is to strictly limit the spectrum of acceptable opinion, but allow very lively debate within that spectrum — even encourage the more critical and dissident views. That gives people the sense there's free thinking going on, while all the time the presuppositions of the system are being reinforced by the limits put on the range of debate.

— NOAM CHOMSKY

TWELVE

"A plague. And just when I thought things were back on track." Delta Kingman addressed the wilderness. He took in the expanse of forest that fell away to the east. In the far distance a checkerboard showed where lumber companies had clear-cut hundreds of acres of Montana virgin timber. "Lord, you gave us this world, this universe. Told us to take charge. And that's what we're doing — and, even if I say so myself, I think we've made a damn good start. But now, you've sent us a plague, a bunch of pacifists. I don't understand why, but I promise you this, Lord, I promise you we will defend your people against the treacherous deceit of those from other worlds."

Kingman wore a sheepskin coat that came to his knees. Beneath it were blue jeans and a plaid flannel shirt. Cobra skin cowboy boots and a western hat completed his outfit. He smoked a long cigar, one from his latest batch of imports from Cuba. He had finished breakfast and come out to greet the arriving Governors.

The men of the World League communicated regularly using their computer network, but met face-to-face infrequently. This meeting was an exception forced by the recent turn of events. It had originally been scheduled to review progress at LNR's desert facility, now it would focus on the alien beings in their midst. Nine of the twelve Governors headed one or another of the affiliate groups; the other three were involved with administering the affairs of the World League; each had a publicly recognizable position in society; and each had taken an oath to maintain secrecy and to cooperate with the others until death.

His right hand grasping the gold handle of his cane, Warren Ophir shambled to where the retired General stood. "I don't think it's all that bad," he said. "People aren't going to rise up against the establishment — just because some no-navel alien tells them to."

"I hope you're right. But people may not see all the good that's being done for them. And we can't give them the whole picture — they'd freak out if they knew somebody was collaborating with off-planet forces. Hell, they'd freak out if they knew we existed."

"They're comfortable," Ophir said. "Pacified with television, movies, booze, and dope. Entertainment, that's what counts. Entertained people don't inquire, don't rebel — the Romans figured that one out."

"Yeah, got to keep them comfortable. That way they'll go along. 'Do not rile the populace.'" It was one of the World League's tenants that Kingman loved to quote. "And don't step on their beliefs. Right or wrong, their beliefs are what count."

"Some are clinging to the notion there's a God." Ophir enjoyed pushing that one at Kingman. He already knew the older man's reaction. Many years ago, when his mother had disowned him, Ophir had decided that he did not believe in God, or any other power greater than his own wits. In fact, Ophir distrusted anyone who said they "believed" in anything.

"That's right, and that is mighty good for us," Kingman said distaining Ophir's avowed point of view. "The more on our side the better."

Delta Kingman was not about to throw away his religious convictions, just because he knew this planet was not the only inhabited one, just because he had met an alien. He could not explain how it all fit together, but that did not worry him. The critical thing was he knew that the World League was doing God's work. The aliens with whom the World League was cooperating had reinforced the idea of the dominion of humans.

"I don't like what happened with Boyle," Ophir said after Kingman had not spoken for over a minute. "Every one of his advisors gave him the standard picture: Terrorism, international power politics, precarious economic conditions, and threats from hostile aliens. In the meeting, he seemed to buy it all; then the next day he goes and declares those Colorado aliens 'ambassadors.'" The last word left a bitter taste in Ophir's mouth. He leaned over the railing and spit on a sapling.

"Somebody got to him," Kingman said. "By gawd, I'd sure like to know who."

"We've been monitoring Ryan Drake's phone calls," Ophir said. "Seems he and his old friend Sam Wellborn have gotten reacquainted. I think those two may be the source of Boyle's backbone." What he did not say to Kingman was that Ryan Drake had talked directly to Boyle, that Ryan Drake had escorted the aliens to meet with Boyle, and that Ryan Drake had engineered the whole business of Ambassadors from Phantia.

"Ryan Drake, huh? That damn pipsqueak?"

"Yeah."

Kingman turned back to gazing at the pines and took a long drag on his cigar. After a few moments, during which he occupied himself with where to steer the conversation, he asked Ophir, "You met with those two aliens face-to-face, what do you think?"

Ophir was surprised that Kingman knew that he had traveled to Boulder to interview the aliens. He hesitated, and then said, "They just wanted to talk about their idea that the universe is friendly. Apparently they don't know about our alien connections."

"Drake mentioned it in his speech the other day," Kingman injected. "They know all right. The real question is how much they know."

"They insisted they were here to help us evolve this planet to a place of enlightenment." He snickered as he said the last words.

"Godless infidels." Kingman shook his fist. "A curse on all of them. They're here because they know we're the chosen ones."

On one thing the governors of the World League agreed, they all agreed that aliens were trying to manipulate humans for their own objectives, objectives that had never been made totally clear.

"Peter Jones said he believed in God," Ophir said, still pushing the religious thing.

"They'll say whatever they think people want them to say. They're using that mind stuff of theirs to deceive everybody, including their buddy Ryan Drake. At least with our alien friend, we know where he stands."

And indeed Ophir did know where the World League's alien friend stood. Their alien contact had told them of his race's fight with the celestial overseers, with the other so-called peaceful races of the universe. It was all about freedom, he had assured them, freedom just like Americans had fought for.

Warren Ophir had arrived yesterday before Kingman. He and the head of the military affiliates were in charge of security. Each had brought a contingent of ten men who were now positioned in the nearby woods. Two of them, dressed in hunting garb, stopped every vehicle that came up the dirt road. Kingman and his personal security detail had arrived after dark.

The World league had built this hunting lodge forty years ago. It had overnight accommodations for all twelve Governors and their assistants. Security people were housed in cabins surrounding the main structure.

Arranging a gathering of this importance was challenging. Each member of the Board of Governors had to devise surreptitious transportation to this remote location. Each traveled with his second in command and security personnel. According to prior agreement, only one Governor could fly on a particular airplane. The small airfield nearby could accommodate only single engine aircraft and the nearest airport capable of handling jets was Kalispell. A sudden collection of private jets at this regional airport was sure to draw attention.

In addition to Kalispell, Kingman had orchestrated arrivals at Missoula, Helena, and Great Falls. Ophir and his military counterpart, George Stephens, had flown into Missoula and Helena respectively. Their contingent of men had arrived by commercial airlines. The other nine Governors were scheduled to arrive within the hour.

"How did you leave things with Drake?" Kingman asked.

"Told him we'd back off if he'd keep the rest of the diary to himself. His reply was that he wants us to put our program to a vote."

"A vote? Ha, ha, ha." Kingman crushed the remainder of his cigar into the wood of the deck. "By gawd, that's really choice. He wants a goddamned vote, huh? How about we vote him one with the wrong end of a bullet?"

"After that press conference — it'd just make him a martyr." Ophir had called off the assassination squad he had sent after Ryan Drake.

"We've got to keep an eye on Boyle." With the sub-freezing temperature, Kingman's words came out in a frosty haze. When Ophir squinted just a bit, he could imagine the general as Zhu Di, the legendary emperor of China, spitting out orders to construct the Forbidden City and elongate the Great Wall. Kingman had likened the situation of America today to that time when China was the most technologically advanced and economically strong power in the world. Zhu Di was Kingman's hero.

Ophir hit the redwood railing of the deck with his cane. "Can you believe it? Diplomatic recognition — you don't give diplomatic recognition to things that aren't even human, to things that would love to eat you for lunch."

"What about the medical reports?"

"Medical reports be damned," Warren Ophir said. "The doc's hedged it in Denver, and they're hedging it now. Our guys from Wright Paterson know better. They've had alien bodies for years — but not like these two. Their latest is they think they're some kind of cross breeds or walk-ins."

"We've got to stay on track," Kingman said. "I say we shut the borders, throw out the undesirables, clean everything up."

Ophir was sure that Zhu Di would not have approved of Kingman's last statement. After his reign, China had isolated itself, retreated from its position as the preeminent world power; it had never recovered from the decisions of Zhu Di's successors.

"I like your plan," Ophir smiled. "Problem is then there'd be nobody left except the two of us, and then I'd have to start worrying about you."

Kingman's grin was more of leer than a smile. Ophir knew the other man did not trust him, and would make sure it never came down to just the two of them. Kingman said, "It was that damn memo that started it."

"What memo?"

"The one that woman, Wheeler, wrote. She got the stuff those alien's put out, digested it into a plan, and that damn Boyle bought it, bought it before he was even elected. I'm telling you, Warren, those aliens are setting us up — some playing good guys, some bad."

"Testing our resolve, our defenses," Ophir said. "We still need conventional military stuff, in case they invade before we're ready. Plus it helps make other countries think it's all we've got. We don't have enough of the good stuff, yet — can't get Congress to authorize money for big budget hardware they can't admit exists." He pointed upward. "If they come at us before we build enough —"

Kingman cut him off with a raised hand. "How many ARV's are operational?"

Ophir knew that Kingman kept the number in his head, nevertheless he replied, "Twenty ready, three more under construction. A couple of older ones that still work."

"Could make quite a splash with just those," Kingman said. "Governments all over the world'll fall in line — real fast. They'll realize all they've got are warehouses of outdated stuff."

"I think we need a hundred."

Kingman watched as two SUVs approached. "What's your take on the affiliates?"

"The media group is on its butt," Ophir said "Vanderbush's been slow to take charge. You need to push him."

"I advised him to get moving, before we find somebody else."

"As for the other affiliates, the medicals are scrambling to figure out ways to keep their base of support. The energy guys are worried about something new coming along to replace oil. And the financial gang is busy laying bets on the probable winners, backing any promising idea."

"Sounds like business as usual. Old farts looking after their own asses. Maybe it's time to clean house a little further. There's more than Steiger that aren't with the program."

He did not react to Kingman's comment. Like the leadership structure of China, the maneuverings of the triad were a mystery. Succession of leadership was determined in secret and orders were carried out without question. Warren Ophir was determined to be one of the three who made those ultimate decisions, one of the three who gave the orders to terminate.

When the other two members of the triad arrived, Kingman went into a secure room to huddle with them. Two teams of men, one from intelligence and one military, had swept it for bugs that morning.

The three were joined by an off-planet being who arrived in transportation suitable to his mission — a silver disk from which he alighted. A very human like being accompanied him. Today the white-haired man was dressed in black jeans, a western shirt, and a heavy wool jacket. The role of the off-planet being was to encourage those gathered to maintain their grip on the reigns of the shadow world government.

As he watched the alien enter the building, Ophir wondered if he was part of the group who had offered to begin negotiations, part of the four-sided pyramid. He had not disclosed this choice piece of information to other members of the triad, nor had he received another indication from the aliens.

When the other Governors had gathered, the conclave convened. The off-planet being and his escort departed before the full group began its formal deliberations.

The discussions lasted well into the afternoon. At lunch, they feasted on wild game from Canada, Australian lobster, Italian pasta, French wine, and tropical fruits, all flown in especially for this gathering. Kingman had brought his chef to oversee the cooking. The security personnel who accompanied each Governor kept an eye on the food preparation and did the serving.

Although the main topic of their meeting was how to contain the exposé that Ryan Drake was pushing. Of secondary interest were the voices of the increasingly vocal members within their organization who wished to go public with their own unveiling, to tell the public the truth about extraterrestrial contact. Their off-planet contact had insisted that it would be a mistake; the triad resolved the discussion in favor of continued obfuscation.

By late afternoon, all but the intelligence and military security teams had departed. Ophir waited until the others departed, then he collected his recording devices.

John deBeque had received the call from Ophir last evening. "I want to meet with you first thing in the morning," Ophir had said. From the background noise, deBeque could tell that he was calling from his airplane.

"Where?"

"Usual place."

DeBeque stomped his feet as he waited. The snowplow had scraped the walkway a few moments earlier. His black wingtips had gotten damp when he stepped off the path to give it room.

This morning the coordinator for the media affiliates wore a black cashmere overcoat over his dark pinstriped suit. He was bare headed, but had slipped on black gloves.

The daily cue of visitors to the Washington Monument had begun, when a black limousine pulled to the curb. Warren Ophir rolled down the window and said, "Get in."

When deBeque had settled into the warmth of the dark interior, Ophir handed him a mug of steaming coffee. "Light on the cream, heavy on the sugar."

"Thanks." DeBeque smiled in recognition of the intelligence man's detailed knowledge of his personal habits. He suspected his every action was monitored either by an employee on Ophir's payroll, or by electronic eavesdropping of one sort or another. He had no illusions that he had any privacy.

"I have some startling news. I want you to help spin it."

DeBeque nodded. Since accepting the job with the media affiliates, he had met with Ophir numerous times. The intelligence operative always began his latest disinformation tidbit with these same words. DeBeque understood that it was his job to frame the wording just right and then get the information into the right hands. Ophir drew upon contacts within governments, domestic and foreign. Those sources regularly found it convenient to "leak" information to the media. DeBeque was unable to distinguish between genuine information and disinformation. Ophir never indicated which was which.

It had been deBeque's custom to bounce things off Ernest Steiger. The old man had a terrific sense of what would sell to the public, and how to craft it just right. This was the first time he had talked to Ophir since his stepfather had died.

He had not reconciled with the old man, yet at Ernest's funeral, two days ago, he had spoken of his mentor in glowing terms. He, along with Nick, Richard, and three other men had carried the heavy casket to the burial plot in front of the ten-foot high headstone.

He had thought it strange that none of the other media affiliates had attended the funeral, nor had Warren Ophir. Now as he sat in the intelligence man's car, he wondered about his stepfather's accident.

It seemed ironic that a truck loaded with cattle would be on a Chicago side street. It seemed even more mysterious that Ernest's regular chauffeur had been sick and that his replacement had not been able to dodge something so huge, particularly since there was no other traffic on the street. The driver had been killed along with his passenger. Ernest always referred to the ordinary people as cattle. Was there a message here? And who had sent it?

"Are you warmed up?" Ophir's words brought him out of his thoughts.

"Sure."

"Here's what I got. It seems the true results of the medical examination of the aliens weren't released to the public. The doctors felt pressured to release something before they left Denver, so they said what they said. Now that they're safely back at their respective hospitals, they want to tell the real story.

"They believe that these so-called Phantians are really the results produced when aliens mate with humans. They can't prove their theory because they weren't allowed to do invasive examinations to get at the aliens' internal organs. But they think the DNA results speak for themselves.

"What this really means is that these so-called Phantians are fooling everyone, and in particular Ryan Drake — or maybe he's also one of them. Which brings me to the second theory. It may be that Sarah Smith and Peter Jones are really humans, but that their bodies have been taken over by an alien presence. Some people are calling them 'walk-ins.' This could explain Ryan Drake and his conviction about who they are. Maybe Ryan Drake's body was also invaded when he was out in the desert with them.

"So, who can we get to break this? I want it to be big — maybe, 'alien body invaders.' Or 'aliens scout Earth in preparation for attack.' Mix it with that comment that Sarah Smith made about 'worldwide contact events.'"

"Sounds a bit too science fiction for me," deBeque said, "but let me work on it. I'd say any number of our favorite reporters could be convinced. I'll give one of them a call — after I spin it a bit."

"Go to it. John, this stuff is hot. I want you to stay on top of it. Maybe you should go to Denver to be close to the action. I'll have my men keep you updated on their movements."

There were times when John deBeque knew the intelligence man was manipulating him. He had that feeling right now. But, as Ophir asked, he would go to Denver. He understood enough to know that since he had lost his mentor, he needed someone to champion him. At the moment, Warren Ophir was the best he had.

Besides, the International League office ran itself. And he could easily coordinate his media affiliate activities with one of his six 'editorial' assistants. He was still rankled by the sudden disappearance of the computers on the lower floor. He tried to talk to Ophir about it, but there were always more urgent things.

Not too far away, in the Hoover Building on Pennsylvania Avenue, Special Agent Jake Ashton was meeting with James Orr, one of the two agents who had interviewed Peter Jones and Sarah Smith in Boulder. Ashton had been summoned to Washington after Ryan Drake's press conference and the issuance of diplomatic recognition to the Phantians.

"You are going to be our point man on these reputed ETs," Orr said. He was the Special Agent in charge of extraterrestrial investigations for the FBI. "As you know, we have other claims of contact with ETs. My force is stretched to the limit. Plus, it would appear that Jones and Smith — I'm sure glad they aren't demanding we call them by their real names — have found a friendly ear with our new President. We need to treat this situation with a little more respect than just another weird sighting or crazy abduction case."

"So you believe them?" Ashton asked.

"I didn't say that. I said only that we will treat them with a little more respect."

"You interviewed them. What do you think?"

A long pause, Orr straightened his dark blue tie to make sure it hung in line with his belt buckle. He picked a piece of lint from his dark blue suit jacket. "Jake, I don't know. I've been looking into this stuff for years. Most witnesses describe ETs as something far different from those two. Most people are scared to death by the mere fact that they might have encountered something from another planet. Jones and Smith just seem too human. I have new info from the medical team. Now they're saying that Jones and Smith are humans who have been invaded by ETs.

"This is where you come in. I want you to stay real close. I can't give you additional manpower, but I can make sure you're not pulled off in other directions. I've cleared your new assignment with the Special Agent in Charge of the Denver Office. Stay on them, and keep me updated."

The meeting ended without Orr asking him his opinion on Sarah Smith and Peter Jones. As he walked out of the Hoover Building, Jake decided it was just as well. James Orr probably would not have wanted to hear what he had to say.

"Do you really think this planet has a chance?" Peter asked.

Sarah and he had hiked into the forest to the west of Boulder. They strolled up the Shanahan North Trail as they spoke. Their plan was to go south on the Mesa Trail, and return on the South Shanahan. It was a three mile round trip.

They had agreed to speak rather than using mind-to-mind communications. If they relied completely on the higher level of communicating, they were worried that they would lose their facility with English.

Afternoon sun cast shadows of ponderosa pines on the frost-covered trail before them. Footprints indicated that others were out this cool winter day. Both Peter and she were bundled in heavy winter coats; both wore gloves.

"Be positive, my mentor," she said. "Remember what our minds send out we will receive back. Frustration will yield only frustration. Recall the many extraplanetary helpers who conspire with us to uplift this sphere. Allow them to pull to this planet elements to support our mission."

Sarah knew that Peter was well aware of this basic dynamic of the universe. But she also knew that he was discouraged by the many diversions from the plan to which they had all agreed before departing Phantia. Peter liked order; so far, their trip to Earth had been anything but orderly.

As they passed under electric power lines that crossed over the trail, Peter pointed to them and said, "Look at what they have done, copper wires everywhere. This so called 'power grid' is so unnecessary. If only they would listen to those who know."

With his hands, Peter indicated an object about the size of a microwave oven. "This could power each house. Copper wires are primitive." On Phantia electricity was gathered from one's surroundings by a number of techniques. In most areas, the burning of fossil fuels had stopped nearly seventy-five years ago. All one had to do was purchase the appropriate instrument and you had as much electricity as you required, without additional fuel, and without tying into a massive grid.

"Earth-humans go to extremes," Sarah said. "They are either extremely independent, or totally subservient to some human institution. In either case they are slow to adopt new ways, slow to heed advice from extraplanetaries."

"This new publicity questioning whether we are really from another planet will cause many to dismiss anything we say," Peter said. "I find it so hard to believe that the media changes their story with each new day. First, they refuse to acknowledge our coming forth. Then, they acclaim us as extraterrestrials and the President of the United States recognized us as ambassadors.

"Now, it seems the doctors who examined us have changed their story. Some of them contend we are faking it, that we are the results of plastic surgery. Others are saying that we are either the result of some forced mating between alien invaders and human subjects, or that we have somehow invaded human bodies. We are being painted as monsters from outer space.

"I don't think I can appear before another audience," Peter said. "The demonstrators at that one yesterday chanted, 'alien child,' the whole time I was talking. I doubt that anyone heard anything I said. Not one person asked a question. I had to slip out the back door of the auditorium."

"I am so sorry this is happening." Sarah laid a hand on the arm of her oldest friend on this planet. "People here are so ready to grab the latest story — almost as if they don't wish to think for themselves. I am not sure what we can do about it."

"Will some at least hold onto the cosmic paradigm?"

"Some. But I fear those who question whether or not we are genuine will dismiss the message along with us."

"What will happen to this world?"

"I do not know," Sarah said.

"They don't seem to understand that they must 'pull themselves up by their own bootstraps.' No universe personality is going to come along and save them from the error of their ways." Both Peter and she knew that, except as a last desperate move to preserve the balance of the universe, no off-planet civilization was allowed to come to Earth's rescue, to physically intervene. If that happened, a planet of weak dependents would ensue and the evolutionary process would start all over.

"The sad thing is that most people don't have the slightest idea of what needs to be done."

"All that is required is a critical mass," Peter said, "a few hundred, a few thousand who will stand up regardless of the consequences. It's called commitment, courage, or, in their vernacular, guts."

He switched to his Humphrey Bogart voice. "Guts to admit they have problems. Guts to admit they don't know everything. Guts to look elsewhere for answers. Guts to put aside their comfortable lifestyle, admit to the larger picture, and then build their lives based on that revised worldview. Guts to risk ridicule, risk being shunned, risk being imprisoned, risk being killed. Real guts."

"Ryan has guts," Sara said.

"Yeah, Ryan has guts. But he doesn't know the final ingredient. He's all caught up in opposing evil, and protecting you."

"I think the humility part of it will be the hardest for them, particularly Americans," Sarah said. "They have worked so hard to build the dominant paradigm, it will be difficult for them to admit they are wrong, that there is a better way. So when do we tell Ryan about the final pieces to this puzzle?"

"Soon, Peter said, "I have been giving him a chance to figure it out for himself. In the meantime, he can concentrate on gathering people with the courage to speak out. When there is a committed core, the people of this planet will understand that they cannot solve the situation by using the same tools that created the problem in the first place, that they need to find a new way. When they are humble enough to ask for help, then we can explain the final ingredient."

"Well said." Without warning or even the slightest movement of air, Dr. Adamson appeared and strolled beside them. They had just turned the corner onto the Mesa Trail. "You now understand why Sarah and you were needed here: To provide the people of this world with an off-planet solution, a non-physical solution, a big picture solution."

"And the final ingredient?" Sarah asked. "When do we tell them that they must abandon their ego orientation? When do we tell them that they are doomed to repeat their mistakes until they align their decisions with higher, wiser, celestial powers? When do we confront them with the fact that they were never intended to be 'the masters of the universe?'"

"They will see it as an attempt by aliens to gain dominance over them," Peter said. He kicked a large rock. It landed in brown grass, a few feet off the trail. "And they'll fight us at every turn. Then, before you know it, some of them will start worshipping us like gods. Making us gods should play real well with the fundamentalists. I can see lots of believers in Islam supporting that idea."

"Peter, you overstate the situation," Sarah said. "I think they will accept us for who we are: Elder brothers and sisters with a better grasp of the bigger picture."

"I doubt it."

"Therein lies your challenge," Dr. Adamson said. "Help them see they cannot solve their problems by themselves, by relying on traditional solutions. Show them that help is available, has been available for eons. All they have to do is ask. Help them see that by admitting their limitations and aligning their intent with the wisdom of The Divine One they can come out of their never-ending cycle of violence, power plays, and greed. Help them see that you and other extraplanetary beings — spirit or material — are not gods, and that you do not wish to dominate them."

"How can we possibly do all that?" Peter asked. "At the moment, most people find it hard to believe that we are from another planet or that our message is true. What most people know about ETs comes from novels and movies. We do not fit their preconceived notions. For those who believe that life beyond this sphere is savage and foreign, we offer a challenge to that belief. For those that believe in life after this sphere, we offer a point-of-view that totally contradicts the heaven of traditional religion.

"Now they are being told that we are not genuine, that we are some sort of aberration. This is, somehow, easier for them to believe — it fits the fictional portrayal, keeps them in their existing paradigm. Then they do not have to accept the challenges the cosmic paradigm proposes. Then they can go back to living in comfort and safety."

"But the truth," Sarah said. "What about the truth?"

"And courage," Peter said. "What of courage and commitment?"

The threesome paused to allow Sarah to re-tie the lace on her left boot. "For many, there is no absolute truth," Dr. Adamson said. "Some even believe they create their own physical surroundings. As long as they are comfortable and safe, they really don't care what they believe. Believing and behaving that way requires little courage."

"I must speak to you of a theory I have developed. It involves the diaphanous cocoons in which the people of Earth exist," Sarah said. "This is something strange to both Peter and me. People on Phantia do not possess them."

Dr. Adamson looked perplexed. "I believed that mortals of all planets had these psychological constructs. Here on Earth they have existed since I was born."

"How is it that you understand them?" Peter asked.

Dr. Adamson thought for a moment and then replied, "Soon after a child is born, even before it becomes verbal, he or she quickly learns what is acceptable, what pleases their caregivers or not. This is the beginning of a shield, an armor, which enables them to cope. As they progress through life, their shield develops — from others around them, friends, school, church, television, movies, and society in general. In not too many years, it is fully formed and becomes their 'identity.'"

"What happens to the real them?" Peter asked.

"The real person, their soul, their essence, the spark they receive from The Divine One, is all hidden away deep within their shell — waiting to be discovered. It becomes a life-long process to uncover their true selves."

"What a strange situation," Peter said. "We have nothing like that on Phantia."

"But there is something more," Sarah said. "I think it is connected to Ryan's dream of the transparent jail. My theory is that these constructs interact with each other, that they self-organize into some sort of a structure, that through their constructs people actually help those who would control them."

"Interact? A structure?" Dr. Adamson stopped and stared at her. "That's not possible. They are merely facades, psychological tools."

"I think it is true," she said. "And I think that explains why people are having so much trouble retaining our message and acting on it. Their constructs feel threatened and the constructs of others reinforce that fear."

"If the constructs interact with each other..." Dr. Adamson's words trailed off.

"Yes," Sarah went on. "When the constructs gang up, they produce a closed society, a society that subverts the real person, a society that functions on appearances and fear. And people do not realize their willing participation in all of this because it is their facades acting in place of the real person."

Peter threw up his arms. "If Sarah is correct, this explains why people resist the on-going assistance from extraplanetary and intraplanetary beings.

"The number of celestials residing on this planet is extraordinarily large. Then there are the mortal extraplanetary beings who hover here making contact. Again the level of involvement is unusual. Finally, we have been transported here, and have now gone public with the cosmic paradigm. With all of this, and they still don't get that they are watched over, loved, beckoned to grow up."

"I think it's the constructs," Sarah said, "the interlinked constructs."

"Peter, Sarah, there are some who have internalized your message," Dr. Adamson said. "They see the true purpose of the universe of time and space; they understand the Journey to Paradise; and they wish this planet to take its place in the universe. Maybe they are the ones who have set aside their constructs. Find those and nurture them."

We have earned the hatred of entrenched greed.
— FRANKLIN DELANO ROOSEVELT

THIRTEEN

Ryan rang the doorbell for the condominium in Solano Beach, California. It was tarnished from the salty air of the nearby Pacific Ocean.

A man opened the door. He had to be six five, way taller than Ryan. And he had the build of a professional athlete. Only his eyes gave him away; they reminded Ryan of Sarah's large gray eyes, but you had to know what to look for.

"You must be Ajax," Ryan said.

"And you're Ryan. Dr. Adamson told me to expect you. Come in."

Ajax Johnson looked just like his pictures in the newspaper. Longish blonde hair combed straight back from his high forehead. It contributed to his unique appearance, and to his reputation.

Johnson ushered him into the condominium's spacious main room with a balcony that overlooked a broad swath of the ocean. Ryan's eyes were immediately drawn to the pictures on every wall, pictures of Johnson, and pictures of a beautiful, dark haired woman. The posters of Ajax Johnson were either in sweats or in his San Diego Chargers' uniform. He looked like a football star; he did not look like an extraplanetary being.

There were even more photographs of Ethete Johnson. They sparkled from many colors and shapes of frames. She had a delicate mouth and nose, flawless skin. Something about her reminded Ryan of Sarah, but this girl looked like she was twenty-five. In the photos she wore a variety of clothing, wore them like a high fashion model. Dr. Adamson had told him that she had been auditioning for movie and television roles before she became hooked on drugs. Like many in Hollywood, she had changed her name. Her "stage name" was Hunter McKenzie. Like Ajax, she had planned to become famous and then reveal her origins.

Ryan recalled where he had first been introduced to Ajax and Ethete. Sarah had pictioned them for him at that restaurant on Phantia.

"So, the big game's just a few days away," Ryan said.

"Next Sunday," Johnson replied. "I was just about ready to leave to meet up with the team." He pointed to two bags next to the door.

"And you'll make your announcement after that?"

"Within a few days."

"Does anyone suspect?" Ryan asked. He did not need to add the words, "that you are an extraterrestrial."

"Not as far as I know." Johnson produced a wide grin. "As far as my team's concerned I'm just a walk-on that made good. I've managed to deflect inquiries about my high school and college ball playing by simply stating that I had not played before trying out for the Chargers."

"You're pursing a risky course," Ryan said. Unlike Sarah and Peter who had tried to stay out of the light of publicity, Ajax Johnson had sought out the media. He just had not told them who he really was, at least not yet.

"Hey, looks like it's working. Wouldn't you say?"

"We'll see." Ryan had seen what publicity had produced for Sarah and Peter, had seen the way their story had been twisted.

"Now that Sarah and Peter are public, it shouldn't surprise anyone that there's more than two ET's around."

"Where's Ethete? Or should I say Hunter?" Ryan asked.

"She and her friends took off. She hates football. She never has come to watch me."

"Where'd she go?"

"A little cruise, down to Mexico." Ajax's teeth were perfectly aligned and very white.

"Her instructions were to stay in the United States."

"She probably won't even get off the ship, probably so spaced out on drugs she won't know where she is. Probably won't even remember she went to Mexico." Ajax spat out the comments.

Ethete and Ajax had come to Earth as partners. They were not married. In fact neither had been mated on Phantia, neither had children. They were selected for their physical youthful appearance; like Sarah and Peter they were years older than they looked. Dr. Adamson had told Ryan that Ajax was almost fifty; Ethete was in her early forties. They had agreed to come to Earth because they saw it as an adventure.

Ethete was a Native American name meaning "good." Ajax's name was derived from Greek mythology and indicated valor and prowess.

Dr. Adamson had assigned them to Southern California because he felt they would be able to interact with people there without raising questions as to their origins. Like Sarah and Peter, their plan was to get to know people and expose them to the cosmic paradigm. Unfortunately their outstanding looks and, in Ajax's case, physical ability, immediately led them to associate with the wrong crowd.

When friends of Ajax Johnson had first invited him to play a game of touch football, he was reluctant. But he wanted to establish a rapport with them, let them get to know him. After seeing his speed and agility, they had prodded him to try out for the San Diego Chargers. The first series he ran at training camp convinced the coaches; they signed him to a season contract the next day. As the season finished with San Diego leading the Western Division, Ajax Johnson was generally acclaimed as "the best wide receiver in the game today, maybe ever." He had surpassed Jerry Rice's statistics during his best year with the Forty Niners. After whipping New England and Miami in the playoffs, Ajax's team was headed to the Super Bowl.

Naturally thin, like most Phantians, Ajax Johnson had tried steroids to increase his bulk. Due to his off-planet metabolism, the drugs had worked with amazing speed, but the side effects were devastating. Turning to dietary supplements, he added the necessary weight to play in the NFL.

Ethete was not so fortunate. She saw the amazing effects that drugs had on her partner. She convinced the dealer supplying drugs to Ajax to let her try something. He gave her some ecstasy. Her metabolism instantly addicted her. Now she craved it constantly and was never completely removed from its influence. Since that first dose, she had been unresponsive to her partner's pleadings, or to any guidance by Dr. Adamson. She had become friendly with the Mexican boss of the local drug dealer. He kept the beautiful senorita supplied at little cost.

"Gone? What do you mean gone?" President Carlton Boyle asked. He stood in the Oval office, eyes blazing.

"Tiffany and I went to the archives, same location as before." Sam Wellborn motioned to the Executive Office Building, a short distance from the White House. "I know I'm right. I made a careful note of its location last time. The entire file box was missing, just a black hole on the shelf. This whole thing is a little amazing since the file was in the wrong box to begin with."

"Who's responsible for those files?"

"That room in the archives is controlled by Gloria Limon. Everything's been classified as secret at one time or another; most still is. She's been at that job for the past nineteen years. Knows her way around that labyrinth, a real gatekeeper."

"And what does she say?"

"Says she doesn't know how it could have happened. The archives are open from nine to five weekdays; locked tight the rest of the time. They're inside a very secure building. Whoever removes any folder from the stacks has to sign for it. No originals leave the secure area. She has no record of anybody signing out anything from those files, since I made a copy.

"In her section, all the files are still restricted, haven't been fully released under the Freedom of Information Act. Only a very few people even know this section exists. Only the right people can sift through the files. I had to work a special deal to make one copy. When I showed her the hole that the missing box had left she was horrified. She's going back over her records of everyone who was in the archives for the past two months. But I'm not optimistic. Mr. President, someone snatched those originals, and it's not going to turn out to be someone on Gloria's list."

"So we have no corroboration of Ryan Drake's story? You convinced me to grant diplomatic credentials to some so-called ETs without making sure they were genuine? The opposition is going to have a field day with this."

"Mr. President, you met them."

"And they seemed damned human."

"And I interviewed them. Believe me, they're genuine." Tiffany and Sam well recalled the pictioning session that Sarah had done. On the way back to Washington, they had discussed nothing else. They both agreed; Peter and Sarah were the genuine article.

"You're sure?"

"Positive."

"What about the newspaper articles? The doctors who examined them are making some pretty strong statements."

"I don't know where they're coming from. I talked to those docs right after they had examined the Phantians. At that time, they were quite sure that they had just examined two genuine extraterrestrials. Sure, the public statements they made were hedged a little — normal conservativeness — but in my conversations with them they were quite sure. Joe Ide, one of the docs from Wright Patterson, was the most emphatic. There was no doubt in his mind. He said that the eyes and hands of the Phantians were way out of the range of anything that could be called human, and their reproductive organs were definitely non-human."

"Fly him here. Don't tell him it's to meet me; don't even tell him it's about this subject. Have someone else make arrangements. Just get him to Washington, on some pretext. Then we'll see what he says."

"I think I can arrange that."

"Sam, where are you on all of this ET stuff?"

"Mr. President, you and I both know that we are not the only inhabited planet. I've believed it for years. Our most recent polling data shows that two-thirds of the American people believe it too. Many foreign governments have an official office of investigations. What I now know, as the result of my meeting with those two Phantians, is just how interested everybody else out there is in our little planet. I also know that the rest of the universe is generally a friendly place — they've figured out how to solve problems without violence.

"Extraterrestrials have been coming here for centuries. Until we developed radar, they pretty much had the skies to themselves, went largely unnoticed. They still have us under intense scrutiny, but now they're a bit weary of our ability to shoot at them. Most of the time they hang out in the non-physical end of the spectrum, but that doesn't stop them from contacting millions of people.

"I think the most important thing for you to consider is that we are not alone in the universe, and that the United States is not the most powerful force on this planet."

"Some Americans might take exception to those words," Carlton Boyle said.

"No, Mr. President, what I'm saying is true. The humans of this planet are not the most powerful or wise beings in the universe. It's time we recognized that and started acting as if we did. We can get a lot of help from extraplanetary beings, people whose civilizations have already been through the situations we're caught in. All we have to do is ask."

"Ask? Sounds like giving in."

"Asking for help doesn't mean we're surrendering, just means we're asking, like asking consultants."

Sam exited the Oval Office as a group of Senators from Midwestern States entered.

"Let's talk," Sam said as he passed Tiffany Wheeler's office. When she had entered his, he motioned for her to close the door and sit down.

"I want you to find a medical conference, or a military gathering in Washington." He went on to explain how he wanted Major Joe Ide, MD invited and then about a private meeting with him. He did not mention that the President of the United States would be involved.

Sam then called Martin Bollander, the head of the Central Intelligence Agency, and Chuck Brown who headed the Federal Bureau of Investigation. He scheduled a meeting with each.

The next day, President Boyle sat facing Martin Bollander. The CIA chief had been appointed by the prior administration in the wake of renewed terrorist attacks. Although nothing as dramatic as the World Trade Centers had occurred, terrorist threats to America had continued. Bollander's organization had come under fire for its inability to predict the fall of the twin towers, but the intelligence apparatus had been credited with preventing further major attacks on American soil. In addition to Bollander and the President, Sam Wellborn was present in the Oval Office.

"Give us a rundown of our intelligence operations," Carlton Boyle said. The President had now been in office for ten days. This was the second time the two men had met.

"As I have already informed you, Mr. President, our major focus at this time is on cutting the terrorists' financial support. In addition to intelligence gathering, I have a sizeable contingent of my people working with every major bank and financial institution in the world. We've plugged all contributions from the G-seven. Their only remaining cash now comes from religious fanatics in the Middle East."

Sam watched as Bollander rattled on about terrorists. He wondered how much of what the CIA chief was saying was based on fact, and how much was show for the new President. His musings were abruptly redirected by the President's next question.

"I want everything your agency has on UFOs, extraterrestrials, and reverse engineering projects."

For a moment Martin Bollander just stared back at the President. His face paled and his left eye twitched. "Mr. President, I can't speak of these things in front of other people." He indicated Sam.

"He is privy to discussions on this matter," the President said.

Boyle had told Sam that Bollander had strenuously objected when he had granted diplomatic status to the two Phantians. And he was not the only one: Several Senators, a handful of Congressman. Two of Boyle's own appointments had threatened to resign. But Boyle had held firm — on the basis of Sam's recommendation.

"Mr. President, with all due respect, Mr. Wellborn is not cleared for this conversation."

"Sam has a top secret clearance. Look, Martin, we all know this subject has been hushed up for decades. I'm determined to get to the bottom of it."

"Yes, Mr. President. But, these things can only be discussed on a need to know basis. Mr. Wellborn does not have that need."

"And if I say he does?"

"That will have to be submitted in writing."

On his way back to his office, Sam poked his head in the door of Tiffany's office and said, "Apparently a top secret clearance isn't good enough. Bollander refused to say anything while I was present."

Sam turned just as Martin Bollander strolled past. They did not speak.

A few minutes later, the President requested Sam's presence.

A half-hour after that Sam walked into Tiffany's office and closed the door. "I want you to develop a list of names for CIA Director. Seems Bollander refused to give the President access to any information about ETs — claimed the President wasn't cleared, didn't have a right to see it. The President demanded his resignation.

"All hell's going to break loose over this one. Bollander has developed quite a following over his handling of the terrorist thing. I'll be interested to see what happens with my old buddy, Chuck Brown." Sam and Chuck had been fraternity brothers at Princeton. They had not seen each other until Sam had moved to Washington, DC. Since then, they had met for drinks a couple of times.

The scenario was repeated an hour later with Chuck Brown, Director, Federal Bureau of Investigation. This time, the President made some progress. Brown admitted that his people had been pursuing the arena of UFOs, aliens, abductions, and paranormal phenomenon since the 1950's.

The FBI Director complained that he personally had been systematically excluded from information on the subject. No answers had been forthcoming to his inquiries. Probes into suspected covert operations had been thwarted. Brown told the President that he had assigned an agent to monitor the two supposed extraterrestrials that were living in Boulder. He was of the opinion that there was, as yet, insufficient evidence to determine whether, or not, they were what they said they were. Brown pledged his full cooperation.

After Brown left the Oval Office, Sam said, "Now there's a man who wants to keep his job."

"But I wonder if he's telling the truth. And I wonder if he talked to Bollander?" the President asked.

Sam Wellborn arrived at his suburban Virginia home at about 10:00 PM that evening. Since coming to Washington, he had insisted on driving himself, declining the limousine provided to someone of his importance. Sam felt that the twenty-five minute drive relaxed him.

He and his wife had moved in just after the election. When he pressed his remote, the garage door did not respond. Unwilling to struggle with it at this late hour, he stepped into the dark driveway and headed for the front door.

He had taken only two steps, when a hand grabbed his shoulder and wheeled him around. Another hand grabbed his other arm. His briefcase fell into the snow.

He found himself looking into the black ski mask of a third man. The men on either side pinned his arms and lifted him a few inches from the ground. At 190 pounds, Sam was no lightweight. Relaxing his body, Sam gave the impression that he had decided it was futile to struggle.

"Hello, Mr. Wellborn. If you listen real close to what I say, maybe we won't have to meet like this again."

"What do you want?" Sam smelled expensive cologne. In the moonlight, Sam could see the black ski mask belonged to a man of average height and build. He wore a dark suit and dark tie with a white shirt. His words were those of an educated person.

As the man came closer, Sam thrust his knee into his groin. The black ski mask doubled over in pain. Sam wrenched his right arm loose and brought it around to stab at the man holding his left arm.

The two men jumped Sam and hauled him to the ground. There they both started hitting him. Sam fought back, landing one or two punches and a few good kicks.

"Enough," the man in the black ski mask groaned.

The two other men pinned Sam to the snow.

The black ski mask came and stood over him. "We understand that you and President Boyle are making inquiries where you shouldn't be. There are certain things that don't concern you, and never will. Forget about UFOs and aliens. You have a real nice house here, a real nice lady inside. It would be a shame if anything happened to either.

"Next time you're tempted to inquire about this stuff, you think about what I just said. Next time you put your nose into places it don't belong, somebody's going to get hurt." The black ski mask aimed a kick for Sam's groin but landed only a glancing blow.

"Now I expect, after our little talk, you'll take all kinds of security precautions. But, just remember, we can take out your wife any time. She can't hide. Neither can you, or the President."

"You're threatening the President of the United States?"

"Did I say that? Oh, gosh, I got a little carried away, didn't I. Mr. Wellborn, you have no idea what you're fiddling with. You and the President take care of running this country. We'll take care of the aliens."

The black ski mask drew a syringe from his coat pocket. The two others sat on his arms and legs. Sam felt the prick as the needle passed through the fabric of his suit and into his thigh. They continued to hold him down. At first he felt woozy, then everything went blank.

Is courage — strength of character — desirable? Then must man be reared in an environment which necessitates grappling with hardships and reacting to disappointments.

— THE URANTIA BOOK

FOURTEEN

"Sam. Sam, speak to me." Maggie was standing over him. He was in a room with a white ceiling and white walls. He could barely focus on her image. The gentle touch to his cheek told him it was his wife. Slowly her image became clearer.

"Where am I?"

"In the emergency room. You must have slipped on the ice at the side of the house. I heard your car pull in. When you didn't come in the house I went out and found you in the snow. You were unconscious so I called nine one one."

"Have the doctor do a blood sample."

"Why dear? Are you worried about alcohol?"

"Just do it. Tell them to look for drugs."

A few minutes later, a nurse appeared and drew two burgundy samples from Sam's arm. He was still feeling woozy. An hour later, Maggie drove them home; it was 1:30 AM.

The next morning, he had an eye squinting, head pounding headache. Sam downed three aspirin with his morning coffee, grabbed his briefcase, kissed his wife, and stepped into the chilly air.

When he arrived at the White House, he immediately conferred with the head of the Secret Service. Arrangements were made for a limousine. Extra precautions were put in place to protect the President. The blood test results showed that he had indeed been drugged.

Sam called Chuck Brown at FBI headquarters and told him of the events of the prior evening. "This is not good," Brown said, "but I'm afraid it's not the first time. Other senior people, who started to get interested in the subject of UFOs, have been threatened. They all backed off."

"I'm not backing off," Sam said.

"I figured as much."

"What do you recommend about Maggie?"

"The Secret Service can provide protection. I'd feel better if you lived in a less remote location."

"I can tell you right now, Maggie is not moving. We've only been there a few weeks."

"Have you told her about the threat?" Brown asked.

"Not yet."

"Better tell her. The Secret Service will have men out securing your home in short order. You're getting a limo?"

"Yeah."

They talked for a few more minutes. Brown said he would assign men to investigate the incident. He also recommended a security service that could keep an eye on the house and on Maggie.

Sam called Maggie and explained the real story of his fall. She chided him for lying to her; he apologized. He then called Ryan Drake at the hotel in Boulder. Sarah Smith answered the phone. "He's on his way to Mexico," she told him.

"Have him call me as soon as you talk to him."

"It might be a day or so. I can..." She did not finish her sentence.

Sam suspected he knew what she was referring to, knew she had extraordinary powers, knew she could probably track down Ryan if there was urgency.

"Not that urgent," Sam said. "Tell him to watch himself. Have him call when he can."

Sam knew he had to grab the initiative on the extraterrestrial issue quickly. It was either that or become bogged down in Washington politics like so many other idealists. One of the main reasons he had associated himself with Carlton Boyle was because he thought the newly elected President had a chance to make a difference. Sam never envisioned it would be a change of this magnitude.

Sam next met with Carlton Boyle and related the events of last evening.

"They threatened you?"

"Yes, Mr. President." Sam did not tell President Boyle that they had also threatened him.

"Any idea who?"

"I could hazard a guess."

"Don't. I have Martin Bollander's resignation. We'll find someone to replace him and then we'll get to the bottom of this."

"I don't think it's that easy, Mr. President," Sam said. "I think this thing's been going on for so long that it's buried very deep. Even Bollander may not know the whole story. Give me some resources and some latitude. I want to take a crack at breaking it open."

"You mean outside of here?" The President motioned to indicate the confines of the White House.

"Mr. President, this is too big to ignore. I want time to pursue it. And I don't want to drag you into it, distract you from your Presidency." Sam thought that by distancing himself from Carlton Boyle, he might somehow avoid another visit from the guys in the ski masks, and he might avoid an attempt on the President's life.

But Carlton Boyle did not buy Sam's proposal. "Maintain your office here. I'll get you resources. Keep me informed."

When Sam told Tiffany about their new assignment, she smiled and said, "Good, I won't have to hold you to that promise you made."

Ryan left his hotel early. This morning he was dressed in the shorts and short-sleeved shirt of a tourist. The gigantic tour ship with Ethete on board had slipped into port during the night. It would ferry passengers to shore about 9:00 AM. If, like many others, she came ashore to shop, he didn't want to miss intercepting her.

He walked down Boulevard Marina, the only divided road in Cabo San Lucas. CARLOS AND CHARLIE'S. He passed by the closed restaurant on the west side of the street. He had eaten there last evening — best ribs in Mexico, maybe the best ribs anywhere.

Palm trees with lights left from the Christmas Holidays. Girls in string bikinis, young hard bodies. CABO DE PLATA, STERLING SILVER. Neon lights in the store beneath the sign had just flashed on. Groups of American tourists in shorts and sandals, bright shirts, and bright hats. The smell of sunscreen. Across the street, a tall building was under construction; American-style graffiti decorated its unfinished concrete. Dark skinned Mexicans, some without shirts. 3 T-SHIRTS for 9.99 US. The store beneath the sign was still shuttered tight.

Cabo San Lucas was a playground for Southern Californians. If Ryan squinted a little, he could easily transport himself to San Diego or Los Angeles. Familiar restaurants and hotels populated the highway from here to the airport. Cabo stood in sharp contrast to Mexico's underdeveloped cities and countryside. One billboard advertisement for Cabo called for visitors to enjoy its hedonistic allure.

On the other hand, Americans had forced change on this formerly sleepy fishing village. Sanitation and health services had been upgraded to a level beyond the rest of the country, way beyond the level of most third-world countries. And tourists provided jobs for many. Sure they were not glamorous jobs, but Mexico was slowly developing a prosperous middle class. Many of the shops and restaurants belonged to local entrepreneurs, and many of them were successful.

Every time Ryan visited a foreign country, he came to the same conclusion: the influence of America was a mixed bag. His country's tourists forced backward cultures to upgrade, to adopt new technologies, new methods. In the process, they also obliterated some of the native traditions and brought with them that uniquely American mixture of opulence, self-indulgence, and arrogance. Not all good; not all bad.

Maybe that was the real reason that Dr. Adamson had sent him here. So that he could see that American influence needed to be tempered, to see why America needed to examine its behavior in light of the cosmic paradigm. Wherever they went, macho Americans made things happen, forced change on others. Now America itself needed to be changed, from within.

He turned right at the KFC and walked down a broad "V"

shaped walkway toward the ultra-modern Marina Cabo San Lucus. When it rained, as seldom happened in this blissful paradise, this canted walkway would carry the runoff from the town into the bay.

More than a hundred white fishing boats. The locally owned fleet catered to deep-sea fishermen. Nearby waters offered some of the best sport fishing in the world. Sailboats with nautical blue trim displayed homeports like Lake Havasu, Newport Beach, and Bull Head City.

Street vendors were busy setting up colorfully painted dishes and ceramic birds for the crowd from the ship. Beggar kids sold Carrels. When he was a kid, they had called them Chiclets. A disheveled youngster approached him every fifty feet. Ryan finally gave in and purchased a cellophane wrapped package of four squares. He gave the tiny, bare-footed girl with the missing teeth five pesos.

As he strolled along the cracked concrete bordering the Marina, the ground suddenly swayed. Glancing around, he saw that none of the locals paid much attention to the minor earthquake. Checking to make sure he did not walk near any tall structures, Ryan continued toward the dock where people from the ship would be deposited. Having lived in California for a few years, earth tremors of this magnitude gave him only momentary pause.

Sooner or later, a real earthquake would hit the area. The San Andreas Fault ran somewhere under the Sea of Cortez. Ryan hoped he would be far inland, preferably Colorado, when that event happened.

The first of the day-tourist craft motored across the calm waters of the bay to a dock shaded by white, Teflon coated canvas canopies. Dr. Adamson had confirmed that Ethete was aboard the huge Vision of the Seas. This was its first stop since departing the Port of Los Angeles. From here, they were scheduled to visit Mazatlan, and Puerto Vallerta before heading back to Los Angeles.

Ryan positioned himself at the end of the dock. A Baja Medical Response ambulance was parked to one side. Its attendants, in khaki pants and blue hats, smoked cigarettes and waited. The captain of the ship must have radioed ahead that someone was sick, or maybe this was just standard for every visit by the ship.

Passengers from the launches unloaded and pushed toward

the shopping afforded in Cabo. The crowd filed past Ryan, toward the stalls of a palm-shaded shopping area loaded with local merchandise, and into the town. He studied every attractive woman. From the pictures in her apartment, Hunter McKenzie would not be hard to spot. Sarah was beautiful; Ethete was gorgeous. Since she did not expect him, she had no reason to avoid him. If she did not alight, he was prepared to talk or buy his way aboard the ship and search for her.

A member of the crew rushed to the ambulance attendants and spoke in hurried Spanish. They grabbed a stretcher and ran toward one of the launches. Ryan studied more women, some beautiful, most plain, some young, many old, many overweight. None matched the photos in Ethete's apartment.

He would have paid no attention to the woman on the stretcher, if a slight breeze had not ruffled her black hair. But the instant he caught a glimpse of her face, he knew it was Ethete Johnson, Hunter McKenzie. Her eyes were closed and her skin had a gray cast, but it was her. His first impression of Sarah, as she lay on the cold floor of the basement of Ernest Steiger's mansion, flashed though his mind. Ethete had that same gray pallor.

He tried to get the attention of the attendants, but they were preoccupied and his Spanish was not good. A Mexican man, one who had obviously come from the ship, barked orders at the stretcher-bearers. When the gurney was settled in, the man jumped into the back of the ambulance alongside Ethete. They took off in a blaze of sirens and lights.

Ryan looked for a taxi. Several were parked near the exit the ambulance had taken.

"Hospital," he said as he jumped into the first taxi in line.

Whatever her problem, he had to stop them from using standard medical practices and medications. Sarah's recent medical examination confirmed how sensitive the metabolism of a Phantian was. Did her Mexican companion know she was an extraterrestrial? What would a doctor do when he examined her?

The taxi twisted through traffic. The wailing of the ambulance in front of them had evaporated. In a few minutes, he arrived at Cabo's modern hospital.

When he inquired about the senorita who had just arrived by

ambulance, he was directed to a waiting room. There he found Ethete's Mexican companion pacing the room.

"I saw you come off the ship," Ryan approached the man.

"Si, Senor," the dark-skinned man replied.

"You were with Senorita Johnson?"

The man did not respond

"Senorita Hunter McKenzie?"

The man looked at him and grew wary.

"She's a friend of mine," Ryan said. He forced a smile and thrust out a hand.

The Mexican did not clasp it.

"Actually she's the cousin of a close friend. Saw her come off on the stretcher. Had to find out what happened."

The man's dark eyes hardened.

At that moment, a doctor opened the door to the room. "You are waiting to know about the young lady?" He walked directly to Ryan. He had assumed that the pale skinned American girl had been Ryan's companion.

"Yes."

"She will be okay. A few days rest, nothing more. But I wish to keep her here for observation."

"What's the problem," Ryan asked the doctor.

"It appears to be a drug overdose. We pumped her stomach. No other procedures were required."

At that point, Ethete's Mexican companion intervened. He directed a string of Spanish at the doctor that left the man apologizing profusely. Both men glanced at Ryan with distaste.

"I do not know who you are Senor, but you have no business with my patient," the doctor said. "Please leave my hospital."

"I have as much business as this man."

"That is not what he is telling me."

"We'll see what the police have to say about that," Ryan said. "This woman was kidnapped from her home in San Diego."

The doctor looked stunned.

Ethete's Mexican companion walked to Ryan until he was within an inch of his face. "The woman is traveling with me voluntarily." His words were American, without a trace of Spanish accent. "Stay out of it, or you will be hurt."

Ryan smelled cigar. The man had smoked one this morning.

"I will inform the policia," the doctor said.

"No," Ethete's companion said. He then rattled off another string of Spanish.

When he had finished, the doctor's only reply was, "Si, Senor." He turned and left the room.

Alone with Ryan, the man turned to him. "You need to leave." He pulled a gun from under his jacket. "The woman, Hunter McKenzie, is my responsibility. I intend to deliver her to Senor Viejo. You will not interfere. Do you understand?"

"And just who is this Senor Viejo?"

"My cousin. You have not heard of Raul Viejo? He is a very, very powerful man, recently returned from your country."

"Where can I find him?"

"Enough. Get out." He motioned with the gun.

After Ryan talked to the Cabo policia, he returned to his hotel. He found his friend, Evan Bromley, sipping coffee near the pool. His feet were on the railing as he watched the swim suits a few yards away.

"Couldn't resist the view," Bromley said when Ryan sat down next to him.

Ryan looked at tanned skin on shapely bodies. Young girls came by their curves naturally. Older women spent hours at the spa in an attempt to recapture their youth. He had to admit many of them looked desirable. But then that was the whole idea, wasn't it?

He wondered how many of the sunning people realized they had a spark of the Creator of the universe within them. Would they behave the same, self-indulgent way if they knew that this was the first step of their celestial Journey, if they knew that the decisions they made today that would be with them for eternity?

There was nothing wrong with relaxing and enjoying life, but where did one draw the line? Where did sunning by a tropical pool become self-involvement, particularly when the world was on the brink of self-destruction? And what of the hard working Mexican people? How many of them had opportunities like this? How many of them resented the wealthy gringos? Yes, Americans had lifted the living stand and quality of life for some in Mexico, but it was a byproduct of their self-indulgence. Americans had not intended to lift the ordinary people of Mexico. And it was by examining intentions that the higher realms judged mortals.

Ryan Drake and Evan Bromley went back to their days in Viet Nam. Bromley had flown helicopters; his had crashed. Ryan had spent two days wandering in the humid jungle as he helped Bromley to safety. Bromley insisted that he owned his life to Ryan.

Bromley was part owner of a charter airplane service operating out of Jeffco Airport, near Boulder. His company, Westward, owned three airplanes all of which were leased to corporations on an "as needed" basis. Bromley regularly ferried the top executives of those companies around the world.

Ryan had called his pilot friend as soon as he knew he was headed for Mexico; they had not talked since returning from that quick trip to visit Carlton Boyle in Illinois. With no immediate assignment, Bromley had agreed to meet him in Cabo San Lucus.

"Any luck finding the girl?"

Ryan explained the morning's events.

"This Viejo character is probably some sort of a drug lord," Bromley said. "The police are on his payroll. Besides you're a gringo, not a Mexican."

"So what do we do?"

"I suggest we go back to the hospital. Try to talk to her."

"What about her buddy with the gun?" Ryan asked.

"Come on. I know a little Spanish."

Bromley approached the front desk of the hospital, and in smooth Spanish that surprised Ryan, began to chat with the attendant, an attractive Mexican woman. She basked in the attention of the handsome American. In a few moments he had Ethete's room number.

As they approached the first-floor room, the door opened and Ethete's Mexican companion emerged with another man. Ryan spun his back to the corridor and asked Bromley to describe what was happening.

Bromley watched over Ryan's shoulder. The two Mexicans talked and it became obvious that the second man was staying. Ethete's Mexican companion left by a door at the end of the hallway. The other man sat down on a chair in front of the door to

Ethete's room.

"Do you suppose he's armed?" Ryan asked.

"Wouldn't surprise me," Bromley replied. "Let's see if I can distract him."

Due to Bromley's darker skin and dark leather flight jacket, the Mexican was not immediately alerted by his approach. The two exchanged greetings. When the guard saw Ryan, he reached into the pocket of his jacket. But Bromley was faster and slapped the gun out of his hand with a chop to the wrist.

With the guard's arm behind his back, Bromley pushed him into Ethete's room. Ryan picked up the gun and followed.

Ethete was awake, her drowsy eyes flickering at the disturbance.

Bromley and he tied the guard with strips of towel; then Ryan approached the bed.

"Who are you?" Ethete's eyes squinted in the bright light of the hospital room. There was a glow to her skin that had been absent yesterday.

He offered her a pair of dark glasses. She eagerly grabbed them. "I'm a friend of J'Li and Dr. Adamson." Sarah had told Ryan to use her Phantian name and coached him to pronounce it correctly.

Ethete looked at him with faint comprehension. "I feel awful."

"What happened?"

"Don't know. We were having a good time partying on the ship. Then I woke up here. I feel so awful, and I'm real tired." She laid back and closed her eyes.

"No. Don't go to sleep." Before he could act, Ryan needed answers to two questions. Dr. Adamson had warned him that he could not coerce Ethete. She had to make her own decision. "Are you ready to go back to Harmony?"

"Harmony?" Ethete pronounced the word with difficulty.

"Yeah, Harmony, Dr. Adamson, J'Li."

"I think so. Anything but this. I feel so awful." The girl's face was vacant, her words slow.

"Okay, I'll take that as a yes. Will you let me help you?"

"You seem nice enough, but..."

"How much do you know about your Mexican friend?" Ryan

asked.

"He was taking me to see his cousin in Mazatlan, Senor Raul Viejo. A famous movie producer." Her speech picked up in anticipation of a star-studded career.

"Yeah, right. More like a drug dealer looking for a playmate."

"No. He promised me. I am to be a famous movie star."

"What do you know about him?"

"Diego says he is very famous. He will make me a star."

"What about J'Li and Dr. Adamson? Your mission?"

"The mission." She bit her lip.

Ryan suspected that this was the cleanest Ethete had been for a long time.

Something clicked. "I must go back," Ethete said.

"Another yes. Okay, lets see if we can get you out of here. Do you have your passport?"

"My purse." She motioned to the rack on which her clothes hung. There was no purse in sight.

Ryan finally found it in the bedside stand. Her Antigua Passport was in it, along with a few American dollars.

He produced the bottle of lotion that Peter had given him. "I'm going to rub a little of this on you. You do remember the lotion don't you?"

She nodded.

While he kept one eye on Evan and his captor, Ryan rolled up the sleeves of her hospital gown and rubbed in generous globs of the revitalizing lotion. Sarah and Peter suspected that Ethete had not been diligent with her required daily lotioning, and that this was one reason the drugs had produced such a powerful effect on her. Peter had formulated an especially potent batch for Ryan to use.

When he motioned for her to sit up and turn around, she looked suspiciously at him. "For your back," he said.

She lazily complied; he rubbed additional globs on her through the opening in the hospital gown. Sarah and Peter performed this ritual for each other daily.

The lotion glided over her smooth skin and was immediately absorbed like dry ground sucking up new rain. The Phantians' skin was more absorbent than skin of Earth-humans. As embryos, they used it as the primary path for nourishment.

"How are we going to get out of here?" Ryan addressed the question to Bromley who sat watching with obvious fascination.

"Can't risk the hallway," the pilot responded. "How about a window?" He stepped to the sliding glass and slid it open.

"Let's gag this guy." Ryan motioned to the Mexican guard. He did not need to verbalize the need for a head start to the airport where Bromley's airplane awaited them.

After a quick stop for customs and immigration at Nogales, Arizona, Bromley landed the twin engine Cessna at the small airport at Kayenta. In route, Ryan had used the plane's radio to call Jake Ashton at the Denver Office of the FBI. He told Jake that he could find Raul Viejo in Mazatlan.

A Navajo was waiting with a car to transport them. Ryan climbed into the rear with Ethete.

This was the first time Ryan had seen the area around Harmony since he fled into the desert with Peter and Sarah, four months ago. Little had changed. Black Mesa to the west of the valley retained only one small patch of snow. Winter moisture was as scarce here as in Colorado. Fortress Mesa to the east of Harmony looked as formidable as ever. He was still amazed that Cody Tsotsie had led them up and over that rugged terrain. Out there, in that desert wilderness, his life had changed forever.

When they reached Harmony Center, the front gate was wide open. Several large trucks were parked in the gravel lot. Ryan noticed new panes in the geodesic dome. A few hardy plants in the greenhouse seemed to have survived the government's occupation of the facility. To his right, men were working on the solar array. The tall cliffs of Fortress Mesa dwarfed the entire facility.

Dr. Adamson was waiting in front of the large terracotta Hogan, the main entrance to Harmony's underground facility. Ryan picked up Ethete and carried her inside and down green-carpeted stairs.

The doors to the main room were open. The long table with its dozen chairs was intact, but bore many scars. No place settings, no evidence of food service. As before, the lighting in the room was dim. The solar array and the battery back-up system must have been somewhat intact.

As they walked through the facility, Ryan saw workmen patching holes in the walls — evidence of the destruction wrought during the INS raid of four months ago. Sections of stained carpeting and tile had been ripped up and were being replaced.

Ryan carried Ethete to one of the bedrooms in the underground labyrinth. Except for immigration, she had slept the entire trip from Cabo. A Navajo woman came and made her comfortable.

As they walked back to the main room, Dr. Adamson said, "Thank you. Now, you understand why I needed your help."

"Do you suppose you could arrange for things to settle down for a while?" Ryan asked with a smile.

"Sure." Dr. Adamson returned his smile.

He rejoined Evan, and they headed back to the plane.

When they passed through Kayenta, Ryan phoned Gordon Moore and asked him to come to Harmony. He wanted a doctor's opinion on the effects of the drugs that Ethete had ingested over the past months, and a procedure for ridding her system of them. Given Gordon's recent oversight of Sarah and Peter's examinations, Ryan reasoned that he might understand Ethete situation and be the best to help.

"I'd be honored to help," Moore said. Without using the word extraterrestrial, he asked, "Does she have the same metabolism as Sarah?"

"I'll pay whatever you require," Ryan said.

"Nonsense, I am happy to help. Give me an excuse to get away from my patients."

"You're sure?"

"I'm sure. All in the name of furthering the cosmic paradigm."

Now this is not the end. It is not even the beginning of the end. But it is, perhaps, the end of the beginning.

— WINSTON S. CHURCHILL

FIFTEEN

"Our system is seeing tremors all over the Gulf east of Cabo San Lucas. They are relatively minor. Nothing to worry about," John MacDonald of the National Earthquake Information Center said. The caller was from a wire service. His newspaper had received reports of earthquakes on the Baja Peninsula; they wanted his expert opinion.

After he hung up, he went to his superior's office, the man in charge of NEIC. "It's another piece of the pattern I've been watching," MacDonald said. "Repeated shocks along all edges of the Pacific Plate."

He laid out a map that depicted Earth's tectonic plates; his computer had plotted the disturbances recorded over the past six weeks. The juncture between the North American and Pacific Plates was black with dots depicting recent earthquakes. Similar representations dotted every edge of the Pacific Tectonic Plate.

"Any ideas?"

"My guess is the melting of the ice cover over northern Canada and Alaska, Siberia, and Antarctica," MacDonald replied. "We're not seeing it where the North American intersects the Eurasian, because the ice cap over Siberia is melting at a similar rate. I think we should issue warnings."

His boss looked at him. Ice melts had been dismissed years ago as a possible cause for the shifting of tectonic plates. However, the persistence of global warming — an unfortunate coincidence of natural climate cycles and hydrocarbon emissions — had caused unprecedented melting over the last ten years, more quickly than at any time in recorded history.

"Good work. Keep me posted."

Disappointed at the man's reaction, MacDonald went back to watching his charts.

Sarah saw that it was 4:43 PM. In a little over an hour, she was to meet Peter in Denver for an interview with independent television station.

"It is time for me to go." Sarah said. She had spent over an hour with this learner.

"Can you wait a few minutes?" The young man pleaded. "This is so fascinating. I have a couple more things."

She felt a sense of urgency. "I must go." She opened the door of the hotel suite for him. "We can talk again next week."

When she stepped outside the hotel, she encountered a blizzard. She started Ryan's Jeep and got back out to scrape ice from the windshield. She was glad that the Jeep had been repaired in time for her to use it while Ryan was away.

Peter was coming from another meeting and would meet her at the studio in Denver. He was driving the car that Ryan had rented after his crash on the turnpike. She hoped that Peter would drive carefully. He was not as adept with Earth vehicles as was she.

Both Peter and she were now free from the constraints of having a sheriff's deputy escort them everywhere. Their diplomatic status was an effective shield. Plus everything was now public, including the many confusing interpretations of who or what she was.

In place of a sheriff's car, a small troop of reporters followed them everywhere. Recent articles questioning the legitimacy of their claims to extraterrestrial origins, or emphasizing their evil intent, had increased the number of journalists.

When she pulled onto US 36, headed east out of Boulder, rush hour had ended, but traffic crept along on the slick pavement. On the long grade out of town, she hesitantly pulled around a snowplow and back into the right lane. The van with her media troop followed two cars behind.

Five miles east of town, as she approached the Superior exit, traffic halted. Ahead, a Colorado State Patrol car, red and white lights flashing, blocked both lanes. A uniformed officer directed every vehicle to exit at McCasslin Boulevard.

As she crested the rise of the exit ramp, she saw a bright blue on the side of the divided highway a half-mile to the east.

She gunned the Jeep across McCasslin, onto the entrance ramp back to US 36, and maneuvered it forward until cars blocked her way. She skidded to a halt, behind a light blue van with lettering denoting it as a media vehicle. Tears welled in her eyes. She flung the door open and ran.

It appeared the rental car had slammed head-on into the concrete support. She remembered how Ryan had commented that he thought this was a particularly dangerous spot in the otherwise broad divided highway.

Flames engulfed the wreckage. The reporters and camera crew that followed Peter were already at the scene.

No one could approach the wreckage. The fire, welding-torch blue, seemed to be fueled more from the driver's seat than from burning fuel. The doors of the rental car were smashed shut. Sarah's heart fell, and she began to cry.

She felt a light touch on her cheek. She said farewell to Peter as he departed.

The blue fire was the heat from the spontaneous combustion that occurred when Peter's physical form was of no further value. The bodies of most people on a highly evolved sphere like Phantia disintegrated in this manner, rather than experiencing deteriorating physical health or a traumatic end.

Vehicles stopped everywhere, the Denver-Boulder Turnpike ground to a halt. In the face of blowing snow, many people got out and walked toward the intense blaze. In the westbound lanes, not one vehicle zipped-by without lingering to investigate the intense blue light glistening against the falling flakes. Many cars pulled to the side of the road. A Highway Patrol Officer tried to hustle them along, few complied.

No one in the gathering crowd said a word. Despite her anguish, Sarah could tell that people sensed something remarkable was taking place. They made a circle around the burning wreckage, treating it like a funeral pyre.

Snowflakes contributed a peculiar glow; the piercing blue light could be seen for a great distance in either direction. Sarah stayed at the front of the crowd, as close to the intense heat as possible. Now, after Peter had left for the next level of his celestial Journey, Sarah felt incredibly alone, abandoned on this violent planet.

One of the reporters from her entourage approached her; she shooed the woman away.

"He wasn't a bad driver," Sarah said to a man standing close-by. When she recognized him as one of the journalists who followed Peter, she said no more.

"That semi almost ran over him," the man said.

Alerted, she stared at him. "How did it happen?"

"Real slippery out here." He pointed to the icy roadway on which they stood. "Big rig pulled in between us and Peter." He motioned over his shoulder to the blue van behind which she had parked. "Must have been going sixty — way too fast. Pushed Peter's car off the road, right into the abutment. Never slowed down."

Sarah grabbed the sides of her chest, slipped to her knees, and cried.

It must have been the same truck that had almost killed Ryan.

Peter had been so brave to come to this far-off planet.

She had convinced him to accompany her on this mission.

To die this way...

She heard someone near her say, "I wonder who was in the car?"

"A man with a message for this planet." As he spoke the words, the white-haired man, dressed in western clothes, urged her to her feet. He wrapped his arms about her. They stood together in silent mourning.

'*His soul departed quickly,*' Dr. Adamson communicated to Sarah. '*You can be with him on the Between worlds.*'

Fire trucks wended their way through the halted vehicles. Their flashing red lights added new reflections to the falling flakes.

For almost 20 minutes, the pyre resisted the firefighters' stream of chemicals. Then in an instant the intense flame was no more.

When the charred automobile stopped glowing, a stretcher and black bag were pulled alongside. Firefighters cut open the still warm doors.

"You've gotta see this," one firefighter said. He motioned to his chief who was standing not far away.

After he poked his head into the car, the fire chief said with surprise, "Usually there's something left."

Spontaneous combustion had consumed the Phantian's body; only the bottoms of his charred shoes remained.

Another fireman said, "Hottest fire I've ever seen."

Sarah pushed forward and looked into the blackened interior. On the floor, in the back, was one of Peter's maroon books, untouched by the flames. She reached into the vehicle and placed it under her overcoat.

Evan Bromley was giving Ryan a ride back to his Boulder hotel. After fighting an upslope condition, that was bringing moisture from the south and depositing it as snow along the Front Range of the Rockies, they had landed at Jeffco Airport, east of Boulder.

Evan drove cautiously on the slick streets. The wipers on his car were barely able to keep up with the big flakes. Neither minded the weather; this was the first snow in months. It had been an extremely dry winter, following a season of statewide forest fires. The rest of the state would probably remain dry; an upslope condition meant snow only in the foothills west of Denver.

They were merging onto US 36 when Ryan noticed the white van with the lettering, HUBBLE PLUMBING. It was in the left lane, also headed west. Ryan caught a glimpse of the driver's long shaggy hair. He couldn't tell whether it was a man or a woman.

"Evan, that's the white van." On the way back from Cabo, Ryan had told his pilot friend about his brush with death.

He checked around for the tractor rig before he said, "Let's see where he's going in such a hurry."

Evan speeded up to keep pace with the white van.

Traffic slowed as they passed Flatiron Mall, to the south of the highway. The buildings of Storagetek peeked over the hill to the north. He watched as the white van swerved from one lane to the next. The guy was taking real chances on maintaining his traction; cars were moving out of the van's way as it flashed its headlights.

Ryan noticed the collection of bright lights on the eastbound side at the same moment he received Sarah's frantic communication, *'Ryan, help, I need you.'*

'Where are you?'

'On the highway to Denver. Something terrible has happened to Peter.'

"Evan, pull over — up ahead." Ryan strained to see through the blowing snow.

By the time they pulled to one side, and crossed to the median, the flashing lights of the fire trucks were all that illuminated the gathering darkness.

Ryan pushed through the crowd. He saw Sarah next to the wrecked auto and gasped.

For a moment he thought she had been in the crumpled car. Then he saw her straighten and walk to Dr. Adamson.

Out of nowhere, something brushed his cheek. He raised his hand to the spot. It felt warm.

'I will see you soon, my friend,' Peter communicated. *'Please care for Sarah.'*

Tears welled in Ryan's eyes. He understood the meaning of Sarah's earlier message.

Ryan glanced around. The driver of the white van stood at the median watching. White overalls smeared with paint or grease. When he caught Ryan's stare, he ran back to his vehicle and drove off.

Rather than go after him, Ryan jumped over the median and ran to Sarah and Dr. Adamson. Without words, they mourned the passing of a man who had come from a distant planet, a man who wanted only to help the people of this world.

Warren Ophir stood waiting, the collar of his black cashmere coat turned up against the sharp Scandinavian wind. He wore gloves and a Russian Federation fur hat. Each breath was plainly visible in the pale light of the long winter night.

He stepped over to the edge of the stone wall and looked at the frigid seawater. It was twelve feet below. When the wall had been built, the water had been much higher, within a foot or two of the top. Then it had been used as a dock for small fishing boats. The natives insisted that the land here in Stockholm, and in the rest of the peninsula that embraced Sweden and Norway, had risen as the weight of the glaciers was lifted. They also told him that the winters were just as long, but they were not as cold.

"Warren, my friend, it is good to see you." Kosma Uvizheva stepped out of a crowd and came to meet him. As usual he puffed on an American cigarette. He had picked up the habit when he was stationed at the Soviet Embassy in Washington. Uvizheva was Ophir's main contact within the Russian intelligence community. He was also a member of the intelligence affiliates.

"How goes your little problem with the two ETs?" the Russian asked.

"I have just received word, one of them was killed in a most unfortunate automobile accident."

"A pity. But then, as we say in Russia, 'life is tragedy.' What of the other?"

"As you and I have speculated, there may be others roaming around. I predict that she will live to make contact with them. Now, what I came to discuss is of some urgency, may I proceed?"

"Of course, my friend, of course."

"I have discovered that an atomic device will be detonated about five hundred miles above the southern hemisphere. It is a routine test of our space defense, but it will be unannounced. I wanted you to know."

Uvizheva frowned. "Will there be fall out? Radioactive debris?"

"Some. It is only a small device."

"And when is this to take place?"

"I have been unable to obtain the exact date," Ophir said, "but soon. As you know, the military in America does not cooperate with our intelligence service as does yours."

"I understand. You will notify me? We too have people in the lower half of the world." The Russian took a long draw on the remainder of his cigarette and then tossed the butt into the sea.

"In the usual way."

"The scientists in my country have detected an increase in earth tremors around the Pacific. Are your people aware?" the Russian asked.

"Yes, we know."

"Are your scientists going to issue warnings?" Uvizheva asked.

"Many of your people could be at risk."

"No." Just this morning, Ophir had received a query from his contact at the National Earthquake Information Center, the senior man at the Golden, Colorado facility. He had instructed the man to continue to sit on the information. No predictions were to be issued.

"Our plan," Ophir continued, "is to use the fear and horror generated by such an incident to further tighten controls, controls such as you have in Russia. You know that many in the World League admire the way in which your government has controlled its populace for so many years."

"Yes, but that is now history. You must be very careful that you do not exceed your people's tolerance. Tighten, but just enough. Remember you need their concurrence to create a strong economy. My country is a mess because we went too far for too long, created too many dependents."

The memorial service for Peter Jones was held in Boulder's largest church. The minister had been in the audience at the Phantian's first presentation, two months ago. He had become convinced of the celestial paradigm and worked it into his sermons. He had insisted on donating the space for Peter's final Earthly event.

Ryan turned his head and scanned the pews behind him. The church was one-third full. He noted two reporters; one of them was Colette DuPree. He had issued her an invitation. No cameras were allowed. Tom Ertl was the highest-ranking local official. Jake Ashton, of the FBI, sat next to Doctor Gordon Moore. Six Sanitas employees clustered around Brauk; one of them was Karen Borden-Banes. Ryan recognized acquaintances from the business community and old friends.

The two tall people from Portland sat directly behind where he was seated. In the row with them were a number of men and women he did not recognize. For a moment, he though Ethete had traveled from Harmony to be here. No, this very attractive woman, dressed in winter white, resembled Ethete; she could be her sister, but it wasn't Ethete. The woman looked toward Ryan and smiled.

'She too is from Phantia,' Sarah communicated.

'How many?' Ryan asked.

214

"Seven.'

'Ethete should have been here, and Ajax.'

'Doctor Moore said she was still too sick to travel. I have not heard from Ajax.'

Other than the Phantians, few others had come from out of state; it was primarily Boulder-Denver folks who were here to honor the extraplanetary revealator. Ryan knew several who had stayed away, fearful of being identified with extraterrestrials, or fearful of being associated with a hoax. Unable to see to the rear of the church, he turned back.

Sarah sat next to him in the first row. She wore her long white robe, gathered at the waist with the simple gold chain. Around her neck hung her medallion; her hair was drawn back into a severe bun. She was very beautiful, but the enduring look of a much younger woman was gone.

Just before they shut the doors at the rear of the chapel, a man in his late thirties squeezed in. He was dressed in a dark blue pin striped suit with white shirt and red tie. The blonde woman in the pew behind nudged Ryan. He looked around and she pointed. He was just in time to catch site of the man as he sat.

'Guess who just showed up,' Ryan communicated to Sarah.

'John deBeque,' she communicated without turning to look. *'He was directed to stay close to us. It will be interesting to see his reaction to this graduation ceremony.'*

Ryan studied the mass of flowers at the front of the church, over a hundred arrangements. Peter had made an impression on many, many who had sent flowers because they would not risk coming. He smiled as he thought of Peter's eccentricities, although they probably were not considered such on that far-away planet of his origins. Peter Jones, the emigrant, had tried so valiantly to appear to be just another human of this planet. He remembered that Peter always left the toilet seat in the up position. He contended that way it was fresh for the next man or woman who desired to use it. He abhorred public men's rooms and refused to use them. And Peter instinctively used both feet to drive. He insisted that using only the right foot was a waste of motion. Another quirk of Peter's was his taste for cool, but not iced, coffee. Peter never drank anything hot or iced. And then there were the caraway seeds that he sprinkled on everything.

"Peter Jones was a great man by any standard, a giant among the people of his home planet, a crusader for the people of this world," the words of the minister interrupted Ryan's musings. "He chose the common name, Peter, to blend-in with the humans of this planet. But his Phantian name was Z'Rv." After coaching from Sarah, the minister had learned to pronounce Peter's Phantian name like Zoraff. "In the language of Phantia, Z'Rv means wanderer. But Z'Rv was not a wanderer; rather he was a leader, a man who was showing this world the way to a better life. I used to think the missionaries of my church sacrificed a lot when they went to Africa. Their sacrifice was nothing compared to that made by Z'Rv."

"I know that Peter was from another planet. And I know that there are many other spheres on which human beings live. Despite their somewhat different appearances, I know that the lives of extraterrestrials are closer to ours than they are different. Through Z'Rv I have come to know that off-planet personalities have families, societies, desires, loves, and, yes, dislikes.

"The celestial paradigm, and all that it implies, touched me deeply. Through Z'Rv, I have come to know The Divine One who is a trillion times larger and more wonderful than my old God. A Universe Father who dispatches a fragment of himself to dwell within each of us.

"Z'Rv sacrificed family, career, and everything else familiar to him in order to come to this planet of ours. The celestial paradigm must not die with him, for it is the best hope we have to take charge of our future. No longer can we allow fear and self-centeredness to rule our lives. No longer can we depend on some magical 'force of nature' to correct that which we are unwilling to do for ourselves. No longer can we proclaim ourselves victims of something that happened a few hundred thousand years ago, or a few thousand years ago, or yesterday. No longer can we shy from our responsibilities as the caretakers of this planet.

"If you would honor Peter Jones, Z'Rv, then take his message into your lives, into your hearts. Z'Rv has graduated, but his soul and his message live on."

As Ryan listened to others speak about Peter, he contemplated his own situation: next to him was one of the most wonderful creatures in the galaxy. She had come to depend on him, an ordinary mortal of this planet. Along with Peter, she had coached him about the celestial paradigm and exposed him to a very human-like person from a trillion miles away. He had felt those experiences transform him.

At the request of the celestial messenger, and at the urging of Peter and Sarah, he had agreed to help lead a movement dedicated to remaking his world, remaking his world before it was too late. He was strengthened by the idea that, no matter who opposed him, who did what to him, he had already begun an incredible celestial Journey that would take him to The Divine One, and then to the farthest reaches of the cosmos. This realization gave him the courage to oppose the hierarchy of the status quo.

Sarah and Ryan both spoke. They expressed their love for Peter and said that they planned to carry on with unveiling the cosmic paradigm. Ryan dedicated the Cosmic Paradigm Center to Peter's memory. He then talked of the ground swell that the bald Phantian had initiated and told of small groups forming to pursue his plan of transformation.

As Ryan spoke, he caught faint images of a host of off-planet personalities present to honor Z'Rv: celestials, non-materialized extraterrestrials, and intraterrestrials from this planet. They were present in quasi-physical form. Many had come to honor Peter, many more than the two hundred Earth-humans in the pews and the seven from Phantia.

When Sarah spoke, she explained how Peter would have wanted this to be a happy occasion, a celebration of his graduation to the Between worlds.

After Ryan and Sarah finished, a white-haired, white-robed man appeared at the front of the church and without the benefit of a microphone filled the space with his words. "Make no mistake, The Divine One who created, nourishes, and controls this world will not abandon this planet until His plan for it to become a world evolved to peace and enlightenment is fulfilled. It is only a matter of time.

"Now, I ask each of you to stand and take the hand of the person next to you. Be sure you are connected to another and that everyone is connected to me."

Ryan moved to one side of the white-haired apparition and placed his arm around Dr. Adamson's back; it immediately felt charged. On his left, he found the hand of the minister. As people shuffled and stretched to accommodate Dr. Adamson's directions, two of Tom Ertl's deputies locked the church's doors so that none from the outside would disturb the gathering. Then they too held the hands of another in the web.

Ryan watched the barely visible off-planet personalities position themselves behind those who held hands.

"Now, please close your eyes." Dr. Adamson said.

Despite some rustling of discomfort, everyone complied. Ryan felt a familiar feeling of warmth and comfort pass through him to others in the unbroken chain of hands, felt the pulsating energy around the room. He wondered how Jake Ashton was going to handle this. How would John deBeque react?

It has become appallingly obvious that our technology has exceeded our humanity.

— ALBERT EINSTEIN

SIXTEEN

In the mind's eye of everyone present in the church, its top disappeared and they were lifted upward. The experience seemed so real that the minister clenched Ryan's hand. As they sailed upward, he heard gasps of astonishment from others around the circle. In a moment, each person was high above the Earth, looking down as the magnificent globe rotated beneath. Soon it was a dot against a starry background.

They were transported to the first of the Between spheres. Earth's green was exchanged for violet. The air was filled with pleasant fragrances. They visited buildings and amphitheatres of that wondrous world and saw its multitude of teachers and learners from all manner of other planets, quasi-physical beings of many shapes and sizes, all radiant, all beautiful. In addition to classroom work, the graduated mortals were employed in tasks from minding a nursery to intricate landscaping to art and music. Their homes were only slightly dissimilar to those on Earth. They passed over purple landscape to stand on the shore of a broad glass lake; its surface reflected a cloudless sky.

They were whisked to a second Between world where they saw a setting advanced from the first. Former mortals from the evolutionary planets of space and time were more radiant and less physical. They passed on to a third, and a fourth. Each new sphere was more beautiful than the prior. The buildings and landscape became more ethereal as they ascended from one world to the next.

On the fifth Between sphere they found Peter Jones. Z'Rv, stood in the middle of a great lecture hall, debating with the celestial at the podium. The more nearly spiritual form of Z'Rv paused, turned toward the group from the church, smiled, and saluted the travelers with a wave of his hand. Ryan did not want to risk breaking the experience, or he would have raised his hand and waved back.

Then they returned to the familiar blue water, green and brown land, and patchy white clouds of their home planet. In barely a moment they were settled in their places in the church.

"You can release each other's hands now," Dr. Adamson said loudly enough to be heard at the back of the church.

It was several moments before people began to open their eyes and move about. Many were reluctant to return from the peace and beauty of the trip. Then they began to share what they had experienced with each other. Many had recognized loved ones. Some of their deceased family members had communicated with them. Others related how they had felt a powerful hand on his or her shoulder.

Ryan looked to his right; Dr. Adamson had disappeared. Glancing around he saw that the non-material beings were also gone.

Sarah beckoned him to her side. They stood there, arms around each other's back, as those gathered quietly departed the building.

When Ryan and Sarah walked from the church, a crowd of well-wishers surrounded them. Tom Ertl led Jake Ashton to them.

"We have a lot to discuss," the FBI man said to Ryan and Sarah. He was smiling.

"Whenever you are ready," Ryan replied.

"I hope you're ready for what he's offering," Tom Ertl said

"After what I just experienced — I'm ready," the FBI man said.

"Me too," said Gordon Moore who stood at Ashton's side. "I'm interested in getting to the bottom of what the government is hiding on this whole subject. I know a few military types. Think I'll do a little snooping around."

Ryan made another mental note to find out the connection between Ashton and Moore.

"This show just keeps getting better and better," Brauk spouted, interrupting their conversation. "What's next?"

"Stick around," Ryan said, "and you might get to see what comes next."

The blonde man and woman from Portland waited until the crowd thinned and they could approach Sarah privately. After they had held her for a long time, she turned to Ryan and communicated, *'I would like you to meet more of my friends from Phantia. They have been working quietly and have convinced many of the cosmic paradigm. I envy their privacy.'*

Without words, Ryan communicated, *'I seem to be meeting you Phantians everywhere.'*

'Thank you for what you did for Ethete," the blonde woman communicated. *'How is she?'*

'She is recovering at Harmony. The doctor thinks she will be fine in a couple of weeks.'

Colette Dupree waited until the crowd around Ryan had thinned, then she approached him and said, "You set me up."

"I know. And there's more. I have some material that your New York bosses, and certain other powerful men, are not going to like. I want to find a way to make it public. How can I do that?"

"I don't know if I'm the right one to help," she replied. "To get anything on national TV, you're going to have to knock down some brick walls. I'm sure they are watching you very closely and anything that comes from you will be tagged. But, let me think about it — I'll call you. What happened inside was very impressive."

Ryan turned back to the remaining well-wishers. There had to be a way to get the rest of Steiger's diary public, to help people see how they were being manipulated, to get it out before the World League suppressed it.

Ryan noticed a man seated on a nearby wall. Recognizing him, he approached the hunched figure.

"Are you all right?" Ryan asked.

"That was really something," John deBeque said. Ryan saw that his eyes were red. "I have to know more."

"For yourself, or for the media affiliates?"

"For myself. What I just experienced raises some real questions about everything I've been taught, everything I've been doing for the last eighteen years. I need to understand what went on in there."

"Truth," Ryan said, "that was truth."

"I know, and I want to know more."

'I believe he is genuinely interested,' Sarah walked up as Ryan and deBeque exchanged guarded words.

Ryan studied the other man for a long time. Neither spoke. John deBeque's eyes held steady under Ryan's gaze.

Finally Ryan said, "You know where Harmony Center is. Find your way there. Don't let any of your media affiliate buddies know where you are going. Call me when you have it arranged. I'll meet you." Ryan gave deBeque ways to leave messages.

When all had departed, Ryan and Sarah were left alone, although both knew they were not really alone, only that they were the only humans present.

'Come sit with me,' Sarah communicated. She pointed to a bench under the wide branches of a leafless elm tree.

'So where do we go from here?' Ryan asked.

'From here,' Sarah motioned to the church's courtyard, *'from here, we continue to help transform this world.'*

Ryan reached across and placed his arm around her slim shoulders. For a while they sat together, remembering Peter Jones, and wondering about the next step.

Ryan began to massage Sarah shoulder with his right hand. She turned, and he began to knead her muscles with both hands.

'You are very important to me,' Sarah said. *'It is much more than just the mission in which we are engaged. You have become my strength, my protector, and my friend. I love you Ryan.'*

He stopped his motion, placed both arms around her, and pulled her tight. The vanilla scent of her body filled him. She was indeed the most incredible creature in the universe.

The Arizona high desert in early February can be quite cold. Walking along the dirt road from Harmony Center toward Ben Tsotsie's archeological excavation, Ryan Drake and Sarah Smith were bundled against a sharp wind that blew from the north. The sun, high in the southern sky, provided little warmth.

Sagebrush, TS'AH, lined the sides of the road. Where brush and grass did not cover the ground, red sandstone jutted forth. An occasional, stunted juniper, GAD', grew where it found water in the dry soil. Despite its harsh outward appearance, Ryan found the desert appealing. He had learned to love it when he attended Arizona State University.

Since coming back to Harmony, Ryan had been able to see their situation more clearly. All their hard-won publicity had been twisted and defiled. True, more people now recognized that extraterrestrials lived among them, but it had not made much difference in their day-to-day lives. Many people were now prepared to believe that Sarah Smith was a human whose body had been invaded by some sort of an evil spirit. At best, only a small number were convinced of the cosmic paradigm, and a smaller number yet were willing to do anything about it.

Ryan had learned from Dr. Adamson that indeed there were Earth-humans who had surrendered their non-physical and that the soul of a non-human had entered the body. This occurred most often as the result of some tragic accident or near-death experience. Like many phenomena, which were dismissed by the prevailing paradigm, this appeared to be more common than acknowledged, and generally resulted in a highly conscious person.

Peter's death had brought it all home. He now understood that virtually everything he said, everything he did, was being monitored by some agent of the World League. He could no longer shield Sarah, nor could she hide behind diplomatic status. Neither Sarah nor he could hide behind Sheriff Tom Ertl. If the League decided they were expendable, that would be the end of it. Why then were they still alive?

Ryan spent his time trying to figure a way to get the rest of Ernest Steiger's diary published. He was convinced that the names and events on its pages would turn heads, and with that they might recruit a few more activists to their team. In addition to merely making it available, he had to maintain the credibility of the document, had to bypass the defense mechanisms set up to defeat material critical of the status quo, and, most importantly, had to make a real splash.

Since returning to Harmony, Sarah had spent long hours in meditation. This morning she strolled next to him with an air of confidence. She had combed out her long blonde hair; it cascaded to her shoulders. Her cheeks displayed a healthy glow. He noted one of her phantasmal guardian, a little off to the left.

"I wish that Peter were here," Sarah said.

Ryan looped his arm around her. "I know that you miss him. I do too."

This walk offered them a brief respite. It was the first time since returning to Harmony they had ventured beyond its fifty acres, beyond the listening devices that the World League had planted around the property. A half-mile up the road toward Ben's camp, Ryan said, "Ethete seems better. I hardly recognize the woman I rescued."

"The effects of the drugs are finally wearing off," Sarah said. "I think you got to her just in time. If she'd fallen into Viejo's hands, we might have lost her."

"Can you believe the irony of it all? We're here, where we first met. Harmony is returning to normal. But Raul Viejo, who was in the business of transporting illegal Mexicans, the man who tried to destroy Harmony and caused you to flee into the desert, is wealthy, living in Mexico, and kidnapping beautiful women. Don't you find this just a little strange? I think the celestials who are supposed to be orchestrating everything need to work on their end of it."

"Viejo is most certainly not the work of celestials," Sarah said with a knowing smile. She had learned to recognize when Ryan was teasing, but had not yet learned how to respond in kind.

When Sarah had announced her plans to leave Boulder, only a few members of the media elected to accompany her. After a week in the isolation of the desert, most had departed. The two remaining were now camped out at a motel in Kayenta. These two had been at Peter's graduation ceremony and had developed a certain fondness for Sarah and her saga. With no telephone service into Harmony, they made daily forays to where the dirt road left the main highway. Since ninety-five percent of Harmony's facility lay underground, inaccessible to the outside world, there was little for an inquiring reporter to do.

Sarah walked the mile from Harmony's underground facility to talk with the two reporters each morning, always bringing a thermos of hot coffee and paper cups. She took great pains to explain something new and to encourage them to come back the next day. This sunny afternoon, they were not in sight.

"Do you think they are watching?" "They" was never the media; "they" were the operatives of the World League, the ones who had submerged the cosmic paradigm in a twisted discussion about her authenticity.

"Oh, I'm sure 'they' are keeping an eye on us." Ryan motioned to the clear blue sky. "Given their resources, I'm sure they know this is you and this is me." He waved to the spy satellite that he was sure observed them. Even if the World League did not have funds for a satellite of its own, he felt sure they had sufficient influence to convince some government agency to snap pictures."

"So what can we do?" she asked.

"Be as open as possible. Publicity, such as it is, is our friend; it's their enemy. Even with questions about your authenticity, there is still interest in you, and what you do. And what happens when we introduce Ethete?"

"Dr. Adamson said that Ajax is likely to show up at any time."

Ryan smiled. "I guess, since his team lost the Super Bowl, he's a little less interested in playing football."

They walked over the last rise and peered at Ben's camp. It had changed little since Ryan's time here. Ben's new truck was parked not far from the road; along side it were three aging vehicles. Ryan had made a donation to the dig that enabled Ben to purchase the F-150 pickup.

The camp with Ben's trailer and the cooking tent was deserted. Ryan and Sarah walked a few yards to the site of the excavation. There they saw Ben supervising his crew. Ryan saw that the trenches were a foot deeper and had been extended in new directions since he had been here last fall.

"Found any old bones?" Ryan asked as they approached the archeologist.

"You need a new line," Ben replied. "You also need practice to walk quieter. I heard you coming a quarter mile away."

"Maybe you'd like to give me a few lessons?"

"Sure." Ben walked to Sarah and gave her a huge hug. "How about we start with Sarah?"

"No way. Don't harass the ambassador."

"All right you two," Sarah said.

Ben feigned admonishment and bowed toward Sarah. "I yield

to the ambassador from Phantia."

"Anything new?" Ryan asked Ben in a more serious tone.

Before answering, Ben turned to Sarah and said, "I was sorry to hear about Peter. He was a good man."

"Yes, he was," Sarah said. "Thank you."

Then Ben said to Ryan, "There is a new man in town, staying at the Holiday Inn in Kayenta, checked in yesterday. He drives a rental. Wandered around a bit to familiarize himself with the area — drove past the turn off, but didn't stop." Ben pointed to the high-way running through the valley. The road to his excavation and to Harmony turned off it. "Someone saw his car by the side of the road last night."

"FBI?"

"Don't think so, we've learned to recognize them. For a while, they were all over the place."

"You'll keep me posted?"

"Yeah."

"Come for dinner," Sarah said. "Tonight?"

"Okay."

It was a dark night, no moon; stars blanketed the clear desert sky. The frosty temperature had subdued the noisy creatures of the night. The two men stood looking at the firmament.

After dinner with Sarah and Ethete, Ryan had walked Ben out to his truck. They took no notice of the dark automobile parked between Harmony's van and Ryan's Jeep. Other vehicles belonging to Harmony's staff were scattered about the parking lot. Harmony had no exterior lighting; the thumbnail of a moon provided little illumination.

"Seen any ET craft recently?" Ryan asked.

"Nothing the past month," Ben replied. "Don't get too many like the one that showed off for you. Dr. Adamson and his friends really set you up, didn't they?" The Navajo chuckled and slapped Ryan on his back.

A figure in dark clothing alighted from the rear seat of the dark vehicle. The interior lights had been turned off, so he tele-graphed no warning of his movements. His eyes, a phosphorous green, watched the two men as they talked and gazed around. He crouched behind the pickup and moved a step toward the two. When he emerged from behind Ben's truck, the two men were gone. He stood upright and looked around, his night vision goggles aiding his survey.

Suddenly he was knocked to the ground. Before he recovered his senses, he was pinned to the gravel by two heavy bodies.

"Well, well. What do we have here?" Ben asked. He sat astride the prone figure. With a free hand he ripped off the man's night vision goggles.

"Welcome to Harmony," Ryan said. He relaxed his grip on the man's arm.

"Yeah, thanks a lot."

"Ben, this is —" Ryan was about to blurt out John deBeque's name, but he restrained himself. "This is a friend. I think you can get off him, now."

Ryan looked around for observers. He was sure Harmony was under constant scrutiny. And it would be just like someone from the League to be prowling around at night.

"Come on." Ryan held out a hand to the prone man. "Let's go find Sarah."

After deBeque brushed off, he and Ryan walked to the larger Hogan and down to the dining area. Sarah, Ethete, and Dr. Adamson were seated at the long table. The Navajo serving crew had just finished cleaning off the dinner dishes.

"Look who I found in the parking lot," Ryan said.

Like a graceful queen rising to greet one of her subjects, Sarah held out her hand and said, "Welcome, John deBeque. I am pleased you are here."

Motioning to the white-haired apparition, she said, "I don't think you have formally met Dr. Victor Adamson."

John deBeque thrust out his hand. Dr. Adamson did not extend his. Instead, he came forward and placed his left arm around the young man. Ryan recalled that this was the way he had initially been greeted by the bear of a man.

"Hello, John deBeque," Dr. Adamson's deep voice rumbled. "Know that you are welcome here."

"I did my best to avoid being followed," deBeque stammered. He glanced at Ryan. "Coming here at night, and all."

DeBeque's eyes darted about the room and settled, not on Ryan, Sarah, or Dr. Adamson, but on Ethete. She had walked around the end of the table.

"My name is Ethete." The slim, dark haired Phantian extended her hand to deBeque. "Like Sarah, I too am from Phantia."

John deBeque was speechless, caught not only in the charm of a beautiful woman, but also trying to reconcile the words of an extraterrestrial.

"Tell me what you need from your car," Ryan interrupted, as if he were a doting parent overseeing his teenage daughter. "I'll bring it down for you."

Without taking his eyes from Ethete, deBeque said, "Just my two bags." He fished for the key to the car.

"Can we offer you something to eat or drink?" Sarah asked.

"Sure."

Sarah motioned deBeque to a seat at the table, then headed toward the kitchen door.

The Navajo cook quickly produced a plate of fried chicken, mashed potatoes, and peas. Everything was sprinkled with caraway seeds. While John deBeque picked at the food, drank a little iced tea, and glanced at Ethete, the others made preparations for his stay.

"Why did you come?" Sarah asked.

"I'm afraid I may have put you all in jeopardy. If my bosses find out —" He did not complete his sentence, but paused to again assay the members of the group. "I have to know what's going on, what's true."

"Then tomorrow we will begin," Dr. Adamson said. "You will see if what we have to say is of interest."

"We will explain more about the organized, nurturing, and friendly universe," Sarah said.

"Are all ETs friendly?" deBeque asked.

"Only a very small percentage are not. We will be sure and talk about that."

"You and I will talk about the three great tragedies that have befallen this planet," Ethete said. She laughed and added, "I've experienced the results of them, first hand."

"You're not worried I'm some kind of a spy?"

"John, even a spy can change his mind by discovering the truth," Dr. Adamson said.

"And I have lots of additional pages from your stepfather's diary," Ryan said.

DeBeque told them about his three days of travel to arrive at Harmony. He had driven a rental car from Washington, DC to Philadelphia. Once there, paying cash, he had taken a series of busses to Chicago, getting off at stops and waiting for the next bus. When he arrived in Chicago he had flown to Phoenix. In Phoenix, he had rented the car that had brought him to Harmony. He believed he had not been followed, and believed it would take his friends in the media affiliates a while to find him.

Throughout John deBeque's getting acquainted, Ryan noted that Ethete did not shy from his obvious infatuation with her. A stunning woman, Ryan understood how she had attracted the attention of so many in Hollywood.

"What should I do about my rental car?" deBeque asked.

"I'll take care of it," Ryan said. "If you need to use a vehicle, you can use one of Harmony's. I think it's best if you remain inside; this facility has everything you'll require. But, know that you are free to leave whenever you wish. Just say the word."

Think of the universe as a great white canvas of peace and love, upon which are scattered dots of fear and violence.

— DR. VICTOR ADAMSON

SEVENTEEN

"Before you retire for the night, I thought you might like to hear the story of my origins," Dr. Adamson said when John deBeque had finished eating.

"Your origins?" John deBeque had finished eating. "I thought you were an alien."

"Not alien," Ryan corrected him. "Extraterrestrial, or my preference, extraplanetary. And Dr. Adamson is none of these. He is an intraplanetary."

A confused expression engulfed John deBeque's face. He glanced at the others around the table, eyes coming to rest on Sarah.

"John, over the next few days, you're going to learn many things that you will totally reshape your view of this world," Sarah said. "There is a lot more going on here than visits by extraplanetary mortals. May I suggest that you remain as open as possible? Now to Dr. Adamson's story." She motioned to the white-haired man who sat next to Ryan.

"All right, sure." John deBeque relaxed back into his chair.

"My great grandparents, on my father's side, whom I never met, came to this world about thirty-eight thousand years ago," Dr. Adamson began. "By the way, I know that some of the things I'll mention will raise questions. I suggest that you hold them until I finish the story.

"My great grandparents had been raised for the specific purpose of going to a world such as Earth — in order to biologically upgrade the native population. They were members of the third physical series — fair complexion, light hair, and blue eyes — were a little over eight feet tall, and left behind fifty sons and fifty daughters on their planet of origin.

"They committed to a plan that had been exhaustively discussed with the universe administrators and were fully aware of the less than ideal conditions of this troubled world. Their initial home was a beautiful garden that had been prepared for them by some of the more advanced residents of Earth. It was on a protected peninsula that jutted out into the Mediterranean. When they rematerialized, they were welcomed with great ceremony and expectation. My grandfather, their first child of this world, was born in this beautiful garden.

"For one hundred and sixteen years, they worked at developing an advanced civilization, instructing both their own children and people of the resident races about sexual equality, the golden rule, and health. They modeled play and humor, and showed their children how to find competitive substitutes for fighting. And they worked toward establishing a representative world government. Incidentally, establishing a world government is still a requirement for this planet to be accepted as an equal by the other planets of the universe.

"But I digress, back to my story. Their efforts worked well with their own children, and with those living within the garden, but those members of the resident races who lived beyond its boundaries did not accept their advanced concepts. This was due in large part to the efforts of former planetary authorities, and their teachings of unbridled personal liberty.

"My great grandparents' efforts to blend their superior biologics with those of the races of Earth were further thwarted by the existence of certain retarded and defective human strains, and by the floundering of the resident races in the spiritual darkness and confusion resulting from the rebellion against universe authority. In an impatient impulse to overcome these obstacles, and contrary to the agreed-to plan, my great-grandparents mated with members of the resident races — this type of mating was a task that was to have been reserved for their children's children."

"You know, this sounds like a lot of science fiction," John deBeque said.

"Let Dr. Adamson finish," the lithe Phantian said gently.

Dr. Adamson continued, "My great grandparents' actions caused the universe authorities to demote them to the status of ordinary mortals. Not long after, in the face of an invasion by an army of the resident races, my great-grandparents fled the garden. In the face of this debacle, their offspring were given the opportunity to leave the planet. Two thirds of their children, and their children's offspring, chose to leave. The original garden sank into the Mediterranean.

"A second garden was established, between the Euphrates and Tigris rivers, in what is commonly called Mesopotamia. My great-grandparents spent their remaining years there. Hundreds of seeds and bulbs, from the first garden, were planted in the land between the rivers. In a program to uplift the evolved races, one thousand six hundred eighty two of the most highly developed women from the resident races were impregnated with my great grandfather's life plasm. He died at the age of five hundred thirty.

"Incidentally, that is the way in which Type A blood was introduced into the Earth-human species. It was the mating between my great grandparents, and their offspring, with the resident races. Type A stands for the fact that my grandparents introduced the concept of agriculture to the races of this planet.

"My grandfather, who had fathered thirty-two children during the time of the first garden, found the second garden was far from satisfying, primarily because his mate and all his children had been among those who elected to depart this planet. Traveling north, he found and married a wonderful and beautiful woman, a direct descendant of the former planetary authorities.

"She and my grandfather had sixty-seven children. But now we come to the most interesting part," Dr. Adamson paused to make sure those around the table were still with him, and to make sure they focused on his next words. "Every fourth child of theirs was very special; most often they were quasi-physical."

He paused again. "By inter-marrying these special children, one thousand, nine hundred eighty four 'intraplanetary beings' were born. I am one of them. We have the ability, without technology, to exist in either the physical or quasi-physical. You have watched me appear and disappear.

"We remained with my grandfather until he died, at which time, thirty-three of us decided to dedicate ourselves to the service of the planetary overseers who had taken over when my great-grandparents defaulted. Unfortunately, my other brothers and sisters chose to lead a rather unorganized existence, causing mischief, until a couple of thousand years ago, when they were finally brought under control.

"Those of us who dedicated ourselves to planetary service have kept my great grandparents' truth and skills alive for the humans of this planet. Despite repeated setbacks, when barbarians overwhelmed advancing civilization, or when mankind allowed itself to degenerate, we have kept the path of civilization on an upward slope."

"Are you speaking of technological innovations?" Ryan asked.

Dr. Adamson smiled, and said, "If you are referring to the genius of an Edison, no. Such breakthroughs are introduced in cooperation with celestials and other extraplanetary beings. What I am referring to are such things as the skill of meditation, and the value thereof in connecting to the non-physical."

"I suggest we take a quick break," Sarah said standing. "I'm sure you have other questions. Dr. Adamson will answer those in a few minutes."

When Ryan glanced back to where Dr. Adamson had been speaking, the white-haired apparition was no longer visible. John deBeque sat staring at the spot where he had been a moment before.

Ryan looked at deBeque to access how the young man was holding up his first evening at Harmony Center. He had, apparently, abandoned a promising career as the spokesman for the International League, not to mention his secret activities with the media affiliates. There was a part of Ryan that found him just a little hard to believe. Was deBeque a spy for the black ops?

As they munched on apples, oranges, nuts, and cookies, Dr. Adamson reappeared and took the seat next to deBeque. With a broad grin, he said, "All right. Now for your questions."

"I'll start," deBeque said. He had stopped eating when the white-haired man made his sudden reappearance. Now he clasped his hands on the edge of the table. "So, you're trying to tell me that you've been around here for thousands of years?"

"Yes."

"I find that hard to believe. You look pretty normal to me, except for that disappearing thing."

"You remember the trip you took to see Peter on the Between world?" Dr. Adamson asked.

"Yes, very well. It's the reason I'm here."

"All right, close your eyes." Dr. Adamson placed his arm around deBeque's shoulder. "I'm going to let you see what the world of thirty-three thousand years ago was like. At that point, I had only been alive about five thousand years."

Ryan watched as deBeque's face mirrored what his mind was seeing. At first it was pleasantly relaxed, then not so pleasant, then ugly, horrible, shocking. The trip took but a few minutes. Ryan finished his snack of nuts and fruit as he waited for the young man to return to present time.

When John deBeque opened his eyes, he had that stunned look of someone who had just emerged from a frightening movie, or a close encounter with death. He tried to pick up his water glass but his hand shook and spilled most of it in his plate.

Ethete placed her hand on his arm to calm him.

"The place I took you to was what you now call London," Dr. Adamson said.

"So now what do you think?" Ryan asked.

"I had no idea." DeBeque raised his hands palms up. "They were little more than animals." With that he shook his head, and leaned back into his chair.

'Aren't you rushing things a bit with John?' Ryan communicated to Sarah and Dr. Adamson.

'When we introduced you to these things, in the desert, you did not know that Peter and I were extraplanetary beings,' Sarah communicated. *'John knows that we are from Phantia. He almost expects something outrageous to happen.'*

"So, there's truth to the story in the Bible?" Ryan asked.

"Yes, my great grandparents really did exist." Dr. Adamson

said. "The Bible relates the story of the temptation in the garden in the form of a conversation with a snake. Now that you understand the true story, I'm sure you can see that the forbidden fruit was sexual intercourse with a member of the resident races."

"I like your version," Ryan said. "Makes a lot of sense, but it's more complicated."

"The larger truth is sometimes more complex than that which was told thousands of years ago. One does not tell a child as many of the details as one is able to disclose to an adult."

Ryan thought for a moment, and then asked, "Who are these former planetary authorities?"

Dr. Adamson smiled at Sarah and Ethete, as if to say, "here we go," then he said, "The former planetary authorities and their staff, a mixture of celestials and mortals from far-off planets, assembled here five hundred thousand years ago. They set up the original civilization for this planet: agriculture, animal domestication, trade and industry, sanitation and hygiene, and the beginnings of religion. Recruiting students from all colors and strata of the primitive humans of that long-ago time, they built an advanced city that housed thousands. There was a fair amount of mating that occurred between these 'gods' and the ordinary people. Because these off-planet beings had the ability to exist in the quasi-physical, many of the legends and myths of Earth-humans are based on the happenings of these distant times.

"Due to their influence, civilization progressed in a fairly normal manner for almost three hundred thousand years. But their leader had a fault; he was ultraindividualistic. When his superior, a celestial in charge of many planets, decided to rebel against the higher universe authorities, the leader of the off-planet beings on Earth joined him. Earth was isolated from other planets and the celestials, extraplanetary beings, and members of the resident races who were here were forced to choose between the rebellion and the Grand Plan of The Divine One. Many of them chose to join the uprising.

"It took seven years for the higher universe authorities to reestablish control of Earth. In that interval, the rebels attempted a radical reorganization of the civilized world, along the lines of the uprising's 'declaration of freedom.'"

"Declaration of freedom?" John DeBeque asked. He was slouched in his chair, taking in the discussion.

Dr. Adamson said. "In the declaration of freedom, the rebels charged that The Divine One did not exist. They also contended that Michael, the creator and governor of over a million occupied spheres had unjustly assumed sovereignty in the name of this hypothetical Divine One. They attacked the celestial Journey, contending that far too much time and energy was being spent on a scheme that led to a presumed goal of attaining Paradise, the home of a non-existent God. Individual self-determination, equality of all beings, and denial of universe structure were the basis of their declaration."

"Sounds like the Declaration of Independence," deBeque said.

"Yes," Dr. Adamson said, "in some ways, it does — with two important distinctions. The Declaration of Independence of the United States was made in opposition to oppression by other humans; the declaration of freedom made by the rebels was against the vast hierarchy of the cosmos, against beings who had lived for billions of years, beings of incredible wisdom and power, against the very creator of the rebels. That is quite different from rebelling in opposition to other humans who seek to suppress you. Also, the United States' Declaration of Independence did not deny the existence of God; it embraced it."

"So what happened to the rebels?"

"The affairs of the universe move slowly," Dr. Adamson said. "So slowly that even I have trouble comprehending. It took two-hundred-thousand years for the rebels to be completely brought under control."

"But I thought the universe authorities were so powerful," deBeque said.

"Powerful, yes, but also wise enough to wait and see if the rebels would recant. In time, many of them did re-embrace the Grand Plan."

"But our ancestors were left with a real mess," deBeque said. "Sounds to me like we got the short end of the stick."

"John, despite the uprising, the celestial Journey remained intact. Those that chose to participate in it were, and are, welcomed and well cared for. If you can come to understand that this mortal life is but the forerunner of things to come, you will see that the circumstances of your life here matters little. What matters is what you do with what you have been given. If you see this life as the first step of the celestial Journey, if you see this world as an integral part of a interdependent, complex universe, then the residual effects of an uprising of two hundred thousand years ago fades away.

"What matters is that you live a life based on truth, cosmic truth, not the clouded truth promoted by a self-absorbed few who would dominate you, who would re-write history for their own ends. What matters is that you discover the spirit within you, listen to it, and develop your soul accordingly. Those humans who would dominate this planet are playing according to the declaration of freedom made by the rebels of two hundred thousand years ago. The game of power, greed, and violence is a very old game. Cosmic truth helps you see beyond these old ways of behaving.

"As regards the rebels, the forces of evil, if you will, they are in no way equal to the forces of good, not even close. I hope that I can help you see that the overwhelming posture of the universe is good, from The Divine One to the spark of that same God that dwells within you, from distant galaxies to the smallest sub-atomic particle, from the first moments of the universe of time and space to the eternal future. The Divine One is a God of love. Such evil as exists, within the ranks of mortals, is but a small dark dot on the otherwise white canvas of the cosmos."

Dr. Adamson paused to make sure Ryan and John deBeque were following his explanation. Ryan nodded that he was following. John shrugged his acknowledgement.

"You see the legacy of the declaration of freedom everywhere," Dr. Adamson said. "Their legacy is the diaphanous cocoon within which you try to function, a cocoon that masks your true self. People are self-involved, concerned about taking care of themselves, isolated in cocoons, focused on the present. Almost no one acts as if The Divine One exists, and few really treat others as their brothers and sisters. Yet, it is the celestial Journey for which the entire universe of space and time was created — as a stage upon which your ascendancy to The Divine One is played out. It is the only reason you were given life. A life based on anything else is wasted."

Ryan was taken back by Dr. Adamson's uncompromising

words. He saw their implications. He also noted that John deBeque was struggling even more. Ethete and Sarah sat with closed eyes. Ryan felt sure, that among the mortals at this table, Sarah alone had lived the last few months with the Grand Plan of the universe uppermost in her mind.

"Sounds to me like celestials want to run everything," deBeque said.

"Celestials do run everything," Dr. Adamson said. "Beyond this planet, the universe is organized and highly structured. Celestials administer this galaxy, and the other occupied galaxies."

"So what about my freedom?"

"You may believe you have freedom to do as you please, but in the final analysis, you have the freedom to follow the celestial Journey, or not. It is your ultimate choice.

"How can you say you have freedom, when you do not know the whole truth? True freedom can come only after you come to rely on the larger truth. True freedom comes with giving to your brothers and sisters that which they need, with helping to evolve this planet to a place of enlightenment.

"Nor may you tamper with the free choice of another. The cabal for which you used to work seeks to perpetuate the rebellion's self-centered declaration. They would institute a world government based on violence and power."

"I don't see any celestial world government," deBeque said.

"At the moment, the celestial government is largely invisible. Because of the uprising and my great grandparents' default, your world has been left without a visible superhuman government. If the uprising had not occurred, your world would not have been subjected to two hundred thousand years of lies about the true nature of the universe — lies that have become ingrained in every culture, lies that have resulted in the façade behind which you hide. If my great-grandparents had not defaulted, they would now head your world government, a government that would have peacefully evolved over the last forty thousand years.

"In place of such a government you now have powerful men vying for control, imposing their desires on others — using economic force, using violent methods. In place of such a government you have intraplanetaries like myself, millions of celestials, and, more recently, many off-planet mortals. All of us are trying to nudge this world to a place of enlightenment, and do it before it self-destructs."

"That's not exactly an optimistic picture," Ryan said. He thought of the resources of the power elite arraigned against the group at this table, a power elite dedicated to their own self-preservation and aggrandizement. He though of the abuses to the planet's ecosystem due to environmental pollution, global warming, and resource depletion. His former company, Sanitas Technologies, had been at the forefront of reporting on these.

"This planet is an aberration in the otherwise friendly, organized universe," Sarah said. "Vast numbers of non-human conscious life forms are ready to assist the positive transition of this sphere. It is a race to see whether an enlarged awareness can overcome the forces of greed. Be pleased that you are aware of the larger truth. For in the end, the peace of the cosmos will prevail. What we are struggling with is the potential of an intervening dark time, or worse the destruction of the planet."

"Think of the highly evolved being you will be a million years from now," Dr. Adamson said, "think of the example you can set for those who struggle on this sphere, think of the wisdom you can impart to other struggling planets."

These last words, like the charge from Michael's celestial messenger humbled Ryan. He felt his body relax, felt his shoulders sink, felt himself center inward on the spirit at his core, felt his resolve to continue reinforced.

"This sounds to me like the story of Atlantis," John deBeque said.

Dr. Adamson smiled. "Yes, the legend of Atlantis is a mixture of the memory the first garden, which did submerge beneath the sea, and that wonderful, highly advanced city of the long-ago planetary authorities. If either of these advanced civilizations had persisted, this planet would already be a full member of the universe."

"So the stories about extraplanetary beings mating with our ancestors are true?" Ryan asked.

"Not all of those assertions are factual," Dr. Adamson said. "It is true that Earth-human carry genetic fabric from more than one off-planet source."

"And stories about elves and fairies?"

Dr. Adamson grinned. "My errant brothers and sisters."

"So who's this Michael?" John deBeque asked.

"Michael is the ruler of this portion of the galaxy." Dr. Adamson's face took on a serious cast. "Along with a host of celestials, many of whom he created, he oversees more than a million planets that are inhabited by intelligent, free-choice mortals."

It was 2:30 AM when Dr. Adamson bid the group a good night. The two Earth-humans and the two from Phantia straggled to their sleeping quarters. Ryan wondered how long John deBeque would last at Harmony.

America is a vast conspiracy to make you happy.

— JOHN UPDIKE

EIGHTEEN

"Well, they're off the front page." Delta Kingman rubbed his hands together in a confident gesture.

It was 10:00 AM on the East Coast. Kingman sat in Warren Ophir's office at DIA. It was a rather plain office, standard government-issue furniture, bare walls. Other than a few subordinates, few people ever visited. When one ran a black op, one did not advertise that they controlled a budget worth billions.

Among his other tasks, Ophir directed a team of special operatives who were the first at the crash of any alien craft — the, so called, "Men in Black" — and another team who intimidated people in the name of "National Security." What was most unusual about these operatives was that the government did not employ them; rather they were paid and directed by a private intelligence organization indirectly owned by the World League. This allowed maximum flexibility, virtually zero accountability, and pay scales comparable to commercial firms.

Terrorist attacks, continued military action in the Middle East, and people's fears had enabled the World League, and its affiliates, to increase their grip on certain vital areas. Working through the organizations in which some of their people surreptitiously resided, they had made sure those organizations had excuses to control the personal freedoms of people in the United States. Patterning themselves after these creeping restrictions, many foreign governments had tightened controls on their populations.

241

The financial world, working in cooperation with government authorities, had ostensibly closed the routes for all but the cleanest of money. This, of course, left room for favored fund managers, such as Jonathan Olson, to make choice investments. It also left room for the operatives of the intelligence affiliates to continue their highly profitable ventures in illegal drugs.

Legitimate branches of law enforcement took advantage of curtailed citizens' rights against search, seizure, and unlawful detention. What had been circumspect monitoring of communications and the Internet had now become routine. To pursue their nefarious ends, the affiliates of the World League had only to tap into these new operating procedures.

Against this background, the appearance of the two extraterrestrials, and now the death of one, had made but a small impact. The media affiliates had managed the potentially damaging information well. Most people were back to worrying about their everyday lives. The blackout of information about the extraterrestrials had effectively blunted Sarah Smith's ability to deliver her message to all but those with whom she maintained personal contact.

"I think that one out in the desert still bears watching," Kingman said. "I don't think we've heard the last from her."

Warren Ophir relished these one-on-one sessions with one of the triad for the World League. It enabled him to impact the League's direction, and to demonstrate his usefulness based on knowledge he regularly collected from the members of the intelligence affiliates.

To Ophir the situation was like one of those five hundred piece puzzles: The pieces fit, but it took time to find the right one. His aunt, who had raised him when his mother disowned him, had done puzzles with him. That was one the few happy memories he had of his school years.

The other memories were not so nice. A father who died when he was ten. His mother's successions of wealthy playboy friends. He had eventually mastered the city neighborhood to which his mother had banished him, and he had avoided drugs, except those he sold to others. The only way he had made it to this lofty position was his mind — it was the one worthwhile gift his father had given him. His mind had led him to finish high school, go to college, and complete a stint in the military as an officer. His mind had allowed him to dispel those awful teenage years.

Well, he was almost there; he was almost at the top. Just one push on Kingman and he'd be sitting in the other's chair. Just one push and he'd be the one calling the shots for the World League.

"We could disable Caesar." Ophir tossed out the suggestion anticipating Kingman's reaction. Part of what Ophir did in any circumstances was float trial balloons. Sometimes, he got an unanticipated response; mostly he got expected replies.

"You're talking treason." Kingman reacted instantly. "I won't be a party to it."

Ophir studied the man's reaction — an anticipated answer, little new information. In his day Kingman had been a great military leader, dedicated, strong. He still harbored allegiances to the chain of command. If the time came to remove Caesar, it would be done without the ex-general's involvement.

He quickly changed the subject to his real interest. "How about Von Hedemann's idea," Ophir said. "Wipe out a bunch of UFOs; take out a couple of satellites in the process. Make it look like the Chinese are preparing to attack. A little escalation of tensions. I doubt that Caesar is ready for that one."

"Interesting, but dangerous. No telling how the aliens might react. I don't think anybody's ready for an attack from space."

"That's what I don't understand, why don't they come at us? We know they've got the capability. Why wait for us to copy their technology, to become a credible power? Why?"

"It's been going on for a long time." Kingman dismissed Ophir's concern. The former general had been party to UFO incidents long before Ophir became aware of the subject. "Making us aware of their presence, then backing off. Too bad the ones we've captured all died. Maybe they could have told us something. Now all we have is the word of those who say they're 'helping us.' I think the ETs that come zooming in here see we've developed some serious weapons; makes them skittish. They go around pretending they're all nice and peaceful, but I know they've got weapons. I can hardly wait to bust their pacifist asses."

"How about interrogating this so-called Sarah Smith?" Ophir asked.

"What did Steiger get from her?"

"The diary talks about his frustration. She insisted she wasn't technical. He had just given the go-ahead to start drugs when the diary ends. Must have been when she was rescued."

"What have your guys got on her?"

"Nothing. The whole gang pretty much stays underground. Just the usual Navajo crew coming and going."

"Any electronics?" Kingman asked.

"The listening devices our construction guys planted have been disabled — don't know how they found them. And our remote viewing and psychotronics don't work in their underground maze."

"Sounds like a dead end."

"Tuck this away, I'm keeping our tricksters active. Helps keep the natives restless. Maybe we can recruit a frightened Indian."

Kingman brushed off Ophir's last comment with a wave of his hand. The general, a man geared to direct confrontation, had never been a big advocate of the abduction scenario. But Ophir, the intelligence man, knew the impact that alien abductions had produced. After forty years, a whole segment of the population, from California to the East Coast, was convinced that aliens were hostile. Yes, he would keep his tricksters on the job.

"How is the deuce doing?" Warren Ophir asked.

"Talked to him last week."

"And?"

Delta Kingman eyed the intelligence man before replying. Only the League's triad was supposed to know the full list of their friends and operatives. Ophir knew that it irritated Kingman to know that he had discovered the identity of their most highly placed confederate. "I would characterize him as 'reluctant.'"

"But if called upon, he will act?"

"Let's just say the circumstances would have to be just right."

"Let's go back to Von Hedemann's idea." Ophir knew if he continued to surface bigger issues, he was likely to get a go-ahead on what he really wanted. "I have acquired a small nuclear device."

Kingman thought for a long time, then he said, "Could help keep the international situation off balance. Give Caesar something more to wrestle with, keep him and his lackey, Sam Wellborn, off us. I'll discuss it with the others."

Organized chaos increased Ophir's power, made it a little more likely that he would soon become one of the triad. And then, then he would create a chaos from which only the most powerful and ruthless would emerge, and then he had a good chance of becoming the unchallenged ruler of the world.

"Now I have something else," Kingman said. "Several of our best supporters in Congress are backing away. Any ideas?"

"Not off hand. Let me think about it."

Ophir was already aware of the situation, and had been thinking on it. He also had reports from his people on the President's staff that long private meetings were being held with a number of Senators and Congressmen. This was somewhat strange as they were the ones that would have generally opposed the new President's agenda. After the meetings, they had uniformly muted their criticism of the new administration. Ophir was in the process of cross-referencing these individuals against those that the media affiliates had compromised. But he was not ready to share any of this with Kingman.

Kingman said, "Do you suppose there's any more of those aliens around?"

"Hard to say. So far it's just the one, and, of course, Ryan Drake. As I say, we're watching and listening. If there are others, they'll make contact."

"What about Adamson?"

"What about him? My sources tell me he's been around forever. He's one of those intraplanetary critters. There's nothing anybody can do about him. Besides, he's harmless."

"Why not just terminate the female alien?"

"So you liked the way I did the other one, eh?" Ophir smiled. "Nice and clean, no tracks."

"Yeah, except you created a martyr. People are going to his memorial every day, flowers and all kinds of stuff. We don't need another one of those. Next time, just make them disappear."

"The last one did disappear," the intelligence man chuckled. "Didn't stop them from having a funeral service."

"Damn aliens, by gawd, I wish they'd go away and leave this planet to us."

"By the way, John deBeque has taken an unscheduled vacation," Ophir said.

"Unscheduled?"

"Yeah, left his secretary a note; didn't say where he was going. She says he got real upset when he found that his computer center had been moved while he was out of the office." Ophir laughed, "He walked in and there was just the tiny server for the International League left."

"Where'd he go?"

"Don't know, yet."

"You're working on it?"

"Yeah."

"Where's the equipment?" Kingman asked.

"We found a nice corner in the basement of the NSA complex. One of my guys'll keep tabs on it."

"I don't like that."

"So what do you suggest?"

"I'm thinking about a private facility, somewhere there's not a bunch of spooks nosing around."

Now that he had it, Ophir knew he could not allow the communications hub to be removed from under his control. If Kingman or one of the others of the triad took over, he would lose a vital means of spying on their activities.

Sarah Smith was chatting with the two reporters. It was a cold morning, and she sat in the rear seat of their sedan sipping the hot coffee she had brought. Earlier one of them had relayed a problem she was having with her boyfriend. He did not like the idea of her remaining out here in the desert.

The red Corvette skidded as it turned onto the gravel road leading to Harmony. It pulled up next to where they sat talking. From her vantage point Sarah could not see the driver until he alighted.

His blonde hair was long and shaggy. He was taller than she, probably five inches over six feet, broad shoulders, a thin waist, a physically fit man. Wrap-around sunglasses hid his eyes, but when he turned to look directly at her and smile, there was no mistake. "J'Ms," she blurted out, pronouncing it like "Jarmin."

In one fluid motion Sarah was out of the car and into her

brother's outstretched arms.

The smell of his cologne filled her head, as she stepped back to survey him. This was a very different Ajax Johnson than the one who had left Harmony eighteen months before. The biggest change was the additional weight he carried, weight he had added in order to play professional football.

They had communicated mind-to-mind a few days ago, and she had remote viewed him as he told his team good bye. The coach and his teammates could not understand why he would give up such a promising career. Without him, they would have little chance to repeat their successful season.

A week ago, he had blanked her out, rebuffed her communications, and refused to allow her to remote view his space. She had replayed his final message over and over in her head: *'I'll see you at Harmony.'*

When Sarah turned, the two reporters were outside their car. "I want to introduce you to some friends," she said.

"Hi, I'm Ajax." He stepped forward and eagerly extended a hand to each of the women.

His words and hands were out before Sarah had a chance to say anything. Harmony's prodigal son had learned a lot from the spotlight of fame, from radio and television appearances.

"Are you who I think you are?" one reporter asked.

"I think we just got a scoop." The other slapped her leg with delight.

"This is the Ajax Johnson of football fame. This is also J'Ms, my brother. And, yes, he is from Phantia. You are ready to go public, aren't you?" Sarah asked with an older sister grin.

"I guess this is as good a place as any." Ajax motioned to the surrounding bleak landscape, the high façade of Fortress Mesa to the east, Black Mesa to the west. He had spent his first months here at Harmony, acclimating himself to the nuances of this planet's environment and culture.

For the next half hour, they talked. He answered questions about his extraplanetary origins, why he had played for the Chargers, and why he had decided to stop playing professional football. The two journalists were not sports reporters, but they had the instincts to know a great story when it was handed to them.

"So why wait until now?" the one reporter asked.

"Who's going to believe a guy living in San Diego? You people," he indicated the two reporters, "barely believe me when I'm standing next to an extraterrestrial hangout, next to my extraterrestrial sister."

"They went on one of Dr. Adamson's little trips to the Between worlds," Sarah said.

"Ah ha."

"And Sarah showed us Phantia," the other reporter said.

"Well, see what you can make out of my story," Ajax said. "If others want me, I'll be right here."

When Ajax entered Harmony's main underground room, he encountered Ethete seated alone at the long dining table. Sarah watched as the dark haired Phantian remained sitting, barely acknowledging him.

Ajax dropped the bags he was carrying and went around to where she sat. "Hi."

She stood and slapped his face. "Why did you let this happen to me?"

He grabbed her arm. "Hey, you made your choice. You wouldn't listen to me."

"But you saw what those drugs were doing to me. You didn't stop it." Ethete struggled to free her arm.

"I tried, but you weren't interested." Ajax grabbed her other arm before she could strike.

"You could have forced me to stop. But no, you were too busy playing football."

The two of them were glowering at each other when John deBeque entered the room. He saw a stranger holding Ethete's arms and rushed to her defense. "Let go of her."

"I don't know who you are, but stay out of this," Ajax said without turning to deBeque. "This is between me and my partner?"

"Partner?" DeBeque stepped back.

"Yeah, we came a long ways together."

"You're not my partner any more," Ethete said and wrenched her arms loose.

At that point Sarah intervened. "John, I'd like you to meet my brother. This is Ajax Johnson."

"Ajax, this is John deBeque. He is staying with us to learn about the cosmic paradigm, and how it produces 'high minded' people."

The two shook hands. If John deBeque recognized the Ajax Johnson of football fame, he said nothing.

"Why don't you let me show you to your room?" Sarah said.

"I know where my room is."

"Ajax, I said let me show you to your room."

The star receiver for the San Diego Chargers walked over and picked up his bags. Without another word he headed for the door to the living quarters. Sarah followed him out of the dining hall.

It took only a few hours for reporters and broadcast vans, with giant rooftop dishes, to gather at Harmony's front gate. Lacking any wire or cellular connections in this remote area, their only recourse was satellite links. Several tried to sneak into Harmony's property but the Navajo staff chased them off. From their position at the front gate, the media could see only the top of the geodesic dome. They clamored for Ajax to make an appearance.

By evening, Ajax Johnson had conducted a formal news conference, had agreed to a book deal, and had been interviewed on two national sports talk shows.

"Do you feel like you're in any danger?" one reporter asked.

"If they wish to take my life," Ajax replied, "I would willingly give it to them. My mission is what is important. Once you embrace the celestial Journey, you no longer fear for your mortal body — it is to be used for a greater good."

With the exception of Sarah, who Ajax introduced as his sister, the other residents of Harmony remained inside. With live feed going to the networks, the news about "Ajax Johnson the ET" was broadcast before the media affiliates could stop it. The men and women of the Navajo staff were the only people allowed into the underground complex; they did not speak to the reporters.

Sarah reported that a sedan and a van, both black and both definitely not part of the media, had joined the throng at the gate. By remote viewing them she determined that the men in the van were using sophisticated electronic monitoring equipment to scan Harmony, to monitor all conversations outside the underground facility, and they were in constant communications via satellite with others. Based on their reaction to a brief chat she had with Ajax in the parking lot, she said that they appeared to be able to pick up conversations from sensors placed around the grounds of Harmony. Had they heard anything that gave them cause to invade the underground facility?

Men who try to do something and fail are infinitely better than those who try to do nothing and succeed.

— LLOYD JONES

NINETEEN

"Can you believe this?" Delta Kingman slammed the newspaper on Warren Ophir's desk. The headline read, SUPERSTAR ADMITS HE'S ALIEN.

Unannounced, the retired general had burst into his office a few moments after 10:00 AM. With all the supposed security at the DIA's building, Ophir was always puzzled at the way in which the ex-general was able to move so easily within this facility.

"Poor Chargers," Ophir chuckled. "The NFL will probably take their AFC championship away from them."

"Screw the Chargers. This wasn't supposed to happen." Delta Kingman shook a large finger at Ophir. His face had the ruddy glow of anger. "You were supposed to keep track of these goddamned aliens."

"Do you know what this means?" Kingman tossed out comments as he paced the small room.

"A whole new round of inquiries into anything alien.

"Ajax Johnson was big news as a football player.

"Ajax Johnson the alien is even bigger.

"Goddamn it all.

"Damn you.

He turned a ruddy face to Ophir. "So how are we going to get him off the front page?"

"My atomic's ready to roll," Ophir said. "Just say the word.

251

We can put something different on page one."

Kingman glowered at him, then slowly replied. "All right, this does it for me," he pointed to the headline. "I'll get the others to agree."

He walked toward the door, then turned and asked, "Any word on deBeque?"

"Nothing." Ophir was immediately worried that his response had been a little too quick. He watched Kingman to see if the ex-general reacted. There was no twitch at the edge of his mouth signaling he was suspicious.

Through rental car records, Ophir's people had tracked deBeque to Philadelphia. Then they had lost his trail. But just this morning, one of his analysts had found that John deBeque had used his driver's license to rent a car in Phoenix. Ophir's man was headed to Phoenix to question the rental car company.

"His absence is worrying me, too," Ophir said. "Do you suppose somebody took him out in revenge for Steiger?"

"Who loved Ernest Steiger that much?"

"Don't know, but I'm pursuing that angle."

"Any good news?" Kingman paused in the doorway.

"I've seen some reports about unusual seismic activity all around the Pacific Rim, lots of small tremors. The people at NEIC want to warn the public that it might be signaling major quakes. I've told them to sit on it."

"Good. That's the sort of thing that could distract people — take their minds off Ajax Johnson." As Kingman shut the door to Ophir's office, he said, "I'll get back to you on the nuke."

The automobile's headlights illuminated the deserted road. Sarah Smith and Ryan Drake were traveling north on AZ 591, a gravel road that connected to US 160 at Kayenta. No other vehicles were in sight; it was 11:30 PM. Thinking that it would be less identifiable than Ryan's Jeep, they had taken the green Ford Taurus, one of the vehicles that belonged to Harmony.

Driving down this deserted road, late at night, made Ryan realize how much of his life was based on trust. Tonight he trusted that no animal, no huge boulder, no unforeseen anything would impede the progress of his vehicle. Tonight he trusted that Sarah would lead him through the promised adventure. Yes, trust was one of life's most valuable ingredients.

Although they had little hope of evading anyone using sophisticated equipment, they had turned off AZ 59, the paved road that ran north and south a mile to the west of Harmony and connected to US 160. In addition to the media's renewed interest in everyone's movements, he knew that the World League was monitoring the whereabouts of Ajax Johnson. Ryan was surprised that they had not tried to storm Harmony.

Puffy cumulus clouds filled the night sky. It was too much to hope for that they might interrupt any spy satellite's tracking of their route.

'John has really come around,' Ryan communicated. *'I think he's ready to give the media a dose of real insider truth.'*

When John deBeque was not engrossed with the others, he and Ryan had worked their way through the disclosures contained in Ernest Steiger's diary. At first deBeque had been merely curious. But as he read further, and as Sarah, Dr. Adamson, and Ethete helped him see the truth of the cosmic paradigm, he had moved from curious to crusader. He was able to explain certain remarks with which Ryan had struggled. John deBeque was now prepared to correct the misinformation, lies, and manipulations he had so recently helped to construct.

'He is also occupied with Ethete,' Sarah communicated.

Ryan had noted that Ethete was very careful to give the impression that Ajax Johnson and she were only teammates. The implication was that they had not been intimately involved, and that John and she could be.

John deBeque had now been at Harmony for ten days. One of Harmony's Navajo workers had taken his car soon after he arrived and had returned it to Phoenix the next morning. He had not left the underground facility. With no wire or cell phone available, Ryan was quite sure the young man had not contacted the media affiliates, or anyone else in his old office.

John had told Ryan that he had left his secretary a note saying that he was taking an unplanned trip to visit relatives. It was a suspicious action; people in his profession did not take unplanned trips.

After a week of watching the young man, Ryan had decided

that John's presence was more than a knee-jerk reaction to Peter's funeral. After a day and a half of resisting their explanations, he had finally caved in and began to demonstrate a genuine interest in everything.

The biggest surprise for Ryan was deBeque's lack of insight into the World League. Yes, he had been the Secretary of the International League, and he had been part of the media affiliates, or thought he had been. He still wasn't sure which of his media contacts were members of the media affiliates, or even if they knew about the media affiliates. As deBeque poured through the pages of his stepfather's diary, it made him angry. He became increasingly determined to set it right.

He had told Ryan that his primary source of information was from a man known to him as Warren Ophir. Ophir had told deBeque that he worked for the Central Intelligence Agency. When he had questions, he contacted Ophir by leaving a message at a phone that only he answered.

When deBeque read pages from Steiger's diary, the young man was truly startled. For the first time, he saw himself as an unwitting cog in the work of the World League. He read about men who he thought were members of the cordial International League, but were really members of the sinister World League. He read how Ernest Steiger had manipulated him into his job so that he, Steiger, could keep track of who was doing what. And he saw that Warren Ophir worked for the DIA, not the CIA, and in reality Ophir ran a program within DIA that even his superiors knew nothing about.

On the one hand he was disappointed that they had not trusted him with their secrets. On the other, he was now grateful they had not engulfed him further in their nefarious work.

'*He appears to be won over,*' Ryan communicated. He knew that riding in a car for an hour without saying anything had undoubtedly aroused the suspicions of those tracking them. But he was not going to chance giving anyone a hint of John deBeque's whereabouts.

'To the mission, or to Ethete?'

'You have questions?'

'He has yet to prove himself.'

'*I think he's just coming out of shock. It took me weeks to feel nor-*

mal. I watched Aza and Tom Ertl after you pictioned for them. They were barely able to function. I think one of the major values of the Cosmic Paradigm Center will be as a recovery site.'

Sarah's smile was visible in the lights from the dash. 'So you still think of me as an extraterrestrial?'

'Yes and no. I see that you are far advanced beyond people like me. Your level of consciousness is something I can only hope to achieve. I also see a beautiful woman, a beautiful woman who I have come to love.'

Sarah reached across and gently placed her hand on his thigh. 'Ryan, I also love you. And I think you are more advanced than you give yourself credit for.'

They rode through the town of Kayenta without further communications. Neon signs illuminated the main commercial area along US 160. TEEDIUDEEH Shopping Center. 35 MPH. Ryan paused once to allow a scrawny reservation dog to cross before them. The curbed, four-lane highway was an improvement over the dirt sidewalks when he had first visited here in 1970, as a guest at Ben Tsotsie's parents' home.

Beyond the streetlights along the main road, the town lay in darkness. Ryan knew that beyond this fancy new lighting, Ben Tsotsie's Navajo family, Ryan's earthly brothers and sisters, lived on dirt streets, in minimal housing provided by the Federal Government.

Sarah communicated, 'I believe John will never return to being the media affiliates' information manipulator. What he will do next is less predictable.'

'I loved his story about being denied information about the computers at his office. He was sitting on top of the World League's data communications center, and he didn't realize it.'

'Yes, and that story about Ernest Steiger, his stepfather, coming out of his coma.'

'He's really been jerked around,' Ryan communicated. 'The disinformation he received about you and Peter, the whole UFO cover-up. Layers and layers of intrigue and manipulations, he thought the media affiliates was as deep as it went.'

'I feel sorry for him.'

'Don't feel too bad; he had a hand in all this. Things just don't happen that easily, unless you're willing to look the other way, willing to *compromise your ideals.'*

"We are, after all, totally responsible for what happens to each of us." Ryan switched to verbal conversation; he still was not completely comfortable with communicating mind-to-mind. When he saw Sarah stare at him, he said, "I need a break."

'Ryan, it is most important that you focus on communicating mind-to-mind. Please stay with it a little longer.'

He nodded that he had understood her, then communicated, *'Whenever he surfaces, I think he'll be in jeopardy. The men from the League will brand him as a traitor. I have no doubt they'll target him.'*

'As they tried to kill you?'

'Yes, but even more so.' As Ryan stretched an arm against the top of the sedan, he concentrated on using mind-to-mind communications. *'John deBeque is not a high visibility individual. Killing him will not raise the questions that surrounded my accident.'* The Colorado State Patrol was still investigating the circumstances surrounding the auto accidents of Peter Jones and Ryan Drake. They had established that there was no Hubble Plumbing in the Denver area.

Sarah had told him little about what to expect tonight, only that it was an important meeting. The overseerers of the planet were concerned about an impending event. She had advised him to dress warmly as they would be outside for a time.

A full moon, peeking from between the thick clouds, softly illuminated their desert surroundings. The road gently twisted through a valley surrounded by tall mesas. Not far north of Kayenta, the cone of an extinct volcano thrust itself from the valley floor. Ryan was reminded of Shiprock, in New Mexico. There, a larger version of this rock formation had guided both Native Americans and early pioneers. He also remembered Lobo and how Sarah, Peter, and he had narrowly escaped from the authorities in the town of Shiprock. That was four months ago.

Soon after they crossed the Utah state line, Ryan turned the car east on the paved road into Monument Valley. Plywood shacks, the home of Navajo souvenir vendors, dotted both sides of the road. Wood smoke rose from two of them. In the winter, few of these shops would be open to tourists. For some families, these sales of jewelry and snacks provided their only source of income beyond the monthly handouts from the U.S. government.

The full moon, now at its zenith, peeked though the cloud cover and illuminated one of the two massive buttes guarding the entrance to Monument Valley. It was as if they were being welcomed.

The thickness, hardness, and homogeneity of the sandstone layer in this area had created buttes like no others in the world. Their vertical sides jutted five hundred feet above the surrounding desert. And these were just the guardians at the entrance of the Navajo Tribal Park.

Ryan could just make out the visitors' center at the end of the road. Moonlight, reflecting off the asphalt ribbon that stretched before them, beckoned them forward. Always on the lookout for grazing wildlife, Ryan drove down the middle of the deserted two-lane road.

They approached the gate at the entrance and slowed. A steel barricade blocked their way. The sign on it read: PARK HOURS 7:00 AM TO 8:00 PM. Except for locals who dwelt within the park, or an occasional movie shoot, after hours visitors were excluded.

As if detecting their presence, the metal arms swung open allowing them to pass, then silently closed behind them. Ryan had the feeling that they had just entered an area protected by some unseen presence.

"Here we are safe from being overheard," Sarah said.

"It feels good to talk again." He took a deep breath and exhaled slowly.

"Go there," Sarah pointed to the left.

They drove through the parking lot at the visitor's center. During the day, vehicles belonging to tourists and tour buses would occupy the spaces. He guided the car onto the narrow dirt road that led deeper into the park. Ryan had navigated the road before, but this was his first nighttime experience. He maneuvered through the two well-worn hairpin turns and the dark shadows beneath the overhang on the side of the road. He would have felt better behind the wheel of his Jeep; the road was barely manageable in a low-slung automobile.

As if some powerful wind had suddenly pushed away the overcast, the sky above them opened, and stars were visible. Looking in other directions, the more-or-less solid cloud cover was still in place. The moon, riding high in the northern sky, illuminated the majesty of Monument Valley.

For a brief moment, when he was able to take his eyes off the deeply rutted road, he saw Mitten One Butte jutting from the floor of the valley. The sheer walls of its vertical cleavage, illuminated in moonlight, glowed without their usual terra cotta hue. In daylight, Monument Valley was impressive, the most photographed site in America. At night it was mysterious, filled with shadows and dark recesses. Ryan returned his attention to the rough road.

When they reached the valley floor, Sarah said, "Turn in here." She pointed to a small sign next to the road, PRIVATE HOME, NO TRESPASSING.

Now their passage was along two ruts amidst miles of sagebrush. Viewed from the Park's overlook, it was the route to the home of a Navajo sheepherder. Ryan drove around a series of potholes and proceeded forward. As they bounced along, weeds scraped the underside of the car and pebbles pinged against it.

"Stop here." Sarah indicated a spot to the side of the road.

She reached into the back seat for her fur lined parka and gloves. Both of them wore hiking boots.

"Come with me." She sprang out of the car and headed into the sagebrush.

The path you're on is made by walking it.

— Antonio Machado

TWENTY

Ryan followed blonde hair glistening in the moonlight. He caught a faint whiff of Sarah's vanilla lotion. Sagebrush grabbed at his jeans as they bashed their way through thick clumps of it.

After a hundred yards, they emerged into a flat area. In the dim light, he could see that the bushes had been flattened, almost as if a heavy object rested on them.

Ryan felt a cold breeze. Both Sarah and he buttoned up and pulled on gloves.

Sarah beckoned to him. After a brief embrace, she moved to his side. They stood, hand in hand, watching the splendor of the night sky.

Dr. Adamson joined them. "Let us come together — the representatives of humans from this planet, of extraplanetary residents, and of its permanent occupants." After they had formed a tight circle, Sarah and the white-haired intraplanetary closed their eyes; following their example, Ryan did likewise.

After they stood this way for a few moments, Ryan became warm. He felt Sarah shed first her gloves, then her coat. He opened his eyes and did the same.

Looking upward, Ryan saw the moon and stars, but they were distorted. It was as if he were looking through a window frosted with crystals. The moon was no longer quite round. The stars had squiggly patterns to them. And there was no wind.

As Sarah squeezed his bare hand, he noted that she was trembling with excitement. He could see her comely face. Perfectly aligned white teeth, framed by a wide smile, glistened in the moonlight. Her expectant eyes darted about, like those of a child on Christmas morning.

In an instant, tiny blue-white lights appeared all around them.

In another instant, the extraterrestrial craft that had enveloped them materialized.

Ryan found himself in a domed room. Beings of many sizes and shapes were communicating in a jumble of phrases and thoughts that flooded his mind. He stared at the extraplanetary beings; most did not resemble humans. They were all different, all exceedingly handsome, and all humanoids. One or two resembled the stereotype greys with their dark almond eyes; others he could not have imagined. The creators of Star Trek and Star Wars would be envious of the magnificent specimens arranged here. He saw the tall praying mantis whom he had encountered in the desert outside Phoenix.

'*This is an emissary craft from the overseers of this planet.*' Sarah touched his arm. '*All who have a vested interest in the fate of this sphere are represented.*'

"Wow." Ryan said. He was too overwhelmed to communicate.

His utterance caused a tall extraterrestrial to turn in his direction. The life form with green eyes towered over Ryan.

He gasped.

Then he looked harder and fine features came into focus. He, or she, wore a tailored jacket and pants, and was extraordinarily handsome. The reptilian visage did not repulse Ryan, but the reality of this moment set his heart to pounding.

'*You are Ryan Drake, yes?*'

Ryan concentrated very hard and communicated, '*Yes.*'

The extraplanetary being turned away.

Dr. Adamson walked to the far side of the area and spoke to a small being. Not more than three feet tall, and looking very old, he could easily have been a painter's model for a wise old elf. Dr. Adamson seemed to know him well. The short being seemed quite agitated about something.

'*He is the chief of this planet's life carriers,*' Sarah communicated. '*He was here long before Dr. Adamson.*'

Then Ryan saw him, a magnificent being, robed in white. He

was more materialized than he had been in the shower stall, but he still seemed to float above the surface on which Ryan stood. The celestial ambassador turned to face him. *'Welcome, Ryan Drake.'*

Ryan was too overcome to speak or communicate. He felt a surge of overwhelming love fill his heart. This was the same being who had appeared to him as he showered in his hotel room in Cambridge, Massachusetts three months ago. This was the celestial messenger from Michael to whom he had made a commitment, a commitment to help lead a movement that would transform his world.

'You have accomplished much since we last spoke. We are pleased.' The celestial ambassador then turned to greet others.

He felt a tug on his hand. Sarah indicated a seat within the circle of comfortable chairs. He sat down next to her. Dr. Adamson came and sat on his other side.

A young woman with red hair, wearing jeans and a blue-checkered shirt, came and sat on the other side of Dr. Adamson. She looked familiar.

'Who is that?' Ryan communicated to Sarah.

'A surprise.'

'She looks so much like Danielle.'

'Yes.'

Calling Ryan's attention to the celestial at the center of the space, Dr. Adamson communicated, *'Michael sends his emissary because he is occupied with the affairs of several million other planets.'*

'Other planets have problems too?'

'Even enlightened planets have their problems, and each of his millions are somewhat different.'

As the others took their places, the celestial ambassador remained standing in the center of the circle. In a directive to all, he communicated, *'We are gathered here to receive your assessment of the situation'*

The tall reptilian promptly stood and communicated, *'Your eminence, I wish to state my disgust with the Earth-humans. I think I speak for many at this gathering.'*

The emissary recognized the speaker and motioned for him to continue.

'Over the past two hundred years Earth-humans have succeeded in

fouling the air of this sphere, almost beyond repair. In a process that is now escalating out of control, the planet's protective shield has been damaged, its store of water is melting at an unprecedented rate, sea levels are rising, and disaster looms. We recommend immediate intervention to shut down all forms of hydrocarbon pollution.'

Ryan was amazed that he could understand these communications. Apparently, everyone was using a universal language that transcended individual spoken words. No wonder Sarah had been so keen on his learning to communicate mind-to-mind. He was quite sure the ideas were not being expressed in English, yet he thought he comprehended most of what was transpiring.

'*Furthermore,*' the reptilian humanoid continued, '*we recommend intervention to capture all nuclear weapons and to decommission them. We have tracked such devices since their manufacture and are quite certain we can account for all.*'

'*We further recommend that we immediately establish a planetary government. This race has shown that it is unable to grow beyond its cycle of fear and violence. Repeatedly they have slipped backward just before emerging into the new paradigm, before joining with the enlightened community of the universe. We do not foresee any improvement in conditions unless outside assistance is employed. With all due respect to my colleagues from other worlds, and for reasons not understood, their program of guidance and nurturing has not worked over the last ten thousand years. I see the Earth-humans treating each other as badly as they did when they were little more than animals.*

'*As regards the disaster that looms, it is too late to prevent it. If a planetary government were quickly empowered, it could alleviate some of the aftermath.*'

The tall reptilian returned to his seat. Ryan saw several heads nod in support of his position. Until this moment, he had not understood the degree of involvement of extraplanetary beings in the affairs of his planet. They knew where every nuclear device was located? He wasn't sure that the makers of the devices knew that.

'*There are many who agree with his position,*' Dr. Adamson communicated to Ryan. '*They see our planet as a laggard within the universe. What should have been accomplished thousands of years ago is still left unfinished. Our advances in technology have far outstripped our spiritual maturation.*'

'*So is he an evil alien?*' Ryan had read about those who were trying to conquer Earth for their own purposes.

'*Far from it, he and his allies wish only that this planet would mature. But as you see, their patience is wearing thin. The rogues who seek their own advantage by conspiring with the cabal are outlaws, a tiny fraction of the non-human conscious life forms who are involved with this planet. They were invited, but declined to attend this gathering.*'

'*How can they decline?*'

'*All mortals have free choice.*'

'*Your eminence, I would like to speak for others among us,*' a tall, very human-like being stood. He had been seated in a sector of the circle next to two shimmering beings who resembled the humans of Earth. In Ryan's opinion, no one else in the room could walk the streets of Earth unnoticed, as did Sarah or Dr. Adamson. The life carrier who Dr. Adamson had spoken with sat within that cluster.

Sarah must have noticed his staring for she communicated, '*The two seated are pure spirits, celestials. Some of your people would call them angels. They represent the one billion who attend to the needs of mortals of this planet. Like the celestial ambassador, they are visible to you within this space, but they are never material. The one standing works closely with Dr. Adamson.*'

'*You may address the assembly.*' When the celestial ambassador pronounced the non-resident life form's name, it had most closely sounded like "Jasper," but Ryan was sure it was not an Earthly name. Apparently not every word translated into something that Ryan could understand.

'*We believe that any interference in the affairs of this planet cannot succeed. As all of us who have helped for eons know, the people of this sphere are most independent, a lingering result of the rebellion. In the tradition of their reliance on violence, we believe they will physically resist any attempt to force a government upon them. Their likely reactions to outside direction will only serve to reinforce this behavior.*

'*More important than their instinctual reaction, if we were to successfully intervene, they would become overly dependent upon us. The only way in which they can grow and take their rightful place in the cosmos is through their own efforts, through their own free choice decisions. We foresee that the full measure of the maturation process may take centuries. But then, we have already been at it for centuries.*' He motioned to

263

those who sat on either side of him. *'While we restrain their technology and weapons, we work to heal this planet through empathy, love, and forgiveness. We call on the higher celestial powers to soften the hearts of those Earth-humans who oppose the path to awakening, and to strengthen the hearts and wills of those who would lead us into the light.*

'I would now address an event of immense proportions, and of immediate concern.'

'What event is he referring to?' Ryan communicated to Dr. Adamson.

'You will learn.'

'One of the things we are here this night to discuss is the extent to which it is possible to influence its outcome. In the past, the efforts of my race have saved many of this planet from natural disasters. But the magnitude of this pending event is beyond our scope. I request that the planetary energy controllers be directed to prevent its occurrence.'

'The energy controllers are not here,' Sarah communicated. *'They are living energy and gravity orchestrators who are strategically positioned around Earth. Theirs is a full time job. They implement the laws of physics dictated by The Divine One.'*

'We are all aware of your efforts to nurture this world, and thank you,' the celestial ambassador communicated to Jasper. *'On behalf of Michael, we wish to express our deep appreciation for the risks that you and all your comrades take with your continued presence here.'*

Extending his arms to the others in the room, he communicated, *'We do understand that this sphere's natural evolutionary pattern has been repeatedly interrupted. Even the legacy of Michael's bestowal has yet to work itself out. Nonetheless, each millennium the consciousness of the mortals of this planet evolves. At the same time we are well aware of the continued degradation of the planet's biosphere, and understand that it has reached a place where disastrous results loom. As has been expressed here, this planet is truly at a critical juncture.*

'I now ask Dr. Adamson for his opinion.'

The white-haired intraplanetary stood and collected his thoughts. *'As you know I have labored for many ages with my charges. It has been challenging. Despite the many problems of my planet, its lack of maturity, its contorted sense of free will, and its stubbornness, please bear in mind the incredibly tough graduates that arrive on the Between worlds. Where else can we harvest such beings? I oppose any attempt to impose a* planetary government on my people. It saddens me deeply to say it, but I believe we must let events take their course. How else can the consequences of my people's actions be demonstrated?'

'J'Li D'Rona, new resident of this sphere, what do you say?'

For a moment it puzzled him who the celestial had addressed. Then his solar plexus tightened into a knot as Ryan realized he too would be called upon to make a statement. What he might say in the next few minutes could affect an entire planet. Was he up to the task? He had no training in international diplomacy, let alone interplanetary diplomacy. Why had he ever agreed to be part of transforming his planet?

Sarah rose and communicated, *'I have lived among the people of Earth for only a short time. I see how they struggle without the benefit of a world government and without the wisdom of the celestial overseerers. Yet there are those among them that are searching out a higher way to live.*

'My charter was to live among them, setting an example. For a variety of reasons, this has been most difficult, and I have been able to influence but a few. Others of my team have had marginally better success. Despite all of this, I remain optimistic.

'I do not think we should force solutions upon the people of this planet. And, if natural laws are not to be abridged, I can accept the consequences. However, I would like to warn as many as possible of the impending disaster.'

Sarah's statement was followed by a babble of comments. Some agreed with her, some opposed. The celestial ambassador called for quiet.

'Thank you, noble representative from Phantia, we all acknowledge the sacrifices you have made to live among the mortals of this sphere." He next motioned to Ryan. *'And you, Ryan Drake, resident of Earth. How say you?'*

Ryan cast a brief look at Dr. Adamson and at Sarah. Both smiled and motioned for him to stand.

Ryan's whole body trembled as he stood and concentrated as Sarah had taught him. *'Most of my race are good people,'* He was pleased to find that he had little trouble expressing himself. Glancing at his audience, he found everyone attentive, leaning forward to take his measure.

'Most of my race love their families, try to be respectful of others,

and search out, in their own way, a set of ideals and beliefs. Most of the people of Earth are good people.' He found words spilling from him without any movement of his lips. More importantly, they represented his heartfelt thoughts and feeling.

'In recent months I have learned of the cosmic paradigm. It has changed my view of my world. I wish that more of my brothers and sisters could also learn of it.

'At the same time, I have come to understand that my race has been misguided, that we are caught in schemes that do not operate in the best interests of either the individual or the vast majority. Selfish humans, a small percentage, dominate all. It appears to have been this way for ages. The voices of the many are strangled, sacrificed, ignored, and obfuscated by the few. I do not see a way out of this situation. I can only hope that we find one, soon. I am also aware of the environmental damage inflicted on Earth by my race, and understand that we are in danger of destroying our home.' Knees shaking, Ryan fell into his seat.

The celestial messenger then nodded to the red-haired woman next to Dr. Adamson. *'You would say something to this gathering.'*

'Her name is Julie Benjamin,' Sarah communicated with a grin.

The young woman spoke with a heavy English accent, *'I bring you greetings and encouragement from the planet Earth one hundred and twenty-six years hence. I have come back into this time to be present at this meeting.*

'The message I carry from the Earth of the future is that your efforts did result in the transformation that you all so earnestly desire. Although it is not completed, the Earth of the future is becoming the beautiful, peaceful, and plentiful world you now dimly envision.

'We, the descendants of those living on Earth at this moment, applaud your efforts. We plead that you stay the course, difficult though it may seem. Speaking for myself, I am honored to have a forbearer who helped make the transition possible.' She motioned to Ryan.

'Is she staying here to help?' Ryan inquired of Sarah and Dr. Adamson.

'No, she is present only for this gathering,' Dr. Adamson communicated. *'In order to support you in your efforts, you have been granted the special privilege of seeing and hearing her. She was named after J'Li.'* He nodded in Sarah's direction. *'You may tell no one of this.'*

The discussion went on for what seemed like a long time. The extraplanetary reptilian and those seated near him advocated an immediate "event." Such an event would place the planet under a world government, stop the burning of hydrocarbons, and eliminate nuclear weapons. *'The consequences of environmental degradation is nothing compared to unleashing nuclear weapons,'* the reptilian stated. *'Although the time traveler communicates otherwise, we foresee a third world war with the physical forms of the entire population of this planet either terminated or genetically mutated beyond recognition. Let us not forget, it has happened before.'*

Those who thought the situation should be allowed to work itself out through evolutionary processes, with only nurturing and guidance from extraplanetaries, made their case in quieter, but no less persuasive, communications. They did not deny the dire warning of the reptilian, but contended that rising consciousness would save the situation. With difficulty, Ryan followed the arguments made by the two sides.

The celestial ambassador called for an end to the debate. The room became still and everyone closed their eyes.

After a few moments he spoke, *'I have heard from all and I have relayed all to Michael. It is his decision that events on this planet be allowed to run their course. Free choice is paramount. A planetary government will not be forced upon this sphere.*

'Michael has consulted with the energy controllers. They have reminded him of the interlocking effects of their work. To even momentarily disrupt the laws of physics would impact not only this planet, but also every other inhabited planet in this star system, and beyond. It would cause unanticipated calamities of enormous proportions. They are strenuously advising against causing repercussions that they would be unable to control. Needless to say, we are very saddened by this situation, but the workings of the energy controllers cannot be disrupted.

'All of you are free to provide a warning of the impending disaster, but you may not make use of any special powers to provide assistance.'

Dr. Adamson stood and spoke. *'I would ask one exception to your ruling about special powers. May we attempt to save Carlton Boyle, the new President of the United States? He has potential as a great leader, and he has shown that he is open to the mission which concerns all of us gathered here.'*

The celestial ambassador cocked his head and waited. When

he had received a new communiqué, he said, *'It is foreseen that Carlton Boyle may be instrumental in future events.'* He pointed to Ryan. *'If you, and your Earth-human friend, wish to attempt this, it is permitted.'*

'You may piction for him our discussion, nothing more.' He motioned to Sarah.

The elfish being stood and asked to be recognized. He had not spoken during the discussion. For lack of a better name Ryan decided to call him Mulligan, in honor of the leprechauns his mother had told him about when he was growing up.

Sarah elbowed him when he communicated the nickname to her.

'Yes, honored one, you may assist their efforts.' The celestial ambassador bowed to the life carrier.

He then straightened and announced, *'This convocation is now ended.'*

Everyone stood to acknowledge acquiescence to the pronouncements. The celestial ambassador's brilliance increased until it was hard to look in his direction. Then in an instant he was gone.

Julie, the time traveler, walked to where Ryan stood.

Throwing her arms around him, she whispered, "Thank you, great-grandfather."

Then she stepped away and was lost to his sight.

A few moments thereafter, the overseers' ship dematerialized about them. Ryan found Dr. Adamson, Sarah, and himself standing in the open area among the sagebrush. Their coats and gloves lay where they had discarded them.

He reached down and handed Sarah's coat to her. "That was really something."

Dr. Adamson pointed upward.

Above their space, a collection of ET craft silently hovered. Ryan saw disks, cylinders, and triangles. As he watched, some noiselessly took off; others simply winked out. One left a light trail as it zipped into space. "Michael's messenger," Dr. Adamson said.

"Let's get to the car," Sarah said. "We have only a short time."

When Ryan next looked around, Dr. Adamson was no longer with them.

"Will I get to see Julie again?" Ryan asked as they ran to the car.

"Not in this life."

"She sure is pretty, and powerful. Looks a lot like Danielle. I'd like to spend time with her." Ryan slammed the door and started the engine.

"You will see Julie again on the Between worlds."

"You're sure?"

"Yes."

As soon as they were underway, Ryan asked, "Can you clarify something for me? These planetary energy controller thingamajigs couldn't be reprogrammed to avoid whatever is about to happen? If Michael is so powerful, couldn't he just make it happen?"

Sarah smiled. "Energy controllers are like the drivers of teams of horses. They must keep a tight rein as they go about their job of delicately balancing all the various pieces and parts of the universe. It is a ticklish process. The celestials could not risk overriding this.

"For me this illustrates how interconnected is all life. That is part of the reason that this meeting took place, why all we extraplanetaries are present. If Earth self-destructs, all life in the universe will be impacted."

As to the immediate problem, Sarah explained that the gradual warming of the Earth was causing polar ice to melt at an unprecedented rate. What had been a gradual rising of a millimeter per year was now inches. This shifting of water was about to cause a massive readjustment in the Earth's tectonic plates. When it took place earthquakes and tidal waves would take place all over the planet.

Dr. Adamson had been monitoring the movements of President Carlton Boyle, as he did with any new president. He knew that Boyle had flown from Washington, DC to his ranch in Oregon. Earlier, before they had begun their discussion, Mulligan, the wise old being, had told Dr. Adamson that the West Coast of America would soon experience a tsunami. Sarah told Ryan that the Western White House was only slightly inland from the ocean.

"Ryan, those you just saw are but a very small fraction of the many beings — off-planet overseers, permanent residents of this planet, and transplants like myself, material and spiritual — who are assisting the transformation of —"

"Stop." He pulled off next to the shacks of the Navajo souvenir sellers; they were about to turn back onto US 163. He switched to communicating, *'We have to assume that everything we've said since passing through the Monument Valley gate has been overheard.'*

'What have we said that they don't know already?'

'I don't know, but at the very least we've made ourselves targets who know too much.'

Sarah pointed left, down the road back to Harmony. *'We have no choice but to proceed.'*

'To warn everybody, sound the alarm?' Ryan communicated.

'Yes.'

'And we have to get to President Boyle, convince him. As soon as I can get to a phone, I'll call some newspaper people.'

A man does what he must — in spite of personal consequences, in spite of obstacles and danger and pressure — and that is the basis of all human morality.

— JOHN FITZGERALD KENNEDY

TWENTY-ONE

Ryan and Sarah raced back to Harmony. The cloud cover had thickened as soon as they left Monument Valley; now the moon lighted neither the road nor their surroundings.

They hatched a plan whereby they would drive to the nearest airport, Cortez, Colorado, and fly to the airport nearest President Boyle's ranch in Oregon. Ryan did not believe anything less than a personal pictioning by Sarah could convince the President to leave his residence, and to undertake a massive warning to other countries around the Pacific Rim.

As they passed through Kayenta, Ryan used his cell phone to place calls. He was unable to raise either Sam Wellborn or Tiffany Wheeler. He left messages with both that he had a critical need to talk and would they please leave their cell phones on. With no telephone or cellular service available at Harmony, Ryan knew he would have to initiate further contact. Both Sarah and Ryan knew they had to get to Carlton Boyle as soon as possible.

They were five miles south of Kayenta when Ryan noticed the bright lights closing on them from the rear. Since he was doing 50 MPH on a dirt road that was made for twenty-five, he reasoned it was the Navajo Police and slowed.

Suddenly, all of the warning lights on the car's dash blinked on. Then, they went blank. The engine stopped and he lost power steering and power brakes. Ryan wrestled the car to a gradual stop on the edge of the road.

The lights from the rear were extremely bright, maybe from a light bar atop a SUV. At least the vehicle had seen them and was stopping. He could not imagine what had happened to the car. Surely these folks would be happy to lend a hand. They needed to get to Harmony, alert Ethete, Ajax, and John deBeque to their plan, and leave at once. The airport in Cortez was two hours away.

He saw shadows moving against the bright lights. Someone was coming toward them.

An expressionless silver head with large almond eyes appeared at his window. Ryan jumped. Had one of the extraterrestrials from their meeting followed them? Had they interfered with the car? Was this some kind of rebellion against the decision of the celestial ambassador?

'Be wary,' Sarah communicated. *'This is not what it appears to be.'*

When the silver skinned being yanked open his door, he understood what Sarah meant. This was not one of the peaceful extraterrestrials he had met in the overseerers' craft. This was something very different.

Before he could move something stunned him.

Silver coated hands disengaged his seat belt and locked onto his arms to pull him from the car. Dizzy, Ryan grappled with his attacker.

Another expressionless face had appeared at Sarah's window, similar large almond eyes. Ryan glanced at her as she calmly opened the door.

"Don't," he yelled.

But it was too late. Sarah was already out of the car. He watched as she fearlessly reached her hand out to the tall being.

A second after he clasped it, the being stumbled and fell to the ground. Sarah released the hand. She then placed one of her hands on either side of the being's head. He relaxed into unconsciousness.

The sound of a train whistle filled the night air.

Strange, Ryan thought, the only railroad was fifty miles to the west — an electric powered line for transporting coal.

The figure with whom Ryan was struggling pulled away and sprinted to the craft behind. Ryan heard a noise like the slamming of an airline door. Then without a sound, the intense lights blinked out and they were left alone in the blackness of the night.

Ryan struggled to the passenger side of the sedan. "What was that?"

"They were going to 'abduct' us," Sarah laughed. "This is no alien."

She stooped down and pulled the head covering off the being on the ground. His head had been shaved along with his eyebrows, but he was definitely a human of this planet.

Ryan breathed a sigh of relief.

"Look at this," Sarah said. She pointed to the almond eyes of the mask. Around the edges you could see stitching.

He paused for a moment to clear his head and then communicated, *'We could have some real fun with this. But who do we tell? The Navajo Police and FBI already think we're crazy. And I have a hunch those guys in the black vehicles are there to stop the media from going public with anything they don't like.'*

'We need to get to President Boyle,' Sarah communicated.

'Give me a minute.'

Ryan began hatching a plan. He knew that they needed to get to Oregon. Carlton Boyle had to be convinced to sound an alarm before the tectonic plates shifted. But they had an unconscious man on their hands, one who had been posing as an alien. They needed to turn him over to some credible authority. And they had to tell John deBeque, Ajax, and Ethete what had happened. It wouldn't take long for the fake alien who got away to trace this car's license.

Ryan reached down and began dragging the unconscious man into the rear seat of the car. *'I say we drive this guy to Boulder, give him to Tom Ertl. How long is he out for?'*

'Three or four hours.'

'Good.'

'But how long will it take to get to Sheriff Ertl?'

'We'll have Tom meet us half way.'

They stretched the metallic-clad body across the rear seat. Sarah scooped up the man's mask and placed it on the floor of the passenger compartment.

In the early hours of the morning, they awakened the others at Harmony. Ryan told them of the botched abduction and the plan to take the fake alien to Tom Ertl. Ajax volunteered to draw off the black vehicles and the press by driving out the front gate with the top of his car down. He was sure they would recognize him and follow.

John deBeque said he wanted to get to a major city where he was prepared to release items from Ernest Steiger's diary. Ethete volunteered to go with him.

"What if major newspapers were to publish pictures of your captive? DeBeque asked. "That way, regardless of what happens, the information about him will get out. As long as we're publishing things from the diary, why not add a picture or two."

There were several mentions in Ernest Steiger's diary about alien abductions and how the media affiliates had successfully blocked the stories. One of the entries explained how people who insisted they had experienced benign contact were set up to be ridiculed.

"Let me get my camera," Ryan said.

At 7:00 AM the procession lined up. The sun was hidden under a cloud blanket that had thickened during the night. They had waited until the first of the media were positioned outside the front gate.

Ajax went first, stopping to engage the reporters in a story about heading to Gallup, New Mexico, to make an important announcement at the television station there. He invited them to come with him. Most of those assembled did as he suggested. The black van followed Ajax, but the black sedan remained behind.

Ryan and Sarah departed next in Ryan's Jeep. John deBeque and Ethete followed them in a pick-up belonging to Harmony. Both vehicles turned north. They had left the green Taurus parked in Harmony's gravel lot with a note on the windshield, "ETS ARE THE GOOD GUYS." The black sedan followed them.

In the Jeep's rear compartment, along with Ryan's backpack and small suitcases for the two in the front, the silver suited man lay unconscious. His hands and feet were bound with duct tape. Despite Sarah protests, Ryan had gagged his mouth.

Harmony's pick-up followed them as far as US 160. There it

headed west to Flagstaff.

When the black sedan chose to follow Ethete and John deBeque, Ryan breathed easier. "I'm torn between taking our friend to Tom Ertl, warning everyone about earthquakes, and getting to President Boyle," he said.

"Convincing President Boyle will save lives," she said.

By 9:00 AM, they were approaching Cortez, Colorado. The airport, that Ryan and Sarah had originally thought they would use to fly to Oregon, was to the west of the highway. With a renewed sense of urgency, they drove past it. They passed the Anasazi Motor Inn, on the east side of the highway. On the same side of the highway, further north, was the Cortez Middle School.

They stopped at the Burger King where US 666 split off from US 160 to head north. Ryan ran into the restaurant to get coffee.

Before he returned to the Jeep, he stopped at the pay phone and called Sheriff Tom Ertl. He told Tom about the attempted abduction and asked Tom to relieve them of their prisoner. At first Tom had a hard time believing the story, but after a few moments of discussion, and more than a few expletives about Ryan's antics, he agreed to take custody of the fake alien. Ryan asked the Sheriff to meet them in Grand Junction where Sarah and he could catch a flight to Portland.

Just before he rang off, Ryan had a second thought. He was fairly sure that this out-of-the-way pay phone was not bugged, but he was not so sure about the phone in Tom's office. "Remember that restaurant where we always stop and get those great burritos after fishing. I think the name of it is Buffalo something or other."

He could almost hear the gears as Tom recalibrated their meeting place. At last the sheriff said, "Are you talking about the one with the great coconut cream pie? Cute waitress, named Sandy? Just north —"

Before the Sheriff could say more, Ryan said, "You got it. Last time we ate there, you had a steak."

"I think I know the one you mean, but —"

Ryan cut him off again. "I'll meet you there. Probably take us three and a half to four hours."

He then dialed Collette Dupree. He explained about the forthcoming earthquakes. She promised to take the story to her editor and to others who might believe. He tried the other Denver newspapers, but failed to get anyone's attention.

He had parked the Jeep in a corner of the parking lot, away from other vehicles. Sarah had the silver suited man propped up. His hands and feet were still bound. She was holding a cup and allowing him to drink water.

Ryan offered the man an empty coffee cup. "I won't let you out to pee, but here's a cup."

When he nodded, Ryan cut his hands free.

He lashed out, clawing at Ryan's head. But Sarah touched the man's shoulder and he relaxed. While he was still groggy, Ryan replaced his gag.

"Get it over with," Ryan said. "If you try anything else, you'll be a long time waiting."

"Hurry," Sarah said. "I think people are getting curious." She motioned to the door of the Burger King where a young couple stood watching.

The man tried to use a free hand to pull off the gag. Ryan caught him.

Then the man unzipped the crouch of his aluminized garment. When he had filled the cup, Ryan dumped it nearby.

Sarah once again placed her hands alongside the man's head. He immediately slumped to the floor of the compartment. Ryan rebound his hands.

East of Cortez, Ryan was in the left lane preparing to turn north onto CO 145. This would take them through Dolores, Ridgway, and Montrose on their way northeast. It was also a fairly easy way through the San Juan Mountains.

'Don't go that way,' Sarah communicated. *'They are waiting for us.'* She pointed to a globe about six inches in diameter. It hovered about three feet off the surface of CO 145, about twenty yards up the road. It alternately pulsed red and silver.

'What's that?'

'A friend, from last night.' She raised her hand about three feet off the Jeep's floor. *'Mulligan.'*

'It didn't take the cabal long to figured out who has their alien.' Ryan

276

pointed to the rear compartment. He pulled back into traffic and headed east on US 160 toward Durango.

'I hope you weren't too explicit with Tom.'

"Tom knows where to meet us." Then he added without speaking, *'And it isn't anywhere near Grand Junction.'*

When they had roused Ethete, Ajax, and John deBeque, Sarah had briefed them on their meeting with the overseerers. She had told them of the plan to rescue President Boyle. Ethete and Ajax understood instantly. John appeared skeptical until Ethete persuaded him.

Now with the appearance of the shining globe, Ryan was again reassured. He had to admit that the globe had been there; he had seen it with his own eyes. The meeting last night at Monument Valley was not some kind of a dream.

"Damn," Ryan said. He reached over and switched off his cell phone. "No telling how many tracking devices they've planted on this Jeep."

Sarah said. "Pull over at the next deserted road."

They sped through Mancos. Beyond the town, Ryan turned off on a side road lined with tall pines.

"Now what?"

Sarah held up a hand to quiet him as she communicated with some invisible ally.

In a moment she nodded at the silent directive and said, "Step out of the Jeep. Leave the doors open. Open the rear compartment."

After they had moved away from the vehicle, a golden sphere, about four inches in diameter, appeared. It zipped around the Jeep and through its interior. Four times it stopped and emitted a piercing sound. One of these was over the unconscious alien pretender, another over Ryan's backpack.

Next it came to the two humans. It squealed loudly at Ryan's billfold. Then it took off into the woods.

Ryan felt warmth against his skin. He pulled out his billfold. One of his credit cards was crinkled, as if had been melted in a microwave oven. He edged it out and tossed it on the ground.

The un-manned ARV was armed and readied for launch. At his Washington office, Warren Ophir watched last-minute preparations at the Utah facility on a secure picture phone.

The ARV silently hovered three feet off the concrete floor. The ground crew had just secured the opening in its silver skin. The craft they were using was third generation. It was faster and more stable than the one the tricksters used, but not as maneuverable as the latest models coming off the production line.

The hanger, under its protective lip of cap rock, opened into the Utah desert. Ophir could just make out the junipers on the mesa across the valley. What a desolate wasteland. He was happy they had found a fitting use for it.

Over the years, LNR had used a number of unmanned ARVs. Their controls were the same as those used in pilot-less drones. Whenever they wished to probe deeper into space, or test the flight characteristics of a new design, an unmanned craft had been used.

Ophir and Von Hedemann were convinced the aliens would see this vehicle as just another experimental craft, and would come to investigate — just as they shadowed every other space flight, ARV or rocket propelled. Nuclear power sources had been used on other satellites and space probes. They hoped the aliens would think the nuclear material on board this ARV was a power source. Furthermore, they hoped a large number of them would be in the vicinity when the bomb detonated.

Von Hedemann had been delighted when Ophir had called two days ago. The nuclear device was fitted into the ARV within twenty-four hours.

Kosma Uvizheva had received an email from frog137@aol.com. His was a blind carbon copy of a message sent to other intelligence affiliates. The email address of the sender would be used once, and then discarded. The message read, "Your cousin, Alfred Simmons, will be playing goal tender for the All Blacks. His first game, against South Africa, will be the day after tomorrow. You may want to contact him and wish him well. Best, Uncle Frog." When decoded he had read the communiqué as: "In forty-eight hours, a nuclear device will be detonated high over the Southern Hemisphere. Take necessary precautions for your people."

In addition to killing a few aliens, the explosion would cripple any number of communications satellites. Anticipating this, the aerospace companies that owned LNR were already building replacements that would soon be ready to launch aboard conventional rockets. There would, of course, be an expedite charge added to the multi-billion dollar tab — after all replacing vital communications links in record time did not come cheaply. What they would not tell the procurement people was that each new satellite would carry concealed receivers and transmitters reserved for use by the World League.

Ophir saw a familiar face on a guard in the launch area. Günter Hauptman's skills were being put to good use.

"Prepare to launch," the voice of the control center's director boomed through the small hanger. Unlike the massive organization required to launch a conventional rocket, a small team would manage this trip. When the director finished inputting the coordinates, he leaned over the lone control console and readied his hand over a simple joystick. The five technicians stepped back a few paces. Hauptman slipped out a side door.

Almost as if it were a hologram in some video game, the ARV silently advanced out of the hanger and hovered over the valley. But Ophir knew this sleek craft was not a hologram; this space ship was very real.

The director moved his joystick and the craft took off, straight up into space. A picture of the video feed from the craft replaced the camera image on Ophir's screen. Ophir knew communications were not quite real-time because commands and video between the LNR facility and the ARV were done using a satellite link at Vandenberg Air Force base in California. This caused a three-second delay in communications, each way. Today, because the craft was due to be positioned over the Southern Hemisphere, satellite earth stations in Australia and South America would be used. They would relay the command signal from Vandenberg, causing a few more seconds delay. It was not unlike overseas reporters waiting to reply to a question from someone in New York, or waiting for a slow computer modem to receive email — response time was extremely sluggish.

Ophir watched as the small craft shot through the atmosphere. Its charged surface enabled it to travel thousands of miles per hour without encountering the friction experienced by conventional aircraft. Its zero-point energizer supplied all the power it would ever need — without chemical or nuclear fuel.

The curvature of the Earth receded to form a globe. In a matter of seconds, the ARV settled in near a geostationary satellite.

Three alien disks arrived in a matter of moments. They circled the ARV and the satellite.

"Are we ready to detonate?" It was the director's voice.

"Hold. I'm hoping for more visitors." Von Hedemann's voice was hushed as if the circling saucers could hear him.

The picture on Ophir's desk went blank. But for the crackling of the audio, he would have believed he had been disconnected.

"What happened?" Von Hedemann asked. "Did you detonate?"

"We've lost contact, sir."

"Anything from Australia?"

"Nothing, sir."

The picture of the control center returned to Ophir's display. The flight director was hunched over his console, frantically punching keys. Von Hedemann stood over him. Ground personnel huddles around waiting for word.

"Detonate now!" Von Hedemann's voice took on a note of panic. "Now, do it now."

Ophir's video returned. Outside the hanger opening, the opposing mesa shimmered in the dry desert air. In the upper corner of his screen Ophir glimpsed the ARV. It was just outside the hanger, surrounded by three disk shaped craft.

The ARV quietly slipped into its pre-takeoff position above the concrete floor. The three disks winked out.

A second or two after that, Ophir's screen went blank again. This time the audio died also.

After repeatedly dialing LNR's underground facility with no success, Warren Ophir called the offices of the International League. "I'm sorry, Mr. Ophir, but Mr. deBeque is not back from vacation," the receptionist said.

"I know that, damn it. Patch me through to Patty." Warren Ophir knew exactly where John deBeque was. His men had seen him leave Harmony's facility that morning and followed. At this moment he was somewhere in Arizona traveling west on US 160, about three hundred miles south of the former LNR underground facility.

When Patty Nelson answered the phone, Ophir asked, "Who's available to do a work-up?"

After he had arranged for work to commence on three very different stories, Warren Ophir called the members of his team at DIA. They were to report back to him immediately with any information about an explosion in Utah. He then dialed the senior members of the intelligence affiliates. When all that was in place, he picked up the phone and called Delta Kingman.

"A what?" Carlton Boyle asked. He stood next to a desk that had been in his family for several generations. It was quite a bit smaller than the one in the Oval Office, but this one had a familiar feel to it. The room also had a familiar feel to it. As a boy, it had been his bedroom; now it served as his office away from the White House. For an hour that morning he had ridden around the ranch that had been in his family for three generations.

"A nuclear explosion, Utah," the President's National Security Advisor replied. Raymond Nazem was one of the skeleton staff Boyle had brought with him. "Our orbiting sensors picked it up at 10:05 AM."

"A test? I didn't authorize anything like that."

"Not a scheduled test, Mr. President. It was nowhere close to the Nevada Test Site. We're not sure what it was."

"When will we know more?"

"A DOE team is on its way to the site," Nazem said. "With your permission, I suggest we get troops out there and cordon-off the whole area."

"Yes, yes, of course."

"You will need a statement for the press. May I suggest we get someone working on it?"

John MacDonald's instruments recorded the nuclear explosion. Using triangulation, he was able to pinpoint its exact location in Utah. During the era of testing in Nevada and the Pacific, the National Earthquake Information Center had developed techniques that allowed them to distinguish between an earth tremor and a nuclear explosion. MacDonald waited for the press to call.

Of equal interest to him, and the other scientists watching their instruments and computers that morning was the unusually large number of tremors from every edge of the Pacific Tectonic Plate. Over the past days, the number of small quakes reported in California towns along the San Andreas Fault had risen steadily. Their equipment was also sensing tremors in Northern California, Oregon, Washington, and British Columbia. As he watched, tremors were being reported in Japan, the Philippines, and New Zealand.

In analyzing the 1960 quake in Chile, his group had noted a similar pattern of small tremors leading to the final earthquake. The pattern around the North American Plate looked similar. MacDonald was ready to bet that one would occur, very soon.

MacDonald was frustrated. Earlier that day he had gone to the head of the National Earthquake Information Center and explained to him his prediction about earthquakes along the edges of the Pacific Plate. He had been told, in no uncertain terms, that he was not to speak to the press about theories. The role of NEIC was to report, not to predict.

The phone rang. The woman on the line, an old friend, was with the National Oceanic and Atmospheric Administration offices in nearby Boulder. She told MacDonald that readings from their tsunameters were going wild. Her request for permission to alert state and local governments along the West Coast had been denied on the basis that it would cause panic. In the opinion of her bosses, tsunameter technology was just too new to be trusted. In their opinion, a mass evacuation was sure to kill hundreds. She confided in him that the low-lying coastal areas of Japan and Taiwan were being quietly evacuated.

Jake Ashton, Special Agent from the Denver office of the Federal Bureau of Investigation, had been unable to take his morning run through the foothills west of Denver. Just after 6:00 AM, he had taken violently ill with stomach cramps and vomiting.

He could not connect it to any food he had consumed. Neither his co-workers nor family were sick. His wife had pointed out an article in yesterday's Denver Post about tainted hamburger from a local meat packing plant. But he had not had a burger in days and they had eaten at home the prior evening. He called the office and returned to bed.

At 9:32 AM, Sheriff Tom Ertl called and invited him to an emergency meeting with Ryan Drake.

After Ertl explained the situation, Ashton had agreed to travel halfway across the state. He called the Denver FBI office, requested a contingent of men. They were to meet him and Sheriff Ertl at the intersection of US 40 and Interstate 70, near Golden, west of Denver. From there they would head west on Interstate 70 to Grand Junction.

When he drove from his house, the FBI agent spotted a dirty white van. There were no identifying marks or lettering on it. It was parked in the cul-de-sac in front of a neighbor's house.

The young man in the driver's seat wore a dirty blue T-shirt; his long brown hair was tied in a ponytail. He appeared to be watching the FBI agent depart the house as he talked on a cell phone.

As Jake drove down the hill from his home, another cramp doubled him over. In a daze, he pulled to the side of the road. After a moment his stomach was okay, but he felt dizzy. He dismissed it as further evidence of his flu, and drove ahead slowly. At the bottom of the hill, he jumped onto I-70 and headed to his meeting. In a stupor from his bout with the food poisoning, Ashton did not pay attention to the white van that followed him.

There are two worlds: the world we can measure with line and rule, and the world that we feel with our hearts and imagination.

— LEIGH HUNT

TWENTY-TWO

When Sarah Smith and Ryan Drake arrived in Durango, forty-five minutes after the globe had sanitized the Jeep, and an hour after arranging to meet Tom Ertl, Ryan turned north on US 550, this highway led through the heart of the San Juan Mountains. Since they had been stopped from going north at CO 145, this was the shortest route to their meeting with Tom Ertl. It was also a route that the locals avoided during winter.

Ryan desperately wanted to rid himself of the alien imposter. He was sure the man was like honey to a gang of hungry bears.

He stopped at a pay phone and dialed Sam Wellborn. He was told Sam was out of his office. He asked for Tiffany Wheeler.

"Hi, Ryan, how are you?"

"In trouble, as usual."

They talked for a few moments until he was sure the person on the other end was Tiffany, and then he said, "I need to talk to Sam."

"He's out at the Western White House, with President Boyle."

"That's what I was afraid of. Listen, I need you to call Sam, tell him I'm flying out to see him and President Boyle. I'll be there as soon as I can. Tiffany, this is very important, Sarah Smith needs to meet with the President as soon as possible."

North of Durango, as they gained altitude along the twisting highway, Ryan pointed out the absence of snow to Sarah. His spirits swelled. Maybe the highway across the high mountain passes wouldn't be so bad after all. Durango Mountain Ski Resort, a half-hour north of the town, was closed for lack of snow.

They drove over Coal Bank Pass and Molas Pass without finding snow or ice on the roadway. Only the remains of an occasional snowdrift signaled that winter was in process.

When they arrived at Silverton, a red pulsing globe blocked US 550 over Red Mountain Pass to the north. Sarah pointed ahead. He could just see the hood of a black automobile, about a half-mile up the highway.

Ryan pulled the Jeep into the parking lot at the visitor's center, just west of the town.

"Now, what?" Sarah asked.

"I guess we could go back the way we came. Or try the impossible."

"What's the impossible?" Sarah asked.

"Over those mountains." Ryan pointed to the snow capped peaks to the east of Silverton. Even though the snow pack was far below normal, they appeared mostly white. "It's a gamble, and it's also a lot longer."

"I say we follow our friend," Sarah said. She pointed to a golden globe that waited for them at the exit to the parking lot.

"Okay. Let's hope it knows what it's doing."

Sure enough, the globe led them east into the town — escorting them toward the impossible route.

Sarah and he had agreed that they were likely to be intercepted somewhere along the way. As soon as the cabal found out what had happened, Sarah and he knew they would be the subjects of a nation-wide manhunt. Although legitimate law enforcement would not be recruited to track them down, the cabal had plenty of its own resources.

In the rear compartment of the Jeep, they held the answer to the mystery of alien abductions, to the way the cabal had induced fear in those it wished to terrorize.

Ryan had become tired of this game of cat and mouse. First it was Steiger's men; now it was the men from the World League. It seemed like everyone wanted to stop them. He reasoned that if they were in Boulder, he'd have ways in which to fight back. But he was in the middle of the San Juan Mountains. He was not sure what kind of law enforcement Silverton had; surely it would not stand up to the might of the World League.

At Sanitas, the Department of Commerce had challenged him over exporting technology. He'd been able to prove that the technology could not be used for military purposes and was not a threat to America's national security. The lesson he'd learned was to pick battles he could win. He planned to win this one.

So far, it had been a light snow year in this part of Colorado, the tenth year of a drought. But it was February. Would this winding road be passable? If not, their bodies would be found when the snow melted in the spring.

The globe led them east on Greene, the main street of Silverton. PROSPECTOR MOTEL. MINER'S TAVERN. Everything appeared closed. The winter population of this isolated mountain town was slightly more than two hundred.

He looked back. No black vehicles; no vehicles at all. They headed east on San Juan County 110. Of the two routes north out of Silverton, this one was less known and seldom used as a travel route — never in winter. It was a rough dirt road that wound its way to thirteen thousand feet and skirted the Uncompahgre Wilderness — even in summer, it was unlikely that anyone would select it to go anywhere quickly. A small blue sign with a Columbine flower read, SCENIC BYWAY.

They drove east through a wide valley with few trees. Two miles from town, they passed the SUNNYSIDE MINE. Its rusting metal structures, dating from the 1920's, had become a tourist attraction. The asphalt turned to gravel. Overhead ore cars clung to a rusted cable. Many years ago, when the facility was operational, its mine and processing plant had been on opposite sides of the valley.

In two miles, they came to a group of cabins. A hand lettered sign on a telephone pole read GENERAL STORE. Metal highway signs read WELCOME TO THE ALPINE LOOP, SPEED LIMIT 25 MPH. Ryan was going forty. Clouds obscured the mountains on either side of the valley.

There were steel mine buildings on both sides of the road, then an old wooden miner's cabin to the left. The road turned to washboard and Ryan devoted his attention to guiding their vehicle through the least severe sections. Nevertheless, everything in the Jeep that was not fastened down shook and rattled.

The sides of the valley closed in. The road hugged the barren hillside. In the early 1900's, the valley floor had been dredged for gold. It left a signature: wide stretches of rocky rubble — a scar on the otherwise pristine landscape. He glimpsed the polluted stream as it meandered through black foliage. The acid used to leach precious metals from ore had blackened the bushes. Heavy metals had killed the fish.

Yellow tailings scarred the mountain at the head of the valley. Some sort of stone structure stair-stepped up its face, more remnants of turn-of-the-century mining activity.

They crossed a concrete bridge and climbed. The heavy overcast sky threatened snow. The road turned from gravel to a single lane, dirt road. He slowed the Jeep to 25 MPH and focused on the road's deep ruts.

The road crossed a landslide where rubble from the mountain had cascaded into the valley. Basketball-size boulders above and below the road; snow in the cracks between. Hikers called it scree, hell to cross on foot. It covered the tops of many of Colorado's fourteeners.

A Jeep loaded with cross-country skiers came the other way. He pulled off in a wide place and let them pass. How far up the pass had they been? Surely they had not come from Lake City on the other side. That was too much to hope for.

Past that point, a pristine stream flowed down the valley. They had left the most recent mining activity behind. Ahead, small piles of tailings dotted the hillsides. Many of these high altitude mines had been the working of a single man and his burro. He had read somewhere that early miners found the purest metals at the highest elevations. During that era, the road they now traveled had been a path for mules bringing miners and their treasures to Silverton.

The discussions they'd had at Harmony had sure helped to clarify why this planet was so screwed up. Two hundred thousand years while the rebels roamed the planet convincing whoever they liked that they should get it all here and now. It helped him understand some of his business acquaintances who did not believe there was anything beyond this life, who took greed for granted, who were "sharp" in their dealings with others. If he ever got out of this mess, he'd try to help them understand what was true.

And Dr. Adamson's great-grandparents, the two who knew ahead of time what they were getting into, who knew the planet was screwed up, who were supposed to hang in there until they made it right. They screwed it up even more. Ryan couldn't remember the last time he got into something knowing all about it going in. That hadn't been the case in business; it sure wasn't the case when he got involved with the Phantians..

"Here they come." Sarah was glued to the Jeep's side mirror.

"Damn." Ryan saw two dark sedans, a quarter mile behind. With carloads of operatives, his only chance was to out run them. "Ya'al hold on," Ryan instructed them mimicking his friend Jimmy Lee from Texas. "We are agoin' ta have some fun." He increased the pressure on the throttle. The Jeep accelerated to 50 MPH. Dust spewed out behind them. The Jeep lurched from side to side on the narrow, rutted road.

"Gooooo Ryan!" Sarah laughed and tightened her seat belt. The voice of an excited young girl had replaced the soft controlled voice of the extraterrestrial. For a moment, she reminded him of his daughter. Danielle had loved to ride with him on Jeep trails, the scarier the better.

"This road's gonna git a little rougher," Ryan announced. As they careened along, he visualized the bottoms of the black sedans as they scraped boulder after boulder, fought to remain in ruts carved by SUV's, fought to keep going.

CINNAMON PASS. ENGINEER PASS. ANIMAS FORKS. The golden globe beckoned; Ryan followed the sign for the steeper, narrower road that lead up the side of the mountain. The road's surface was free of snow. He glanced ahead: snow capped mountains peeked through the clouds.

The tops of mountains always attracted more snow than the valleys. Ryan knew that air pressure decreased with elevation. He had recently learned that temperature also decreased, at the rate of about three degrees per thousand feet gained. This combination caused moisture to condense into rain or snow and fall more at greater heights. In a geographic region, the annual precipitation was always greater at these higher elevations. This feature was known as orographic precipitation.

It began to snow, a few flakes at first, then steady. The road became muddy, ruts filled with slush. They rounded a sharp turn and the Jeep's back end fishtailed. The passenger-side rear wheel slipped into a shallow ditch; Ryan heard the scraping of metal against rock — more bodywork. He switched on the windshield wipers.

The black car pulled within a hundred yards as the Jeep paused in the ditch.

"Are those gun shots?" Sarah asked. It was the first time she had heard the report of a real gun.

A bullet pierced the rear window.

"Should we stop?" Sarah asked. She had scooted down in her seat.

"We'll lose them real soon." Ryan gunned the Jeep and pulled back onto the roadway.

The Jeep's blades flashed across the glass and cleared off muddy snow. Before them, a steep rough road climbed up a barren hillside. The lush grass and wildflowers of summer were covered with a foot of snow. ALPINE TUNDRA, the small sign flashed by.

The distance between the Jeep and the black cars widened as the first sedan navigated the sharp turn. As both right wheels slid into the ditch, it ground to a halt.

The second car slowed and navigated around the first car. With tires vomiting gravel and mud, it charged the hill — a toy in the hands of a five-year-old.

The road was so steep and narrow that any oncoming vehicles would have to wait at one of the hairpin turns. San Juan County had not worked this road for years, never plowed it in the winter. In the summer it provided a nice living for Jeep tour companies who wanted to frighten their passengers as well as show off the scenery. In the winter only the hearty ventured up to find unspoiled ski slopes.

"Can we —" Sarah left the rest of the sentence unspoken.

"At the very least we'll get further than that car behind us. But I don't relish hiking out of here. And we'd have to let our alien go."

They wore warm clothing, but their bags contained no survival gear. Ryan had his ever-present backpack, but it held clothing and rations for one.

The narrow road clung to the side of the mountain. The Jeep occupied its full width. On their left was a steep drop-off with no trees to slow a fall, only white-capped rocks interspersed with brown grass. Ahead, the mountain rose three thousand feet.

The low-slung sedan lost ground as it jockeyed around protruding boulders. Ryan could almost hear its undercarriage scraping on the rocks.

They rounded another switchback and headed higher. The Jeep struggled to maintain the speed Ryan demanded of it. The angle of the climb increased, and Ryan heard the Jeep's motor laboring. He remembered this road — on a nice sunny day, it was a demanding four-wheel adventure. Today, it was near impassable, and he was driving it faster than he cared to think about.

"They'll have to give up soon," Ryan uttered through clinched teeth.

As he maneuvered over a large boulder, Sarah was tossed against the right door.

They heard the report of additional gunshots, but nothing impacted the Jeep.

Ryan discovered he was enjoying his game with the cabal. For the last thirty years, he'd obeyed the rules, calculated the results, and made sure they were accomplished. Now, he dug deep and found that old sense of freedom he'd enjoyed as a protester during his college days. He jammed the accelerator to the floor.

On the bright side, cell phones did not work here, and in all likelihood satellite phone transmission was blocked by the heavy clouds.

The Jeep rocked from side to side as they pitched between protruding rocks and deep ruts. Ryan swerved to miss the worst of them.

Ryan heard a scrape as a boulder scored the Jeep's underside. At each wide spot he could see where vehicles had turned around, unwilling to chance getting stuck further up the mountain.

The steep, treeless mountain fell away from the road to the valley floor, a dizzying 2,500 feet below. In places, the Jeep's tires tracked inches from the edge of the road.

Controlling the steering wheel took all his strength and concentration. The Jeep climbed at an angle of 30 degrees. They had slowed to 15 MPH.

They entered a bank of low hanging clouds; the snow slackened. The Jeep's headlights reflected off gray mist. He slowed. His eyes sought the edge of the road. He was pleased that Sarah could not see the sheer mountainside they had yet to navigate.

The golden globe preceded them. It seemed to beckon them forward, to indicate the center of the obscured road.

"They stopped," Sarah said. She had her eyes closed. "Their car is stuck."

"Thank you, Mulligan." He eased off the gas; the Jeep slowed to 5 MPH.

They rounded another curve. The road canted to the left side. Ryan glanced out his side window at the edge of the road and calculated the height of the sheer drop-off. Visibility decreased to ten feet.

Ryan zeroed in on the road's ill-defined boundaries. White blanketed everything. The wiper no longer cleaned the windshield; freezing snow clogged it.

The Jeep plowed into a snowdrift and stopped with a jerk. Snow blocked the road in front of them.

"You okay?" He directed the question to Sarah.

They heard a moan from their passenger in the rear.

Ryan got out and dislodged ice from the wiper blade. The golden globe hovered twenty feet ahead. He walked through the drift until he saw that the road ahead was passable.

Back inside, he cranked up the defroster and backed up. With two cars-loads of operatives behind them, they had no choice but to proceed up the mountain into the blizzard.

"Hang on. Here we go." With a running start, the Jeep blasted through the drift and continued on toward the top.

After a tortuous half hour in the white-out and several more drifts, they emerged on top and Ryan pulled over — close enough for Sarah to see: ENGINEER PASS ELEVATION 12,800.

Six inches of new snow had accumulated on top of the sign. The golden globe pointed east, the way down from the top. Now if they could just hook up with Tom Ertl and get rid of their unwanted passenger.

Genius is only the power of making continuous effort. The line between failure and success is so fine that we scarcely know when we pass it...

— ELBERT HUBBARD

TWENTY-THREE

Sarah Smith studied the mountains and compared them to those on Phantia. Blowing snow limited her visibility. The road down the east side of Engineer Pass was less snowy and there were fewer switchbacks, but it was not without its tense moments. Ryan had to blast through several drifts — always wondering if the Jeep would make it out the other side.

In Tibnap, on the far side of her world, there were mountains that rose this high and appeared as formidable. She had visited there, once, an extended vacation with M'Adan and their two teenage daughters, A'Dr and B'Tric. She and her mate had enjoyed the trip, however their two girls could not wait to get home to their friends.

"I think this is one of the most beautiful places in Colorado," Ryan motioned to the surrounding snow encapsulated vista. "Maybe we should stay awhile."

This time she knew he was joking and said, "In the summer."

Sarah returned to meditating. During the ride from Monument Valley, and continuing since they had left Harmony, she had been communicating with the others who had come from Phantia. To each she relayed a general warning of mighty earthquakes and tidal waves. She asked each to contact their local media to warn of the pending event. Now she was receiving the results of those earlier communications. Everywhere the media had rejected their desire to warn people. Neither newspapers nor television stations were willing to start an unfounded panic. Local government officials were equally unwilling to assume any leadership role — every one knew you could not predict an earthquake. Even recent readings from the seismometers and coastal tidal gauges that scientists had placed on the ocean floor were insufficient to convince authorities to order an evacuation of low lying coastal areas.

When she opened her eyes again, low clouds continued to shroud the mountaintops. The presence of knurled pine trees indicated they had descended below timberline. Ryan saw that she was looking around and explained that Bristlecone pines were the heartiest and survived at the highest elevations. The trees were twisted and tilted in their fight against the fierce wind.

Ryan pulled off at a wide spot and said, "I want to take care of something."

Sarah followed him out of the vehicle. She stretched as he wandered off into the woods. It felt good to move about.

"You were clever, you know — using that rough road to escape," she said when he returned. "I viewed those men hiking down to their one functioning vehicle. They abandoned the other one in the middle of the road."

"Perfect. Nobody else is getting up that road tonight," Ryan said. "Maybe not until spring."

She studied the man who had rescued her so many times in the past six months. In the gathering darkness, as he strained to see the road, small wrinkles formed at the edges of his eyes; they complimented the gray at his temples. The signs of aging did not detract from his otherwise handsome face. Her celestial-allies had told her that he had recently turned fifty — on Phantia he would have been taken for a man of seventy-five. That made him six years older than she, in terms of physiological aging.

They rounded a turn in the road, when she saw it — a flashing red and silver globe, a few hundred yards ahead. She also glimpsed the golden globe off on the side road.

"Turn here." She pointed down the narrow road into the pine trees. The sign read, ROSES CABIN.

"Why?"

"Quickly. Do as I say."

He followed her instructions.

They had barely pulled into the trees and shut the Jeep off when two black vehicles came racing up the road to the top of the pass.

After an hour they arrived at a small village, Lake City. Its streets were almost deserted; like Silverton few people remained for the winter. Ryan stopped at a pay phone and called Tom Ertl's office in Boulder.

Ryan talked to his assistant. "Relay this message to Tom. 'Engineer Pass was a little slow. I'll buy dinner to make up for it.' Don't say who it's from. Don't use my name. He'll understand."

Tom and he had camped out in the Uncompahgre Wilderness. The Sheriff knew what kind of a road it was and would know they had been delayed getting to their meeting. Ryan hoped Tom had taken whatever evasive action was necessary. He also hoped the forces of the cabal were focused on Grand Junction.

In another forty-five minutes they crossed a bridge and were at the intersection with US 50. They had encountered no other vehicles.

A red globe blocked the way west; Ryan turned the Jeep east, the direction opposite from Grand Junction. They had lost more than two valuable hours by going over Engineer Pass; they had also out-maneuvered the cabal.

As they approached the west side of Gunnison, they encountered a roadblock, two Sheriff's cars, with flashing lights. Ryan had no choice but to stop the Jeep.

They spoke with two jittery Gunnison County deputies. Their instructions were to question anyone but locals. When Ryan identified himself, the taller deputy said, "Thank God. We were beginning to wonder what happened. They're waiting for you at the Buffalo."

And indeed they were, Tom Ertl's car and four FBI vehicles. As Ryan pulled into the parking lot, his Jeep was surrounded by uniforms and men dressed in dark suits.

"About time you got here." Tom Ertl said as Ryan alighted from the driver's seat.

"Did you really go over Engineer Pass?" Jake Ashton asked. He extended an arm to Sarah who had come around the Jeep. "We were concerned until we got the call from Tom's office."

After Peter's memorial service and before Ryan and she had departed for Harmony, Sarah had spent several hours with Jake Ashton. He had come to understand the cosmic paradigm, and they had become friends.

"Let me introduce the rest of the high altitude gang to you," Ryan said with a grin.

Two of Ashton's men pulled the silver suited alien from the rear compartment. He was disoriented from his ride in the back of the Jeep, but otherwise healthy enough to stand.

"This completes his costume." Sarah handed the man's head covering to Ashton.

"Do you two have any idea how much trouble you're in?" Ashton asked. Holding up his hand he ticked off the offenses. "Kidnapping. Interstate transportation. Violation of civil rights. Undue force." When he finished, he grinned at Ryan.

"Be careful with him," Ryan said. "And I think you'd better get on with interrogating him. Once they find out where he is, they'll come after him."

"We'll see about that." Ashton motioned to the six men in dark jackets with large FBI lettering. Each of them held an automatic weapon at the ready.

"Anyway, thanks. This helps explain a lot." Ashton held up the head covering. "I'll make sure the right people find out. What can you tell me about their craft?"

"We couldn't see it very well," Sarah said. "The lights were really blinding."

"It didn't make any noise," Ryan said. "I'm sure it wasn't a helicopter. Our friend should be able to tell you. Just don't let the cabal get their hands on him."

"Word has it that there was quite a gathering today in Grand Junction," Ertl said. "Lots of black vehicles."

Ryan said to Tom Ertl, "We have to get to the airport, and fast. Can you give us an escort?"

"Come on, ride with me. You can tell me all about it."

Ashton turned to his men, "Get him in the van."

Ryan tossed his keys to Andy Milliken, the Sheriff's deputy he knew best. "Leave it at the office in Boulder." Ryan and she climbed into Tom Ertl's vehicle.

Ryan pulled out his cell phone and dialed Sam.

Sam Wellborn was in the trailer that served as his temporary office. A few minutes ago President Boyle had asked him to go to Utah and personally investigate the mysterious atomic explosion.

He had secured transportation and was packing his briefcase when the call from Ryan Drake came in. Ryan told him that Sarah and he were on their way.

"The President has asked me to go to Utah," Sam said. "There's been an explosion at an underground alien base. Can this wait?"

"Sam, if you leave now, there may not be a Western White House to come back to. Also, I'm positive there is no alien base in Utah. I'm guessing that was where the cabal was assembling the alien reproduction vehicles."

When Ryan and Sam had chatted about the World League, Ryan had mentioned the extensive reverse-engineering efforts the cabal had undertaken since the Roswell UFO crash. Steiger's diary had indicated their success with recreating an extraterrestrial type craft. But Steiger had not been included in that aspect of the League's activities. In an attempt to get closer to the center of decision-making, he had maneuvered John deBeque into the Washington office of the media affiliates. It was also why he had decided to capture Sarah Smith without involving the other Governors of the World League.

"I'll keep that in mind. What's this about no Western White House?"

"Sorry, I'm calling from a sheriff's vehicle. We're at Gunnison, in the middle of the Colorado mountains. What I said was that the coast of Oregon is going to be wiped out. You've got to get the President out of there."

"He's not due to leave for another two days."

"This impending disaster isn't going to wait."

"You're positive?"

"I'm bringing proof."

"It had better be good."

"Oh, it is."

"When can you get here?"

"We're just catching a flight." Ryan explained how they

planned to get to the ranch.

The ride from the Buffalo Restaurant to the Gunnison airport had taken less than five minutes. As they paused at the terminal, the two-way radio in Tom's car crackled. "Sheriff Ertl, this to Jake Ashton. Please come in."

Ertl grabbed the mike and responded, "Tom Ertl here."

"Thank god," Ashton said. "Is everybody okay?"

"Yes."

"A black helicopter — fired rockets at us — just missed the van with our guy, but rolled it over. Drake's Jeep was blasted to smithereens. Over and out."

Ryan looked at Tom Ertl.

The Sheriff's jaw was tightly clinched. "Andy Milliken was driving —"

Ryan felt the same sinking feeling as he had when the explosion at his house had killed the fire investigator. How many more would die to maintain the power of the cabal? He knew the answer: if they didn't get to the President in time, lots.

Success may generate courage and promote confidence, but wisdom comes only from the experiences of adjustment to the results of one's failures.

— THE URANTIA BOOK

TWENTY-FOUR

Ryan and Sarah waited only a short time for the commuter flight from Gunnison to Denver. The other seats were filled with skiers griping about the lack of snow.

True to his word, Sam had arranged for priority tickets at United Airlines in Denver. The nearest airport to Boyle's ranch was Eugene, Oregon, but the next flight was not for another five hours. They ran to catch a flight to Portland that was already boarding. Exhausted from the past sixteen hours, they dozed the entire two and a half hours.

Ryan was standing in line at the rental car counter scanning the morning newspaper. He was disappointed to see there was nothing about an impending earthquake or tsunami. It brought home to him that not only did the media manage information about extraterrestrial contact, but also the information gatekeepers were oblivious to anything beyond their carefully contrived box. There was no scientific proof that earthquakes or tidal waves could be predicted, so nothing got printed. Was it possible there was another reason that the media was not responding to the warnings provided by the many people whom Sarah and he had alerted?

A man wearing a dark suit approached him. "Mr. Drake?"

"Yes."

"Jack Glenn, Secret Service. Sam Wellborn asked me to transport you to the President."

Sam and he had not discussed this part of their trip, but it made sense. It would save them valuable time getting to President Boyle. No telling when the tsunami would hit.

He motioned to Sarah who was waiting with their two bags.

"Sarah, this man is from the Secret Service. He's going to take us to the President."

"My vehicle is outside, Madam Ambassador." He pointed to the nearest door and reached for the bags.

The man made sure they were comfortable in the rear seat of the long black limousine; then he closed its door and went to the driver's seat. As they pulled onto Airport Blvd, the door locks clicked and the chauffeur raised the privacy window back of his seat.

'Something is not right,' Sarah communicated. 'I do not believe this man will take us to President Boyle.'

'What are you saying?'

'Someone has found out about our mission. We must get out of this car immediately.'

Ryan glanced out the window as they drove onto Interstate 5. Unfamiliar with Portland, it was not until they were crossing the Columbia River and he saw the welcoming sign for the State of Washington, that he knew Sarah was right, again.

"Don't we need to go south?" Ryan spoke into the intercom.

No reply.

"We're headed the wrong way," Ryan knocked on the glass partition and yelled at the driver. "We need to go south toward Eugene."

The driver did not even nod his head.

He tried the door handle; it would not move. 'What can we do?' he communicated.

'I'll see if I can get us some help.'

They had traveled another five miles north, when the motor of the limousine died. The driver brought it to a halt on the side of the interstate. Ryan watched as the Secret Service imposter tried to get the vehicle restarted. Failing that, he pulled out a cell phone and dialed a number. He nodded once, then burst from the front seat, and ran down the embankment of the freeway to a side road.

Ryan tried to kick the glass that separated them from the

driver's compartment, then tried kicking out a window. Nothing succeeded. Outside traffic zipped by at 65 MPH. Ryan felt helpless. He was in a panic; President Carlton Boyle was the other direction.

"You told me that you wanted the car stopped," Sarah chuckled. "You didn't specify that we had to get out of it."

He shook his head and gave her a disgusted look. "So how did you do that anyway?"

"Our earth energy friends have known how to disrupt electrical circuits much longer than the men in that ARV."

As they waited for help, Ryan puzzled how they could have been intercepted. He could only conclude that his conversation from Tom Ertl's car had been monitored. He wondered what had happened to the silver suited imposter now that the cabal had figured out where he was.

They were startled when a Washington State Trooper knocked on the side window. He motioned for Ryan to open the door. Ryan finally got him to understand that they could not open it, that they were stuck. The trooper went to the door of the front compartment; it too was locked.

The trooper went to his patrol car. Ryan saw him talking to the dispatcher. When he returned he used his nightstick to break the window of the driver's side. Then he released the door locks.

Ryan and Sarah stumbled from the rear seats. "Can you give us a ride?" he asked the trooper.

Carlton Boyle's ranch encompassed two thousand acres of river bottom and gently sloping land between the small towns of Tiernan and Cushman. It was directly east of Florence, a large town on the coast of Oregon. The entry to the property, which Boyle had inherited from his family, was off OR 126. The Siuslaw River flowed through one corner of the land.

The only reason that newly inaugurated President was at his ranch was to check on its reconstruction into a secure government facility that would serve as the Western White House. Blustery wind, cold rain, and chilly temperatures had kept his wife of thirty-three years, Margaret, in Washington. Boyle was determined to avoid an environmental debacle as the Secret Service and other agencies added their facilities to the existing ranch buildings. According to

Sam, the President had arrived two days ago and was planning to leave the day after tomorrow.

When Sarah and Ryan arrived at the gate of Carlton Boyle's ranch, a U.S. Marine guard stopped their rented car. "We're here to see Sam Wellborn. He's expecting us."

After a call, the guard came back to their car. "I need to see your I.D.'s."

After a long discussion on the phone of the guard shack, the gate opened, and they were directed to the large ranch house that served as Boyle's home away from the White House.

An addition was being added to the main ranch house. Plastic sheeting protected the work area from the frequent showers that swept in from the west. Foundations for several outbuildings were being poured. These would house the added security, communications equipment, and personnel required by the Presidential presence. In the meantime, five portable offices were lined up to serve that function. A ten-foot high chain link fence had been erected to enclose all the buildings except the barn. The President had refused to allow anyone to commandeer that or the ranch hands who worked there.

Another Marine indicated where they were to park. He escorted them to the reception area, formerly the front porch of the ranch house; a portion of it had been enclosed.

A uniformed man behind a government-issue desk said, "Mr. Wellborn left an hour ago. He told me to tell you that he had to get to Utah. Said you'd know what that meant."

"Actually, we are here to see President Boyle," Ryan said.

"Yes, sir, Mr. Wellborn told us that's what you'd want. I've informed them that you are here." He indicated the interior of the ranch house.

Nothing happened for what seemed like a long time. The phone on the guard's desk was silent, but Ryan heard other phones within the building ring, along with un-intelligible conversations. Several people came and went. He paced; Sarah stood with her eyes closed.

'The event is about to begin,' Sarah communicated.

Finally, a man came through the front door of the ranch house. "I'm Raymond Nazem, the President's Security Adviser. I'm also his appointments secretary for today. I'm afraid the President is occupied with a crisis. Is it possible that you could come back to-morrow?"

"Did Sam tell you that our business was urgent?" Ryan asked.

"Yes, but the President has many urgencies. As I said, he is occupied."

"None as urgent as this one."

"Can you tell me the nature of your visit?" Nazem asked.

"With all due respect, this is not a social visit. And I don't want to exaggerate the situation, but we are delivering a message that may save the President's life. We don't have a lot of time to fool around."

"The President's security is a matter for the Secret Service."

"No," Ryan said, "in this case, it's a matter for the President."

"I see. Well, the best I can do is to deliver your message. It will be up to the President to determine when he can see you. His sched-ule is quite full. As you can see, we are understaffed."

"Please tell the President that the Ambassador from Phantia requests a few moments of his time." Sarah's words were delivered with an authority that startled Nazem.

Ryan saw the Security Advisor's crusty exterior relax a notch. Without a word, he turned and walked through the door to the interior.

'The event will begin very shortly,' Sarah communicated to Ryan.

'I hope we can convince him to leave. Are we in danger?'

'The tsunami will engulf this entire area.'

'Let's hope he'll listen.'

Ryan went back to pacing. Standing very still, Sarah closed her eyes. Ryan checked his watch every minute. Time seemed to stand still.

'They are coming for us now,' she communicated to Ryan, just before the door opened, and Nazem motioned them in.

They went through the main area of the ranch house, down a short hall, and entered a room that had been set up as an office for the President.

"Ambassador Smith," President Boyle smiled and extended his hand. "How nice to see you again. And Mr. Drake."

This was a very different Carlton Boyle than they had met at Richard Tyler's farmhouse in Illinois. His face looked strained, his eyes tired. The stress of the Presidency was showing already. But there was something more; Carlton Boyle was severely conflicted.

Sam Wellborn had told Ryan that many in Boyle's Cabinet did not approve of him granting ambassador status to Sarah and Peter. He had also told them that the President's science and intelligence advisors constantly pointed out the evilness of extraterrestrials — abductions, mutilations, and implants. They tried to convince him that he was the leader of the most powerful nation on Earth, and as such he could not tolerate anyone, even visitors from another planet, telling him what to do. The most vocal of these voices was that of Vice-President Richard Tyler and Raymond Nazem.

"Mr. President, I'll get right to the point," Ryan said. "We are here because this area is about to be inundated by a tidal wave. Sir, you must leave immediately, and we want you to warn others."

"What are you talking about, we're miles from the ocean," Nazem said.

"I'm talking about the largest earthquake and tidal wave to hit the continent in the past ten-thousand years."

"Says who? Everybody knows you can't predict earthquakes."

"It has been foreseen —"

Sarah's words were clipped off by the first shock. The earthquake lifted the house as if it were a small boat rolling with a stormy sea. Ryan lost his balance and stumbled into the President.

Two Secret Service agents flung open the door and surrounded Boyle, brushing Ryan to one side. "Sir, we have to get you to the helicopter."

With a Secret Service agent on either side, the President bolted for the rear door. Another agent held it wide.

Ryan grabbed Sarah's hand and they ran after the President.

Just as they reached the open space, where the helicopter already had its rotor in motion, a much larger shock hit. The helicopter flipped on its side. With a cloud of dust and a grinding sound, its rotor dug a trench in the ground not far from the President.

The agents pointed to their vehicles, and in unison said, "Over there." They pulled Carlton Boyle in that direction.

Before they could move more than a few feet, a gigantic shock opened a gash before them. All were thrown to the ground. From their prone positions, they watched as their vehicles toppled into the crack like a pile of kindling sliding down a steep embankment.

"We've got to get to higher ground," Ryan shouted to the two agents who were pulling President Boyle to his feet. He motioned to the west, toward the ocean. "Tidal wave." He turned and pointed to a small hill at the back of the ranch property.

The agents stood fixed. They had been trained for such a catastrophe, but this was an unfamiliar place. If they had been at the White House, or even at Camp David, procedures were in place, shelters nearby, alternate escape routes mapped out. Carlton Boyle had insisted on this impromptu visit, long before they were completely ready to protect or evacuate him.

Ryan ran to them, "We've got to move." He pointed to the hill.

The agents ignored him, looking around for any transportation not smashed or engulfed by the chasm.

Sarah came alongside. In a steady voice she said, "You must take the President to safety." She laid her hand on the arm of one of the agents.

He glanced at the slender fingers. His training rebelled at the thought of a possible enemy agent touching him. He reached for Sarah's hand, but paused.

In an instant he turned to the other agent and said, "We need to get to higher ground. Head for that hill." He pointed to an opening where the tremors had knocked down the perimeter fence.

When the Army helicopter bearing Sam Wellborn approached the site of the nuclear explosion in Utah, the pilot pointed to the ground and said, "Sir, the crater is over there. We'll be landing to the south to stay out of the radiation drift."

"How close can you get me, before we land?"

"If you want, I can make a pass directly over it."

"That would be good."

Sam saw a crater in what had been the top of a juniper and sagebrush covered mesa. The exposed area was about two hundred yards across, an indication that much of the blast had occurred underground.

Men in radiation protective garb were gathered around the periphery of the hole. Some were taking photographs; others were measuring radiation levels with various instruments; still others were taking soil and rock samples.

At one side of the crater, an enormous cavern opened into the side of the rock formation. Twisted strands of the rebar and steel beams that had formed the roof and walls of an underground facility lay exposed. Chunks of gray concrete contrasted with the ruddy colors of the mesa's natural sandstone.

The helicopter descended for a closer look. Inside the opening, Sam could just make out the shape of a flying saucer. The report had been right; this was an alien base. But what was it that Ryan had said? Something about someone manufacturing alien reproduction vehicles?

Ryan should be with Boyle by now. He asked the pilot to get him a line to the President. After several tries, the pilot reported that there was some difficulty with communications. Sam decided to try again when they landed at the Army's base camp.

Immediately behind the buildings at Carlton Boyle's ranch, the land sloped upward, a forested hill about a hundred feet high. President Boyle, urged on by the two Secret Service agents, detoured around uprooted trees and started to climb. Sarah and Ryan followed. Two other agents followed them. Glancing back, Ryan saw little movement among the collapsed structures of the ranch and the mangled vehicles.

They climbed for a few minutes, gaining precious vertical feet. Immediately ahead, the tree-covered slope slanted sharply upward. A cliff, about forty feet in height, imposed itself between them and the top of the hill. Seeking an easier assent, Boyle and the two agents slanted their path to the left.

'We must go there,' Sarah communicated to Ryan.

'Where?'

'Watch.'

As Ryan looked, an opening appeared in the face of the cliff. It had not been there before, before it had been a solid rock face. Now there was an opening, an opening through which a person could squeeze. At its entrance glowed a small golden globe.

"In there," Ryan shouted and pointed to the opening. The full force of the tsunami could not be far off. "We'll be safe in there."

Boyle and the two agents hesitated just long enough for Sarah to catch up with them.

"I'm not so sure about this," the one agent said.

Again Sarah placed her hand on his arm.

After a moment, he said, "I think this might be okay. I'll check it out." He ran into the entrance, unaware that, moments ago, it had been solid rock.

A minute later he emerged. "There's a cave in here. Plenty big enough." He motioned the party forward.

Ryan just managed to squeeze through the entrance when a rockslide closed the opening. The cave plunged into darkness. The two Secret Service agents following Ryan did not make it into the cave.

Ryan stumbled forward until he ran into Sarah and they both fell to the dirt of the cave floor. He swept her into his arms. Thank God she was okay. He had been so focused on Carlton Boyle that he had almost forgotten his primary responsibility, and the one person who mattered more to the future of this planet than the President of the United States of America.

One needs to be slow to form convictions, but once formed they must be defended against the heaviest odds.

— MAHATMA GANDHI

TWENTY-FIVE

The intersection of the North American Tectonic Plate and the Juan de Fuca Plate, known as the Juan de Fuca Ridge, lay off the west coast of the United States and Canada. In a billion-year old process, the North American plate was slowly inching its way on top of the diving Juan de Fuca plate, which was being pushed north and east by the Pacific Plate, and forced under the North American Plate. The subduction zone, beginning at the Juan de Fuca Ridge ran many miles inland; in ancient times it had formed the line of volcanoes known as the Cascade Range.

During the last twenty years, as polar ice melted at an unprecedented rate and the resulting water flowed into the Pacific Ocean, the load over that portion of the Juan de Fuca that lay under the ocean had increased, while at the same time the load on the North American Plate had decreased. This had enabled the North American Plate to continue to edge its way over the Juan de Fuca. The process had caused minor earthquakes all along the subduction zone.

The Pacific Tectonic Plate had been the major recipient of water from the melting polar caps. Estimates were that the Earth's oceans had risen by as much as six feet over the past five hundred years. During that period the tectonic plates had gradually adjusted themselves. In a process similar to that of the Juan de Fuca, the Pacific Plate had been adjusting itself along the San Andreas Fault that extended through California into the Gulf of Cortez. In recent years the movement between these Plates had diminished; small tremors had failed to relieve the building stress.

On February 15th, the North American Plate jumped two feet over the Juan de Fuca. That was a more rapid movement than either plate had experienced in the last fifty thousand years. A chain reaction went out in every direction.

A hundred miles east of the coast, forty to fifty kilometers below the surface, the crust was rent and hot magma from the liquid center of the Earth forced its way to the surface. It found old passages such as had created Mt. Hood, Mt. Adams, and Mt. Ranier. These long extinct volcanoes spewed hot lava from their tops. The magma found other cracks in the structure of the North American Plate and began building new mountains. Some of these new volcanoes were in places where people lived.

The Pacific Tectonic Plate, one of Earth's most extensive, took this opportunity to adjust itself vis-à-vis every surrounding tectonic plate. Gradual adjustment turned into a sudden jolt. The Pacific Plate suddenly slipped — depending on the nature of the contact with an adjacent plate; the slippage was anywhere from a few inches to a foot. Earthquakes hit every landmass bordering the Pacific Plate; tidal waves rose up to pound every coast.

At the tip of the Baja peninsula, Cabo San Lucas experienced both earth tremors and rising seas. Fissures opened in the middle of streets as the land adjusted itself. The fancy yachts in the marina found themselves beached amidst the rubble of fallen structures; others were speared by concrete pilings. On all sides of the peninsula, hundred-foot waves lashed the patios of homes, elegant and dilapidated. When residents ventured into the shopping area they would find one yacht neatly parked in front of Carlos and Charlie's restaurant, as if its owner had stopped off for a plate of ribs.

The San Andreas Fault ran to the east of Los Angeles. There the Pacific Plate and North American Plates adjusted themselves as they had done periodically over the ages. The adjustment this time was a six-foot wide fissure that ran for hundreds of miles. Railroads and Interstate highways were closed. Water and natural gas lines burst. Telephone and electrical service was disrupted. Three oil storage tanks in San Pedro, south of downtown Los Angeles, burst; flames soon ignited them and a nearby refinery. In the hours following the initial shock, the entire Los Angeles metropolitan area was essentially shut down.

Nine hundred and sixty miles to the north of Los Angeles, and two hours north of Boyle's ranch, a mighty wave of seawater ran up the wide valley of the Columbia River, inundating the city of Astoria under a hundred feet of water. It had spent most of its force by the time it reached Longview, some thirty miles inland, but the level of the river continued to rise as seawater mixed with fresh. In its path the tsunami had scraped the riverbanks clean of all natural and manmade objects.

People in Portland experienced earth tremors more than the rising water that flooded the city's wharf. Tall buildings collapsed, carrying hundreds to their death. Many were trapped in auto pile-ups and in the rubble of structures. In the hours that followed, smoke from burning rubble clouded the sky.

Further north, along the coast of the State of Washington, a peninsula with little elevation jutted into the Pacific. To its north was the inlet from the Pacific Ocean known as Grays Harbor. To the south, Leadbetter Point, a state park, and the town of North Cove, formed the entrance to Willapa Bay. Three state parks rested on the Pacific Ocean side of the Peninsula: Westhaven, Westport Light, and Grayland Beach. With typical winter weather, and many of the houses occupied only as summer residences, few people were at the parks, and only hearty locals were wintering in the towns of Westport, Grayland, North Cove, and Tokeland.

The tsunami flooded these towns under a hundred feet of water; further inland, it washed over the timber farms of Weyerhauser uprooting most of the trees. The oyster beds along the shores of Grays Peninsula were churned into a muddy mass. The fifty-foot wall of seawater quickly inundated the city of Aberdeen. The bridge for US 101 was swept eastward on the crest of the gigantic wave. When the water reached Elma, it had spent its force.

Ken O'Neal was having lunch at the Spouting Horn in Depoe Bay, Oregon, an hour north of Carlton Boyle's ranch. He felt a slight earth tremor and looked out to the west. Nothing unusual, just another minor shock. He went back to eating his chowder.

Five minutes later, he looked again. Water from the harbor was rushing through the narrow entrance. He had never seen the tide this low. He checked the ocean to the west and watched as the sea rose above the horizon. Then he heard what sounded like the roll of distant thunder. Everyone in the restaurant became quiet. The wall of water came toward the shore with the sound of a hundred on-coming freight trains. Mesmerized by the awesome spectacle, O'Neal calmly laid down his spoon.

The tsunami hit the town of Depoe Bay with its full fury. For a brief second the front window of the Blue Heron held before im-ploding into the display of Swarowki ceramics. The flower box crash-ing through the window of Gracie's Sea Hog was the first its patrons knew of the wall of water. The Spouting Horn and the Oregon Coast Aquarium Store along with their customers and staff, were quickly submerged, crushed, and deposited under the waters that crashed into Depoe Bay. The concrete of the US 101 bridge across the narrow entrance to the bay was fractured. Its fragments were deposited five miles inland alongside boats, houses, and automobiles.

South along the Oregon coast, the tidal wave mashed the town of Florence. From there it marched inland, up the Siuilus River Val-ley, sweeping all before it. Cattle, horses, dogs, cats, chickens, and people were mixed with the debris of structures and autos that the gigantic wave had picked up. Supports for the railroad bridge, four miles inland, were tossed about its crest like mere chips of wood. The tsunami slashed telephone and power lines like a cougar rip-ping into a new kill. Homes, beautiful and plain, were submerged along with their occupants. At Mapleton, thirteen miles up the twist-ing river valley, it spent the last of its force, but not before it cleared out the Siuslaw Marina and flooded the Davidson Lumber Mill.

The group of five, President Carlton Boyle, his two secret Ser-vice agents, Glenn Koslowski and Tony Santori, along with Sarah Smith, and Ryan Drake felt the ground shudder as the force of the tsunami swept over the land. In their black vault, there was little they could do but wait. For over thirty minutes, the smell of the ocean permeated the air, but the entrance to the cave held.

Glenn played his flashlight over the walls of the cave. It dis-closed writing on the smooth walls, lettering that none of the Earth-humans had seen before. Glenn and Tony went to examine the entrance. They found it blocked by three huge boulders. They put their backs against them, but they did not budge.

When Sam Wellborn's helicopter landed, he used the base phone to place a call to Raymond Nazem. He wanted to check to make sure that Ryan and Sarah had been able to meet with the President.

After several attempts to get through to the ranch, he called Tiffany Wheeler at the White House.

Without waiting for him to say anything, Tiffany burst out, "Sam, we just received word."

"About what?"

"President Boyle, everyone, they were caught in an earthquake and a tidal wave." Tiffany broke into sobbing. "We can't get in touch with anybody."

"I'll head out right now. Keep you posted." He ran to the helicopter. It headed for Hill Air Force Base.

"Do you want the good or the bad?" Warren Ophir spoke into his cell phone. He could barely contain his enthusiasm. Without waiting for a reply he said, "Here goes the good. The satellite observing Carlton Boyle's ranch in Oregon reported that it was hit by a tidal wave."

"When?" Delta Kingman's voice was filled with a mixture of curiosity and glee.

"I just got the news. I'm sure he was at the ranch."

"I hadn't heard."

"It just happened. I keep telling you, my people are good," Ophir smiled his crooked smile. "Delta, think about it. This may be our chance. Of course we'll have to wait until they find his body. Then again, maybe not."

"I see where you're headed, but let's not get ahead of ourselves. Find out what happened to Boyle."

"Now, are you ready for the bad?"

"Go ahead."

"Ryan Drake got one of our phony aliens; turned him over to the FBI."

"I already know about that," Kingman said with a note of disgust.

"But we have a couple of problems. First, there's an FBI guy by the name of Jake Ashton. He's refusing to turn over our guy. His superiors are pressuring him, but he's refusing to give him up until he gets concrete assurances that the whole affair won't be buried."

"Stop calling him our guy. This whole alien abduction business was your idea."

"Hey, it worked great for a long time."

"Yeah, and now we have a problem. I'll see what I can do about getting your alien back for you. What's the second piece of bad news?"

"Somebody has pictures of our alien, my alien. The papers, and I mean all the papers from the New York Times to the San Francisco Examiner, are going to hit the street in about an hour, and they're going to have a big fat picture of my alien on page one."

"How could that possibly have happened?"

"All of our safeguards were bypassed," Ophir said. "It had to be an inside job. I'm guessing that John deBeque's been turned."

"DeBeque? I though he'd dropped out of sight."

"Dropped out of sight? Yeah, but I'm guessing he's back. And he's not on our side. And you know what else they're printing?"

"I can hardly wait." Kingman's voice had become quieter.

"Pages of Steiger's Diary, including pages from before February Sixteenth Nineteen Ninety Eight, pages I've never seen before."

"That's just great. What about the explosion in Utah?"

"Nothing points to us," Ophir said. "The media are calling it an alien base."

"Get it on page one."

"It'll be there, but not until the morning edition. In the meantime the networks are talking about the captured alien."

The next morning, sunlight shining through an opening at the top dimly illuminated the cave. Ryan Drake estimated that the area in which they were trapped was an oval about fifty feet at its major axis. The rounded top of the cave looked to be about thirty feet above its floor.

Ryan had found a spot on the soft dirt of the floor next to Sarah. Using the jackets with which they had departed Harmony as pillows, they had snuggled close throughout the night. Despite the rock walls, the temperature in the cave seemed to be a comfortable seventy degrees.

He was about to get up and explore further when Sarah touched his cheek. *'I think we did well. Search parties are already on the way to us.'*

'Pretty close call if you ask me.'

'We are safe for now.'

By the time the others roused themselves, the light shining into the cave from the hole in the ceiling was sufficient to see details without the benefit of Tony's flashlight. The concave walls were without protrusions; so smooth that Ryan could see no hope of climbing to the opening at the top of the cave.

The cave extended into the hill and ended in a narrow passage, at the end of which was a small trickle of cool, fresh water.

"Any idea how we get out of here?" Carlton Boyle asked.

"Mr. President, I'm sure they'll come looking," Tony said with an air of bravado.

Glenn checked his two-way communicator, but received only static in response to repeated attempts to call.

"Save your battery," Tony said. "There's probably no one out there."

"So we wait." Boyle addressed the comment to the group. "I wonder how many survived?"

"If the water got to the top of this hill —" Ryan did not finish his statement.

President Carlton Boyle sat on the dirt floor of the cave and buried his head. "What a disaster. And I'm not out there to help. That's what they elected me to do, help. And I'm trapped in this damn cave."

"Better here than dead, Mr. President," Glenn said.

"I just feel so helpless."

An hour later little had changed. Sarah sat down next to Carlton Boyle and said, "Mr. President, may I tell you of my home?"

He managed a weak smile and said, "Sure, in fact that would be welcome. Take my mind off of this." He waved a hand at the walls of the cave.

For the next hour Sarah talked about her home on Phantia, about the family she had left behind, about her friends, and about her teaching career. With nothing else to occupy them, Carlton Boyle, Tony, and Glenn listened.

Ryan could barely make out the faint image of Sarah's guardian as it stood behind her. He tried to see if the others in the cave had guardians, but none were visible to his soft eyes.

She reached out and rested her hand on the President's arm. "May I show you a picture of my planet?"

Tony edged forward ready to place himself between them. Boyle waved him off.

"Little hard to see in here, but sure."

"Close your eyes. It will appear."

Thirty minutes later Carlton Boyle's eyes blinked wide open. "I had no idea." Amidst tears rolling down his cheeks, he said, "I had no idea how beautiful it could be. There is no violence, no pollution. It is so peaceful.

"Damn Joe Ide, and the rest of them. Things are so different than the way they kept explaining it to me. They kept talking about the terrible things you'd done to people who you'd abducted, that you couldn't possibly be friendly."

"Who explained these things to you?" Sarah asked gently.

"My, so called, advisors. They said you were evil, a threat. That you were a scout for an invasion."

His ramblings and questions flowed for an hour. Finally, exhausted, he leaned back, closed his eyes, and slept.

'I think we have made a start,' Sarah communicated to Ryan who sat not far away, observing the entire procedure.

'And this clever shelter we're in?'

'Courtesy of Mulligan.'

'When do we get out?'

'When someone finds us.'

'Will they?'

'Oh, yes, when the time is propitious.'

"So is the President okay?" Glenn asked. He and Tony sat nearby. Neither had been trained for these circumstances; neither had been trained to handle an extraterrestrial experience.

"He is fine," Sarah replied. "Just resting."

"So what did you do to him?"

"I showed him my home planet, Phantia."

314

"I didn't see any photos."

"I pictioned it for him," she said.

"Pictioned?"

"Yes, I replayed views of my planet as I remember it. If you will give me a few minutes, I can do it for you also."

"I don't know."

"It didn't seem to hurt President Boyle," Ryan said. "Ask him if it was worthwhile."

"I just want to get him out of here," Glenn said.

By the time the light faded from the hole in the ceiling, President Boyle had talked to Ryan Drake not only about the media affiliates, but also about the World League. Despite hunger, the five people stranded in the cave were reasonably comfortable. They had water and the cave remained remarkably warm.

"When are they going to find us?" Tony kept asking.

"I just want out of here," Glenn echoed his sentiment.

Both Ryan and Sarah urged the two Secret Service agents to relax.

Sarah wandered to the back of the cave. After a while, Ryan became concerned and went to find her. She was squatted not far from the trickle of water. Her head was buried in her hands, and she rocked back and forth. As he got closer, he saw that she was sobbing.

When he laid a hand on her shoulder, she looked up. He could make out tears streaming down her face. "What's wrong?"

"So many," she said. "So much destruction. Why didn't they listen? I don't understand why they didn't listen. Why did so many have to die?"

"How many?"

"Millions."

"Millions?"

"Millions of my brothers and sisters — all around the world. We tried to tell them." She went back to sobbing.

"How do you —" But Ryan knew the answer, knew that she had remote viewed the death and destruction.

MILLIONS DIE PRESIDENT LOST Headlines screamed across the front page of every major paper, except those on the West Coast.

They were not functioning due to earthquake damage. In accompanying articles, pictures and words described the devastation in Oregon and Washington, California, and British Columbia. Earthquakes and tidal waves had killed an estimated twenty million people in the United States, wiping out smaller towns along the Pacific Coast, severely damaging larger cities. They had also closed all ports on the West Coast. The eruptions along the Cascade Range had destroyed both lives and property. Search parties and relief efforts were hampered by the total breakdown of communications and transportation.

Earthquakes had also hit all landmasses bordering the Pacific Plate. The damage was most severe in Japan, New Zealand, and the Philippines. But the greater damage was from tidal waves. Satellite sensors estimated that the greatest adjustment for the Pacific Plate was relative to the Antarctic Plate that had heretofore been covered by thousands of feet of ice.

Reports were slowly coming in from around the world; current estimated deaths were in excess of one hundred million. The toll would have been greater if the authorities in Japan and Taiwan had not acted to evacuate their people.

A separate article, without a large headline, reported that Vice President Richard Tyler had assumed the reins of government. He had declared the entire West Coast a disaster area. Tyler had not been sworn in to replace President Boyle. Since no trace of the President had been found, it could not be confirmed that he was dead. The Supreme Court was meeting to decide the precedent-setting situation. A hundred searchers were combing what remained of the President's former ranch. Since the President had not been evacuated, they were not optimistic about finding him alive.

A smaller front-page headline stated, ATOMIC BLAST AT ALIEN HIDEOUT. A picture of the Utah site was immediately below the headline. The article accompanying it told about human bodies, identified in conjunction with the UFOs that were under construction at the underground site. Although no alien bodies had been found, the conclusion was that the humans had been the slaves of their alien captors. It was the discovery of an alien base on U.S. soil that had led Tyler to raise the Homeland Security Threat Level to a code red.

Never before have we had so little time to do so much.

— FRANKLIN DELANO ROOSEVELT

TWENTY-SIX

"We got ourselves a President," Delta Kingman declared. This was not news to the twelve Governors of the World League, but he said it anyway to those assembled in the penthouse of the St. Regis Hotel in Washington, DC. "I'd say we're in good shape."

"More important, the President of the United States reports to us." Jonathan Olsen, head of the financial affiliates, raised his wine glass in a toast. "And that private enterprise is now firmly in control of the largest economy in the world."

"Hear, hear." Several applauded their remarks. Acting President Richard Tyler was not among those present.

The thirteenth member of the group did not react. As was customary, the off-planet being remained expressionless. He communicated with no one other than the members of the triad. Warren Ophir had seen him several times; this was the first gathering of this sort he had attended.

In one corner, the off-planet's escort waited patiently. Today the white-haired man wore a black cape over a black shirt and pants. He appeared to somewhat ethereal, less than fully materialized.

"Warren, tell us where the search for Boyle stands," Kingman said.

Ophir was startled out of his focus on the off-planet being. "My people are in the area, with the search parties. They report that the ranch buildings were completely destroyed, pieces of them were found a mile away. Lots of bodies; none identified as Boyle."

317

"And what if Boyle shows up?" Jonathan Olson asked.

"The court says Boyle'll be President again," Kingman said.

"Damn Court. There are two of its members that I'll welcome being gone," Warren Ophir said. "I don't want Boyle coming back." What he did not need to say to those gathered was that his people working with the search team had orders to make sure Carlton Boyle did not show up alive.

"I've got a list of several Senators and Congressmen who have overstayed their welcome too," Oliver Vanderbush, head of the media affiliates, said. "Bastards don't want to play ball."

"Okay, everybody, hold on," Kingman stood at the end of the long table. "We need to focus on our plan. In an hour, Tyler will direct all military and Federal law enforcement agencies to begin rounding up 'suspected terrorists' and anybody that resembles an alien. Now this could include some Governors, Senators, Congressmen, judges, and businessmen, not to mention the very popular Ajax Johnson, ex-football player, and of course that damned FBI agent in Denver. Oliver are your people ready for this?"

"Just like the script." Vanderbush pointed to the bound document that lay on the coffee table. Earlier each Governor of the World League had signed off on new controls over the media, as a part of the World League's soon to be published "declaration of freedom."

"I hope you can do better at this than with Steiger's diary and those damned pictures."

"It's been squashed; no further reference in any major media," Vanderbush said. He had been particularly embarrassed as many of his own newspapers and television outlets had been a party to the dissemination of the diary pages and the pictures of the phony alien.

"The second part of this is Warren's area." Kingman said. "There are a whole bunch of folks that we'd rather not arrest. Warren's going to see to it that they contract some very serious diseases. Have I got that right?"

"Correct," Ophir said. "If you will check page twenty-seven of your folders, you will see the list. We have determined they are not worthy of trials for treason, and we don't want to take the chance any of these activists might be freed on some legal technicality. As we have discussed, they will never know how or when they contracted cancer."

"What about our Utah facility?" Joe Randolph asked. As the head of the corporate affiliates, he not only supervised LNR, but also acted as the main contact for corporate executives allied with the World League.

Delta Kingman replied, "Fortunately, it is so contaminated with radioactivity that no one can get very close. I've told the Army to stand down, let it cool for a few years."

"So, no one can tell it was ours?"

"That's right, not for months, and maybe never," Kingman said. "Until we decide different, it's a goddamned alien base on the soil of the United States of America."

"We need to re-start production," Randolph said.

"Pick a site," Kingman said. "Now that we control the U.S. Treasury, we can build one anywhere we goddamned please — anywhere except the West Coast. We wouldn't want an earthquake to disrupt things." He chuckled at his last words and drained his glass.

Under orders from the World League, Acting President Tyler had been slow to order assistance to California, Oregon, and Washington. The League had determined it was better to use the government's resources to make sure the rest of the country continued to function normally.

Jake Ashton almost refused the call, he did not recognize the name, and then it registered. This was the guy who had been at the presentation that Peter Jones had given. He had seen the sleaze again at Peter's funeral. Looking for a little relief from the incessant pressure from his boss, he picked up the handset.

"I don't know if you remember me, but I'm helping Ryan Drake and the Phantians," John deBeque said.

"Oh, I remember you from Peter's presentation, all right. As I recall it, you're Ernest Steiger's stepson."

"You're right, and I was with Steiger's organization. More recently, I'm the guy who got the picture of your phony alien in all the papers and on the TV."

"So what do you want?" Ashton asked.

"They're coming to arrest you for treason. You may want to

make yourself scarce."

"How do you know?"

"Our extraplanetary friends."

"I'm not abandoning —"

DeBeque cut him off. "Neither am I. But I am being smart about things."

The forty-eight hours of internment for the five in the cave passed quickly. Sarah Smith spent every moment that Carlton Boyle would allow schooling him in the truth of the cosmic paradigm. After observing, the two Secret Service agents allowed her to piction Phantia for them. For Boyle alone, she pictioned the extraterrestrial gathering at Monument Valley.

During that time, Sarah explained to the President what she had discovered about people's psychological constructs. She started out describing how parent "train" a small child, and how each child builds a protective shield. She went on to describe how the construct of an adult was their identity, hiding their true self, instinctively acting on behalf of the true self. And how constructs interacted, totally apart from the true self, to keep everyone in a prescribed "safe" box.

When she tried to attribute current power structures to the interactions of constructs, Boyle objected. "This cannot be. We in government act in the best interests of the people."

"But Mr. President, what if people are so unconscious that they don't know what is true, what they truly need? And not knowing, what if people automatically yield to those more powerful? What if the whole scheme is built on fear, on false premises? What if people unconsciously support the gradual crumbing of what is right and true through the collective actions of their constructs? And what if the constructs think they are doing the right thing in protecting their charges?"

The discussion went on for many hours. Ryan joined in, describing his dream of the transparent jail and what he had discovered in a careful reading of Steiger's diary about the manipulations by the World League.

"How do we get rid of our constructs?" President Boyle asked.

"We're still working on that." She pointed to Ryan and herself. "When we do, the illusion that supports the current political and economic structures will crumble, real people will emerge from their cocoons, and this world will transform into the beautiful, peaceful and plentiful place it was created to be."

As the first light of the third day shown through the hole in the roof of the cave, Dr. Adamson appeared. By then Carlton Boyle was used to amazing disclosures; the apparition's sudden appearance did not startle him. On the other hand, Tony and Glenn greeted him with guns drawn.

After everyone settled down, Dr. Adamson proceeded to tell them about the destruction wrought by the earthquakes and tsunamis. He told Boyle about the actions of Vice-President Tyler, the involvement of the World League, the many arrests, the psychotronics that were being used to induce cancer, and the truth about the nuclear explosion in Utah. He also warned everyone that, outside this protected space, there were men intent on killing the President. This last piece of news made an immediate impression on Tony and Glenn.

Carlton Boyle said to Sarah, "You are the most amazing person I have ever met. If we get out of here, I want you to become my top advisor."

"Not if, Mr. President, when," Ryan Drake said. "I think it will happen very soon. Our protective shield has been lifted." He pointed to the cave walls and to the boulders at the entrance. They had lost their smooth appearance; now they were the ragged edges of a cave that had been chiseled from solid rock.

Ryan now understood that some sort of a membrane had ensured their safety. The temperature in the cave began to drop and the air became stale.

Sam Wellborn and a crew of Washington State Troopers and federal agents from the Secret Service and FBI had searched the wreckage of Boyle's ranch. The Air Force had flown him into the airport at Eugene, Oregon. There he had found emergency workers stretched thin, hospitals overwhelmed, and the route to the coast closed. In the midst of this chaos, it had taken almost twelve hours to assemble a team and equipment to begin the search for President Boyle. At dawn the day after the tsunami, they had helicoptered in and begun to probe the first of the collapsed structures.

The search mission had recovered most of the bodies of the staff that had been with the President. They had been discovered under piles of construction materials, under collapsed structures, in vehicles, and in the tops of trees. It had been a grisly business; Sam had been the one to identify many of the dead. The injured had been taken to hospitals in Eugene. With the exception of Carlton Boyle, and two Secret Service agents, almost everyone had been accounted for.

The whereabouts of Ryan Drake and Sarah Smith remained a mystery. Sam was not even sure they had been at the ranch. Communications were still down. Rescue shelters were jammed with the injured and homeless.

On the hill to the east of Carlton Boyle's ranch, the tsunami had deposited pieces of buildings, vehicles, and human body parts. The tidal wave had carried them from as far away as the town of Florence. Sam stood there looking at the remains of the destruction, a jumble of twisted wood and metal. The area had begun to smell like rotting fish, probably accounted for by the seaweed and fish carcasses that lay at his feet.

"Perhaps if you look over there," the white haired man said. He pointed to a rocky area at the dome of the hill. The man was dressed in a western shirt and jeans that were remarkably clean for someone who was participating in the dirty business of recovery. "I believe I saw a hole in the ground."

Sam wasn't quite sure why he listened to this bear-of-a-man; he seemed somewhat familiar. He climbed to where he could see what it was the man was pointing to. Sure enough, there was an eighteen inch-wide hole. He could not see its bottom and assumed it might lead into a cave. The tsunami had probably filled it with water.

"Anyone down there?" Sam shouted. He felt a little ridiculous shouting into a hole in the ground, but he did it again anyway. "Anybody hear me?"

"Well it's about time," came the familiar voice of the President of the United States.

"Mr. President? Are you okay, sir?"

"Fine. But we're ready to come out."

"Sam, go down the hill to the rock slide." It was Ryan Drake's voice. "There's an entrance to this cave under there."

"Mr. Wellborn, get everybody but the Secret Service out of the area," Tony yelled. "Tell them it's a code red."

In the dim light, Ryan went to Sarah and hugged her. She returned his hug and kissed him gently on the lips.

An hour later, the last boulder was dragged from the entrance of the cave. The glaring light of mid-day greeted those inside.

Tony squeezed through the opening. The chief of White House security greeted him. A phalanx of Secret Service agents surrounded the opening.

Carlton Boyle straightened his tie and smoothed his hair. He was ready to greet the reporters and cameras that he knew awaited his resurrection. When Tony was satisfied, he motioned for the President to come out.

The first person the President saw was his wife. Margaret ran to him and engulfed him in a warm embrace.

Then Carlton Boyle went to the bank of microphones and prepared to speak. Ryan and Sarah had followed him into the bright light.

'There is a man with a gun.' Sarah pointed to a collection of vehicles about a hundred yards distant.

"Tony, Glenn, watch out — gun," Ryan shouted. He pointed in the direction Sarah had indicated.

The President was about to tell everyone what he had learned during his three days, when Tony pushed him from the microphones. They landed in a tangle.

Ryan heard the report of a distant rifle shot. He pulled Sarah behind one of the boulders that had been removed from the mouth of the cave. Five Secret Service agents remained standing around the prone President. Then there were shouts and other guns fired.

It was not until they pulled Tony's body off the President, that they saw the blood. He had taken a bullet in the shoulder, a bullet intended for Carlton Boyle.

Secret Service agents surrounded the President and escorted him to a waiting helicopter. It took off immediately.

Ryan pushed his way through the throng around Tony. Reaching for the wounded man's hand, he said, "Thank you for everything."

Tony looked back and said, "You're welcome. Good luck with your mission." Then the paramedics pushed his stretcher into a second helicopter.

The arrests and psychotronics had been going on for twenty-four hours when Richard Tyler got word that Carlton Boyle had been found alive. The first one hundred arrested, accused of being aligned with alien terrorists, were in custody in various federal facilities around the country. They were being held without benefit of counsel. In many cases their families did not know their whereabouts.

Without waiting for the President to arrive back in the Capital, Richard Tyler commandeered Air Force One and flew it to St. Louis, Missouri. From there, his Secret Service contingent drove him to his family farm. When he arrived there, he went into a closet, retrieved an old pistol, and placed its barrel in his mouth.

BOYLE ALIVE The headline screamed across the front page of the newspaper that Ryan held. Sarah and he were in Kayenta. The smaller print went on to tell how, after spending three days trapped in a cave, Carlton Boyle had been rescued through the tireless efforts of searchers. Despite the hardships of being without food, the doctors at Walter Reed had pronounced him fit. The article identified the other people who had been with Boyle, pointing out that one of them was the alien, Sarah Smith. The article went on to tell about the sniper who had been apprehended after he attempted to kill the President. Tony Santori, a Secret Service agent guarding the President was recovering in the hospital from a bullet wound he had received.

Boyle's first official act was to rescind his former Vice-President's orders regarding suspected domestic terrorists, and to order their release. He invited those who had been arrested to Washington for an informal "kitchen cabinet" get together.

His second action was to instruct the military and a panel of civilian experts to probe the underground facility in Utah. He appointed Sam Wellborn as his special representative to oversee the effort.

His third act was to declare the entire West Coast a disaster area, and to order immediate assistance for the victims of the earthquakes and tsumanis.

Carlton Boyle's fourth move was to issue arrest warrants for the twelve members of the Board of Governors of the World League. The article said that the charges were treason against the elected government of the United States of America and against its people. They would be tried individually in Federal District Courts. He encouraged the trial judges to allow live televising of each trial. As of the dateline of the newspaper article, a newly invigorated FBI had found six of the twelve.

In an unusual move, President Boyle issued a decree of amnesty for those men and women who had in any way participated in the cover-up of extraterrestrial contact, who had engaged in secret "black" projects involving reverse engineering of extraterrestrial technology, or who had been part of the effort to institute mind control, media manipulation, and other illegal intelligence operations. They had only to submit a written deposition, within the next forty-five days, with any federal, state, or local law enforcement agency. If they were deemed in need of witness protection this was to be provided. He also offered Federal grants for the commercialization of energy sources derived from extraterrestrial technology. He asked Congress to quickly pass legislation ratifying these actions.

Boyle said that his heart went out to those who had died in the earthquakes and tidal waves around the globe. He pointed out that melting polar ice, due to global warming, had aggravated tectonic plates movements that had led to the worldwide disaster. He promised executive orders to move this country to non-polluting energy sources as quickly as possible, and asked Congress to enact legislation to support him in this. He offered to support similar actions in other countries around the Pacific Rim.

Ryan passed the article to Sarah. "Looks like you made quite an impression on the President."

"Although he is a politician, he is intent on doing the right thing. Now we will see if he can use his office to help the cosmic paradigm become a reality."

"You all set to go to Washington, next week?"

"Yes, the President and I have agreed to meet once each month."

The two Secret Service agents assigned to Sarah stood not far away. They followed the pair as Ryan's new Jeep pulled out and headed to Harmony.

EPILOGUE

Ryan Drake had turned off the light next to the bed in his room at Harmony. He pulled the blanket under his chin and turned on his side. The room was a little cooler than he liked it, but Sarah insisted that they maintain the temperature in this underground facility to a level that "suited people who came from a planet where there was considerably less sunlight." He had adjusted with sweaters and extra blankets.

He recalled his second reaction to Sarah and Peter — after he had gotten over the shock that they were extraplanetary beings. His second reaction was to question how he was going to relate to such superior beings, how he was going to avoid becoming subservient to their every wish, avoid treating them like gods. But Peter and Sarah had solved that for him; they had not tried to lord it over him. Rather they had developed a working relationship that respected his ability to translate their message into terms that could be understood by Earth-humans and to translate the things of Earth so that the Phantians might better understand them. And it had worked; his world was now ready to transform itself.

The door softly opened and a tall slim figure entered. She stood for a moment next to the bed, then pulled back the covers and settled in next to him.

'*I need your company tonight,*' She placed her arm gently over his pajama-clad torso and snuggled closer.

'*I've been waiting for you for months.*'

'*I know.*'

'*I may not be able to restrain myself.*'

'*I know. I also know that I love you. But I would just snuggle like*

327

this for a while, before you turn my way.'

'Sure, as long as you like.'

'This means that you and I are mated.'

'I know, until we graduate and then on the various levels of the Between worlds.'

It seemed like forever, but in a little while Sarah slipped her hand under the edge of his pajama top and touched the bare skin of his stomach. He tried not to react.

Sarah felt the hair on his body. She had seen it before, seen it at the swimming pool at his mountain house, seen it before he slipped on his shirt. Phantians had little body hair. They had descended from a different animal line. She did not mind Ryan's hair, in fact, now that she was touching it, it felt rather nice.

Ryan felt her hand on his skin, the hand of an extraterrestrial. This was the hand he had studied trying to prove to himself that she was indeed from another planet. Her fingers were a bit longer than would be normal for a woman from his planet, but not so much as to be unpleasing. Now, as she wound them through the hair on his belly, he experienced a delight he had never known before.

Ryan turned on his back, pulled her head to his, and kissed her lips. They were much softer than the lips of men from Phantia. They lingered together, electricity passing between them. At that moment, nothing else mattered. Her mission to this violent planet receded.

At the last moment, before her emotions took total control, she pulled away and caught his eyes in the dim light that crept under the door to the hallway. *'Ryan, know that by making love to you, I may decrease my powers of awareness, and my abilities to remote view and piction.'*

Ryan felt his body tense. "Should we be doing this?"

"Yes." And before he could question her further she covered his mouth with hers.

As Sarah and Ryan ate breakfast at Harmony's long dining table the following morning, the main door opened; Ethete Johnson and John deBeque walked in.

After warm hugs were exchanged, John began to tell them how they had managed to use the media affiliates network and protocol against his old employers. The major media had accepted the picture of the phony alien because it appeared to have the imprimatur of the media affiliates. The same had been true of the pages of Ernest Steiger's diary. He had managed the entire escapade by tapping into the media affiliates network with his laptop computer. Things were going well until someone in the World League figured out what was going on. Then they abandoned the information dissemination project and ran.

Throughout the tale, Ethete held onto John's hand. Even when food was served, and they began to eat, they continued to hold hands.

Unable to resist longer, Sarah asked, "Ethete, while John was busy with his disclosure project, what were you doing?"

"Taking care of him."

Sarah looked as if she was ready to reproach her young team member when Ethete added, "The World League's surveillance picked us up as soon as we left here. I could feel it, so I scanned the vehicle and found the tracking device. Then we were almost stopped at a roadblock on the outskirts of Flagstaff. But I managed to maneuver us through it. While John was doing his computer thing, I detected someone trying to remote view him. Well, I put a stop to that right away. Should I go on?"

A noticeably softer Sarah smiled and said, "It would seem that the effects of your drug addiction are gone."

"What about Ajax?" Ethete asked. "The last I viewed him, he was in some jail."

"They released him. He's on his way here."

"So what happens now?" John deBeque asked.

"Now, John? Now we all go about the work of transforming this world."

ACKNOWLEDGMENTS

This book is a parable. It integrates the experiences and discoveries of many people and the truths they have derived from those experiences and discoveries. I am one of those experiencers, those discoverers.

In addition to that, the writing of this book has been a collaborative effort. I feel more like its editor than its author. I express my gratitude for having participated in its creation.

Many readers of *Trillion* believe the tale told in that book is true. I too have been amazed to discover the many things that became true *after* its publication. I sincerely hope that some of things that I have depicted in *Decimal* remain in the realm of fiction and do not come to pass.

Many of my brothers and sisters are responsible for this work, people who have shared their truth, people who have encouraged me to stay the course, people who have caused me to grow. I would particularly like to thank my spouse, Heidi, for supporting my work, for her counsel and nurturing, and for allowing me the freedom to pursue what I see as the main purpose of my life.

Andromeda, Sara Coulter, Don Daniels, Dr. Steven Greer, Josh Hayward, Gailmarie Kimmel, Arlyn MacDonald, Anna Olsen, Jill Hull Struck, and Linda Willits all contributed to the wisdom contained within these pages, and to the quality of these words. Last and most importantly, I am particularly thankful to a wonderful, professional editor, Patrick LoBrutto, for grasping that which I intended to convey, and for his many suggestions that have improved not only the story but the message.

Mark Kimmel
July 2004

ABOUT THE AUTHOR

Since 1987, Mark Kimmel has studied the messages provided by extraplanetary beings. His writing and speaking is based on first-hand experiences and interviews with people who have had contact with non-human life forms. By focusing on the implications of UFOs, extraterrestrial contact, and paranormal phenomenon, Mark presents an uplifting vision for the future of this planet.

Mark exited a thirty-year career in business and venture capital to pursue his investigation and reporting of what he calls, "the most important event in human history." He has been listed in Who's Who since 1985. He has degrees in engineering, marketing, finance, and psychology.

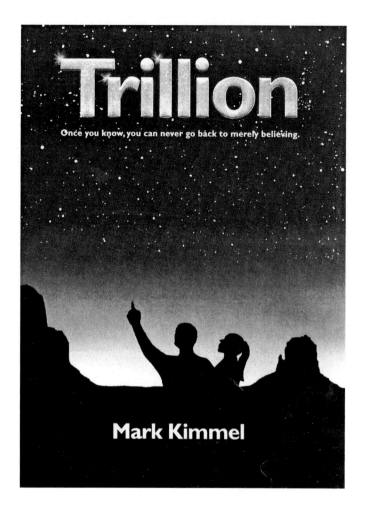

TO THE OWNER OF THIS BOOK

1) If you have information contrary to that presented in this book, please contact me so that I may incorporate it into subsequent publications.

2) All mortals of this universe are on an incredible Journey. Remember that although you are dwarfed by the vastness of this vision, you are a very special person, capable of greatness, important to the fulfillment of the Creator's grand plan.

Knowing the truth changes everything; it did for me. May you awaken to the realization that the universe requests your active participation.

Travel well,
Mark Kimmel

For comments on this book or for questions: MK@montrose.net

Interested in joining a global network of individuals dedicated to awakening this planet? Want to find out more about the Cosmic Paradigm?
Visit www.cosmicparadigm.com